...gged.

"What aren't you telling me?" he demanded.

"It's going to take time to learn everything about him, Dawson," she hedged, trying to redirect the conversation back to a comfortable place. "Maybe it's enough for the two of you to get to know each other. We don't have to do this all in one day, do we?"

"No. Of course not. But I have every intention of being there for my son as he grows up."

"Why didn't you tell me about the baby?" Dawson asked.

"I was scared."

He shot her a look. "Why didn't you really?" She shrugged.

TEXAN'S BABY

BY
BARB HAN

First Published in Great Britain 2016
By Mills & Boon, an imprint of HarperCollins*Publishers*
1 London Bridge Street, London, SE1 9GF

© 2016 Barb Han

ISBN: 978-0-263-91902-8

46-0416

Our policy is to use papers that are natural, renewable and recyclable products and made from wood grown in sustainable forests. The logging and manufacturing processes conform to the legal environmental regulations of the country of origin.

Printed and bound in Spain
by CPI, Barcelona

USA TODAY bestselling author **Barb Han** lives in north Texas with her very own hero-worthy husband, three beautiful children, a spunky golden retriever/standard poodle mix and too many books in her to-read pile. In her downtime, she plays video games and spends much of her time on or around a basketball court. She loves interacting with readers and is grateful for their support. You can reach her at www.barbhan.com.

I owe a debt of gratitude to Allison Lyons and Jill Marsal for the chance to work with you both, the best editor and agent in the business.

Thank you to the entire team at Mills & Boon Intrigue, led by Denise Zaza, for brilliant editorial, art and marketing. I'm blown away every time.

There are a few people who inspire me, breathing joy and laughter into every day. . .Brandon, Jacob and Tori; I hope you know how much I love you. And to John, my one great love, for being the person I can't wait to talk to at the end of each day.

A huge thank-you to Chrissy McDowell for her medical research help and to her daughter, Morgan, for her all-around awesomeness and bright red hair.

Chapter One

Dawson Hill stared at the two-story Folk Victorian across the street intently. It was two o'clock in the morning and he'd been in the same spot at the front window an embarrassing number of hours already. He was staying the night at his childhood home in hopes that he would figure out a good reason to approach her. If he thought he could get a straight answer out of Melanie Dixon, he'd stalk over and ask her outright. As it was, he could only guess why she'd disappeared two and a half years ago, not long after they'd started what he thought was a real relationship. Normally he'd be able to let it go and not look back, but they'd known each other since they were kids and it wasn't like her to pull such a stunt.

Movement across the street caught Dawson's eye. A dark silhouette crossed the front window. Was someone on her porch? Why would anyone be moving around outside in the dark at this time of night? The thought sat in his gut about as well as eating a handful of nails.

Beckett Alcorn, aka The Mason Ridge Abductor—the most notorious criminal in Mason Ridge's history—was in jail where he belonged. That should have ended the terror that had haunted this town for fifteen years. Except that, in return for leniency, Alcorn gave up his partner's name. He and Jordan Sprigs had been running a child abduction ring throughout Texas for the past fifteen years. Sprigs was believed to be out of the state, in hiding.

The town should be able to rest easy. It couldn't. The feds had been brought in to actively look for Sprigs. This was the last place anyone expected to find him. And yet no one felt safe. This case never seemed to close. Maybe that was the reason Dawson didn't believe it was over, either.

Now that Alcorn was behind bars and every available law enforcement officer was seeking Sprigs, the town was supposed to be able to move forward. Go back to their normal lives. And yet little things were still going bump in the night. Or in this case, shadows were moving across windows.

Melanie's parents were on the road, so Dawson already knew she was home alone. Her parents had spent every summer in their RV traveling around the US since retiring from the post office half a dozen years ago.

Because she was by herself in the house and Dawson's creepy radar was on full alert, he slipped out the back door to investigate.

A quick walk around the perimeter followed by peeking in a couple of windows just to make sure she wasn't in trouble would allow him to rest peacefully. Rest? He suppressed a laugh. Knowing Melanie was across the street alone while one of Mason Ridge's most notorious criminals was on the loose wasn't exactly the cure for insomnia.

Making sure she was safe would go a long way toward giving him the peace of mind he needed to sleep, he told himself. And this had nothing to do with the fact that he needed to see her again.

Dawson ignored the little voice in the back of his mind calling him a liar and slipped across the street.

With every step toward Melanie's place, the hair on Dawson's neck pricked. What was that all about? He didn't believe in the hype about black cats walking over graves or bad luck following walking under a ladder. He believed what was right in front of his nose. If he could see, touch or hear it, then it existed.

The front curtain moved as he positioned himself inside the Japanese boxwoods lining the perimeter to gain a better view over the porch. Whatever was on the other side of the wall five feet away had his senses screeching on full alert. The sirens in his head were so loud he'd have one helluva headache if he didn't silence them soon.

Climbing onto the wraparound porch, he listened carefully. The inside of the house was pitch-black, and there was no sound of breaking lamps or noises associated with stumbling into chairs or side tables. Whoever was in there most likely knew the layout. This was knowledge Melanie would have, but why would she creep around in her childhood house in the dark? Didn't make any sense, which was another reason the warning bells inside his head were ringing so loud his ears hurt.

If he covered all the possible scenarios, then he had to consider the notion that she had a boyfriend. There could be a guy in there trying not to wake her.

Dawson glanced over at the carport. All he saw was Melanie's vehicle, which revealed nothing. She could've picked the guy up in order to keep their relationship under wraps.

Thinking about Melanie with another man didn't do good things to Dawson's blood pressure. And yet he had no right to be angry.

There were other possibilities. Melanie had a sister, Abby. Dawson was sure he'd seen her around town yesterday, but he'd assumed that she'd gone back to Austin when her car disappeared last night.

The RV was gone, so there was no chance her parents had returned.

An ugly thought struck. Was Dawson making an excuse to spy on her? Had he really seen what he thought or was his mind playing tricks on him? He quickly dismissed the notion. Even though she'd been more frigid than crab fishermen's waters since their breakup—if he could call it that—he needed to make sure she was safe, especially while Sprigs was still free. Their mutual friend Lisa was still recovering from being attacked in connection with this case.

Dawson peeked through the front window. He couldn't see a thing.

How many hours had he spent inside that house as a kid?

How many since? He and Melanie had started things up between them when she took a job as a paralegal a couple years after she'd graduated from college. Things were going well until she'd abruptly told him it was over and then pulled a Houdini, moving to Houston and cutting off all contact. Said she'd moved on and had meant it literally and figuratively. Her stuff had disappeared from her parents' place where she'd been staying, and she hadn't taken his calls since. Didn't he lick a few wounds over that?

The time or two he'd been drunk enough to torture himself by looking at a picture of her online hadn't given him any more of a clue as to what he'd done wrong. Her privacy settings on her social media pages were set tighter than perimeter patrol at Leavenworth, so he couldn't see much beyond her profile picture.

Dawson slipped around back of the house and onto the screened porch. He'd remind her to keep that locked the next time he saw her. Yeah, he'd be the first one she'd want to talk to. She'd been home four days already and had managed to avoid talking to him so far. Since they shared the same friends, that took effort.

A shadow moved in the hallway toward the kitchen. Based on the size of this one, Dawson assumed it belonged to a male. Shadows could be deceiving.

The figure retreated. Dawson crouched low to make himself as small as possible—which was difficult given his six-foot-three frame—in case the dark figure returned. His eyes had adjusted to the darkness and there was just enough light coming off the appliances to see the kitchen fairly well.

Years ago, the Dixons used to hide a key in a fake rock near the porch. He dropped down to the bottom of the stairs now and felt around. Bingo.

Dawson slipped the key in the lock and then froze. If memory served, the Dixons had had an alarm installed for when they went on long road trips. He had an auxiliary code for emergencies, so he was good there. His grip tightened around the door knob.

Hold on a second.

If the door chime was on, he'd be given up the second he opened that door. He muttered a curse.

The telltale double click of a shotgun engaging a shell in the chamber sounded from behind.

Dawson spun around and stared at Melanie.

"Put that thing away before you hurt me." He waved her off.

"What are you doing here, Dawson Hill?" She studied him intently. Her legs were apart, positioned in an athletic stance, and the determination on her face said she'd shoot if she had to. She had the feral disposition of a mama bear protecting her cubs.

"Hold on there." Dawson's hands came up in surrender.

"Why don't you lower that thing before you accidentally pull the trigger?"

She dropped the barrel, allowing it to rest on her forearm. It was the easiest spot to pull up and shoot from, Dawson noted.

"You didn't answer my question," she said, a look of sheer panic in her eyes. And there was another emotion present that Dawson couldn't quite put his finger on, but it was intense.

"Trying to make sure no one's breaking into your parents' house." His hands still in the air, he stared at her. Damn, she looked good. It was too dark to see all the flecks in her honey-brown eyes, but she still had that dancer's body she'd earned at Nina's Dance Studio in town. Her hips had filled out in the sexiest curves. The silhouette of her long, wavy blond hair said she'd let it grow out since he'd last seen her. He flexed his fingers to distract himself from wanting to reach out to touch her smooth glowing skin and he wondered if she would still quiver if he ran his hand along the lines of her flat stomach.

Given the fact that a shotgun barrel was pointed right at his groin, his thoughts couldn't be more inappropriate. Dawson sidestepped the line of the barrel.

"What makes you think someone's trying to get in here?" The edge to her voice was another slap of reality.

It was clear that she'd rather face down a robber than see Dawson again. Now, wasn't that interesting? Apparently she regretted the time they'd spent together, especially given the way she'd bolted without a word not long after. Personally, he thought the sex had ranked right up there with the best he'd ever had.

Since Dawson didn't want to admit he'd been staring out the window half the night just to catch a glimpse of her, he decided to say, "Woke to a noise across the street and followed it here."

She gave him a quick once-over, her disbelief written all over her expression.

Yeah, he was still fully dressed. She would know that he slept in boxers and nothing else.

Her gaze narrowed as she took him in. "Looks like you just woke up all right. And I'm the tooth fairy."

"That's good to know, because I've been meaning to talk to you about that nickel you left me in second grade." Normally a statement like that would make her smile and then she'd fire a snappy comeback at him. He'd always loved her sense of humor. She wasn't buying in this time. Her glare could crack ice.

"No one's here but me and you. *You* should go." Didn't her tone just send an icy shiver down his back? Who needed air-conditioning with the chill she put in the air?

He needed to man up and ask her what was really on his mind while he had her here. He couldn't pinpoint the reason, maybe it was her mood, but he decided not to push his luck. In her state of mind she might just tell him. Brutal honesty could be the most painful kind, and a small part of him—the part that still had feelings for her—didn't want to know.

"Just as soon as I know you're okay." He took a step toward her. "And you put that shotgun away."

"You're looking at me. Do I seem fine to you?"

He wasn't about to touch that statement. "Let me double-check the place to be sure. I saw someone moving around inside. I won't be able to go back to sleep until I know you're safe."

Her cocked eyebrow and the way she looked him up and down again said he needed to drop the act. They both knew he wasn't asleep before.

"I can handle myself, Dawson. I don't need your help."

Most women would balk at the idea of going inside a house alone if there could be an intruder present. Melanie had always been able to stick up for herself, but she'd never been foolish. What was going on? Did she hate him so much that she'd be willing to risk her own safety just so she wouldn't have to look at him again?

"Then do it for me," he said.

"I already told you no." She moved around to block his access to the door, her back to the kitchen.

If he didn't know her any better, he'd say she was hiding something…or someone.

Reality hit him hard. She wasn't alone.

The last thing Dawson needed to see was the other guy. That would be an image he'd never be able to erase. It would burn into his retinas and his heart. "Suit yourself."

He turned and took a step toward the screen door.

A noise pierced the awkward silence. Then a sudden burst exploded behind him and he turned in time to see a little kid, bawling, running toward Melanie.

What the hell?

The kid had to be at least a year, maybe two. His friend Dylan's daughter was three and she looked much older than this guy.

Melanie swore under her breath, loud enough that Dawson heard but quiet enough to shield the kid.

The little boy moved closer, into the light, and Dawson's jaw fell slack.

Staring up at him was the spitting image *of him*.

Chapter Two

Melanie's pulse raced, her heart hammering on her rib cage as she started toward her son. *This cannot be happening.*

Her entire world was crashing down around her and it was hard to breathe. One look at Dawson and it was clear that he'd put two and two together. Her secret was out in the open.

She examined Dawson's reaction as panic welled inside her.

Pure unadulterated anger fired through his eyes when he glared at her. Melanie placed the shotgun on the cushion of the wicker sofa as she raced toward her son, who was crying and still half-asleep, with her arms open. "It's okay, baby."

"We're going to talk," Dawson said in a low growl that sent a chill racing down her spine.

Returning to Mason Ridge had been the worst of bad ideas.

This wasn't how things were supposed to go down. Abby had been supposed to stay in Houston with Mason, not bring him back to Mason Ridge. Her sister had called saying that Mason wouldn't stop crying and that his forehead felt warm. Even after Melanie had reassured her sister that he was most likely cutting teeth and would be fine, Abby had insisted she come anyway. She'd shown up four hours later.

Fear had gripped Melanie when she thought about Dawson's parents living right across the street and possibly seeing her son. Dawson visited all the time. He was too close, and her worst-case scenario was playing out all around her as she hugged her son closer to her chest and consoled him.

The heat of Dawson's glare practically burned holes through the back of her head. She didn't need to turn around to know he was staring at her. The only surprise was that he'd been mute so far. That scared her the most.

She felt Mason's forehead and frowned.

"He's burning up. I need to take him inside. You already know the way out."

"Nice try, but I'm not leaving until we talk." His tone was lighter than she expected and she quickly realized he wouldn't want to scare the baby. At least that would buy her some goodwill.

She exhaled.

"Fine." She patted Mason's back and he felt warm there, too. He hiccupped and coughed, and his chest sounded croupy.

Dawson followed her inside. His silence was worse than any words he could've thrown at her. She'd almost rather he yell. The guilt that had been eating at her insides for months was about to destroy her stomach lining.

No. She wouldn't do this to herself again. She'd made the right call, she reminded herself, the *only* one she could've made under the circumstances and especially after the warning from Dawson's mother.

And yet Melanie couldn't shake the feeling that everything was crumbling around her.

"Can you get a clean washcloth from the linen closet

down the hall and wet it?" She couldn't worry about Dawson right now. Mason was her priority. She carried her clinging eighteen-month-old son to the couch. He was dead weight in her arms, already in the ninety-seventh percentile for height and weight, and she felt every one of his twenty-six pounds.

Dawson disappeared down the hall, returning a few moments later with the offering. His dark brow creased with worry. He could be intimidating with his tall and powerful frame, and pitch-black hair. He had the face of a warrior…long, strong chin, hawk nose and serious dark brown eyes. But she'd seen the softer side to Dawson and knew exactly where her son got his kind disposition.

Dawson sat on the edge of the solid wood block coffee table.

Normally shy, Mason didn't blink twice at the stranger's presence. But then Dawson wasn't exactly a random person. He was Mason's father. Did her son know that somehow?

A fresh wave of guilt washed over her as she took the wet cloth from Dawson and placed it on her son's forehead.

"Stay right here, baby. Mommy's going to get you some medicine."

"Who's dat, Mama?" came out through a yawn. His normally bright dark eyes were glossy and dull from fever. This was more than teething and Melanie was glad Abby hadn't listened earlier.

"Mr. Hill is a nice man." She risked a glance at Dawson, who hadn't stopped staring at their son. No way could she get him to leave now, not with all those questions brewing behind those dark eyes. "He's going to help us tonight. Okay?"

Mason nodded and then closed his red-rimmed eyes.

"I'll be right back, sweetie."

She returned with a fever-reducing medicine strip that would melt on Mason's tongue as soon as he opened his mouth.

Dawson's body was square with her son, he was leaning forward, and he seemed protective of the little boy already. Melanie couldn't deny how right it felt to see the two of them together, no matter how much the thought she could lose Mason caused her chest to tighten.

When she got close enough, she could see that Dawson was holding Mason's hand. Her heart skipped a beat.

Nothing was ever going to be the same again.

Right now the only thing that mattered was getting Mason's fever down. She'd have to deal with the rest later.

"Open up, baby," she said.

Mason did. He'd always been an easy child.

She placed the small strip on his tongue. "Fifteen minutes and you'll feel all better."

He yawned again and rubbed his eyes. "Sleepy."

"Try to rest." She couldn't help noticing that Dawson still held her son's hand.

Melanie perched on the couch next to Mason, turning the cloth to the cooler side, rubbing his back.

"What's going on with him?" Dawson whispered. Concern deepened his tone.

"At first I thought he was teething but it has to be more." All of Dawson's attention was on Mason. Good. Melanie wouldn't be able to stand it if Dawson scrutinized her. "He's had teething syndrome, which means several of his teeth have been trying to come in at the same time. They've been giving him fits."

"But that doesn't explain the coughing and congestion."

"Exactly."

He looked up at her. Sensual heat crawled up her neck,

and her face heated, which couldn't be more unwelcome under the circumstances. She diverted her eyes to Mason, her safe place. No one could argue she'd been a good mother. Well, no one but her. Apparently delivering a child meant second-guessing every decision. By the time Mason's first birthday rolled around, she realized it was most likely a normal part of the turf.

Growing up watching her own parents live in a loveless marriage, Melanie didn't want to make the same mistakes. She wondered if they'd ever really been in love. Their relationship felt more as if they existed in the same house, like roommates and not husband and wife.

What they had was more of a mutual understanding than a marriage, and maybe a healthy fear of ending up alone.

If Melanie committed herself to a man, she wanted fire and spark and forever. Not someone content to live under the same roof or who was afraid to be by themselves.

And maybe that was a childish notion. Until she was sure about a relationship, she had no problem going solo. But then her last relationship, the one with Dawson, had set the bar pretty high before the unexpected pregnancy and everything that followed.

Fifteen minutes had passed and Mason's skin was beginning to cool. He'd turned on his side and his breathing had grown steady. Sleep was a good thing for her little angel.

Dawson pulled his cell out of his pocket.

"Who are you calling in the middle of the night?" she whispered.

"My mother. She'll know what to do." His voice was low.

She's already done enough, Melanie thought.

"It's too late," she said with a little too much emotion. "And this isn't the first routine fever I've gotten my son through."

"Is it? *Routine*?" The way he emphasized that last word made her realize he had other questions about his son's health, questions she knew would come.

"It's already coming down." Panic skittered across her nerves. His mother's words wound through Melanie's thoughts. If the baby became sick from the genetic illness that had taken his baby sister far too early, Dawson wouldn't survive. Then she'd reminded Melanie that Dawson had been adamant about never having kids of his own. He would never risk putting a child through the same thing his sister had endured. His mother had said that if Melanie told him about the baby, then he'd stick around, trapped, and that he'd resent her for the rest of their lives.

Melanie thought about her parents, who'd been forced to marry after an unplanned pregnancy, about their empty lives.

"He felt so hot when I touched his forehead. He was an inferno. It can't hurt to get a doctor's opinion," Dawson said, forcing her out of deep thought.

"Mason tends to get sick fast and hard, and he gets the worst temps. Luckily, he gets over them just as quickly. He needs rest and plenty of fluids. I'll give his pediatrician a call in the morning just to be sure."

"His name is Mason." It was more statement than question, the fire still burning behind Dawson's eyes.

"Yes."

"How did this happen?" He held up his free hand. "Don't answer that…*that* I know."

Her cheeks flamed.

"The rest is complicated." Her gaze bounced from Dawson to Mason. She didn't want to disturb his peaceful sleep.

"Not from my viewpoint." Frustration and confusion drew his dark eyebrows together.

"I'm exhausted, Dawson. I've been worried about Mason. Is there any chance we can talk about this tomorrow?" She started to turn but was stopped by his strong hand on her arm. She ignored the sensual trill vibrating through her where he touched, shrugging out of his grip.

"I saw a shadow pass by the front window. I should investigate before I leave. Besides, I'm not going anywhere until I know why this is the first time I found out I have a son." His voice carried a subtle threat, but there was no way Dawson would ever act on it. He was hurt, she could see that in his eyes, and he needed time to adjust to this new reality.

"Do we have to go through this right now?" she asked, hoping for more time, time to clear up her churning thoughts so she could speak like a reasonable adult.

The look he shot her could've burned a hole in Sheetrock. "Don't you think you've kept him from me long enough? Or that he deserves to know he has a father?"

"He needs his rest and I don't want to disturb him. We can talk tomorrow," she said as coldly as she could manage with Dawson so close.

"Oh, you really must think I'm an idiot. First, you hide my own son from me for…how old is he?"

"Eighteen months."

"A full year and a half…and then you think you can just tell me to leave so you can slip out of town again. Not this time. I'm not leaving your side until I know everything."

Hell would freeze over before she'd tell him the whole truth. Besides, he was acting as if this were all her fault and that fired anger through her veins. She wasn't just being selfish by not telling him about Mason, she'd been trying to protect him. "It takes two to tango, mister. You had to know this was a possibility."

"But we were careful."

"Condoms are only effective 98 percent of the time. Look who's in the 2 percent." She held her hands up and shrugged.

"They really should put that on the package." His anger was still rumbling along the surface and this was not the time for a rational discussion.

"They do. You'd need a magnifying glass to find it. At least, that's what I used." Her attempt at humor was met with a chilly response. For a split second, she wished for that carefree breezy smile of Dawson's. The way one of his lips curled in a half smile was just about the sexiest thing she'd seen. And it had been great at seducing her. Just thinking about it caused a similar reaction she had to consciously shut down.

She refocused on a sigh. "You already know he's eighteen months, so ask me something else."

"How'd you decide on his name?"

"It was easy. That's where he was conceived." She didn't want to admit to Dawson how very special that day was to her. And it had been.

"The night we spent at Mason Ridge Lake?"

She nodded. Dawson deserved to know that much at least. She had no plans to tell him what had happened a few weeks afterward in his mother's office. Her shoulders relaxed a bit the way they always did when she talked about her son, correction, *their* son. Like it or not, Dawson was most likely going to be part of their lives. For Mason's sake, that was a good thing. But she was worried about Dawson. Had she just condemned him to the fate she'd most feared? "What else do you want to know?"

"I don't even know where to start." Bewildered, he

rubbed the scruff on his chin. "What kinds of toys does he like?"

"The usual stuff babies like. Balls, trucks and baby dolls."

"You let him play with—"

"Don't even say it." She shot him a look that scolded him without another word.

"No. You're right. That was stupid and sexist of me." He paused. "You're sure he's going to be okay? He's so little and seems so…fragile."

The look on Dawson's face spoke volumes about how afraid he was for Mason. Of course, he wouldn't say that if he had to lug the little bugger around all day. But that wasn't really the question he was asking.

As far as Melanie knew, their son was fine. But then, the disease Dawson worried about wouldn't show up until later. There was genetic testing available but Melanie had been too freaked out to take that step. She would. There'd come a point in the near future when she would need to know. Up until now, she'd been able to bury the thought down deep.

"He's strong and healthy," she said for both of their benefits. "His fevers always scare the heck out of me, but he should be good by tomorrow. It's probably a virus and that's the reason for the cough."

"Sounds worse than that." Dawson stuffed his cell into his pocket. "If you won't let me call my mother, then we should take him to the emergency room or something. Mercy's open."

"He needs rest for now." She positioned extra pillows around his sides so he wouldn't roll off the sofa. If she were going to have this conversation or any conversation with Dawson she needed caffeine.

She moved to the fridge, Dawson on her heels, and

pulled out a Pepsi. Normally, she fixed a glass with ice and a lime wedge, but this situation called for emergency measures. The cap was off and she'd had her first swallow before Dawson could fire another question.

"Where do the two of you live?" His face was stone and she had no idea what he was thinking.

"Outside of Houston. We have a two-bedroom apartment there in a suburb."

"What about work? What do you do for a living?"

She didn't want to tell him. He'd judge her. Maybe even call her an unfit mother. Oh, no, would he try to take Mason away from her? Courts might side with him, given that she'd kept their little boy a secret all these months— a fact that she hadn't thought about until now. His family had enough money to wage war if they wanted to. Panic washed over her in a tidal wave mixed with other emotions. All her fears pressed down on her like concrete slabs pulling her to the bottom of the ocean. She put her hand to her chest.

"Breathe." That one word, spoken with authority, was more calming than it should be.

"I need to check on Mason." She took her Pepsi into the living room where she could keep an eye on her son.

Dawson followed.

"Let's sit over here so we can talk and keep an eye on him," she said, pointing to the pair of wingback chairs nestled near the fireplace as she eyed Dawson wearily, praying the caffeine would kick in.

"I'm not going to try to steal him, so you can stop looking at me like that," Dawson said.

"You want coffee or something?" She'd rehearsed this scenario inside her mind a thousand times. Facing him, seeing the hurt in his eyes planted so much doubt about her actions up until now.

"No, thanks. I'll take a Pepsi, though."

She retrieved another bottle and handed it to him as they returned to the wingback chairs near Mason.

Here goes.

Melanie opened her mouth to speak and then clamped it shut. A noise in the other room stopped her cold. "Did you hear that?"

"Get the baby and get ready to run on my word. Don't wait for me to come back. Just go when I say." Dawson was already on his feet, moving toward the kitchen so stealthily with his back against the wall that his movement almost didn't register.

By the second noise, Mason was in her arms and an ominous feeling had settled over her. Her purse was on the foyer table next to the front door, keys inside.

She heard a scuffle and then Dawson shouted, "Go!"

Her need to protect her son warred with her desire to make sure his father was okay.

Dawson had told her to leave.

She dug out her keys from the bottom of her bag, hands shaking, praying Mason would stay asleep on her shoulder.

As she stepped onto the front porch, a shotgun blasted in the other room.

Chapter Three

Melanie's pulse raced as Mason opened his eyes and bawled so loudly there was no covering it. The sound would alert whoever had the gun, and chances were that person wasn't Dawson. A knife pierced her chest at the thought of him being shot, bleeding. She had very much loved him and the two had been inseparable for most of their childhoods.

She bolted across the porch and down the stairs.

Mason wriggled, working up to release another round.

"It's okay, baby," she soothed as she made a run for her car, her legs bogged down by what felt like lead weights as she thought about leaving Dawson behind.

The carport on the side of the house was equal distance from the front and back doors. Anything happened to Dawson—and she prayed that wasn't the case—and the attacker could get to her and Mason easily.

She couldn't allow herself to think that anything could happen to Dawson, no matter how heavy her heart was in her chest, trying to convince her otherwise.

The auto unlock caused her sedan's lights to blink and make a clicking sound. Mason stirred and she feared he was about to wail again giving away their location, but he whimpered instead.

Melanie repeated a protection prayer she'd learned as

a child as she tucked Mason into the car seat. She half expected someone to come up from behind and jerk her away from her son. Or another sudden blast to split the air.

No matter how torn she felt between running to safety with her Mason and staying back to help his father, she would go. Dawson had ordered her to take the baby and run, and she had to believe—no, pray—he knew what he was doing.

Getting the key in the ignition was difficult with shaky hands. Adrenaline had kicked in and her insides churned. She finally managed on her fourth attempt. Mason stirred, crying louder, winding up to release a scream. The energy he was expending threw him into another coughing fit. And there was nothing she could do about it, which sent her stress hormones soaring.

Melanie backed out of the carport with blacked-out lights. She turned the car around so that she could better see as she navigated the gravel driveway.

With the windows up Mason's crying would be muffled to anyone outside the car. Leaving him in the backseat, not being able to comfort him while he cried ripped out another piece of her heart. As soon as she could be sure she'd gotten them out of there and to safety, she'd pull over. No, she'd call 9-1-1 first.

Nearing the end of the driveway, she was almost to the street when a dark figure jumped in front of the car.

Melanie slammed on the brakes and flipped on her headlights.

It was Dawson…covered in blood.

She unlocked the doors, motioning for him to get inside while scanning the darkness for his attacker. Her heart sank. She could get him to Mercy Hospital in twenty minutes.

He darted to the passenger side, opened the door and jumped in. "Go."

No other word was needed. As soon as his door closed, she gunned it, spinning out in the gravel. She eased her foot off the gas pedal enough for the tires to gain traction, cut a right at the end of the drive and sped toward Mercy.

"Dawson, you're shot."

"It's not that bad," he said.

Mason's cries intensified. She glanced in the rearview and saw that his eyes were closed as he tried to shove his fist in his mouth.

"You have blood all over you," she said to Dawson, not masking the panic in her voice as her heart ached to hold her son.

"It looks worse than it is," he said, dismissing her concern and focusing on Mason. "What can I do to help him?"

"There's an emergency pacifier in the diaper bag in the floorboard." She motioned toward the backseat. "I've been weaning him."

Dawson held up his bloody hands.

"There are wet wipes in the bag, too."

Dawson grunted in pain as he twisted around and pulled wipes from the bag. Distress was stamped all over his features at hearing the baby cry.

Melanie had had the same look when her son was born and she realized that she didn't have the first idea how to take care of a baby. A few months later, she'd become an old hand at caring for Mason, and she had no doubt that Dawson would, too.

As soon as the pacifier was in Mason's mouth, he quieted.

"Make a left at the next light," Dawson said, sounding satisfied.

She remembered that feeling well. Those early wins were important confidence boosters.

"You're hurt. I'm taking you to the hospital," she said emphatically.

"No. I'm fine." There was no room for argument in his tone. "A piece of the slug grazed my shoulder. That's all."

"It looks a lot worse than that," she said. Was he downplaying his injury? She wanted to believe he was fine. From her periphery she saw him one-arm his shirt off and then roll it up.

"Nah. I'll be okay."

"I have a medical kit in the glove box. There are a few supplies in there that should help."

"Since when did you start keeping an emergency kit in your car?" he asked.

"Mason was climbing up the stairs to a slide at a playground. A mom asked me a question, distracted me for one second. I looked away. Next thing I know, Mason's screaming and blood's pouring from his forehead. A nice couple brought over a few supplies they'd learned to keep with them. I made my own kit after that."

"The sound of his crying is heartbreaking. He's quiet, but what if he loses that pacifier I put in his mouth? Should I go back there and hold him or something?"

"Not with blood all over you. Plus, he's safer in his car seat."

"You're right. Of course. I don't know how you can listen to him and still drive. It kills me," he admitted.

"Believe me, it isn't easy." She didn't want to say that she'd had more practice than Dawson or remind him of what he'd already missed.

"I'll watch out to make sure we're not being followed," he said.

"Who was it back there?" she asked. "Did you get a good look at him?"

"I didn't recognize the guy. We had a scuffle and he got hold of the shotgun. He pulled the trigger as he ran away."

"I thought for sure it would be Sprigs." Relief flooded her that it wasn't him.

"What would he want with you?"

"He's always given me the creeps," she said with a shiver.

"Ever since he developed that crush on you when you were in middle school and couldn't let it go?"

"Yes. And every few months he felt the need to make sure I knew he still liked me. He was really upset when you and I started dating and sent me a few odd messages through social media. I tightened all my privacy controls when I left town so he couldn't see any of my stuff. I hoped that would send him the message to leave me alone." Learning he was involved in a child abduction ring had shocked her until she really thought about it. Sprigs was creepy before. Now he was flat-out dangerous.

"Why didn't you tell me?" he asked.

"Had no reason to before. I just thought he was a creep. Now, with everything going on I'm scared."

"What makes you think it might've been him tonight?" Dawson asked.

"I'm pretty sure that I got a piece of mail from him at my parent's house the other day. It was cryptic but alluded to the fact that we'd be together again someday. At the time, I thought he might be saying good-bye."

"And now you're worried he means you'll be together now," Dawson said through what sounded like clenched teeth.

She gripped the steering wheel tighter.

Mason stirred, crying without opening his eyes.

Melanie sang her son's favorite song while Dawson worked on his flesh wound for the rest of the ride. The baby settled halfway through the lyrics and fell back into a deep sleep.

Riding in a car helped. How many times had she driven around the block to get him to take a nap in the past year and a half? She'd lost count.

Singing in front of Dawson should embarrass her. For some reason, it didn't. She chalked it up to their history and tried not to read anything more into it.

It would be nice to know what Dawson was thinking. Then again, after all that had happened tonight, maybe not knowing was better.

Reporting the crime didn't take long. The deputy said he'd check the house personally and then lock up using the spare key Dawson provided. He also said that he'd make a note on the Sprigs case about the letter even though he seemed unconvinced the two were related, stating that stalkers acted alone.

"That seemed like a waste of time," Melanie said to Dawson on the way out of the sheriff's office.

"Agreed. Burglaries do happen, but this was not one of them. I have a feeling you're right about Sprigs and he's behind this in some way."

"Like I told the deputy, I'm not going back to that house tonight and I don't for one minute believe that could be random," Melanie said, patting Mason's back as he slept with his head on her shoulder.

Dawson agreed. "We're not staying at my parents' place, either. Sprigs is still on the loose and our friends have been targeted before. We need to take every precaution necessary to ensure your safety."

She wasn't sure she liked the sound of "we." However, she wasn't in a position to argue.

"That's part of the reason I was watching your house earlier." He seemed to realize that he hadn't meant to share that news, giving an awkward glance in her direction. "I was concerned about you, Melanie, and it wasn't like you were talking to me."

"I'm glad you were there, no matter what the actual reason was."

"By the looks of your initial reaction to my presence, you can take care of yourself." His tone was lighter and that was meant to be a joke.

It should be funny.

Being a single parent was more than difficult, even though Melanie wouldn't trade one single day with Mason for the world. If she were being totally honest, though, she was tired of taking care of everything on her own. Or maybe she was just tired. The early months had been a string of missed nights of sleep. Taking care of her son alone had been tough and rewarding and exhausting.

And lonely.

Part of her had a better understanding of why her parents chose to stay together and that scared her even more.

Having an intelligent conversation with a baby about the latest big book or movie wasn't exactly possible. Since her friends were out or asleep when the baby went down for the night, she'd buried herself in being Mason's mom.

"Confession?" she asked.

He nodded, smiled at the reference to the game they used to play when they were about to reveal something they didn't want to or wanted to correct a lie.

"I work at a bar at night so I can spend the days with Mason. I don't feel like I've really slept in—well, if you count the pregnancy—almost two and a half years."

The look of shock on his face had her thinking sharing was a bad idea.

"I know I'm not using my degree," she said quickly, "but I will. As soon as Mason's old enough to go to school, I plan to get an office job. And then we'll have more of a normal life. I didn't want to miss it—miss this stage. I wanted to be there to see him take his first steps, hear him say his first words."

And, yes, to watch over him and make sure he wasn't showing any signs of the disease Bethany had died from. She'd never say that part out loud, but it was just as true.

"Of course, I'm also afraid that I'm doing everything wrong. Maybe I should get a normal job now with regular hours. I worry about being tired all the time. How can I possibly be a great mother on the days I can barely keep my eyes open?"

Dawson's silence was just about the worst thing right now as they got inside the car and then pulled out of the parking lot without him responding.

His mother's words echoed in Melanie's head over and over again until her brain hurt. *Leave my son alone. Let him have a life. Don't trap him with a child that would only make him live every day in fear.*

Well, guess what? The secret was out in the open. The ball was in Dawson's court. He knew he had a son. And now he was as trapped as her parents had been.

"You're a good mother," Dawson said, and the note of reverence in his voice took her back.

"How do you know?"

"The way you look at him. The way you want to protect him. Back on the porch you were ready to shoot me. *Me.*"

"In my defense, I didn't know who you were at the time," she said.

"Exactly my point. You didn't so much as flinch. You'd do whatever it took to keep him safe. You couldn't possibly be a bad mother. But we're not even close to done talking."

She held up a hand as she suppressed a yawn. Yeah, it was a stall tactic. What could she say to him?

Melanie remembered every moment of his sorrow after losing his sister.

Once the baby was born, her emotions had been on a perpetual roller coaster. Should she tell him? Did he have a right to know? Would it break him if the worst case came true? She'd been too exhausted and too emotional to make a rational decision, even though she told herself a thousand times she'd figure out a way to reach out to Dawson. Every time she seriously considered it, an image of him after he lost his sister, the overwhelming sadness had her reconsidering.

Coming back to Mason Ridge had been a colossal mistake. What if Dawson got it in his head that he needed to "do the right thing" and propose? She'd have to refuse. Visions of shared custody and an empty holiday table every other Christmas flooded her and tears instantly welled in her eyes. She was being silly, selfish. She knew that.

A few spilled over, but she'd be damned if she let Dawson see her cry. How many times had she heard her own mother crying herself to sleep at night?

Melanie had no plans to go there. Ever.

"WHERE ARE YOU taking us?" Melanie asked Dawson, his brain still trying to process everything that had just happened.

"Somewhere safe." A place where they could take care of the baby and talk. Dawson was owed answers. He would ask more questions, but he honestly didn't know where to start. Finding out he had a kid was more than a shock and he was trying to wrap his mind around how he felt about the news. Most men had nine months to gear up for parenthood. He'd had the bomb dropped in his lap about an hour ago. Not to mention the fact that he'd missed the first entire year and a half of his son's life.

Anger. Now, there was an emotion. Dawson was all too familiar with that reaction to the world. He'd be all over it now if he thought raging would do any good. It wouldn't. One thing Dawson had learned from youth was that no good had ever come out of losing his temper. He had more experience to back that statement than he wanted to admit.

Fear was another emotion ripping through him. What if his son had the same genetic trait Bethany had? What if Mason developed Alexander disease? A ripple of anger burned through Dawson.

Distrust topped his list, as well. People lied all the time. Dawson was ridiculous enough to believe that he and Melanie had a special relationship. If it had been, she wouldn't have been able to harbor a secret of that magnitude.

The pair had been inseparable as kids. She'd been the only one he could trust when his five-year-old sister had been diagnosed with a terminal illness. His parents had mentally checked out afterward. Not Melanie. She'd been there for him every step of the way.

Sadness and rage had filled the ten-year-old Dawson. He'd been angry at the world for taking away his baby, and she'd been called his baby from the day she was born for how protective of her he'd been.

There'd been endless doctor visits and the agony of watching his baby wither away until she'd closed her eyes for the last time.

Dawson had withdrawn from his friends that year and retreated inside himself into a dark place. Then, out of nowhere, Melanie had shown up. She'd just sat on his stairs every day after school until her parents called her in for supper, never once knocking. Days turned into weeks, weeks into months. Curiosity eventually got the best of Dawson and he opened the door and asked her what she wanted.

"Nothing," she'd said.

He'd closed the door and gone back into his room, stewing over why anyone would sit there every day on his property if she didn't have a good reason.

The next day they had the same conversation. After a week, he told her to leave.

She'd looked at him with the same eyes she had now, shivering, and gave him a flat "No."

When he asked why she wouldn't leave, she'd replied, "Free country."

That day, he'd sat down next to her. "You sure are stubborn."

"I know," was all she'd said. Then she'd pulled out a stack of basketball trading cards from her coat pocket— collecting had been his passion—and asked him what he'd give for a Topps Kareem Abdul-Jabbar 1976/1977 edition.

Dawson, who hadn't looked at his cards in almost a year, started negotiating for the forty dollar prize. As he did, the heavy burden he'd been carrying since losing his baby lost some of its grip. That had also been the first night he didn't cry himself to sleep.

It had taken a little time after that, but he'd eventually regained his bearings. He'd rejoined his friends, the rest of the world, and had shared everything with Melanie since then. He and Melanie had been inseparable until hormones and the demands of his high school girlfriend had split them apart.

Of all the people in the world, Dawson had believed that no matter how much time and space came between them, Melanie would always have his back.

Until now. Until this. Until her betrayal.

Never in his wildest thoughts would he have guessed she would do this to him—denying him his child burned him like a stray bolt of lightning, fast and deep. Hiding his son from him was the worst betrayal. She'd broken every thread of trust that had existed between them in a way that couldn't be repaired.

Dawson forced his thoughts back to the present as he exited the highway. He'd pulled a few evasive maneuvers to ensure that no one had followed them. There was a hotel on the outskirts of town, heading toward Dallas, that would work. They should be safe there for a little while at least.

Law enforcement knew about Sprigs and Alcorn, but Dawson couldn't rule out the possibility that there'd be others involved. Those two might sit at the top of the crime ring, but they had to have a fairly sophisticated network to pull off human trafficking. Any of their lackeys could be after Melanie.

Dawson had a thought. Maybe the guy back at the house was supposed to kidnap Melanie and bring her to Sprigs. With everyone on the lookout for him, he'd have to be crafty. He could've planned to snatch Melanie and then disappear out of the country.

The thought sat hot in Dawson's stomach. Being on the Most Wanted list made all those individuals even more dangerous. And that meant his son was in serious danger, too.

"Who knows about Mason?" he asked.

"My family."

"That's all?" he pressed. He'd picked up on something in her voice when she answered.

"Yes."

With a sick baby, Dawson's first priority would be to

get adequate housing and food. What did a baby eat? Did his son even eat real food? Dawson had no idea. Resentment for losing the past year and a half of his child's life bubbled to the surface along with a very real fear. Thinking about his little sister, her illness, had him wondering again if his son would inherit the disease.

He glanced at the rearview.

Melanie had closed her eyes in the backseat while holding Mason's hand, and a piece of Dawson's heart stirred.

Once again, he was floored at the thought he had a child.

It was a lot to digest, but nothing would stop him from getting there and accepting it. An image of him and Mason playing ball popped up in Dawson's head. Pride filled his chest, accompanied by a feeling he couldn't put his finger on. He recalled feeling something like this for his baby sister when she'd been alive, but the feeling had been tucked away so deep he almost forgot it had existed.

He hadn't allowed himself to think about her in years. He guessed he'd stashed away everything that had caused him pain.

His relationship with his parents had never been the same after her death. Their mourning was so powerful, so strong that they had nothing left to give Dawson or each other.

His mother took it the hardest, staying in bed until Dawson returned from school most days for a year. Grief-stricken, she left her medical practice for almost two years before finally trying to move forward. His father put on a brave mask and went to work. He'd bring food home, keeping the house going, but he never really smiled or laughed after that.

A few years later one of Dawson's friends and her little brother, Rebecca and Shane, had been abducted. Dawson's parents had joined in the search. It was the first thing they'd done together since losing Bethany. With time, they became closer and more involved in Dawson's life again.

But in those dark years when the air had been sucked out of the house, Melanie had brought the light.

If someone had told him that Melanie would betray their history, their friendship, with one act, he wouldn't have believed it possible. She could've gotten away with almost anything and he'd have found a way to forgive her. But this?

Never.

Chapter Four

By the time Dawson pulled into the hotel parking lot, Melanie was asleep in the backseat. He hated to wake her, so he just stared at her for a minute. All those old feelings—good feelings, like nights spent outdoors looking up at the sky and warmth—crashed with the new reality, the one where she'd betrayed him in the worst way.

She wasn't the same person and neither was he. Her skin glowed and he figured something about motherhood had changed her. So much about her was different, especially in the way she carried herself. Her features had softened even more unless her son was threatened and then her protectiveness was written all over her stern gaze and determined stance.

On closer look, he'd noticed the dark circles under her eyes. It seemed she hadn't had a good night's sleep in months, and based on his limited experience with a baby, he could see how that might happen. Dawson didn't think he'd ever sleep again for worrying over his son, especially while the little guy was sick. Plus, everything about Mason seemed tiny and fragile.

The kid had a good set of lungs on him.

And Melanie seemed to think Mason was huge now. Dawson could only imagine what those first few months must've been like while he was even smaller.

"Where are we?" Melanie woke as soon as Dawson cut off the engine.

"We're in a Dallas suburb. Figured there'd be grocery stores nearby where we could pick up supplies for the baby."

She shook her head and blinked her eyes. "Okay. Just give me a second."

Dawson opened Mason's door and waited for her to unbuckle him. Working the car seat was a lesson for another day. He'd need to figure it out soon if he was going to take his son anywhere on his own. The learning curve on caring for a baby would be steep. He'd seen first-hand with his friend Dylan.

Melanie made it all look easy as she clicked a button and gently removed the straps to free their son.

Dawson reminded himself he'd only had two hours of practice, whereas she'd had the past eighteen months to adjust.

"You're tired. I'll carry the baby," Dawson said. No matter how bad things were between him and Melanie, Mason had nothing to do with it. Dawson had no plans to make his son feel uncomfortable when his parents were around each other so he'd have to work on keeping his emotions in check.

"No, thanks. I got him." Melanie scooped their son out of his seat fluidly. She had that same look in her eye that she did on the porch, too.

For now, Dawson wouldn't argue. But she'd learn to give him an inch. Mason belonged to both of them and Dawson had no plans to let his son down in the way his own parents had done him.

Grinding his back teeth, he shouldered the diaper bag.

After ten minutes at the front desk, Dawson had a hotel room key in hand and the promise that a crib was being delivered to the room. He knew enough to make sure there was a fridge and a microwave, opting for an all-suite hotel rather than one with traditional rooms. The inside entry would ensure that Melanie and Mason were safe while Dawson ran out for supplies.

Their suite was on the second floor, another safety precaution he'd insisted on.

"This should give us a place to rest and think so we can figure out our next move." He opened the door, allowing her and the baby in first.

"It might be safer for me and Mason if we go back to our apartment tomorrow. Sprigs doesn't know where I live."

He didn't want to scare her, but he couldn't let her take unnecessary risks with his child, either. "You're stuck with me until they catch him."

All hope that his comment would ease her concerns flew out the window with her exacerbated look. If possible, her stress levels seemed to increase. Hell on a stick. He hadn't meant for that to happen. She had bigger ghosts from her past to be afraid of than him.

Mason stirred, spit out his pacifier and started crying again.

The sound was pitiful and caused Dawson's heart to sink to his toes. He'd do just about anything to make it go away. Watching his son upset with no means to soothe him had never made Dawson feel more helpless in his life, not since…well…dammit…he couldn't go there again about his sister.

Melanie was gently bouncing Mason while she sang the song from the car to him.

The place had everything they needed, including a bedroom with a door that closed, sealing off the room. He figured Melanie would appreciate that feature as much as he did about now. Especially if they had to stay put for a few days.

"Is he hungry? Does he need milk or formula?" Dawson had scooped up the pacifier and set it on the counter.

"No, he shouldn't be. Babies cry when they don't feel good." She kissed Mason's forehead. "He's just telling us that whatever he has isn't fun."

Dawson stripped off his shirt and paced. He oversaw the logistics department for a major online retailer. He could handle this. He thought about his friend Dylan. There was a man who was the second least likely natural father material in their group and look how well he'd done since his daughter, Maribel, had come to live with him. To say the guy had changed drastically was a lot like saying a cow had turned into a dog.

Dawson mentally calculated the age difference between Maribel and Mason. She was three, so the two were about a year and a half apart. Thinking back, she'd come to live with her father when she was about six months older than Mason.

At least Dawson had a friend with experience at being thrown this curve ball. Dylan would be a great resource. Dawson needed to reach out to his friend when things settled down and he was able to spend time alone with his son. As protective as Melanie was, there was no risk she'd leave the two of them to their own resources before she had to.

As much as he didn't like the idea of being forced to spend time with her after what she'd done, he wasn't stupid. He would need her to help him get up to speed. Baby boys probably weren't much different from girls, but Dawson was starting from ground zero with the whole parenting thing, and he needed all the help he could get.

A few minutes of rocking and singing later, and Mason had settled down enough to go back to sleep.

"What time is it?" Melanie asked, diverting her gaze from him as a soft knock came at the door.

If that noise woke the baby, the person on the other side of that hunk of wood had better run. A glance at Mason revealed that he still slept.

Dawson checked through the peephole and saw two men dressed in maintenance jumpsuits standing on the other side. No doubt the crib had arrived.

He opened the door slightly and put his finger to his lips.

One of the men, the one nearest the door, nodded his understanding and then turned to his buddy and repeated the gesture.

Dawson allowed them access.

"Where would you like this set up?" the lead man whispered.

Dawson deferred to Melanie. An act he was sure to repeat more than he cared to in the coming days, weeks, months.

And yet she looked just as sweet and pitiful as Mason with the boy snuggled against her chest. Dawson didn't want to notice either of those things any more than he wanted to feel sorry for her. He did.

HAVING DAWSON AROUND fried Melanie's nerves. Thank the stars he'd gone out for milk and baby food after he washed up and rinsed blood from his shirt. At least now she could breathe normally again—something that was impossible to do when he was in the room.

The maintenance workers had put together the crib. Thankfully, Dawson had stuck around until they'd left, and he was all she could think about since he walked out the door.

She'd given Mason a second dose of medicine according to the directions on the package.

He'd made a good point earlier, though. Why was Sprigs still obsessed with her? There had to be some underlying reason. If she could figure it out maybe she could make it stop. She understood why their other friends had been targeted. They'd been sitting on secrets that, pieced together, could've gotten Beckett Alcorn and Sprigs arrested a lot sooner and broken up the child abduction scheme.

But what had Melanie done?

Nothing.

She'd been careful not to encourage Sprigs. Then again, it wasn't as if she'd remember something that had happened fifteen years ago. Good God, she could barely remember events from last week. Lack of sleep didn't do good things to the memory. Or the brain. Or the body, she mused, looking down at her little pooch. Her stomach muscles hadn't quite bounced back since she had the baby, and most of the time she didn't care. It wasn't as if she was trying to date.

Being in the room with Dawson had made her think about just how much she'd let herself go. Her hair was in a perpetual ponytail and she lived in yoga pants. She had to get dressed up for work, but that didn't count. Forget makeup unless it was time to clock in.

Then she'd force herself into a pair of jeans, put on an actual bra and rotate her three good shirts. Money had been tight and all of hers had gone to taking care of Mason. Another thing she didn't regret.

But speaking of clothes, she'd left her parents' house in such a rush she hadn't had a chance to grab any. Which was fine for now. At least she'd thrown on yoga pants when she heard the noise outside. Other than that, she had on a sleeping T-shirt and no bra.

And thinking about that was just a way of distracting herself from the very real possibility that Dawson would take her son away.

A part of her knew that he could never be that cruel, but if the shoe were on the other foot, what would she think about him?

She pushed the thought aside because she'd been trying to protect him.

Plus, there was no time to worry about that while she was hiding out from a crazy person—a man who stole kids.

A shudder ran through her bone-tired body. She'd been focused on the possibility of Dawson filing for sole custody, but there was another very real threat out there to her son. The Mason Ridge Abductor was more than one person, and the second half of that team seemed intent on harming her.

The door opened, causing her to jump.

"It's me," Dawson said, arms full of bags. "I got whole milk. That's what he drinks, right?"

"Yeah, sorry, I should've been specific."

"It's fine. I looked it up on my cell. Apparently, you can learn just about everything on the internet."

She couldn't help herself so she laughed at his attempt at humor. She shouldn't like the way it made him smile. At this point, she had no idea what his plans were and she had to protect her son at all costs. The thought of not being with him would end her—Mason was the only thing she'd thought about for two and a half years.

"I'll help you put away the groceries," she offered.

"Sit down. I got this." He waved her off.

She bit back a yawn. When was the last time she'd really slept? Certainly not at her parents' place. The idea had been good. Come back to Mason Ridge to help her friend while Abby took care of Mason in Houston. It was the first time she'd been away from him and she'd totally underestimated how much her heart would ache without him there.

A couple nights of sleep would help her be a better mother, she'd reasoned. Had any of that worked out the way she'd planned?

Only if tipping off his father to his existence was part of the plan.

Being away from her baby had only caused her to worry more about Mason, miss him and try to ignore the fact that his father, the man she'd never stopped loving, was sleeping right across the street. She'd known he was visiting because of his black SUV and a part of her had wished he'd been there because of his feelings for her even though she'd feared running into him, afraid of his questions. If he'd seen her face-to-face, would he realize something was different about her? Would he figure it out? Would he care?

Okay, so that last part had been answered with a resounding yes. But it wasn't an emotion reserved for her, it was for Mason. There'd never been a doubt in her mind that if Dawson had known about Mason he would want to do the right thing and be involved. Because he was truly a good guy, he would most likely even propose marriage. In her hormonal state, she might've agreed. And then what? If Mason did have the gene, God forbid, and ended up with the same fate as Bethany, Dawson would be stuck with Melanie forever. The only tie they'd had, Mason, would be gone. And their lives would be empty.

At least her parents had had two daughters as glue for their relationship.

Considering the other side of the coin, say Mason escaped the worst-case scenario. This was the one she prayed for every night. If she and Dawson had married based on her pregnancy, would all the spark between them slowly die with the realization that the only reason they were together was Mason?

Most nights, Melanie sat up worrying, churning over her guilt. She stressed about Mason growing up never knowing his father, about Dawson's reaction if he found out about his son, and about whether or not she was being unfair. And it had just felt like this huge no-win situation. Tell Dawson and commit him to a life of worry. Don't tell him and cheat him out of his son.

How many nights had she lain awake staring at the ceiling? That hamster wheel of questions spinning through her mind? Wishing answers would magically appear?

Working nights mostly after he was asleep, she felt incredibly blessed to have been there for all his important firsts. There would be even more that she had to look forward to, like his first day of kindergarten, his first bike ride and the first book he could read on his own. Based on his taste so far it would be something by Dr. Seuss.

"That about does it," Dawson said. She hadn't noticed the little clanking noises had stopped that he'd made while putting away supplies.

Another yawn rolled up and out before she could suppress it. When was the last time she'd been this tired? Having her body beyond the brink of exhaustion was one thing. Her mind, overthinking her circumstance, had pushed this into a whole new stratosphere.

"Think you can get some sleep?" he asked.

"I doubt it."

"I've never seen you look so tired."

"Comes with the job," she mused, thankful the mood had lightened at least for now. "Thanks for what you said earlier, by the way."

His brow came up as he took a seat on the couch. "And that was?"

"For saying I was a good mother."

"Whatever is going on between us, and believe me, we're going to talk about this all very soon, doesn't affect how I think of you as Mason's mother." He paused thoughtfully. "I meant every word of what I said. He couldn't have done better."

The deep rumble of his voice, the way it poured over her like Amaretto on vanilla ice cream, would cause her knees to buckle if she'd been standing. He'd always had that ability to make her legs turn into rubber.

"It means a lot to hear you say that, Dawson."

"Come sit over here on the couch," he said, motioning for her to take a seat next to him.

She did, feeling the heat swirl as their shoulders touched. He still had that effect on her and she should be concerned about that. As it was, she was just happy that she could feel that way for anyone. To say her love life had been a draught since getting pregnant was the understatement of the year.

Walking away from Dawson had been one of the most difficult things she'd ever done. Until sitting next to him on the couch right now.

Chapter Five

Dawson urged Melanie to put her head on his shoulder as he leaned deeper into the sofa, tabling his anger for now.

If they were going to coparent, they were going to have to learn to work together. None of that could happen in her current condition and his former state of mind. She was run-down, skittish and exhausted, and he couldn't help feeling partly to blame. As it was, he'd been throwing a lot of subtle anger at her. Not that he wasn't still mad.

Right now he acknowledged that it was more important to set his own frustration aside and do what was right for Mason. And that involved making sure his mother took better care of herself.

As soon as he figured out what to do about Sprigs so they could set this ordeal behind them, Dawson would take the necessary steps to ensure that Mason had everything he needed. First order of business would be figuring out an appropriate amount of child support. Melanie was stubborn. She'd argue about taking the money. He could see that it was important for her to feel as though she was taking care of her son.

Dawson could tighten his own belt enough to swing paying her bills.

A noise shot straight through him. He held steady, and

that was a good thing, because that small, honking-like-a-duck sound came out of Melanie.

She was asleep on his shoulder and that shouldn't give him satisfaction.

It did.

MELANIE WOKE WITH a start and quickly scanned the room. Dawson was pacing in front of the window, holding Mason. The image of him shirtless, with their son against his chest, could melt a glacier in Antarctica. She wouldn't be able to erase that picture for a long time, and maybe a little piece of her heart didn't want to. "How is he?"

"His fever is down and he hasn't coughed again."

"That's great news." Maybe life could be like this? Dawson could pitch in to help share some of the load. His mother was wrong. He looked pretty happy holding his son. "I should change his diaper."

"Changed it when he woke up. That wasn't as easy as it looks. On the internet they use a baby doll to demonstrate. This little guy doesn't hold still." Dawson seemed pleased with himself.

Melanie had worked so hard at creating a life for herself and Mason without really including others. She'd moved to Houston to get away from Dawson, but that had also separated her from her family and any help they could give. Her sister was busy with college in Austin. Maybe it was time to let someone else in. "Did you get any sleep?"

"No."

"I can take Mason for a while. Let you get some shuteye." She made a move to get up.

Dawson waved her off.

"Not necessary. I don't need that much rest. Plus, I

was doing some thinking. We should talk." He paused—
so not a good sign—and she prepared for the bombshell
he was about to drop.

"Mind if I get a cup of coffee first?" she asked, needing to put off the conversation until she had enough caffeine inside her to handle what was sure to come next. A
discussion about Dawson in their life, permanently.

"You don't drink coffee," he said.

"I need caffeine and I'd kill for a toothbrush right now."

"You'll find that and toothpaste in the bathroom.
Pepsi's in the fridge. I had the store manager cut up some
limes and there's ice in the bucket." He motioned toward
the counter. Sure enough, ice and a glass waited.

"Seriously?" Okay, now she knew she was dreaming.

A few minutes later, clean teeth sealed the deal. This
felt too good to be real life.

"That's still how you like it, right?" he asked as she
walked into the room.

"Yeah. I just didn't think—"

"What? I'd remember?"

"That you'd care." She pulled out the baggy of wedge-
sliced limes from the pint-size fridge.

"If you doubted my feelings before, then you don't
need to anymore. I'm 'all in' with everything connected
to this little boy." His tone was laced with just enough ice
to send a chill rippling down her back. It wasn't much,
not enough for someone who didn't know him to pick up
on, but she knew.

He bounced the baby on his knee and Mason was too
happy for her to ruin the moment by shooting a zinger
back. Besides, she didn't want to start a fight in front of
him, and since she was about to have her favorite drink
courtesy of Dawson, she decided to let his comments slide
as she fixed her soda.

Ice in a glass, followed by Pepsi and then the lime and this was shaping up to be the best morning she'd had in a long while. She took a sip and could've sworn she heard angels sing. "I slept crazy-good on that couch last night." She glanced at the clock. "Correction, this morning. Thanks for seeing to Mason."

"He needed his breakfast and you have to take better care of yourself."

So much for polite conversation.

Melanie decided nothing would ruin her first Pepsi. She walked over to the small table and chairs nestled in the corner rather than sit in the living area.

Not having to rush around to change Mason's diaper and fix him something to eat left her feeling a little useless. This should be a glorious time. Had she forgotten how to have an easy morning? This wasn't exactly a normal situation. She tried her best to ignore the big presence on the chair, but he seemed intent on sweating her out.

"Okay. Fine. What did you want to discuss?" she asked.

Dawson was on his feet. He made a beeline toward her, and her pulse beat faster with every step he came closer. She set her Pepsi down in time to receive Mason.

"Do you smell that?" he asked, turning his attention toward the appliances.

"No. What?" She sniffed near Mason's diaper, grateful that wasn't the kind of scent he was talking about.

"Did you leave anything on in the bathroom?"

"Like what? There's only a hair dryer in there. I think you'd hear it." She glanced around the room, and must've seen the smoke at the same time as he did.

Dawson raced toward the door to the hallway and placed his hand on it. "It's hot. We're not going out that way."

"That's not good." Melanie tamped down the panic rising in her chest.

"No. It isn't."

"Why aren't the smoke detectors going off?" She motioned toward the sprinkler on the ceiling.

"Good question. The control panel might've been disabled," he said with a frustrated grunt.

"This can't be related to us, can it? How would anyone know we were here?" she asked.

"I thought we'd be safe all the way out here. Whoever set the fire might've located your car in the parking lot." Dawson disappeared into the bathroom and she heard water running. Melanie found a phone and called 9-1-1.

It took two minutes in total to report the fire.

Dawson returned a few seconds later and placed the towels at the base of the door, sealing off the room. "We're not getting out that way, so that means we have to use our other option."

Melanie glanced around the room as Dawson disappeared into the bedroom. She had no idea what options he was talking about.

"I'm going to close this door so I don't scare the baby when I break the window," he said as he appeared in the doorway.

"Okay. I'll gather up supplies." She let Mason stand by himself at the coffee table. He was a good walker but could get ahead of himself and end up on his back side.

Melanie spent the next five minutes packing the diaper bag.

A crash sounded as the sirens blared in the distance.

Dawson appeared in the room a moment later. "We can't leave until the firemen get here. There's no way to get him down safely. This whole scenario makes me think someone's trying to flush us out."

"I hear the sirens." Smoke was creeping in through the vents causing Melanie to cough.

Dawson picked up Mason and held him tight to his chest. "Let's bring him in the other room where the air is clear."

The little boy angled his body toward the floor, started wiggling and winding up to cry.

"He wants down. What should I do?" The big strong Dawson looked at a loss for the first time since this ordeal had started last night.

Melanie held out her hands, trying to see if her son would come to her. Mason let out a whimper and shook his head.

"Come on, baby."

His answer was still no.

She located her keys in the diaper bag and jingled them. He took the bait this time and angled his body toward her.

Dawson jumped into action the second they hit the next room. He wet towels and stuffed them under the door to prevent smoke from filling the bedroom. And then he paced.

The next ten minutes waiting for the firemen to arrive were excruciating.

Dawson was signaling the firefighters in the lot as they roared up to the building.

Once they were discovered, it didn't take but a few more seconds for a safety ladder to be placed against the wall and a fireman to climb the rungs.

Melanie handed over her baby and then followed the fireman down. Dawson was already there by the time she set foot on the ground. He'd wasted no time jumping out the window and had managed to bring the diaper bag with him.

Since it was midday, there were fewer cars in the parking lot. About twenty people stood around, watching the building to see what would happen next. A few others milled around.

With the noise and commotion, it would be easy for Sprigs to hide among the onlookers, so she held Mason tighter to her chest.

Dawson kept her tucked behind him, scanning the lot as he waited their turn to give statements.

"We'll need to stick around a little while. Stay close," Dawson said, his gaze scanning the lot, keeping his body between her and everyone else. He motioned toward an officer and whispered to her, "This place isn't safe and I don't want either of you out of my sight."

Chapter Six

Melanie strapped Mason securely in his car seat. It hadn't taken long to give her statement to the officer a few minutes ago, since it was the same as Dawson's. They'd also relayed their belief that this could be connected to the case in Mason Ridge. The officer had taken notes and then promised to connect to the sheriff's office.

"It might be best to get out of Texas for a few days until this whole thing blows over," Dawson said.

"I have to work tonight and I need this job."

"I'm not sure I like the idea of you going back to work until we sort this out." He moved to the driver's side, so she handed him the keys.

She didn't want to remind him of the fact that she'd had a life before last night that she needed to get back to, a safe life that didn't include home invasions and arson.

"Do you think he's here?" She glanced around. An uneasy feeling settled in her stomach.

"Might be. Either way, we're not taking the chance."

Dawson snaked out of the parking lot and then hopped on and off the highway a couple of times, checking the rearview.

"Sprigs had to be involved with that fire, didn't he? It's too coincidental," she said.

"Do you remember when the Sno-Kone building burned down?" Dawson asked.

"Yeah, I do. It was during one of the hottest summers, late July. They never caught the guy."

"Dylan saw Sprigs watching from in between cars in the parking lot. He set the fire." Dawson changed lanes.

"I remember specifically that they never caught the guy. Why didn't Dylan go to the cops?"

He slanted a look at her and then returned his full attention to the stretch of highway in front of them.

"Right. With Dylan's criminal history they wouldn't have believed him," she said, deflated.

"Or worse, they would've accused him of doing it instead."

"Why would anyone report a crime they committed themselves?" The sheriff's department needed a serious overhaul. She doubted Sheriff Brine would hold office much longer given his personal association with the Alcorns. The senior Alcorn might've been cleared of suspicion, although he had to have been covering, but his son was guilty. And he was going to do the prison time.

"People do crazy things and Dylan isn't stupid," Dawson said. "Which is why he didn't get caught for most of the stuff he pulled."

"I can't believe how much he's changed."

Dawson quirked a glance at her.

"I've been in touch with a couple of the girls. They've been keeping me up-to-date," she clarified.

"He straightened himself out in the military." Dawson changed lanes again. "I'm guessing the attack on your parents' house was a crime of opportunity and that means Sprigs or one of his people is watching you. The guy from last night most likely works for Sprigs. When he didn't get the job done, Sprigs may have decided to step up and take care of it himself at the hotel."

"Except these are just theories. We have no evidence and we can't prove anything," she said.

"True. Rest assured that I have every intention of ensuring your safety personally." His tone left no room for doubt.

"No one knows where I live in Houston. I've kept my address private from everyone but my family, Lisa and Samantha. Those are the only people who can track me down," she said.

"You're going to have to open your circle a little wider, you know, now that everything's changed."

She didn't respond. He was talking about himself and, most likely, his family.

"And I've been thinking about something else, too. I don't want you to work. Not while Mason's little and you have to sling drinks at some bar," he said, matter-of-factly.

"Not a chance. I don't want to depend on anyone else for a check."

"We haven't been off to a good start here and I'll take responsibility for my part. However, I get a say in how my son's brought up from here on out, and I don't want his mother working in a bar. Period."

Period? Did Dawson suddenly get to dictate her life? How would that work out for her? The idea of being home with Mason and not being exhausted all the time was serious nirvana to her, but not like this. Not when she'd have to watch the mailbox every month for a check from Dawson, or set her phone on alert to be notified if he made a deposit in her bank account. Just the thought of being completely dependent on someone else made a hot rash creep up her chest. She'd worked too hard for her independence.

"No can do. End of story," she said a little too emphatically.

"I beg to differ."

"You don't get to step in and tell me how to run my life, Dawson."

"I'm offering you an opportunity here. I thought you'd want to grab on to it. Why does it frustrate you? You said you wanted to spend more time with Mason." That he sounded genuinely confused didn't help matters.

"I do."

"Then why are you being so stubborn?"

Is that what he thought? He didn't have hordes of money stashed in a bank account somewhere. He worked for a living, and he'd started saving for his own ranch when he was a kid. No way would she take his savings away from him. *He'd resent it if I did*, a little voice in the back of her mind said. Owning his own ranch had been his dream since he was a little boy. And he'd been waking up early and driving into Dallas for a job at a major online retailer running logistics that he didn't like for a very long time to make it come true. Even though his parents had more than enough money to fund any venture Dawson set his sights on, he was too proud to take their handout. Precisely the reason he should understand her position.

"It's important for me to take care of us, and I've been doing a pretty darn good job of it so far," she said.

"Just like that?" came out half hurt, half growl.

It was better for her to upset him now than to be the reason he had to abandon his future.

"Thank you, though. I do appreciate the thought. It's just that I need to be able to take care of things on my own."

"Like you have been by shutting me out?" he countered.

"I'm sorry about my decision up to this point when it comes to you and Mason. But my life is a different story. I make the calls. You'll be involved with your son. I get that. And we'll work out a decent schedule for visitation later."

"Visitation?"

"Oh, I assumed you wanted to be part of Mason's life. I totally understand if that's not the case." Was she off base?

"Try and keep me away." His low timbre sent a different kind of shiver down her neck.

Was that a threat? She decided to let it slide. They were both stressed and that had their nerves on edge. Dawson wouldn't stay mad at her for long. And she had his best interest at heart. He'd see that eventually.

In the meantime, this was going to be one long car trip. One hour down, four to go. *Oh joy!*

Mason had nodded off in the backseat, which meant that Ms. Waverly, the babysitter, was going to have an interesting time watching him tonight. Or, more likely, Melanie was going to have a tough time tomorrow considering he didn't do so well when his schedule was off track. Toddlers craved routine.

But then, what if Sprigs figured out where she lived? Would he come for her? Mason could get hurt in the cross fire. Anxiety engulfed her like a wildfire.

"I've done everything I can to keep my information private, but what if he finds me in Houston?" She couldn't keep panic from her voice.

"He won't. And if he does, I'll be there to stop him."

"You can't stay at my place forever. You have work to get back to. Your life is in Mason Ridge."

"Let me worry about that," he said. "Besides, every law enforcement agency is looking for him right now. You're on high alert and he's been getting away with his crimes for a long time because he's not stupid."

"He could hurt Mason to get back at me." Her voice sounded small even to her. "Maybe I should call my parents and ask them to pick him up. He could go on the road with them for a little while."

The idea of being separated from her son even for a short period knifed her heart, but she clamped down the pain. There was no way she'd risk her son's safety just so she could see him every day.

"Let's look at this logically. You could call your folks and have them take him on the road. If Sprigs is determined to get to you, then he could track them down. They're older, unsuspecting—"

"I'd tell them what was going on, Dawson."

"Fine. Even if they know what they're getting into, that doesn't mean they can keep him safer than we can, than *I* can. I don't like the idea of being apart. Not when our son could be used against you."

"You have a good argument," she conceded. She'd be relieved if not for the fear settling over her. No matter how much this felt like a bad dream, this was real and it might not be going away any time soon.

"No one's taking our son." Dawson's words, the determination in them, brought a wave of comfort over her fried nerves.

"You're right," she said. "I'm not going back to Mason Ridge and neither is Mason."

"For now, I'll agree to those terms. I'll tell my family about my son as soon as we get better acquainted and then they'll want to be part of his life, too."

It shouldn't wrench Melanie's stomach that Mason would have so many more people in his life to love him. She couldn't think of that without the selfish thought that meant she'd get so much less of him. No matter how she looked at it, there was no way she could or would deny his father or grandparents visitation.

However, the conversation with his mother might not go as smoothly as Dawson assumed. He didn't have any idea what the woman had said to a newly pregnant Melanie that made her hightail it out of town.

Heck, Melanie had been so naive that for half of her pregnancy she'd expected Dawson to show up, thinking that surely his mother would've shared the news at some point. She hadn't, so Melanie had kept up her end of the bargain. The way she'd read his mother's threat was that she got to keep her son if she disappeared.

Over time, Melanie had let go of the fear his mother would follow through. The woman had only wanted Melanie to disappear.

Dawson would still be in the dark about his son if Melanie hadn't gone to Mason Ridge. Even though she was terrified of the future and of the coming changes, she couldn't regret that decision now.

Dawson knew.

All her cards were on the table for everyone to see, or soon would be. Didn't that leave a sinking feeling in the pit of her stomach? Having Dawson around played havoc with her mentally and physically. And she was already exhausted from both. The thought of bringing more people into the equation didn't exactly calm her stress levels.

The rest of the drive was unsettling save for the fact that Mason slept most of the way. He'd barely coughed and she figured the reason he was sleeping so much was that his body was fighting the virus.

Getting home to her own apartment was the best part of her day.

The strong possibility that Sprigs was still near Mason Ridge made her even happier to be in Houston. In fact, she didn't care what Dawson said, she had no plans to return to her hometown after all that had happened. Not until Sprigs was safely locked behind bars. Maybe not even then.

She didn't care what Dawson thought about her plans, either. He could come to Houston for a visit to his son anytime he wanted to.

Even though it was inevitable, she didn't want to negotiate with Dawson. She still remembered how broken he'd been when he lost his sister, because it was the same look that was on his face when he realized her son was his child, too.

Was his mother right? Would Dawson always hold her in contempt for bringing back those old hurts?

Was it somehow making it all worse that he found out about Mason this way? Heck if Melanie knew what the best path was anymore.

No relationship, no matter how strong or steeped in history, could survive that betrayal. She'd known that on some level when she made the deal with the devil in the first place. She'd been scared, hormonal and alone, and his mother had pounced on the opportunity to put Melanie in her place—a place below the Hill family. In Alice Hill's opinion, Melanie had never been good enough for Dawson.

Seeing the hurt in his eyes—hurt she'd put there—Melanie couldn't argue with the woman's point.

MELANIE'S APARTMENT MIGHT lack in square footage but it made up for it in charm. The place was all her, and Dawson didn't want to instantly feel at home there even though he did.

The living area was open to the kitchen with a large pass-through in between. She'd placed a couple of beige bar stools there. A couch and a pair of chairs flanked the fireplace. The wood mantel had several candid pictures of her and Mason. Dawson could see the age progression in the photos and part of him wondered who'd taken the shots. Jealousy roared through him at the thought of another man being around his son. *And Melanie. Touching Melanie.*

Okay, fine. He didn't like the idea of another man's hands on Melanie, but she wasn't exactly territory he had the right to claim no matter how possessive he felt. Seeing his son in her arms didn't help with that particular emotion and Dawson figured he needed to get used to all this. She wasn't going away. He wasn't going away. And there could be a man in her life…no… Dawson couldn't even go there in thought.

No other man got to spend more time with his son than him. *Or with Melanie,* a little voice inside his head said. Dawson would like to quash that cursed little voice, too. He didn't need to have feelings for her, especially since he was already jealous thinking of a make-believe guy spending time with her and Mason.

Dawson needed to sort out his crazy emotions and come up with a plan for making this arrangement work. If not for his logistics job in Dallas, he'd consider relocating to Houston to be closer to his son. Then again, he could always find another job once the dust settled.

How would Melanie react? That's where the confusion began. It wasn't the fact that he'd had a son with Melanie that threw Dawson. It was that she didn't trust him no matter how well she knew him—and Melanie knew him better than anyone else. Then there was the simple fact that she was the one who'd kept his child from him and *she* looked at him suspiciously anyway.

Forget that he'd been naive enough to think they'd had

a strong bond as kids. A spark had ignited when they'd started a *fling*, wasn't that what she'd called it before she left?

He'd been confused, hurt when she'd pushed him away before, and it made even less sense now. He was, after all, the father of their child and trying to help.

"Would you mind changing Mason's diaper while I get his dinner ready?" she asked.

"Got it." Dawson started toward the little tyke. He ran down the hall, squealing in delight. What a different picture from last night.

After completing the task, he returned. He leaned his hip against the kitchen counter, essentially blocking her in. "How about I watch Mason tonight while you work?"

"You're not serious. And I need to feed him so I can get ready."

"Oh, but I am. Give Ms. Whoever the night off. I'm here. I'll just be fumbling around waiting for you otherwise."

"Are you kidding me? You barely learned how to change a diaper today. It's too much, too soon."

There she was, not trusting him again and it hurt more than he cared to acknowledge. "I can take care of my own son."

"All I'm saying is give it more time."

"You'll save money this way. You'll be at work with a lot of people around you. Sprigs doesn't know where you live, but we can't be too cautious, not after what happened at the hotel." Even she couldn't argue his logic there. "How old is the babysitter?"

"She's old. And you have a point. I don't want to put her at risk unnecessarily."

Capitalizing on his good fortune, he added, "You can write down his evening routine. I'll follow it to the letter."

She stood there for a long moment, contemplating, tapping her toe on the tile. She had that look on her face, the one that said he was wearing her down. Time to be quiet and let her decide. The longer she took to make up her mind, the better for him. At least some things hadn't changed about her.

"Okay. You win." She jotted down a list with a satisfied little smirk, which he didn't quite understand. "It's easier to bathe Mason in the sink than in the tub."

"Got it." He took the list.

"Are you sure?"

"I said I was good to go," he said.

"Okay. You have my number. Call if you have any questions. Anything comes up and I can be home in twenty minutes if needed."

"We'll be fine. Besides, I have this—" he held up his cell "—if I need you."

"That reminds me. I haven't charged my phone for the past twenty-four hours. No way do I have battery left," she said.

"Where's the charger? I'll plug it in while you get ready for work."

"Thanks. That's really helpful." She looked surprised.

"We can get along when we try, Melanie." He regretted the words as soon as they left his mouth. They'd made progress in the past fifteen minutes toward him not being so angry and her actually giving him real responsibility with Mason. Dawson was going to need to figure out how to put the past behind him if he was going to give his son the life he deserved. And Mason deserved for his parents to work together on his behalf. "I'm sorry I said that."

"It's fine." Her chin came up defiantly. "You're right. We're both adults."

"I'm working on it." He tried to make a joke to lighten the mood.

"I hope we can make peace for Mason's sake," she said before disappearing to get ready for work.

That was exactly what he intended to do. He made himself comfortable on the floor, playing cars with Mason.

When Melanie stepped in the room after getting dressed, Dawson also regretted staying home to watch the baby rather than sit at the bar and watch over her.

The jeans she wore fit her like a second set of skin and she had the curves to prove it. Her white blouse over a black bra showed just enough lace to get Dawson's imagination going. Her breasts, though covered, were fuller than he remembered. She had more curves, and his body betrayed him by instantly reacting to her beauty.

With her shiny hair long and loose around her shoulders, he almost decided it was a good time to revisit his earlier argument about her not working at all.

"Ma-ma." Mason bolted across the room toward her.

The blouse she was wearing was buttoned up and Dawson figured that was for his and Mason's benefit. Imagining her shirt opened a little more wasn't a good idea.

"You look fantastic, Melanie," he said, and his voice was deeper than he'd intended.

Chapter Seven

The baby started crying before Melanie got out the door. Dawson wondered how a kid could go from smiling, happy-go-lucky, playing on the floor to full-on tears and tantrum so quickly and suddenly, as if someone had flipped a switch.

Worse yet, Melanie calmed the child long enough to leave. And then the second wave hit.

Loud. Heartbreaking. Helpless.

"It's okay, little guy." Dawson tried to soothe him, unsure if picking the toddler up would make things worse.

The little boy's fist went into his mouth and then he choked on slobber.

How on earth had Melanie figured all this out on her own?

The boy couldn't be hungry. He'd eaten half an hour ago.

All Dawson was supposed to have to do was to give the kid a bath and then put him to bed. It wasn't supposed to be this hard, or gut wrenching. Hearing the little guy cry was ripping Dawson's heart out of his chest. His stress level was through the roof.

His pride wouldn't let him call Melanie for help.

There had to be something he could do to calm him.

Dawson scanned the room for something, anything

that might distract the child. TV. That should work. He located the remote on the coffee table and clicked on the TV.

The cartoon added to the noise factor. Dawson held his arms out toward the boy to see if he wanted to be held.

That elicited a scream so loud the neighbor tapped on the adjacent wall. Dawson didn't want to get Melanie in trouble with her apartment complex. What had she used earlier to calm Mason? Keys. Dawson searched for a set. No, Melanie had taken hers with her. He'd left his parents' place in such a rush to check on her last night that he'd forgotten his own, which reminded him that he needed to call his parents and let them know he wouldn't be back for a while.

No keys.

There wasn't much else Dawson could do, so he brought his son juice. Dawson was so flustered that he stubbed his toe on the leg of the coffee table, bit back a word he couldn't say in front of his son, and then hopped around on his good foot. What he wouldn't give for a strong drink right about then.

Mason laughed.

Dawson thought he might not have heard correctly. So he pretended to hurt his toe this time and was rewarded with a full belly laugh.

"Oh, you like that?"

A pair of red-rimmed eyes stared up at him. So he did the only thing he could…picked up a toy and smacked himself upside the head with it.

Mason roared with laughter.

Making his son happy made something else happen inside Dawson…something he couldn't put his finger on. It was fragile but not fleeting.

Rather than analyze what any of that meant, Dawson asked, "Ready for a bath?"

The little boy's face lit up as he sniffled and then coughed. Crying must've aggravated his chest.

Dawson had never felt so on edge. One wrong move and a torrent of those crocodile tears would be rolling down Mason's cheeks again. Dawson had never felt so vulnerable in his life.

He scooped his son off the floor and into his arms.

There was a resource he'd be tapping into later, his friend Dylan. But Dawson didn't want to share this news with anyone just yet. Not until he wrapped his own mind around it.

Mason started winding up to cry again.

Was there something else Melanie had given him to quiet him? Oh. Right. A pacifier. Dawson dashed over to the diaper bag and located a clean one.

The little boy was satisfied the second he popped it in his mouth.

And that made Dawson very happy.

Melanie had told Dawson it was easier to bathe Mason in the sink.

There were toys in the bath. Mason wiggled in Dawson's arms, indicating he wanted to get down.

Dawson obliged, careful not to set off another round of crying and, therefore, coughing.

He managed to get his son through a bath in the tub with minimal tears, but Dawson was on edge the entire time. Getting on Mason's pajamas was another issue. The little squirt refused.

Trying again, Dawson was pleased with himself when he managed to dress his son only to find his clothes littering the hallway. By the third attempt, Dawson was happy to get a T-shirt on his child.

What was wrong with sleeping in a T-shirt and a diaper?

Putting the kid to bed should be easy, right?

No. That brought on a whole new wave of tears and cries for his mama.

Refusing to admit defeat, Dawson popped a cartoon into the DVD player. Given that there were twenty different DVDs with the same animal on the cover, Dawson figured this was his son's favorite show.

He settled onto the couch with Mason curled up on his chest.

MELANIE EASED HER key into the lock, slowly opened the door and tiptoed across the threshold. It was quarter to three in the morning on a pitch-black night.

Inside, light from the TV filled the space. She stopped midstride when she got a good look at what was on her couch. Her heart squeezed at the sight of Mason curled up on his father's chest, both sleeping.

They looked so natural together. She'd expected at least one frantic phone call while she was at work. Dawson seemed to have handled everything like a pro. And that was every reason she should keep her guard up.

The thought occurred to her that he could have a great case to reverse custody. The courts might just decide in his favor. She would be the one with visitation rather than the other way around. Panic filled her, causing her to shake. She couldn't lose Mason. He'd become her world and that was exactly how she wanted it.

There was another thing Melanie had forced out of her thoughts far too often. The disease that had claimed Dawson's sister so young. Bethany was five when the devastating diagnosis came. Over a short period, Dawson had watched his baby sister lose her ability to walk, talk and smile. He'd said not being able to make her laugh anymore was the worst part. Melanie figured he didn't want to remember those horrible final months until his sister had gone peacefully in her sleep.

She'd seen firsthand how difficult his sister's death had been on his family. Having a child of her own gave her a deeper understanding of just how hard, how unfair, that had been. His mother, a physician, who couldn't heal her own daughter. No wonder the woman had become so bitter.

Melanie didn't think she'd be the same way, but then she hadn't walked in that woman's shoes, either. And that was what kept Melanie from hating Alice Hill.

Instead of dwelling on that thought, Melanie turned off the TV, put her things down and peeled Mason from Dawson's arms.

As soon as the weight lifted, Dawson sat up and his hands gripped her arms.

"It's just me," she said quickly, trying not to wake the baby.

Dawson's tight grip released and he rubbed his eyes.

"I'll be right back after I put Mason down," she whispered.

A nod of acknowledgment came, quickly followed by a yawn.

Melanie moved out of the room, her panic mounting. She kissed Mason on the forehead before placing him inside his crib and pulling the covers over him. "Night, my sweet boy."

Facing the man in the next room was even more difficult with her fears mounting. She took a calming breath and marched into the living room.

Dawson was in the kitchen, making coffee.

"Looks like everything went well tonight," she said. Her normal routine had her eating a bowl of cereal, taking a shower and then flopping in bed. Six thirty in the morning would come early and Mason had always been an early riser.

"We got through it," he said, his tone unreadable as he watched the coffee brew. He turned to her. "Did you notice anything strange at work?"

"No. It was a typical Thursday. We actually do a pretty good business. Kicks off the weekend."

"You work every weekend?"

The coffee finished brewing. She handed him a mug, which he immediately filled.

"Yep. Every Thursday, Friday and Saturday night. Working a weekday is the only way I could get a mostly weekend schedule. Money's good so pretty much everyone wants weekends." Melanie pulled out her late-night snack supplies, Cheerios and milk. She made a bowl of cereal and settled on one of the beige bar stools. "Which gives me Sunday through Wednesday on a normal sleep schedule with Mason."

"Is there anyone else around to depend on? Friends?" he asked, taking a sip.

"I don't have time," she said quickly. Too quickly. "I have my sister to keep me company if that's what you're asking. It doesn't seem to be the same for you, but getting the hang of parenting wasn't so easy for me. I don't do anything besides take care of my son."

Dawson seemed to contemplate that with a look of… relief?

"What time does he wake up?" he asked.

"Six thirty."

"In the morning?"

"Afraid so." She took a bite of cereal and chewed. "Which is why I need to finish eating and shower so I can get to bed."

"That's only three hours of sleep if you're lucky," he said in horror.

"Tell me about it," she said. "We take a nap together after lunch. I try to store up as much sleep as I can on my days off to make up for it."

"It doesn't seem healthy for you or him," he said, and she picked up on something in his voice. Admiration?

Nah. She was hearing what she wanted.

"Thanks for being concerned, but it's actually much easier now that he sleeps through the night. How did he feel, by the way? Any sign of the fever coming back?"

"No. He did fine."

"Good." All her worrying had been for nothing. Was it wrong that a little selfish piece of her wanted them to need her help? She finished the rest of her cereal as Dawson leaned against the counter and drained his coffee mug.

"This is normally when I grab a few hours of sleep," she said after placing her bowl in the dishwasher. "I'm sorry that I don't have a guest room. I'm told the couch is comfortable, though."

"Don't worry about it. I've slept all I'm going to tonight."

"Are you sure?"

He nodded.

"Suit yourself," she said. "I need my beauty sleep. My alarm will go off far too soon."

"Tell me what to do and I'll take care of Mason while you sleep in," Dawson offered, pouring another cup.

"Thanks for offering, but Mason thrives on routine. If he doesn't see me first thing, it could be a rough day." Maybe that was hopeful. He and Dawson seemed to get along fine without her before.

"It's high time I became part of that routine, don't you think?" He pinned her with the way he glared at her.

There was no good comeback to that, so she nodded, fought back tears and said good-night.

The warm water from the shower sluiced over her, soothing the tension in her shoulders. Part of her was glad that Dawson was in her apartment under the circumstances. He made her feel physically safe and no one would watch over Mason more closely. And yet his presence brought on a whole new set of issues, too. No matter how much she fought it, she was still attracted to the guy. Plus, there was the complication of him knowing about Mason.

Had Melanie really believed she'd be able to keep this secret forever?

If she were being honest with herself, the answer was no.

Maybe it was good that they were facing this now. They were both reasonable adults and they could surely come up with a compromise that didn't suck the life out of her.

On that note, she finished washing, dried herself and then dressed in her normal bed clothes of boxer shorts and an old T-shirt from college, keenly aware of the male presence in the next room.

Had Dawson been fishing to see if she had a boyfriend earlier? Why did it embarrass her so much to discuss it with him?

There were other priorities in her life at the moment. Maybe she should have turned the tables and asked about his personal life. Lisa and Samantha had kept pretty quiet about his activities in the past few years and Melanie kept herself from asking about him. She knew there was no good that could come out of knowing about his business because he'd moved on.

Speaking of Lisa, Melanie needed to phone her friend tomorrow with an update. If she heard about the break-in, she would be worried. News would most likely travel quickly.

Her pulse picked up.

The whole town would know Melanie's secret soon enough. And she'd have to face Alice Hill.

Tossing and turning for a good hour, Melanie finally let go enough to fall asleep.

MELANIE BLINKED HER eyes open. The sun blared through her window.

What time was it?

The clock read one fifteen, but that couldn't be right. She listened for sounds coming from the next room as she peeled covers off and slipped into her warm-up pants.

Had she forgotten to set her alarm last night? No way. She distinctly remembered doing it.

A moment of panic seized her. What if something had happened to Mason? Or Dawson? She barreled toward the door. The fact that the house was quiet didn't sit well.

There was no one in the living room or kitchen. Mason's room was empty as was the hall bath.

Melanie tore out the front door to see if her car was still there. It was parked right where she left it. Her pulse raced.

Could something have happened?

Wouldn't she have heard a noise?

Maybe her neighbor heard something. She broke into a run, panic pressing down on her chest, making it difficult to breathe. Nothing could happen to her little boy.

Mr. Patterson opened on the second round of knocking, midknock.

Melanie pulled her arm back. "Have you seen Mason?"

The older gentleman gave her a disapproving once-over. "No. Sure heard him last night, though," he said.

"I'm sorry, what?"

"Could hardly hear my TV for all the crying noise." His nose wrinkled as if he'd tasted something sour.

Had Dawson lied about how well the night had gone? Why would he do that?

Melanie thanked her neighbor, deciding now was not the time to remind him how many times his TV had been turned up so loud that it had disturbed Mason. Instead, she promised it wouldn't happen again. She hoped it wouldn't, at least. Those first few months had been rocky, but she'd figured out plenty of tricks to keep her son calm since then. Sickness or pain couldn't be helped, though. She wished for thicker walls.

Maybe when Mason went to school and she got a better job she'd be able to afford to rent a small house somewhere?

In the meantime, she needed to find her son.

As she turned to go find her cell phone, she heard Mason's laughter. She moved to the parking lot and realized where it was coming from—the playground. Her complex had a small area with a slide and a few swings.

Well, now she was just angry.

She stalked over to the source of Mason's joy, stopping when she saw Dawson smack himself in the head with one of Mason's toys.

Mason roared with laughter.

"What are you thinking taking my son outside without letting me know?" she said, maintaining as calm a voice as she could muster so as not to upset Mason.

"Mama!" Mason exclaimed.

She walked over and kissed his head while the swing stopped. Dawson didn't immediately say anything.

"You're going to give yourself a concussion with that

thing," she said to Dawson, moving behind Mason to give his swing a push.

The boy giggled, clapping his hands. He loved the swings.

"What, this?" Dawson bopped his head again.

Mason laughed so hard he could barely breathe. Melanie giggled. She wasn't thrilled about it, but she couldn't help herself. A grown man smacking himself in the head with a fire engine was funny.

"Is that how you finally stopped Mason from crying last night?" she asked, giving Mason's seat another shove.

"Confession?" he asked.

"Fine. Go ahead," she said, knowing that meant she'd have to forgive him for whatever came out of his mouth next.

"Last night didn't go so well," he said, sounding defeated.

"Why didn't you tell me?" she asked.

"I didn't want you to worry. And I didn't want you to think you had to bring in his babysitter tonight. We survived and I know I can do this," he said quickly.

"Not without being honest with each other." Didn't those words taste bitter?

Especially when Dawson shot her a look and said, "Like you have been with me?"

Okay, he had her on that point. She wouldn't deny that.

"I can't change the past, Dawson. I'm sorry for how everything turned out. I should've trusted you and I was scared." She didn't want to tell him the rest just yet. Not in front of Mason. "We both have adjustments to make if this is going to work. For starters, you can't take the baby without telling me. I was frantic."

"You didn't see my note?" he asked. "I tacked it to

the fridge. Figured you'd get a Pepsi first thing when you got up."

That was actually really thoughtful. She was too busy running around the house like a crazed woman to see it.

"All I did was blast through the place looking for you and Mason. When I didn't hear or see anyone, I panicked." The swing came back a little too fast and hit her arm. "Ouch."

Mason roared with laughter.

"I won't do this again without telling you first. But the same goes for you. I want to know where my son is and what he's doing at all times," he said, firing back.

He made sense. It would be impossible to keep each other updated every second. Wow. This was going to be more difficult than she'd thought. And she hadn't figured it would be a picnic before.

"Leaving a note was the right thing to do," she conceded. "We'll figure it out over time. We're both new at this sharing thing. And you do seem to be doing a good job with him."

"It was dicey until I figured out that me being in pain cracks him up," he said, and she appreciated his attempt to lighten the mood.

"I had no idea he was such a masochist," she said, doing her best to calm down.

"Apparently so." Dawson gave another push.

"I wonder if we should be worried," she joked.

Dawson's half smile tightened a coil low in her belly. It had been too long since she'd been with a man. Suddenly she realized that she must look a mess, and embarrassment heated her cheeks.

Or was the flush caused by something else? Something more primal that accompanied being this close to Dawson?

Chapter Eight

Dawson didn't mean to sound the alarm for Melanie earlier. He'd left a note. The panicked look on her face was the same he felt every time he thought about what had happened to Bethany and the gene he might've passed on to Mason.

Alexander disease might be a rare genetic disorder, but it was a devastating one, taking away everything about Bethany until it had drained her life, too. A burst of anger exploded in his chest as he thought about the past. Sitting on the sidelines with Bethany had him watching a slow death of the brightest star. There'd been nothing he could do to stop it or make it better.

Did Melanie have the same fear?

"Has he been tested?" He studied her, waiting for a reaction.

"No." She looked at him apologetically.

"Have you considered it?" he pressed.

She nodded but didn't speak, and that pretty much told him she didn't want to think about it even though she had.

"When did you feed him lunch?" she asked, and he realized why she was redirecting the conversation. She wouldn't want to discuss something that important in front of Mason.

And she was right. They could talk about it once they got through the weekend.

Dawson checked his watch. "At about twelve. He seemed hungry, so I gave him Cheerios and I cut up bananas. He seemed to really like those."

"I'm impressed. How'd you figure that out?" she asked. He shouldn't allow himself to feel a sense of pride.

"First, I checked in the cabinets. Then I searched my portable nanny here." He held up his phone.

"Of course."

"To be honest, the first thing I looked for was peanut butter and jelly. Thought I'd make him a sandwich."

"His pediatrician wants us to wait until he's at least two. There are so many food allergies now," she said. Then added, "It's about time for an *n-a-p*." She spelled out the last word. "You were so insistent on figuring out everything on your own last night that I didn't warn you how hard it is to put him to bed."

"I deserved that." He could be man enough to admit that.

Melanie gave her son, *their* son, a five-minute warning that they would have to leave the playground.

"I'm guessing the *b-a-t-h* went okay."

"No drama there. The tears didn't start until I tried to dress him after."

"Let me guess. He threw off his clothes and ran down the hallway naked?" Her laugh was musical and Dawson didn't want to notice those little details about her anymore.

"He usually does that?"

"I call him The Streak for a reason. We have a whole thing that we have to go through to get him to bed without him feeling like the world is ending. When I saw you guys on the couch, I worried he might've given you a hard time," she said. "You were so quick to push me out the door last night that I figured you had a handle on it."

Dawson had a lot to learn about his son. He glanced up at Melanie and saw the brightest smile on her face.

Hold on a damn minute. He recognized that look.

"You're gloating," he said.

"Am not," she denied with a twinkle in her eye.

"Are, too," he said. And didn't this argument take him back to their childhood? They'd fought like brother and sister, fierce yet forgiving, except that was where the familial similarities ended. Dawson had never thought of Melanie like a sister.

"Prove it," she countered, and then gave Mason a three-minute warning.

"Challenge accepted," he teased. They both needed a light moment. Even though his heart belonged to his son, becoming a parent overnight was a lot to process. Between that and the very real threat they faced, Dawson could use some levity.

"Time's up, little man," she said.

Dawson steadied himself for the screaming fit sure to come because Mason looked pretty darn comfortable on that swing.

"Are you ready to race?" she asked her son while holding her arms out. Mason's face lit up.

Damn, she was good at this parenting thing. Dawson reminded himself how much more practice she'd had.

He followed behind them, scanning the perimeter of the playground and then the parking lot as they headed back to the apartment.

They'd had a few good moments on the playground and Dawson hoped to expand on that sentiment as they got to know each other as parents.

"I'll just clean him up and tuck him in," she said, looking at him pensively. The awkwardness returned. "Did you want to…"

"Come here, little buddy," Dawson said, dropping to his knees, realizing after watching Melanie that confidence was half the battle with a toddler.

Mason flew into Dawson's open arms, melting any frustration he had about the change in temperature from Melanie. She'd closed up again based on the tension framing her eyes.

After a nice hug, she and Mason disappeared down the hall, hand in hand.

Dawson got busy in the kitchen. Living alone had given him the skills he needed to get by. He'd fed Mason but skipped eating lunch. Melanie was probably hungry, too.

He should still be furious with her, and that emotion simmered somewhere below the surface. However, putting Mason first meant getting along with the boy's mother. That meant setting Dawson's personal feelings aside, because one look at his son and Dawson knew that his own feelings would take a backseat from now on.

For now, he'd focus on lunch. A trip to the grocery store would come later.

From the supplies on hand, he could heat up bean and cheese burritos.

Melanie came in the room, fresh-faced with her hair pulled up in a ponytail. Dawson tried not to think about the full breasts pressing against her white T-shirt or the soft cotton shorts resting on those full hips—hips his finger had trailed down while he admired her body not that long ago.

Even dressed down she looked incredible. Sexy. And woke all kinds of urges inside him. The sex he'd had since was lackluster by comparison.

Based on his body's reaction to thinking about it he needed to think about something else.

Diapers. Now, there was a subject that could kill a sex drive.

"Why are you smiling?" Melanie asked, entering the small kitchen.

"Already fixed a Pepsi for you." He motioned toward the peace offering on the counter. He didn't want to notice the electricity pinging between them or the sizzle of attraction causing his blood to heat. Instead, he focused on stirring the pot of beans.

"That's really nice of you. Thank you," she said as she moved to the other side of the counter.

"How'd you get him to bed so quickly?" Dawson scanned the hallway, half expecting the tot to come running.

"I told you. He loves his routine," she said.

"Which is?"

"For naps I always wash his face and hands and then we race to the bed."

"I'm picking up on a theme here," Dawson said.

"Yep. He loves to run. The more I make things a game, the less resistance I get. I'm all about making things easier and saving the big battles for the important stuff," she said, then took a sip of her Pepsi.

Sounded easy enough. Dawson could do fun.

"What are you making?" Melanie asked.

"Burritos."

"They smell amazing." She closed her eyes and breathed in the scent.

He should've looked away sooner and not let that heart-shaped face distract him. He didn't. And when she opened her eyes again and smiled at him, he lost himself for a second.

"Oh. Watch out for the burner," she said.

Didn't he feel like an idiot? Standing there, staring at her, he'd burned lunch. Dawson pulled the skillet off the stove, set it in the sink and then withdrew his hand.

He'd gotten distracted and now lunch was ruined.

And wasn't that poetic justice?

MELANIE HOPPED OFF the bar stool and sprang into action, opening the window before the fire alarm went off and woke the baby.

"You need some help in there?" she asked.

"No," was the gruff response.

Dawson wasn't being a jerk. He was embarrassed and she felt bad. She could see that, even though he was still processing things, he was making a huge effort to get along and find some common ground. And maybe that meant he wouldn't show up with court documents requesting full custody when the dust settled from recent crazy events.

And would it be so bad to have a partner to help her bring up Mason? If she were being honest the past couple of years had been lonely.

"I can run out and pick something up. You can't imagine how nice it would be to run an errand while Mason's sleeping," she offered.

His eyebrow went up.

"Don't get me wrong, I'm not complaining about caring for him. He's still the best thing that's ever happened to me."

His other eyebrow hiked.

"I'm just saying that I trust you to stay here with him while I pick up lunch."

"Okay. I'll clean up this mess," he relented, waving his hand around the kitchen.

"Turn that thing into a magic wand and maybe the whole place will be clean by the time I get back," she joked, trying to recover the light mood from earlier. Sure, they were stepping on each other's toes and making mistakes. It had only been a few hours.

Dawson surprised her with a sexy little smirk. And didn't a thousand butterflies release in her stomach when he did? Thoughts of his glorious naked male form crowded her mind. So not a good thing right now.

It was a good time to make an exit before her lack of a sex life had her throwing herself at the man after one cute smile.

She grabbed her keys and made it to the car without giving away her reaction and embarrassing herself. No way did Dawson share the same attraction as she did. Okay, that was a lie. Maybe he still felt a spark. It wouldn't matter. She knew the man better than anyone and he'd never forgive her. Plus, she still wasn't being completely honest with him. She needed to find a way to tell him about his mother. Heck, there was so much to talk about. Where did she even start?

Bringing back fast food was most likely the easiest thing she'd do that day.

She returned with burgers, fries and strawberry milk shakes. His favorites. Hers, too, but she didn't want to think about how much they had in common. Right now she wanted to focus her energy on figuring out why Sprigs had come after her in the first place and on keeping Mason safe.

Dawson didn't smile when she handed over the food, and she figured now that Mason was asleep the questions would begin. Dawson had many. She could tell by his expression, and she'd always been good at reading him.

"How long does he usually nap?" Dawson asked halfway through their meal. He must've been starving to wait this long to speak, especially with the way he cleaned his plate.

"Hour and a half if I'm lucky," she said in between bites. "Thirty minutes if I'm not."

"He's a handful when he's awake," he said.

"I'm not complaining," she said defensively, careful not to give him the impression she couldn't handle this on her own.

"It's *me*, Melanie," Dawson said. "Relax, okay?"

That was half the problem.

"What do you want to know?" She eased back on the beige stool.

"What's his favorite food?"

"Easy. Spaghetti," she said, forcing her shoulders to chill.

"Color?"

"He'll tell you that it's blue, but it's actually green." She hadn't thought about how much Dawson had missed of Mason's life. Sharing him would be difficult, but it hit her that it was the right thing to do for Dawson and her son. The two deserved a chance to get to know each other.

Dawson had been taking everything well so far.

"Why didn't you tell me about him?" Dawson asked.

"I was scared."

He shot her a look that said he recognized BS when he heard it.

"Why didn't you really?"

She shrugged.

"I keep thinking about how I'm going to tell my family," he said.

Melanie must've given him a look without trying to, because he pinned her with his gaze.

"What aren't you telling me?" he demanded.

"It's going to take time to learn everything about him, Dawson," she hedged, trying to redirect the conversation back to a comfortable place. "Maybe it's enough for the two of you to get to know each other. We don't have to do this all in one day, do we?"

"No. Of course not. I have plans to stick around. I know we have a lot to work out and he needs to get used to my presence, but you need to know that I have every intention of being there for my son as he grows up." He must've picked up on her discomfort. "And I want to contribute financially, too."

"No, Dawson—"

"I've already given this some thought. All this stuff—" he picked up a diaper and a toy "—must cost a lot. I understand that you don't want to depend on me, but it's not fair for you to bear the burden alone. I have money saved that's sitting there, doing nothing."

"Money that you've been saving since you were thirteen years old. I can't take any of that money. I'll let you help out with diapers and you're welcome to bring him toys—"

"Let me help you buy a condo or small place outside of town. Nothing fancy."

"No way."

"That way you won't have to depend on me for a check every month. Isn't that what you're worried about?" he asked.

"Well, yes, but—"

"You wouldn't have to be if you let me put a roof over your head," he said.

She was shaking her head, which seemed to make him even more determined.

"How much do you pay here?"

"Nine hundred dollars a month."

"For this?" Shock was written across his wide-open eyes as he glanced around.

"It's a two bedroom, and bigger cities have a higher cost of living," she said defensively.

"Then I can save you even more than I thought. You could cut your hours at the bar and spend more time with Mason," he countered. "That way I'll be helping without you feeling like you're standing at the mailbox every month. It's a win-win."

That thought scared her, excited her and gave her night sweats all at the same time. Dawson would be good for Mason, there was no denying that.

She picked up a French fry and chewed on it.

And it looked as though he planned to be there for the long haul.

He'd made that much clear.

"What about your ranch? You've been dreaming of buying one forever," she said. She couldn't argue with his point that it would make her life easier if all she had to work for was groceries, gas and utilities. Her parents had given her their second car last year, since they were on the road so much, so she didn't have a car payment, which had been another godsend.

"You know what they say. Priorities change when you become a parent. Owning a ranch doesn't seem as important to me as making sure my son has everything he needs."

How could she let Dawson give up his dream? His mother's words wound through her head. *He'll resent you for the rest of his life.*

While Dawson's intentions might be good right now, he hadn't really had time to adjust yet. She didn't want him doing something he might regret later.

"That's a great offer, so please don't take this the wrong

way but I can't agree to that right now." Fear hit her that he'd want to bring Mason around his mother. Dawson might want to be part of his son's life, but his mother was a whole different issue.

Heart racing, Melanie decided to set that thought aside. No way could she deal with Alice, this stalker and the fact that her own life had been turned upside down in a matter of hours.

He folded his arms.

"I just want a little time to think about it. This is a lot for me, too. Don't get me wrong, I'd love to spend more time with Mason. That's not it," she said.

"Then what is? Is it me?"

The way he asked that second question nearly tore her heart from her chest. No. It wasn't him. Yes, it kind of was. Everything was all mixed up and she needed a minute to soak everything in.

"This is a lot to digest, Dawson. One minute, I'm home to support a friend and the next a crazed guy is trying to hurt me and you're here." Did that come out right? "I'm grateful for that last part, don't get me wrong."

Relief eased the tension lines bracketing his mouth.

"Good. I was afraid you were going to ask me to leave," he said.

"I wouldn't be that stupid. Or unfair. I need you. Mason needs you. There's a lot we have to sort out for the long run. Right now we need to figure out what Sprigs is up to. I was home and maybe that's the first time he knew where I was. But he's wanted by the law and I'm shocked he would risk getting caught. His life is on the line. Why come after me at all?"

"I can think of one reason," he said. She didn't like Dawson's ominous tone and she knew exactly what he was about to say. "And we already mentioned it."

"He has nothing to lose," she said under her breath.

The rest of their meal was spent in silence. She was contemplating Dawson's offer and how that might change her and Mason's life.

Mason cried, awake too soon, and Melanie excused herself to tend to him. His curls were tousled, his eyes still sleepy.

She made an excuse about needing to clean in order to keep a little distance between her and Dawson for the rest of the afternoon. Besides, she needed something else to occupy her thoughts, and the place needed a good once-over. That didn't normally happen until one of her days off.

Cleaning usually helped clear her mind.

Except one person kept cycling back in her thoughts... Sprigs.

Chapter Nine

More than a week had passed since the break-in at Melanie's parents' house. The few days off Melanie had spent with Mason and Dawson made her dread going back to work the following night even more. They had only broken the ice in terms of figuring things out, but hope was taking seed.

And as much as she didn't want to admit the fact, since she knew how temporary their situation was, having Dawson around was nice. More than that, actually. It was dangerous because she could get used to it.

The man had become decent at putting Mason to bed without any meltdowns.

Melanie had been able to shower without worrying about much of anything besides how warm the water felt against her skin. She pushed aside errant thoughts of the handful of times she and Dawson had made love under jets like those.

By the time Dawson had finished Mason's nighttime routine, she'd settled on the couch with a magazine. He, too, was fresh from the shower. He wore cotton pajama bottoms that he'd bought and no shirt. Water rivulets rolled down his muscled chest.

Melanie forced herself to look away. What could she say? The man was hot. She could hardly blame her body for reacting when he was close. Images of all the places she'd touched that perfect body of his crowded her thoughts. There was precious little she could do to stop those, too. Fine, some things couldn't be helped. She didn't have to wear it on a billboard, she thought, trying to ignore the heat climbing up her neck, flushing her cheeks.

The lights were low, and she hoped that Dawson couldn't see her reaction.

She was never more aware of how little either of them was wearing. Melanie grabbed a throw pillow and hugged it against her stomach as Dawson joined her on the couch.

Thankfully, he'd taken the other side of it.

"Hold on a second." He held a hand up as he disappeared into the kitchen and then returned with two full wine glasses. "Couldn't find that red you used to like."

"That merlot was so good. What was the name of it?" It had been so long she forgot. She also blamed the memory loss on the fuzzy brain that came with having a baby.

But then, when was the last time she'd relaxed and had a drink?

Melanie took a sip of wine and then set the glass on the coffee table, doing her level best not to think about just how long it had been since she'd really relaxed.

"Do you remember that time we caught your mom sneaking a smoke outside when we came home early from school?" Dawson asked.

"I do. We skipped the pep rally so we could hang out at my house," she said. "I was mortified."

"We learned a valuable lesson, though." He laughed. Really laughed. And the sound was sweet.

"No snooping in anyone's business after that," she said. There was the other time she'd come home early and found her mom passed out. The empty wine bottle on the counter had said everything Melanie needed to know about why her mother was facedown, snoring, on the sofa.

Melanie had never asked about either incident. There'd been a few others. Her mother had made such a show of trying to appear like the perfect family that Melanie didn't have the heart to confront her back then.

"I always wondered if Mom was ever truly happy," she said. Every birthday, every holiday, her mother had put on a nice outfit and a smile. She'd spent most of the time in the kitchen while Melanie's dad watched sports on TV. Same story on the weekends. The most sincere thing was the effort her mother put forth in trying to sell the charade to her daughters.

"Did you ever ask?" Dawson took a sip of wine.

"Are you kidding? That was all I ever knew growing up. It never really occurred to me that we were different. I just thought all families were like that." Although her mother had put up a good front, Melanie wondered if she'd ever truly been happy with her father. Did she ever really laugh? Or talk about something that really mattered?

"Funny how families slip into roles and we don't really ever question them," he said.

"Mostly, I remember polite dinner conversation. Looking back, I remember that if anything bad happened we swept it under the rug." Melanie never thought to expect more.

"Now that you mention it, I don't think I've ever seen your parents disagree in all the years I've known your family," he said.

"They are almost like robots if you think about it."

"You don't think they were existing happily together?" he asked.

"Can you think of one time you actually saw my mother laugh?" she countered. "I mean like really laugh?"

"Guess I never thought about it before. I'm sure I've seen her smile."

"Really smile or polite smile?" There'd been such a vacancy behind her mother's eyes and a hollow quality to her laughter. And then there were the times when Melanie's dad went on hunting trips with his buddies and her mother believed Melanie was asleep. Hearing her mother cry at night had been the worst.

"I guess not." He frowned. "How are they on the road together?"

"Probably as polite as ever," she quipped, trying not to think about just how boring that might be.

"Why do you think that is?" he asked.

"Heck if I know." She shrugged. "My family was never very demonstrative of their feelings. I mean, I know my dad loved me. I think he saw his role as the main provider of the family and Mom was there to take care of the girls. When I think back, there isn't one time I remember seeing my parents hug each other. Isn't that weird?"

"Families are complicated beasts," he said.

"At least we became friends out of the deal," she quipped, trying not to think about just how sad her parent's situation had been.

"How so?" His brow went up.

"Well, I couldn't stand being trapped inside my house, so I decided to bug you instead. My sister was too young, too boring." She tossed the pillow at him.

He caught it.

"Lucky for me." He put on one of those killer smiles and her stomach flip-flopped.

"Yes, it was," she teased, trying to distract herself from the sensual shivers rippling through her, centering heat inside her thighs.

"Like I said." He put the pillow behind his head.

"Hey, give me that back."

"You gave it to me." Another devastating grin.

"Everything in this house technically belongs to me, you know. So that makes you a thief." It was so easy to fall back into their old routine. Getting along had never been a problem.

"No way. It was a gift." He turned to give her another ice-melting smile. "And if you want it back, you have to come over here and take it."

She wasn't falling for that trap again.

The last time he'd pulled that card on her, they ended up in bed together. And it had been without a doubt the best sex of her life, which was why she'd done it more. If she closed her eyes, she could still feel his hands on her, roaming her body. She could still see the expression on his face when he looked at her naked. No one had made her feel so adored or so beautiful. This was not the time for her brain to remind her just how long it had been since she'd had sex. She told herself that she was too tired to think about it most of the time and part of that was true. And if she really wanted to be honest, she'd admit the physical act wasn't even what she missed most. Being held afterward, arms and legs in a tangle. Dawson's strong, male form pressed against her. Waking up to him beside her...

"We can always negotiate a compromise." Dawson scooted over beside her, and her pulse sky rocketed.

"For what?" She tried to steady her breathing. He was so close she could smell that unique scent that was all Dawson.

"You want this pillow, right?"

That pitch-black hair. Those serious dark brown eyes. His strong chin and hawk-like nose. He was so close she could feel him breathe.

Melanie forced her gaze away from Dawson's face, his lips, as heat ricocheted between them.

Try as she might, she couldn't stop her gaze from lowering to the dark patch of hair on his chest. Or following the line down to the waistband of the pajama bottoms he'd bought.

"I missed you, Melanie," he said, and his voice was gravelly.

All she had to do was lean forward a few inches and she'd be able to taste the wine on his tongue.

There were many reasons that would be a bad idea, none of which immediately came to mind.

So she didn't resist when his hand came up to her chin and guided her lips to his. They touched lightly at first. He hesitated. Before either of them could decide this was a bad idea, Melanie leaned into the next kiss.

Parting her lips for him, she slid her tongue inside his mouth.

His fingers closed around the base of her neck and she tunneled hers into his thick black hair.

She melted into his touch.

A quick shift in position and his muscled chest was pressed against her and she could feel his weight on top of her.

Getting lost in that moment was as easy as slipping into a sexy outfit. Everything about it made her feel wanted and like a real woman. Breathing in the masculine and clean scent that was Dawson filled her senses.

And she opened her eyes for just a blink. Just enough time to gain her bearings. She pulled back from the kiss.

Dawson responded, quickly pushing up to a sitting position and following her gaze to the hallway.

Nothing was there.

"Did you see something move?" she whispered.

"No." Dawson was on his feet and to the hallway within a few seconds.

She followed a half step behind. They checked Mason's room, her room and both bathrooms and saw no one.

In fact, Mason was in a deep sleep.

When they returned to the living room, she sat down and took a sip of wine.

"I'm sorry. I'm just so used to being on edge." Was that true? Or was she feeling guilty for enjoying herself? Especially with Dawson?

Dawson returned to his spot at the other end of the couch. "It's okay. You're staying alert and that's a good thing. I'm not sorry, though."

DAWSON WASN'T SURE what the hell had just happened, but it was clear that his hormones could run away when it came to Melanie. And unleash more damn frustrating emotions than he needed to deal with while he sorted everything out.

Complicated. Now, there was a good word when it came to his feelings for Melanie.

For now, it was best to keep a safe distance between them, especially because his body seemed to have different ideas. And sex with Melanie would blow his mind. Again. There was no denying that.

There was more than just the two of them to consider now. And Dawson hadn't even broken the news to his parents yet. In fact, he hadn't told anyone from Mason Ridge where he was or what he was doing. In part because he didn't want to take a chance word would somehow get to Sprigs that he was with Melanie or that they had a child.

So far, they'd been safe keeping things quiet. This situation couldn't last forever. Dawson had a life to get back to in Mason Ridge. He had work and friends. Family.

Speaking of his family, he didn't want to tell his parents about his son until he knew for certain that Mason was going to be okay. If he suffered the same fate as Bethany, it would destroy them both. And he needed to bring up genetic testing with Melanie.

So far, his thoughts kept winding back to that kiss and he didn't want to spoil tonight with serious discussion. They'd made good strides toward approaching how they might coparent Mason.

Was he still hurt that she hadn't trusted him enough to tell him when she got pregnant? Hell, yes.

If she'd told him back then, she wouldn't have had to go through all this alone. And he still hadn't gotten her to tell him the real reason she hadn't shared the news.

Melanie had a stubborn streak longer than the I-35. And he was trying not to let that get in the way of their tenuous friendship.

Besides, spending the past week getting to know his son had been right up there with the best of his life.

"I should get some rest," Melanie said.

"You sure about that?" he said. "You barely touched your wine."

"There's no way I can drink the whole glass," she admitted.

"You don't have to. You've never been a big drinker."

"Well, having a baby and working in a bar would've cured me if I had been."

"In that case, I bought playing cards." He set his glass next to hers. "I'm more of a beer and barbecue guy anyway."

Dawson had his work cut out for him. No way could he spend 24/7 with Melanie and have his body not remind him just how desirable she was every time she moved.

Cards might distract him and help keep his hormones under control.

Then again, seeing her full breasts pressed against that white T-shirt made him want to say to hell with silly games.

Chapter Ten

Last night had stirred up all kinds of conflicting feelings for Melanie. The dust would settle soon, law enforcement would find Sprigs and she'd be able to get back to her normal routine. She'd been thinking a lot about Dawson's idea and she couldn't let him give up his dreams so easily.

Facing facts, she needed his help and she understood that a man like Dawson would see it as his duty to contribute both financially and as a hands-on father. She could live with that and, bottom line, the help would be welcomed. As it was, she and Mason lived paycheck-to-paycheck. Without her parents' occasional monetary gift, she wouldn't stay afloat.

Shooting down help would be stupid and selfish. The money would help Mason. What mother didn't want to give her child every possible advantage?

Traffic was heavier than usual on her drive to work, which gave her plenty of time to think about the ways in which she would be comfortable allowing Dawson to contribute. She would most likely still keep her Thursday through Saturday night shifts at the Phoenix Bar. It was only three nights a week and she made good money. Besides, her boss wouldn't let her cut her days back anymore. She already had the best shifts and there'd been grumbling from some of the waitresses with more seniority.

Also, Mason would enter preschool in another year and a half and then she could work more traditional hours in an office setting with paid insurance. Nothing had to drastically change now that Dawson was in their life. If he contributed financially, she'd be able to give their son some extras that she hadn't been able to so far. She'd be able to afford to do more things with him on her days off, like take him to the zoo.

Mason loved animals, and she planned to get her son a puppy some day when she could afford to get a little house with a backyard.

Her typical twenty-minute commute had turned into forty-five. She was relieved when she finally arrived and could slip into her role serving drinks rather than spend any more time getting inside her head about recent events. Besides, the music was far too loud inside the bar to think clearly anyway.

It was usually all too easy to block out the world, getting lost in the rush of shuffling drinks. Except, tonight, Melanie's thoughts kept bouncing back to Dawson and that kiss from last night.

The evening wasn't off to a good start, but by midnight it was elbow-to-elbow and she'd broken a sweat. Those were always good tip nights.

Another hour and a half flew by and, thankfully, it was getting close to quitting time. The crowd was in full swing, a typical Thursday night, which often turned out to be more lucrative than the weekends.

Melanie grabbed her order, a pair of Heinekens for the guys at table three, when the lights blinked, the music blared, and on top of it came a piercing sound.

The fire alarm.

Her heart raced. Everyone had to get out. As Melanie

pushed through the crowd making their way to the exits, she felt a hand on her arm.

Her blood chilled.

No way.

It couldn't be him. Could it?

She wheeled around, preparing to face down the man who she'd tried to avoid for years, whose name brought fear descending around her…who seemed determined to stalk her.

The pressure on her arm eased before she could get a good look at who was behind her. Her heart pounded. Was he there? Was Jordan Sprigs somewhere in the crowd?

Melanie pulled her cell from her front pocket and clamped her fingers around it.

As she moved with the crowd, she pressed Dawson's name on her contacts. The air inside the bar felt as if it had thinned and her chest squeezed from panic.

At least there were plenty of people around. She should be fine if she stayed with the crowd.

"Hello?" Dawson's sleepy voice slid through her, calming her. "What's going on? I hear sirens."

"Fire alarm went off, so we're literally being pushed out of the building by the crowd."

"Get in your car and drive home now." Dawson's voice was too calm, and that was exactly how she knew just how concerned he truly was.

"I can't. My purse is locked in my manager's office."

"Find him. Have him unlock the door and turn over your belongings."

"There's no way," she said. "There are dozens of people jammed in the parking lot."

"Stay near the front door, then," he said. "When we hang up, I want you to call a cab. We can go back for your stuff tomorrow."

"Okay. I'm with a huge crowd of people and I'm right in the middle of them." She didn't share the part where she believed Sprigs had had his hand on her arm. There was nothing Dawson could do from her apartment, she realized, and it probably wasn't him anyway.

"I hear the sirens in the background. Fire department?" he asked.

"Yes. I see the trucks."

"On second thought, stay on the line with me."

"Okay." She talked to him for a few minutes. By the time the firemen cleared the building, which they did remarkably fast, it was past closing time.

"Keep me on the line as you get your purse," Dawson insisted.

"I need to close out first. I'll call you back as soon as I walk out to my car." Melanie tucked her phone in her apron as she followed her fellow employees inside to finish up work and retrieve her bag.

She scanned the parking lot, searching the faces for Sprigs. Then again, he could've sent someone. Any one of them could be working for him.

Her manager, Joel, stood at the open office door. The lights were back on, the room bright, and the crowd was beginning to thin outside.

Once she was safely inside her sedan, she would breathe easier.

Melanie quickly counted her tips and then tipped out the bartender and the busboy who'd worked her station.

"I have babysitter issues and need to get home," she said to Joel. "Will you watch and make sure I make it to my car?"

"Sure thing." Joel pushed back from his computer. He was in his late thirties, had a daughter in kindergarten and saw it as his personal responsibility to make sure those who worked for him made it home safely every night. "How's the lot?"

"Looks like it's emptying out," she said.

Occasionally, one of their customers thought it would be a good idea to hang around and wait for one of the waitresses. There was no shortage of attractive women working, and some men mistook friendly service for something else entirely.

Joel stood at the front of the building, arms folded, as Melanie crossed the lot. She knew to park under a light and felt safer knowing her manager kept watch as she navigated to her vehicle.

There were pairs of people dotted around the lot, standing next to cars. Melanie's nerves hummed as she quickened her pace. She'd call Dawson as soon as she got inside the car and talk hands-free on the twenty-minute ride home.

There were three couples in between her and her car. The odds one of them worked for Sprigs might be low, but adrenaline pumped through her anyway. Hair pricked on her neck and a foreboding feeling trickled ice down her spine. *Joel is watching. It will be fine.*

She used her remote to unlock the car door as she approached, keeping an eye on the pair of people who were huddled close together near a truck four spaces over. Even if one did make a move toward her, she could be inside her car before anyone could reach her.

Melanie wasted no time closing the distance to her vehicle. She turned and waved to Joel. He stood there, waiting for her to back out of the lot.

Dawson picked up on the first ring. "Tell me you're in the car."

"I am," she reassured him, relief washing over her. "I'm about to pull out of the lot."

"Check your rearview. Make sure no one seems too interested in what you're doing or is following you."

Melanie hadn't thought about that. He was right. She wasn't out of the woods yet. She scanned the area behind her. "So far, so good."

There was so much tension coming through the line.

"How about now?" he asked. His voice was a study in focus and she appreciated the sense of calmness moving through her.

"A truck just turned out of the lot and is heading toward me." Her pulse ratcheted up a few notches and her palms warmed.

"Keep an eye on him and let me know if he gets too close. Are you on State Street?"

"Yes. I'm coming home the way I showed you," she said.

"Good. Don't veer from that course unless I say."

"Okay." The light changed and she pressed the gas a little harder than she'd intended to, jerking forward.

"Melanie?"

"Sorry. I'm fine. Just a little nervous." She must've made a sound without realizing.

"You're doing great. Take a deep breath."

She did, making it through the next few lights with ease. It helped that they were green.

The light turned red in the next block. Her shoulders knitted together with tension as she came to a stop and the truck engine whirred behind her.

"Now check your rearview," Dawson said. "See anyone you recognize?"

Melanie strained to get a good look at the driver.

"It's a woman." Relief flooded her. This was racking up to be one heck of a long night.

"A few more lights and you'll be on the highway," Dawson said. "And then you'll be home in another ten minutes."

"Getting home and taking a long, cool shower never sounded better," she said, glancing in her rearview.

"I'll have the water running for you," he said.

The truck's turn signal came on.

"She's about to turn," Melanie said.

"Any other cars out?"

"None that I can see," she said.

"Good. You'll be home free soon." Dawson's voice sounded hopeful.

And that made her feel incredibly optimistic.

"Done. She just turned and disappeared."

"Any other activity around you?"

"None. It's quiet. And dark. I'm about to pull up to another red light, but it looks good so far." A sprig of happiness sprouted inside her.

Foot on the brake, she tapped her finger on the steering wheel. She was so ready to be home. A bowl of Cheerios sounded better than steak right now.

Suddenly, a noise sounded from the backseat and a hand came over her mouth. She tried to scream, but only a muffled cry came out.

A dark figure emerged from behind.

"Melanie?" Dawson sounded concerned.

She tried to shout his name, yell for help, but the hand tightened, making it impossible to form words.

"Melanie?" This time, Dawson sounded stressed.

The call disconnected.

"He can't help you now."

Melanie would recognize that voice anywhere… Sprigs.

She had a half second to think and no bright ideas

came, so she jammed her foot on the gas pedal. She'd bite his hand if she could, but he'd secured a gag over her mouth. *Oh God, no.*

"Brake," Sprigs demanded. His sinewy voice was not more than an inch from her right ear. Her skin crawled where he breathed on her.

Despair pressed heavily on her shoulders. All she could think about was Mason and his father. She was grateful for the crash course she'd given him in taking care of their son, because if Sprigs had his way, she wouldn't be around to do it herself. *Son of a bitch.*

"I said get your damn foot off the gas," Sprigs repeated, high-pitched and angry, leaving no room for doubt how serious he was. "I'll slit your throat right now."

A hard piece of metal pressed against her throat. A knife?

The reality of the situation hit fast and hard. He wanted to kill her? She shook her head. She might not make it out of this alive, but neither would he. No way would she let him walk away and hurt more kids.

He'd die with her.

Melanie slammed the steering wheel a hard right, popped the curb and aimed the front end of her car toward a brick office complex.

Flooring the pedal, she jabbed her elbow into his face to back him off her as much as she could, praying the object pressed to her neck didn't slice through her skin.

His head bucked and he slammed his hand into the back of her headrest.

"Dammit," he said. "Hear me now. If you'd listened to me before, we wouldn't be in this situation in the first place."

Melanie turned her head to the side, closed her eyes and braced for impact.

"Take your foot off that pedal." Agitated, his voice rose again.

I love you, Mason.

Chapter Eleven

The blunt pressure on Melanie's neck eased a few seconds before the air bag deployed and her body lurched forward. Sprigs had to have dropped to the floorboard, because without a seat belt he'd most likely be dead with an impact like that one.

Everything went blurry, dizzy and she was confused, trying to process what had just happened. Seconds ticked by. Or minutes. She couldn't be sure which.

Still dazed, she felt her instincts kick in and she managed to curl her fingers around the door handle and then push the door open with her left shoulder. She spilled out onto the concrete and fell onto all fours, heaving.

There was no time to waste. Everything in her body screamed to run, to get out of there and as far away as possible. Her thoughts immediately jumped to her son and holding him again. An image of him safe with his father pushed its way through her mind, powering her body to move forward. And Dawson.

Hope blossomed as she scrambled to her feet and then took off.

At any moment and with every step she expected a hand to grab her, jerking her back. So she pushed harder.

Because the only other thing she could think about was how much Mason needed his mother and maybe his

father needed her just a little bit, too. She told herself it
was because there was so much she needed to share with
him about their son, but immediately she knew it for the
lie it was.

When she was about to clear the block, she glanced
back, needing to know if Sprigs was right behind her.

He wasn't. There was no sign of him.

Even so, her heart pounded as she bolted around the
corner and then down the residential street. She could
hear highway noise in the distance. That was how close
she'd been and that was most likely the reason Sprigs had
acted when he did.

Dawson must be frantic with worry after their call had
been cut off. Dawson. A piece of her heart broke knowing Dawson would never trust her again.

It was the middle of the night and there were no lights
on in the row of bungalow-style houses. Thankfully there
were no dogs barking, either. At least not at the moment.

How had Sprigs found her?

It didn't matter. He had and now she had to figure out
a way to get help and call police.

Stopping to knock on a door was risky. It could give
Sprigs time to catch up, especially if he was getting close
or coming at her from another angle.

Legs burning, Melanie slowed down and scanned the
street behind her. It was too dark to see clearly, so she
watched for any signs of movement.

Both sidewalks and the street seemed clear. She double-
checked front lawns. Didn't see anything there, either. It
was too soon to breathe easy.

Thank the heavens for her seat belt and for air bags.
She'd been dazed but she'd made it out alive. Surely Sprigs
was unconscious or worse. Was it too much to hope the
nightmare could end? That he didn't survive the crash?

At the very least, he'd been slowed down and she'd escaped. And that was worth something. Tears streaked her cheeks and she didn't have the energy to fight them.

Thinking about injuries, Melanie had no idea if she'd been hurt during the accident. There'd be time to evaluate any scrapes and bruises later. Everything felt numb. No doubt she was still in too much shock to make a real determination.

For now, she could run and had no pain.

If she waited too long to knock on a door, she might be giving Sprigs time to catch up or disappear. Part of her needed to keep running. To put as much distance between she and Sprigs as she could to make sure he couldn't get to her.

On the next block, she stopped at the first door and knocked. A tiny, high-pitched, rapid-fire bark sounded on the other side.

Another dog barked two houses down. And then across the street.

Melanie bit back a curse and prayed like the dickens that Sprigs was knocked out and not searching the streets for her. If he was, he'd no doubt find her thanks to the noise.

She banged on the door again, louder this time, and a light came on. The little dog was going crazy barking.

Melanie could feel her heartbeat in her throat as the door swung open. A sturdy man, midthirties, glared at her from the other side.

"I'm so sorry to bother you, but it's an emergency. There's been an accident." The words rushed out as a flood of tears released. She glanced around, searching for signs of Sprigs. "May I use your phone? Please."

The big guy checked around her as if he half expected someone to jump out from behind her, and then nodded.

"Thank you." Melanie opened the screen door and repeated those two words.

"Who is it, Roger?" A female wearing a time-worn cotton bathrobe emerged from the hallway. Her short dark hair stuck out at odd angles.

"Go back to bed, honey. I'll take care of it," Roger said.

"I'm so sorry to disturb you, but I've been in an accident and there was no one…" A sob tore from Melanie's throat. She suppressed the next one. "I didn't know what to do so I ran here."

No way could she tell them more or let her guard down, not with Sprigs still out there. Even though Roger looked capable of handling himself.

"Are you all right?" the woman asked, picking up the barking dog and shushing it.

Melanie nodded through sobs as Roger flipped on the living room light.

The woman gasped. "Your arms. You're hurt."

"Celia, get a wet towel," Roger said.

"I'm fine. I just need to use the phone," Melanie said, glancing down for the first time. Her arms were bloodred from what looked like burn marks. She didn't have time to worry about them. Burns would heal. She needed to call the police and then let Dawson know that she was okay. "And please don't answer the door if anyone knocks."

"Sit down." Roger pointed to the plaid sofa with a severe look on his face. "I'll get my cell."

By the time he returned, Celia was by Melanie's side, gently pressing the towels to her forearms.

"You said you were in a crash?" Roger said, handing over the phone.

Melanie nodded.

"Anyone else with you?" he asked.

Melanie hesitated. Tell the truth and what would happen? Would Roger go check on the other person?

Lie and she'd get caught. She had to tell the dispatcher who was in the car with her.

"Yes." More sobs released as Melanie called 9-1-1. She didn't realize how badly she was shaking until just now.

"What is your emergency?" the operator asked.

"I was just in a car crash near Northwest Freeway Highway 290," Melanie said.

"Do you need an ambulance, ma'am?" the dispatcher asked, her voice a calming force in the chaos churning through Melanie.

"I don't think so. I was attacked by a man named Jordan Sprigs and that's the reason I wrecked. He's wanted by the FBI and I think he's still at the crash site." Panicked, she glanced up at Celia and then Roger, who were passing a look between them, and Melanie's heart skipped a beat.

Celia patted Melanie's leg reassuringly.

"Are you there with him now?" the dispatcher asked.

"No. I got out of the car and ran a few blocks to get away. I don't think he followed me. We hit the wall hard, he wasn't wearing a seat belt and I have no idea what condition he's in."

"Okay," the dispatcher said. "Tell me what happened. An officer is on his way to the scene as we speak."

Melanie caught a glimpse as Roger and Celia exchanged another worried glance. She heard Celia tell him to lock the door before she whispered that she'd be back as soon as she got dressed.

Roger clicked the lock, and then disappeared down the hall as Melanie recounted the events to the dispatcher.

It had all happened so fast that Melanie couldn't remember all the details, but she drew the best picture she could of the timeline.

Celia returned wearing warm-ups. Her hair had been brushed.

"Can we turn off the lights?" Melanie asked after ending the call. "Just in case he's wandering around looking for me?"

Celia nodded, complied immediately. There was still a glow coming from the electronics and soft wall lights in the room. They provided enough light to see. Celia came over and sat next to Melanie on the couch.

"How are those arms?" she asked.

"Honestly, I don't think the shock has worn off. I can't feel anything."

"We should put something on them," Celia said, her brow creased with worry. "Burn salve."

"Do you mind if I call my boyfriend?" For lack of a better term. "We were on the phone when it all happened and he must be climbing the walls by now."

Roger returned with a twelve-gauge shotgun resting on his arm.

"Go ahead," Celia said. "Can I get you anything else? Water?"

"No. Thank you." Melanie punched in Dawson's number.

He answered on the first ring.

"It's me. I'm okay," she said immediately.

"What happened?" He didn't bother to hide the stress in his voice now.

"He was in the car. In the backseat," she said, tears streaming down her cheeks.

"Sprigs?"

"Yes," she said, taking a gulp of air. She reminded herself that she was okay and to breathe.

"Where are you?" Dawson asked.

"I'm at a nice couple's house. They let me in." Sirens sounded in the distance and Melanie's shoulder slumped forward. For the first time since the ordeal happened, she felt Sprigs couldn't get to her.

"What's the address? I'm coming right now." No matter how determined he seemed, she couldn't let him bring their son anywhere near this place.

"Don't wake Mason. I'm safe. No one can hurt me now. The police are on their way and they'll get him this time," she said in between gulps of air.

"How'd you get away from him?" Dawson asked.

"I crashed the car into a building," she said quietly, ignoring the gasp that came from Celia.

"You did what?" Dawson's voice was incredulous.

"There was no other way to get away from him, so I slammed my foot on the gas pedal and aimed for the nearest building," she said.

"Melanie, are you sure you're okay?" Dawson lowered his voice and his pain was a knife ripping through her chest.

"I did what I had to, Dawson. He didn't hurt me, but he intended to and I knew it." Her voice hitched no matter how strong she was trying to be.

"I know he did, sweetheart. I'm just grateful that you're alive." His voice was so anguished her heart burned.

"He didn't hurt me," she repeated. "And as soon as I give my statement to police, I'm coming home."

For the first time since this whole ordeal had started, she believed those last three words.

"Yes, you are," he said. "And then we're getting the hell out of here."

"Okay." He was right. Sprigs at the very least knew the area in which she lived. It wouldn't be long before he figured out her address, if he didn't already know. She couldn't take any chances when it came to Mason. And she had every intention of living long enough to watch all the milestones he had yet to achieve.

Squad car lights blared outside. A few seconds later, a knock sounded at the front door.

"I better go, Dawson. The police are here."

"Can I speak to the owner of the house?" he asked.

"Sure." She glanced at Roger and moved the phone from her ear. "He'd like to talk to you."

Roger was already at the door when he nodded. He invited the officer inside and then took the phone from Melanie.

Adrenaline must be wearing off, because Melanie started shaking even harder. Celia dabbed aloe on Melanie's arms and then put a blanket over her legs as the officer introduced himself as Special Agent Randall. He asked a few questions as she accepted a glass of water from Celia.

"Is he still there?" she asked Special Agent Randall once initial information had been relayed. "Did they catch him?"

"I'll check." He took a couple of steps toward the door and asked through his radio if the suspect was in custody.

Melanie held her breath waiting for the answer to come. Sprigs had to be there. Otherwise he would've followed her. Right?

She heard the officer thank the responder as he moved near her again.

"He must've fled the scene. Officers are searching for him and we've notified our FBI liaison," Special Agent Randall said.

No. This couldn't be.

"How could he survive that impact?" she asked, still stunned.

"He might've crawled a few hundred yards away into the brush or managed to get into a Dumpster to hide. If he's around here, we'll do our best to find him, ma'am."

Those words, meant to be reassuring, left a hole in Melanie's chest. As long as Sprigs was out there, she'd have to watch every shadow. She'd have to expect him around every corner. She'd have to fear closing her eyes.

And, worst of all, she was afraid he could get to Mason.

The thought sent an icy chill racing down her spine.

"Thank you," she said, tamping down her worst fears. "Is there any chance my purse or cell phone was found?"

"Both of those items are on their way here right now," Special Agent Randall said.

At least she would get those back. The thought of Sprigs getting away with her personal belongings sent a different kind of chill down her spine, like the feeling people described of what happened when a cat walked over a grave.

The officer finished the interview by letting her know that the city would tow her car for her.

She thanked him again.

"Would you like access to medical treatment?" he asked.

"No. I'm fine," she said, fearing she would never be fine again. Sprigs would see to that.

"Can I offer you a ride somewhere?" Special Agent Randall asked.

"I told her boyfriend that I'd drive her home," Roger said.

That must've been why Dawson had wanted to speak to Roger.

"I can't let you do that. You've already done so much," Melanie said.

Roger shook his head. "It's no trouble."

"We want to help," Celia said. "Don't think twice about it."

"I don't want to burden you guys—"

Roger's hands went up. "I'm a man of my word."

"Thank you both. I don't know what I would've done if you hadn't answered the door when you did." The thought of what Sprigs wanted to do to her made her stomach churn.

He was still out there.

DAWSON HAD ALL the essentials packed up and ready to go by the time Melanie walked through the front door.

She ran straight into his arms, where he hauled her against his chest. He tilted her head back and kissed her on the forehead, each eyelid and then her lips.

The thought that she might not come home had eaten away at his stomach lining.

The past few hours had been pure hell.

"You're safe," he whispered as she trembled in his arms.

Anger ripped through him at the thought of what could've happened to her. She'd been quick on her feet and that was the only reason she was here in his arms and not stranded somewhere with that sick bastard Sprigs, or dead.

Her chin came up and there was defiance in her stare. "I couldn't let him take me. I had no doubt he would eventually kill me when he was through with me. All I could think of was Mason growing up without a mother and how much he needed me."

"You did the right thing," Dawson reassured her. And then he just held her, trying not to notice how much her body molded to his or how warm her skin felt against his own. "Is Roger outside?"

"He left."

"I wanted to shake his hand and give him some money for gas," Dawson said.

"He wouldn't take anything from me. He said to tell you not to worry about it. Said he hoped that if something like that ever happened to his Celia, someone would do the right thing and help her, too."

Dawson was grateful to the man and he would find a way to repay him.

Melanie told him what had happened and showed him the card that Special Agent Randall had given her. It had a phone number she was supposed to call if Sprigs showed up again in addition to a case number scribbled on it.

"Your car is evidence, so I'm sure you won't be getting that back anytime soon and even if you did it won't be drivable. My SUV is still in Mason Ridge, so I figure we'll need a rental," he said.

"He got away, Dawson." Her words trembled as much as her body when she said it.

"Not for long," he said. "Even if he could walk after a wreck like that, he couldn't have gone far. They'll catch him tonight or tomorrow. They want him as much as we do." He doubted that was possible but said the words to offer her some reassurance.

"And if they don't?" She pulled back from him a little, and he repositioned so as not to hurt her arms. Wide, fearful eyes stared up at him.

"They will. If not, then I will. He just made a huge mistake when you got away. One I'm grateful for. It's only a matter of time for him now that they have a general vicinity." Dawson held her tighter, not quite ready to let her go.

"I hope you're right," she said.

She leaned into his chest and for one crazy second the world felt right again. Dawson reasoned that recent events had him off balance, and the thumping in his chest meant nothing more than gratitude that Mason's mother was home safe.

"In the meantime, I'm taking you and our son to my family's lake house," he said.

"Your parents still own that place?"

"They do." Although no one in the family had used it since Bethany was alive. His heart dropped to the toe of his boot and he was filled with the same sense of dread he'd felt when the doctor said all they could do was help her rest comfortably. It had been his idea to take Bethany to the lake house, her favorite place on earth, when she was losing her last little grip on life. It was the last place anyone would ever think to look or expect Dawson to go.

That was precisely the reason it would be perfect for the three of them.

Facing that place again was as appealing as swallowing fire. But Mason and Melanie were the priorities now. And Dawson would do whatever it took to ensure their safety.

"The car rental place doesn't open for another..." Dawson glanced at his watch "...forty-five minutes."

"I just remembered that I don't have a car seat anymore," Melanie said.

"Not a problem. They rent those. I've asked for an SUV with a car seat and GPS. Should we wake Mason?"

"Let's let him sleep. I might as well pack his breakfast." She took a step back and started toward the kitchen.

"Already done," Dawson said. "I had to do something productive to force myself to stop pacing earlier."

Melanie turned around.

"How did he find me, Dawson?" Her chin was defiant, but her voice was small.

"I don't know." If there was a way to keep Melanie and Mason safe tucked away somewhere, Dawson would hunt the son of a bitch down personally and make sure he never hurt another woman or child. As it was, he wouldn't be able to leave them with anyone else or let either of them out of his sight. Not even his best friends in Mason Ridge, and Dawson trusted those guys with his own life.

He thought about calling them for backup and that thought died quickly on the vine.

First of all, he didn't want anyone to know about their new location. He wasn't worried that his friends would tell anyone where he was going. That wasn't the problem. He didn't want to take a chance that anyone could intercept the call.

Another advantage Dawson had at the moment was that Sprigs didn't seem to realize that Dawson was with Melanie and the creep might not know about their son, either. For Mason and Melanie's sake, Dawson needed to keep a lid on his new role as father. All it would take would be one look at Mason and Dawson's friends would make the connection.

Second, all of his friends had been through the wringer in recent weeks while authorities were trying to identify and then arrest those involved with the child abduction ring. Everyone inside Dawson's circle had been touched by recent events, and some of them still had the physical marks to prove it.

"I considered the possibility that he would send someone else after me, but I didn't think in a thousand years that he would come himself. Not when he has this much heat on him," Melanie said. "And how did he get in my car? I promise that I locked the doors before. I always do and I'm being extra careful now."

Sprigs was smart and that made him a helluva lot more dangerous. And deadly.

"I've been thinking a lot about that." Dawson shouldn't notice how beautiful her brown eyes were right now or allow his emotions to take over, because they had him wanting to take her in his arms and never let go. He reasoned that he was still shaken up at the thought of almost losing her. He'd spent a good half hour not knowing what had happened to her and fearing the worst. "He may have gone back to your parents' house and found a pay stub lying around."

"I cleaned my purse out when I was there. All he'd have to do is look through the trash," she said.

"Then my guess is that he pulled the fire alarm to create enough of a diversion to get everyone out of the building."

"He had access to my purse," she said. "But we came right back in and got our things. Someone would've seen him coming in and out if he went outside to unlock my car, wouldn't they?"

"He'd only have to use your remote to unlock your doors," Dawson said.

"So that must mean he was watching me earlier when I arrived at work? Otherwise, how would he know which one was mine?"

"All he'd have to do is click the remote and he could see which car belonged to you. In all that commotion and with the fire alarm blaring, no one would notice what was going on in the parking lot." Dawson paced.

"People were leaving left and right after the alarm," she said.

"He wouldn't have to know which purse was yours, either. All he'd have to do is check wallets for identification. The fire alarm would be the perfect cover. He could've hid inside the bathroom until everyone cleared out. Then, with all the racket of the sirens outside, he'd be able to cover the sound of your car unlocking. Was it busy?"

"The place was packed." Her jaw fell slack. "If he checked my ID then he could've taken my driver's license."

Chapter Twelve

Melanie poured out the contents of her purse and located her wallet. Dawson noticed her hands were still shaking. In that moment, he wanted to put his own hands on Sprigs. Preferably around the man's neck.

"It's here." She pulled out her ID. "And my credit cards, too."

"Anything else missing that has identifying information on it?" He also noticed the burn marks on her arms.

"Everything's here." She gasped. "He might've memorized my address. All it would take is one good look and he could remember where I live."

"Even if he did, he won't come here tonight. Besides, I doubt he can walk after the wreck you described. His body would've taken all the impact while he was down on the floorboards. At a minimum, he's shaken up and has gone into hiding until everything cools down. Best case, he's lying in a ditch somewhere bleeding until the feds pick him up and lock him away for good."

It had taken real courage to do what Melanie had done. She'd done good. Dawson didn't want to be *this* proud of her actions. Denying that he was wouldn't change anything, so he chalked his pride up to their history. "Also, he should realize that the feds will be watching this place from now on, which brings me to another point. I should let them know where we're heading."

"You're probably right. The whole thing just gives me the creeps. I've had a bad feeling ever since his name came up in connection to the child abductions, and I haven't been able to shake it. Even though I shut down everything on social media and cut off ties except to those who I was closest to. I figured he would give up on his fixation with me at some point and just go away or find someone else to put his attention on," she said. "It had been quiet for a few years. Especially since I disappeared and had the baby. Now this—this is all just too close to home, you know?"

He knew there was another reason she'd withdrawn from everyone and it had to do with their relationship.

No way was he about to discuss that. This wasn't the time or place.

"You might want to pull together whatever personal belongings you'd like to have with you," he suggested, ignoring the frustration still fresh in his mind at how easy it had been for her to shut him out.

"And Mason's," she said.

"I packed for him." He had an idea of exactly what she would want to take, but it wasn't his place to rummage through her personal stuff. "Are you hungry?"

"I doubt I could eat anything after everything that's happened," she said.

"You have time to grab a shower before we leave." He would pack something for her to eat on the drive. She needed to keep up her strength.

"That sounds like heaven right now." She started to get up and stopped. Her gaze shifted from the floor to him, and something exploded inside his chest the second she made eye contact. "Dawson, I'm really glad you're here."

"Me, too." He dismissed the feeling.

"I mean it. I can't think of a better friend to have around when the chips are down."

"We've been through a lot together over the years." Dawson half smiled. Most of their trials had come from him during his childhood when she helped him through a difficult time, and he didn't mind returning the favor of being there for her.

"Sure have," she said with a sigh.

"It's my turn to have your back, Melanie. I don't think I ever officially thanked you for being there for me when we were kids."

"You didn't have to say the words. I knew," she said.

He smiled at her as she passed him on her way to the shower, ignoring the sliver of light reaching into the darkest places of his soul.

Dawson studied Special Agent Randall's card while Melanie was in the next room. He retrieved his cell and punched in the number.

The agent picked up on the first ring.

"My name is Dawson Hill and I'm helping my friend Melanie Dixon." He'd used the word *friend* for lack of a better term. Besides, it was true. No matter what else the two of them were or had been, they'd always been friends.

"Ms. Dixon mentioned you." Special Agent Randall introduced himself and then the two exchanged greetings.

That fact should make this call go easier than Dawson had expected.

"What can I do for you, Mr. Hill?" Special Agent Randall asked.

"Any word on Jordan Sprigs?" he asked.

"That's a negative, sir. Sprigs is still at large," Randall said. "We're working with local law enforcement and have a lot of resources invested in his capture. The problem with a man like him is that he can easily disappear into the same outlets he uses to move children."

"I was hoping he wouldn't survive the crash," Dawson admitted, wishing he would have better news for Melanie when she finished her shower. She was already so on edge she'd jump out of her skin if so much as a fly landed on her.

"In all honesty, we all shared that hope," Randall said on a hard sigh. "But he's still out there and we're not giving up until we locate him. We know that he's fixated on Ms. Dixon and that leads us to believe that he won't go far. He'll want to be close to her now that he's pinpointed her location."

"He sent someone to attack her at her parents' house in Mason Ridge a week ago," Dawson said. "I was there."

"I didn't see a report come through on that," Randall said, concerned. "When did you say the incident occurred?"

"It was a week ago. We stayed at a motel that night and then there was a fire the next morning. I'm sure it was him. He has a history with fire," Dawson said.

"The second incident was reported to the task force. The fire marshal's initial assessment is that he suspects foul play. He's continuing his investigation to pinpoint the cause and it'll take a little while to process the scene." Randall's voice had returned to an all-business pitch. "Tell me more about the home invasion."

Dawson relayed the details.

"I'll make contact with the sheriff's department and request that incidents involving you or any of your friends be reported to us immediately," Randall said, his frustration evident in his tone. "Ms. Dixon returning to her childhood home could've been the trigger that caused Sprigs to reignite his fixation on her."

"I'm guessing something in his background must be linked to this behavior, but I didn't know the guy very well," Dawson said.

"Can you tell me anything about him?"

"I know that he kept to himself growing up. I didn't even know he and Beckett Alcorn were friends until all this news broke. In fact, thinking back, I don't remember him having many friends at all."

"Which could've been the first problem," Randall said. "And would also make him easy to manipulate."

Randall made an excellent point. If Sprigs was lonely, had some issues, it could make him pliable. Dawson didn't need to work in law enforcement to put those pieces together. "He was older than us and we pretty much stuck to friendships in our grade. The only reason I knew any of the older boys was my friend Ryan's older brother, Justin. You think Alcorn was pulling the strings on that whole operation?"

"That's what we're trying to figure out," Randall said.

"Does seem hard to believe someone so timid could be the mastermind behind a child kidnapping ring."

"What about family? Did you ever have any dealings with the Sprigses?"

"Not really."

"Were there any rumors about strange behavior?" Randall asked.

"His father died when we were pretty young. Can't say what kind of person he was. Heard that his mom was a religious nut of some kind. I have no idea if that's true or not. He got teased a lot, even by younger kids. The only reason I remember his dad was that traffic shut down on Elder Parkway on the day of his funeral. There was a big game on that day and I overheard older folks complain about the inconvenience. Most people in town are decent, so I remember thinking that Sprigs's dad must've been a jerk. Couldn't say for sure one way or another personally, but it did make me wonder. Can't say I remember much else about the family." Dawson intended to ask around on his own. "Wish I could be more help."

"Alcorn might be the key to putting the pieces together. I have another interview scheduled with him this morning. He's given up his partner, but he's protecting information about their routes, and my guess is that they plan to keep business running as usual. He claims that he wasn't involved in logistics, but my experience tells me that he knows more about it than he's telling us. If we catch Sprigs, we might not need Alcorn's information. Either way, we'll have more leverage when both are in custody."

"Melanie doesn't feel safe here anymore after last night," Dawson said.

"That's certainly understandable under the circumstances," Randall said. "I can arrange protective custody."

"We're planning to leave the apartment and I'd like to move her and Mason to a lake house owned by my family. It's isolated there. No one knows that we own it because we haven't used it in years," Dawson said, figuring this was as good. "She's concerned he has her address after breaking into her car."

"To be honest, we're hoping that's true. I'd like to place a female agent in the apartment in Melanie's absence."

"As bait?" Dawson asked.

"Yes. Can you talk to her and get back to me?"

"She won't mind. She'll do anything to cooperate if it means taking that son of a bitch off the streets."

"Good. That will go a long way toward an end to this," Randall said. "I'll notify my surveillance crew of the change. One thing to consider is that she'll be vulnerable during the transition to the new place. I'd like to offer assistance in transporting her."

"That would be much appreciated." Dawson had been concerned about that, too. No way would he put her and Mason in danger unnecessarily. The extra security measures would help ease his apprehension.

"What's the address?" Randall asked.

Dawson provided it.

"Hold on one second, please." The sound of fingers pounding a keyboard came through the line. Randall must be pulling up the location on his computer. "With one main road leading in and out of the property, we'll be able to control access. However, there are a lot of trees and that could make it more interesting to cover the acreage."

Dawson knew firsthand how easy it was to disappear under the canopy. Even after all these years he remembered the layout. Some of his best times with Bethany had been spent running through those woods. "We had a security system installed out there for the house. It was state-of-the-art at one time. Hopefully that will minimize any concern."

"How about the perimeter? Anything we should know about security-wise there?" Randall asked.

"Barbed wire fencing. Nothing that's hot, though," Dawson said. "My mother didn't want to take a chance either of her kids would have an accident."

"How soon do you plan to leave?" Randall asked.

"I'd intended to wait until a car rental place opened, since my SUV is in Mason Ridge and Melanie's car is no longer drivable," Dawson said. He heard the water turn off in the bathroom and an image of Melanie naked, stepping out of the shower, assaulted him. He shoved the thought aside.

"We can provide transportation," Randall offered.

"How soon can you arrange it?" Dawson figured Melanie would be out soon enough and ready to go. He wondered how long it would be before Mason stirred. Thankfully, his son had been well during the past week other than the occasional cough. Melanie had been right. Mason really did get sick fast and hard, and well just as quickly.

"I can assemble a team in about an hour."

"We'll hold tight until then," Dawson said.

"I'd like to pick up the keys to the new location now and send a couple of guys to sweep the place before you arrive." Randall asked.

"Absolutely." Dawson had no problem agreeing to the extra security measures. While he had no doubt about his own ability to handle Sprigs, Dawson had no idea how many others worked for the man. Besides, he'd cooperate in any way if it meant more security for Melanie and Mason. The hours he'd spent pacing, waiting for her, had been right up there with the worst of his life. And he'd endured doozies. He had no intention of making it easy for Sprigs to get to her, and he had no idea what the crazed man would do to Mason.

Dawson had no plans to risk finding out.

Melanie, dressed in a T-shirt and jeans, walked into the room and sat on the edge of the coffee table near where Dawson stood. He acknowledged her with a nod and then turned his attention to the window. He'd have time to fill her in during the drive. Besides, seeing her fresh-faced from a shower reminded him of the things they liked to do to each other in there, and this wasn't the time to think about it.

Dawson thanked the agent and then ended the call.

Sprigs could be anywhere, even outside at that very

moment. He'd been smart enough to avoid capture so far. The fact sat heavy on Dawson's thoughts.

Sprigs's networks had to be pretty sophisticated to pull off something like this, and he'd gotten away with abducting children for far too many years. Calculating back, Sprigs would have had to begin while he was still in high school and practically still a child himself.

What kinds of horrible things had to happen to a guy to twist him up like that so early in life?

It didn't take long to fill Melanie in on the new plan and bring her up to date with the conversation Dawson had had with Randall.

"I have a lot of questions for him," she said.

"He's planning to meet us at the lake house. Or we could call him back if you'd like."

"It can wait. My nerves are still jumbled and that'll give me time to sort everything out in my head," she said.

"He offered protective custody."

"Won't the lake house be pretty much the same thing?" she asked.

Dawson nodded as he heard Mason cry in the other room. He told Melanie to hold on as he went to his son. Mason wanted down immediately, so Dawson complied. The little guy charged into the next room still half-asleep.

Melanie scooped him in her arms, wincing when he made contact with her burns.

"Want me to take him?" Dawson wasn't being territorial. He wanted to give her a chance to heal.

"No, thanks. I got this." She put Mason in his high chair and then gave him a small bowl of Cheerios while she cut up a banana and poured milk in his special cup.

She sat at the table next to him while he ate; then she wiped his face and hands and drew him to her chest, holding him as though she might never see him again.

Dawson understood why she'd want to do that after her near-death experience. She had to have considered the possibility at some point last night.

"I need to make contact with the guys back home." He needed to check in with his friends in Mason Ridge, who would no doubt start to worry if he didn't show up in town soon. Plus, he wanted to pick their brains about Sprigs.

And there were half a dozen other calls he needed to make to keep his affairs in order as he kept Melanie and Mason safe. Keeping his job had never been more important now that he had a child. Luckily, he'd been saving his vacation days and had another week before he ran out of those. The investigation could take longer and he had no idea what he'd do then. No way was he going back to work until Sprigs had been properly dealt with. They'd have to consider protective custody for her and Mason at that point.

Melanie turned her back to him and he assumed she was wiping away tears. She kissed the top of Mason's head. A few seconds later, she turned to face him again. "Speaking of touching base with people, I should call my sister. She'll worry if she doesn't hear from me and I can't have her showing up here unannounced."

"My folks will start worrying soon, too. I've been holding off contacting everyone back home until we're all clear. Not sure if Sprigs knows about Mason and I don't want to give him information he doesn't already have. I figure news will spread quickly that I'm a father." Dawson didn't say how easy it would be for Sprigs to make Mason disappear into his network, and that might be the ultimate punishment to Melanie if he couldn't have her.

Dawson also couldn't help noticing how uncomfortable Melanie was every time he mentioned his family.

THE DRIVE TO the lake house ate up most of the morning. The driver of the van had been pleasant and had put on a movie for Mason to keep him occupied. An unmarked sedan drove closely behind them.

Melanie was still shaken by the events of last night.

Now that Sprigs had shown himself, the feds had a starting point to narrow their search. She would hold on to that thought tightly.

Also, the fact that they would be watching her and Mason twenty-four hours a day was a welcome addition. She had Dawson and several law enforcement agencies backing him up. The only daunting thought was how easily Sprigs seemed to get away and how determined he was to take her with him.

A determined psychopath intent on possessing her was the most frightening scenario she could imagine.

Dawson had been quiet on the long ride to the lake house. Based on his intense expression, there had to be a thousand thoughts like hers rolling around in his head.

She had never been to his family's lake house before and she couldn't remember a time when anyone else had, either. Had the family stopped using the place after Bethany died?

The van parked on the pad behind the house.

Two men wearing camo pants, work boots and T-shirts exited the building. They signaled the driver, which must've been the okay sign because he cut off the engine and unlocked the doors.

Dawson stepped outside first. He helped Melanie out after she unbuckled Mason and pulled him to her chest, wincing as he brushed against her burns.

Luckily, he seemed unfazed by the changes in routine.

Melanie had no idea what to expect once she got inside the log cabin. All she really cared about was a soft bed, good security and a workable kitchen in order to prepare meals for Mason.

"Is there any chance there's a crib in there anywhere?" she asked. If not, she could prop pillows around him.

Dawson nodded, pausing for a second before he opened the door and walked in.

The warm-wood, cozy-cabin feeling extended inside. The great room was anchored by a two-story tumbled-stone fireplace. The windows displayed the lake beyond. She'd half expected there to be dust everywhere, but the place had been perfectly preserved.

The great room was open to the kitchen, which had all the necessary appliances. Everything was in good shape and looked barely used. The white appliances were a nice contrast to the darker tile countertops. There was a microwave and a fridge.

"When was the last time you came here?" she asked, looking around. Dawson was right about one thing. No one would expect them to be there.

He didn't answer.

In one corner of the room was a toy box filled with baby dolls, books and Barbie dolls. There was a pink blanket folded neatly on the tan sectional. A thick cotton blanket was folded over the back of part of the sofa.

Melanie looked at Dawson. He stood there, staring out the window toward the lake, looking lost and alone. Based on the intensity of his expression, facing the place was harder than he wanted to acknowledge. And her heart felt as if it were locked in a vise while witnessing his pain. Breathing hurt.

Mason wiggled in her arms, his gaze locked on to the toys.

"Would you like to take him while I get the rest of his

stuff from the van?" she asked Dawson, hoping that holding his son would help ease his pain.

Having Mason was the most grounding experience of Melanie's life. No matter how deep her pain had been at leaving Dawson behind, she'd held tightly to her little boy.

He turned to look at his son, and the pain in his expression only increased.

Her stress that Dawson's mother had been right sat heavy on her chest. Seeing him like this made her fear the worst. If Dawson had known about Mason, it would have ruined his life. And it was too late to turn back now.

"I'll get the stuff from the van," he said, and his voice was gruff.

Was reality hitting him that Mason might've inherited the gene?

Melanie stared out the window, looking at the view. It was another warm sunshiny day in Central Texas. The waves on the lake sparkled like glass.

The heat would be unbearable soon and she'd never felt more hemmed in than she did right now.

She needed air.

Chapter Thirteen

"Want to go outside and see the water, Mason?" Melanie opened the sliding glass door onto the deck facing the water. The temperature felt much cooler on this side of the house and she figured that was most likely because of the breeze off the lake.

Mason's face broke into a wide smile.

"Ma'am," came from behind her.

The voice startled Melanie. She spun around to find one of the agents in camo pants filling the door frame.

"I'd feel more comfortable if you came inside or allowed an agent to accompany you when you leave the house." He introduced himself as Special Agent Norse but asked her to call him Andy.

The whole moment was awkward and uncomfortable, but if it would keep Mason safe, she wouldn't resist. Going inside, seeing Dawson in his current state, would just break her heart all over again. Besides, she knew him well enough to know that he needed time to sort out his feelings. He wouldn't want Mason to see his father struggling to this degree, and Melanie had no idea how to help. The one thing that always worked for her when life overwhelmed her—focusing on Mason—seemed to make the problem worse for Dawson. After all, it was Mason he was concerned about in the first place.

"I'd like to take my son for a walk," she said.

"Mind if I come with you?" Andy was beside them in a heartbeat.

"Sure." She didn't say what she was really thinking… that she wanted to be alone with her son. Besides, Andy was a nice guy and he was only doing his job.

Melanie set Mason down and took his hand. It would do him good to get some exercise after sitting in the van all morning and he seemed eager to explore the new place.

His smile, which was exactly his father's, had a way of brightening even the darkest situations. And it was that smile that she'd focused on when she'd driven her car into a brick wall last night.

"How old is your son?" Andy asked as they cleared the yard and headed toward a path around the lake.

"He's eighteen months." She owed her life to the person who'd invented air bags.

"Got a newborn at home," Andy said.

"Boy or girl?" She smiled. It was nice to talk about something normal for a change.

"Boy. Can't wait until he can start walking. I tease my wife all the time that he's all hers for now. Once he's old enough, we're heading out camping." Andy wore a proud papa smile and it softened his serious expression. He looked like the camping-outside type. He was tan, despite having light hair and blue eyes, and had to be in his early thirties. He was half a foot shorter than Dawson and was built on a sturdy, muscular frame. As nice as he seemed, she had no doubt he'd be deadly. The gun on his hip reminded her of the fact.

"Sounds like fun." She imagined Dawson doing those things with Mason and it made her happy. No doubt having a man in his life would be a great thing for her son. She could see that so clearly now. *If* Dawson could get past his fears. There had been no doubt that he would earlier. That was before she'd seen his expression inside the lake house with all the reminders of Bethany around.

One thing was clear. He was battling demons, and she hoped that he would win for Mason's sake.

And maybe, just a little bit, for her sake, too.

Andy sent a text. "Need to stay in communication with the guys at base so no one gets their feathers ruffled that we're not at the house."

Mason pointed somewhere toward the middle of the lake and started babbling excitedly.

Something out there had him fired up.

How sad was it that Melanie's first reaction was panic?

"Fish," Mason said clearly.

It was the first time he'd used that word. She bent down to his level to see what he was talking about. It seemed Mason was learning a new word every day. He was growing and changing so quickly that she almost wished she could freeze time.

"Mama, fish," he said proudly.

Sure enough, there was a splash twenty-five feet away from them.

"Did that fish jump, Mason?"

He smiled up at her and her heart melted a little more.

"That's a great fish." Andy bent down on the other side of Mason.

Mason clapped his hands. "Fish."

"Stay down," Andy said quietly as he scanned the lake, no doubt making sure there was nothing but fish around. He studied movement on the other side in the swaying grass.

Melanie's heart pounded against her ribs.

A few seconds later, another small splash came.

"All clear," Andy said.

Mason repeated the last word, which came out more like "kere."

Standing on weak legs, she took a deep breath. Everything inside her wanted to go back to the house, close the blinds and hide. The thought Sprigs could be out there somewhere, watching, sent creepy shivers racing up and down her spine.

But could he?

After that crash, he had to be hurt at the very least. No one had actually seen him since, which could mean that he's dead. Couldn't it?

Worrying about her own safety was one thing, thinking about Sprigs hurting Mason…an explosion of anger blasted her in the chest.

She couldn't even go there.

Andy's phone rang. At least they had cell coverage.

Melanie took Mason to the water's edge to get a closer look, gripping his hand tightly. Her all-too-brave little boy would jump in blindly if she let him. To have that kind of trust again. What was that like?

Speaking of which, she needed to call Abby. Her baby sister would be worried that Melanie hadn't reached out. They normally spoke every few days. Abby's classes at University of Texas at Austin would begin soon and she was most likely sucking up the last few days of sunshine at Zilker Park before another crazy-busy semester began and she stayed glued to her laptop or a book.

Melanie wished she'd brought her phone outside with her. She had a no-cell policy when it came to spending time with Mason, and habit had her leaving hers in her purse.

Andy ended his call.

"Special Agent Randall has arrived and would like to speak to you," he said.

Melanie nodded, and then focused on Mason. "Ready to race back to the house, buddy?"

"Uh-huh." Another smile spread across Mason's face revealing tiny white teeth. He turned, let go of Melanie's hand, and burst toward the path.

"Nice. I'll have to remember that one for later," Andy said with appreciation in his voice.

"I learned by watching other moms at the playground. This little trick saves me from many a meltdown." Melanie jogged past the agent, who immediately fell in step behind.

Inside, Melanie scooped up Mason, balanced him on her hip and then scanned the room for Dawson.

There was no sign of him anywhere and that didn't sit well.

A man who was medium height and build with a serious face, wearing dark slacks, a button-down shirt and brown rubber-soled shoes, walked in the back door. He introduced himself as Special Agent Randall.

She crossed the room, exchanged greetings and shook his outstretched hand.

Mason mimicked the gesture, sticking his hand out.

Randall shook Mason's hand next.

"Nice to meet you, big fella," he said, smiling down at her little boy.

Mason smiled shyly.

It was past her son's lunchtime and Melanie figured he'd be getting fussy soon if she didn't get something in his tummy.

"Can we talk in the kitchen?" she asked. "He hasn't eaten yet."

"Take your time," Special Agent Randall said. "I need to update the others anyway. We'll be by the vehicles when you're done."

"Good luck with your little boy," she said to Andy as he filed out of the room.

"Thanks. You have a sweet kid there." He motioned toward Mason.

Dawson walked into the great room, his gaze moving from Andy to Mason with a frown.

"I'll feed him," he said, and his voice was raspy.

One look at his heavy expression and she could see the anguish and sadness written all over his face. It was the same look she'd witnessed all those years ago at his sister's funeral. And the real reason she'd sat on his steps every day afterward until he came out into the sunlight again.

"Can I hold him?" Dawson asked.

"Of course," she said. Mason was already holding his hands out toward his father.

Dawson took him and held him to his chest for a long moment before kissing him on top of his head and releasing a breath.

Melanie, tears soaking her eyes, busied herself pulling together lunch from the food Dawson had packed.

They'd have to go out for more supplies later, but there was enough to get through the afternoon.

After lunch, she cleaned up while Dawson handled the nap routine.

Bethany's crib was still in the master and that was where Dawson told Melanie she should sleep, since it was already set up.

She didn't argue, not in his current state. But they were going to have a conversation about the arrangements later. No way did she feel comfortable sleeping in his mother's bed. Just the thought of that woman sent angry pins poking through Melanie's skin. A rash would've felt better.

Now wasn't the time to get into it.

By the time Dawson came back, Special Agent Randall had returned and Melanie had poured three cups of coffee.

The trio assembled at the massive knotty pine dining table off the kitchen. She had so many questions reeling around in her mind. The dots she was having the most trouble connecting had to do with how any of this was tied to the original abductions.

"Going all the way back to the beginning, how does any of this tie into Thomas Kramer?" Melanie asked. "He took seven-year-old boys. How is he linked to the ring?"

"He was and that's really what led investigators to the operation in the first place. He'd been identifying younger kids, circling back to help abduct them in some cases. He was one of several spotters the masterminds used to target victims. You already know that he worked in the breakdown crew for the Renaissance Festival."

"Why didn't law enforcement figure him out then?" she asked.

"If he was the only one involved, it would've been easier. The trail of kids would have followed the festival and the pattern. They didn't. Most of the kids were much younger and the spotters waited six months or more after the festival had gone to strike. Another problem was that there were other spotters involved and they typically took younger kids."

"Beckett Alcorn has been protected by his father and his money. That couldn't have made it easy to identify him," Dawson added.

"Which is true. Beckett had his father, and his father had a relationship with both the mayor and the sheriff. It was difficult to make the linkages we needed early on," Randall said. "Kramer abducting those seven-year-old boys fourteen years apart had to do with a personal issue. He became greedy."

"What does that mean?" Melanie asked.

"He had a son who died at the age of seven," Randall supplied.

"So Kramer is out there identifying targets and in some cases abducting young kids and he thinks why not take an older one for myself?" Dawson confirmed. "How any father could do that to another parent is beyond me."

"Which is the reason Shane Hughes was located safely earlier this summer," Randall said.

"And what happened to him?" Melanie asked. "What did Kramer do while he had Shane?"

"Not much. He used his aunt Sally to help raise Shane, and by all accounts, he was well cared for. Of course, Kramer lied to her about how Shane came into his life and she didn't question him," Randall said.

"The other boy they found recently. What was his name?" Melanie looked to Dawson.

"Jason," he said.

"What about him? Didn't they find him living in terrible conditions?" Melanie asked.

"Kramer was aging and starting to lose grip on reality before the car crash that killed him. He was hoarding and he kept the boy at that filthy house with him after he lost his job," Randall said. "The best we can tell he must've been trying to figure out another excuse to give his aunt for bringing home another boy not so long after Shane went into the military."

"It's a miracle that Shane's okay. That he was never hurt," Melanie said, tears welling in her eyes. She couldn't even think about Mason being taken away from her and not finding him again until he was grown. She'd always understood her friend Rebecca's need to search for her brother Shane, on some level, especially because Melanie had a little sister that she loved. Now that Melanie was a mother, she couldn't fathom living through the kind of pain Mrs. Hughes had endured or imagine a life without Mason.

She prayed she'd never have to try.

"Did you get anything else out of Beckett this morning?" Dawson asked Randall.

"He's holding strong to his story that Sprigs is the leader and that it's only the two of them in the operation." Randall shook his head. "We know that for the line of bull it is. The problem is that he's lawyered up. Dad is sparing no expense for his son's defense."

"There's no way they could get away with this for so long if it was just the two of them," Dawson agreed.

"Their networks are too sophisticated. They could be aligned with any number of criminal organizations running other 'products' through the state," Randall said. "We've had our eye on a number of possible links."

"I realize that Melanie was just attacked last night, but I'm guessing that this level of security means you think he's going to strike again soon." Dawson glanced at Melanie, whose face had gone pale.

Randall shook his head. "He might be dead and we're hoping to find his body. However, he's escalating his fixation on Ms. Dixon and we believe it's because of the pressure on him."

"Meaning, he's desperate because he fears he'll be caught soon," Dawson clarified.

"That's exactly right. Common sense says he'd lie low for a while. Get out of the country until things cool down here in the States. But this guy is a psychopath. His name is out in the press because of his partner. He knows he can't truly escape. If he shows up at the airport, security will be all over him. Border guards have his picture posted on their walls by now," Randall said.

"Shouldn't that mean he wouldn't be stupid enough to risk coming after me?" she asked.

"He has to know that it's only a matter of time before he's in custody," Randall further clarified. "With time being his enemy, he'll want to strike now if he's alive. Besides, ever since news broke about him, he knows you'll be on guard."

Didn't that send a fireball of anger shooting through Dawson?

"And he already got to me once," she said in a low voice. Her cup suddenly became very interesting to her.

"We're going to do everything we can to ensure that that doesn't happen again, Ms. Dixon," Randall said.

"Thank you," she replied, but there wasn't a lot of feeling behind the words. From the looks of it, Melanie had gone numb.

"I'll use all my resources to protect you," Randall said.

"If he's coming after me, maybe you should disappear with Mason for a while." She looked up, staring into Dawson's eyes.

He'd started shaking his head as soon as he realized where she was going with this.

"It's something to consider," Randall added.

"No can do. It's safer for everyone involved if we stay together." There was no way Dawson was leaving Melanie alone to deal with this jerk. They had protection and there was no reason to believe anyone would be safer by splitting up. "I'm not going anywhere without you, and Mason will be better off here with us."

There was a good reason wars were won by the simple philosophy of divide and conquer. It worked.

Chapter Fourteen

After Special Agent Randall had excused himself, Dawson urged Melanie to lie down. She'd refused to go upstairs, saying she could rest on the couch, but Dawson had insisted. She'd agreed to sleep in the room opposite where Mason was sleeping.

Dawson had been preoccupied, stewing ever since they'd arrived at the lake house, and he was tired of wallowing in his own anger about the past.

Walking through the door of the lake house had been like stepping into quicksand. Dawson had been caught off balance by the emotions that had begun to swallow him. And, similarly, the more he fought the deeper he sank into the pit, and the more he felt he couldn't breathe. He was sinking fast and his resistance was pushing him down faster. He could feel the pressure of something like a wall of wet sand pressing against his chest in a matter of minutes, and he knew he wouldn't survive if he didn't get out of there or get help.

And yet he felt as though he was alone.

Bethany was everywhere in the lake house. Her dolls. Her books. Her favorite blanket. This was the place she'd kept all her real treasures—the place he remembered taking her out to play on the back lawn while she could still walk and romp across the yellow-green grass.

There were countless times she and Dawson had played hide-and-seek or keep-off-the-floor inside the great room, climbing onto the coffee table and hopping onto the couch.

And when her strength was being drained from her little body, when she became frail and could no longer walk or hop on her own, Dawson had helped her onto his back for a piggyback ride just to hear her laugh again. Bethany's laugh was like a spring flower bursting through the cold. Like the sun, it breathed life into all living things. Flowers were brighter. The grass was greener. And life was good.

Maybe it was because her life was cut too short that she was given the kind of smile that could light up even the darkest cave and, later, the darkest day. No way could Dawson hold on to a bad mood when he was around her, no matter how much trouble he'd gotten into with his friends or how long he'd be grounded.

And Bethany's thought that Dawson simply hung the moon was evident in the way she looked up to him.

Their mother had always said how unfair it was that Dawson could draw a full-body laugh from Bethany with a glance in her direction, whereas she had had to work for it.

Saying the two had shared a special bond was a lot like saying ice cream tasted good.

In losing her, Dawson had lost so much more than a little buddy. He'd lost a piece of his soul to a dark place. And he didn't figure he'd get it back again. His heart had fractured, the pieces scattered. There were too many splinters to clean up.

Mason stirred upstairs.

Melanie was still asleep and Dawson didn't want to disturb her. He took the stairs two at a clip, shaking off his sadness, and got to his son before the toddler could wind up a good cry.

But Mason wasn't crying. He was sitting up, looking around the room with his fist half in his mouth.

As soon as he made eye contact, Mason smiled up at Dawson and a feeling, like a burst of joy exploding in his chest, enveloped him.

Looking into his son's eyes was the first time Dawson thought he might begin to pick up the pieces.

"Want to go outside, buddy?" There were a few places he wanted to show Mason after giving him a cup of juice and changing his diaper.

Mason squealed and clapped.

Dawson took care of business first, then grabbed raisins and a juice box before taking Mason by the hand.

The sunshine warmed his face as soon as he stepped outside. Were it not for the breeze coming off the lake, it might be too hot for Mason.

One of the FBI officers followed, hanging back at least twenty feet in order to give them a sense of privacy. Again, Dawson wouldn't argue the intrusion.

There was something he wanted to show his son, if it was still there. Dawson hadn't been out to the lake house in seventeen years.

"Bug!" Mason exclaimed, stopping abruptly and dropping to his knees.

Dawson followed suit.

"That's a roly-poly." He let the little bug crawl onto his finger in order to give Mason a better view.

Mason tried to repeat the words, but they jumbled in his mouth and it was about the darn cutest thing Dawson had ever heard.

After a few seconds of intense study, Mason popped up to standing position and took off running.

Dawson let the bug slide off his finger and followed after the tyke, remembering what Dylan had said when his daughter had come to live with him. Little kids had two speeds…mach and drop dead.

There wasn't much in between in Dawson's observation.

Mason ran toward the hill that Dawson had wanted to show him. On the other side, there was a makeshift fort.

The little boy stopped at the top of the hill. "Water."

Dawson also noted that every word came out excited when Mason was happy. When he was sad, it sounded like the end of the world. Talk about wringing out his heart.

Thankfully, the little guy was rested, fed and happy.

"When you get a little bigger, we can take a boat out there and go fishing," Dawson said.

"Fish?" Mason looked up at him, so serious.

"That's right, buddy. Fish."

Mason clapped and then took off down the hill, his laugh trailed behind him, carried by the breeze.

That must've been a hit. Dawson couldn't wait to take his little guy fishing. Maybe he could talk to his folks about buying the lake house from them, since they never used it anymore, and he and Mason could spend summers there. It was time to build some new memories in this forgotten place.

"Whoa. Slow down, buddy," Dawson said as Mason neared the water's edge. Based on his all-or-nothing attitude, Dawson figured the little tyke would end up running into the water before he realized he'd left grass. This end of the lake was deep.

Mason turned around and a squeal leaped from his mouth as he must've caught sight of the fort.

The side of the hill had been dug out and Dawson had enlisted his father's help to put a wood frame around it.

He'd boarded up the makeshift cave, leaving just enough room for him and Bethany to climb in between the slats. Of course, Dawson was too big to fit inside now, so he pulled out his phone and turned on the flashlight app to allow Mason a peek inside. The elements hadn't affected the place too much. Years of dirt covered the little bench Dawson had dragged inside before boarding it.

It wouldn't take much to clean it up and get it ready.

Mason immediately started climbing through the woods slats, but Dawson stopped him midclimb.

"Hold on there, buddy. You can't go inside the fort without me."

"Fort," Mason said, peeking through the wood, holding on for dear life.

"Yep. That's all yours now," Dawson said, clearing the frog in his throat.

"Mine?" Mason asked.

"Sure is."

"My fort?" Mason asked.

"That's right."

Mason clawed at the boards trying to get inside.

"Dada has to clean it up for you first, big guy," Dawson said.

"Dada?" Mason froze.

For a split second, Dawson wasn't sure if Mason was about to squeal or cry. He hoped he hadn't freaked the little guy out by saying the word too soon. It had sort of slipped out without Dawson thinking about it.

Mason spun around and Dawson put the little tyke's feet on the ground. He didn't hesitate. He barreled into Dawson's knees, repeating the word over and over again. "Dada. Dada. Dada."

His son calling him "Dada" was about the sweetest sound Dawson had ever heard.

"Let Dada show you something else, okay, buddy?"

Mason threw his arms up. Dawson immediately scooped the little guy off his feet, much to Mason's amusement. There was still a lot to learn about caring for a toddler, but Dawson felt good about his progress so far.

His heart melted a little more when Mason threw his arms around Dawson's neck and gave him the best hug of his life. A little more sunlight peeked through the dark caverns in Dawson's heart. This time, Dawson didn't fight it.

Next, he took his son to his favorite place of all time, save for being on the lake itself…the tree house. The tree house was located near the edge of the five-acre property deep into the woods. Instead of inside one tree, it was built using three trees to secure the base. Dawson and his father had located the strongest trees with deep roots and a sturdy trunk.

Using studs in the ground next to the trees minimized the damage to them. The platform came next, all within arm's reach, and then half walls followed by the safety railing.

They'd built it that way specifically for Bethany so she could use it right up until the end. The base of the tree house was four feet off the ground, safe for Mason, and Dawson could easily grab his son if he fell. He and his father had installed a safety rail for Bethany and that would work perfectly for Mason now.

"What do you think, buddy?" Dawson asked as he pointed at it through the trees.

Mason's face lit up.

"It's a tree house," Dawson supplied.

"Twee-house?" Mason questioned. He repeated the new words enthusiastically.

"That's right. You want to go inside?" Dawson asked.

It had been purposely built on a small, sturdy platform for Bethany when she had been sick. It was her favorite place.

The handmade keep-out sign she'd posted over the door still hung proudly. It had been her contribution.

Dawson choked back the emotion threatening to overwhelm him. It somehow seemed right for Mason to be there, running around on the place that had given Bethany so much happiness. The place that she'd asked to be taken to when she spoke her very last words.

If Dawson had known she would never speak again, he would've told her he loved her one more time. Instead, he'd carried her to her favorite rocking chair on the deck facing the lake and held her hand as the sun went down.

He'd fallen asleep next to her, her small bony fingers clamped around his hand, and was woken by the sounds of his mother wailing.

"Dada?" Mason slapped his hands on the railing in excitement, drawing Dawson back to the present.

"Yeah, buddy." He wiped his eyes with the backs of his hands.

"My twee-house?"

"It sure is." Bethany would have loved Mason. And Dawson knew in his heart that she would want to share her favorite place with her nephew.

MELANIE WOKE WITH a start. Something was going on with Mason. She sat up and strained to listen more carefully.

And heard…

Laughter?

Yep, it sure was. Melanie threw the covers off, hopped to her feet and then pulled her hair into a ponytail. By the time she reached the bottom of the stairs, she saw the funniest sight.

Mason and Dawson were sprawled out on the floor,

arms and legs twisted and tangled in an old-fashioned game of Twister.

How many hours had she spent playing that game with her sister when they were bored in the summer? Countless.

"Is this game closed or can I get in on it?" she asked before she thought about how close she'd have to get to Dawson to play. A shiver skittered across her nerves when she thought about skin-to-skin contact.

Dawson was wearing his usual summer wear, athletic shorts and a T-shirt. She tried not to think about the fact that she had on shorts and a halter top. He looked up, winked and fired off a smile. She couldn't pinpoint what it was, but there was definitely something different about him. A good something.

"Mama!" Mason squealed, breaking form and running toward her.

"I guess this game's over. We can start a new one," Dawson offered, and she could tell he was just being nice.

"That's okay. I don't want to ruin your fun," she said. "How long have you two been at this?"

Dawson glanced at the clock over the mantel. "A long time."

Did he feel the same sexual spark that she did every time they were in the same room? She'd thought about the kisses they'd shared one too many nights when she couldn't sleep. "I need to call my sister anyway. I haven't spoken to her in more than a week."

Melanie kissed the top of Mason's head and set him down. He immediately took off toward Dawson.

"Dada," he said, and her heart skipped a few beats. Did he…just…say… *Dada*?

When he repeated the word, she had no doubt she'd heard right the first time. This was coming eventually.

She had to have known that on some level. So why did it catch her off guard?

Maybe because of their extreme circumstances, everything was moving way faster than she ever imagined it would.

Wasn't that a good thing?

Based on the smile on Dawson's face, it was. She'd never seen Mason look happier, too. And she'd be lying if she didn't admit that seeing the two of them together melted her heart.

Melanie located her phone and called Abby.

Voice mail. Great. Melanie waited for the beep and then said, "Hey, little sister, give me a call when you get this message. Love you."

Melanie was hoping to talk to Abby and bring her up to speed.

"She's not picking up?" Dawson asked, his forehead creased with concern.

"No. I'm sure she's at some place like Zilker Park, taking in those last lazy days before her semester starts and life gets out of control," she said. "She started seeing a new guy and she seems really excited about the relationship. I'll call her again in a little while."

Dawson nodded, his attention diverted to Mason, who was about to pull a box of checkers off the shelf and onto his head.

"Better leave that to me," Dawson said, rescuing Mason just before the dump.

"Mama. My twee-house," Mason said, pointing to a picture.

Melanie tossed a confused look toward Dawson before moving to her son's side. The picture was of a healthy Bethany, who was all smiles, sitting at the entrance to a tree house. "That's wonderful, Mason."

"My twee-house," Mason said with an earnest expression. "Mine."

Melanie chanced a glance at Dawson, careful not to intrude on what could be a difficult moment.

"It's okay," Dawson reassured her, and he looked so much better than when they'd first arrived at the lake house hours ago. "I took him there to show it to him while you were sleeping. I think it's safe to say that it belongs to him now."

Behind his smile a deeper emotion was brewing. Melanie decided not to push her luck.

"Are you hungry?" she asked Mason, turning away from the beautiful little girl's picture. It was hard for Melanie to look, to be reminded of Bethany and the disease that took her life so young.

Melanie hugged Mason a little tighter.

He wiggled out of the hug.

"Mine."

"I know, sweetheart," Melanie said with a smile, letting him stare at the picture.

Maybe she should've scheduled an appointment with a genetic specialist. It wouldn't hurt to find out if Mason carried the gene. But then what would happen? She'd had this argument in her head a thousand times and there was never a good answer. None of it would change the way she loved him or the fact that she wanted him to have a normal childhood for as long as possible. Knowing would just color every day with a dark cloud.

"I've got this. Why don't you take a break?" Dawson asked. It was more statement than question. He left to put Mason down to sleep after dinner and their nighttime routine.

Melanie agreed. If he'd taken their son to the places he'd shared with his sister, then he probably needed Mason more than she did. Dawson had slipped into a comfortable routine with their son, looking so much more at ease than he had in those first few days.

Nothing like a crash course in child care to get a person up to speed, Melanie thought. She'd had the same one when the little guy was born. Or maybe it just came naturally for parents to care for their child. Natural? Melanie choked back a laugh as she put away the last of the dishes. Not exactly the word she would've used to describe those first few weeks at home with Mason after her mother left.

Then again, he was a lot tinier back then. So much more fragile.

She walked past the bottle of wine and made coffee instead. She poured two cups.

Dawson, none the worse for wear, appeared just in time to enjoy a fresh mug.

"Care for one?" she asked.

"Do I?" Dawson picked up his and shot her a sideways glance when he picked up hers, too, and then balanced them while he opened the sliding glass door. "Coming?"

"What about Mason?"

"I'll leave the door open so we can hear him if he wakes. He was pretty tired when I put him to bed, though." He nodded toward the deck. "C'mon."

"Okay." Melanie followed him outside, where he pulled two Adirondack chairs and a side table in front of the door. He closed the screen door behind them to keep out bugs.

"I see you're taking up my bad habit," he said, and she knew he was referring to coffee instead of Pepsi. She'd already had two of those.

"It's not so bad."

"How's this?" he asked, hesitating when his gaze landed on a small white rocking chair.

It was the perfect size for a five-year-old. That had to have been hers.

Melanie's heart squeezed. She touched his arm, ignoring the charge of electricity shooting through her hand and spiking her blood pressure.

"You want to go back inside?" she asked.

"No. I don't." He stared at it for a long moment and then took his seat, focusing on the lake instead. "I want to be right here. With you."

Those last two words didn't help at all with the blood pulsing through her veins or just how aware her body was of him when he was this close. She needed to redirect her energy. "I'm pretty sure you made Mason's day today. He loves it out here."

"I see some of Bethany in him," Dawson said almost so quietly that she didn't hear him.

Melanie took a sip of coffee. She'd seen it, too. She chose to think of it as Dawson.

"Are you against having him tested?" Dawson asked. He took another sip of coffee and stared at the sky.

"I just haven't, I guess."

"Well, have you spoken to your pediatrician about the possibility?" Dawson pressed.

If there was a right answer to this, Melanie sure didn't know what it was. Just talking about it with Dawson had her hands sweaty and mouth dry. She took another sip of coffee to relieve the itch in her throat.

"Believe it or not, I'm not trying to be a bastard by asking," he said.

"I didn't say you were," she snapped back too quickly. Did this topic make her uncomfortable? Yes. It did. Did that make her an awful mother? Dawson could judge her all he wanted to. She hadn't brought it up and hadn't had him tested. There. Sue her.

"You don't have to be defensive. I know we got off on a bad start, but in case you hadn't noticed I've been trying to work with you," he said, and his tone was indignant. "It's not an unrealistic conversation to have, Melanie. I need to know."

"Would it matter? Would you love him less?" She hated how shaky her voice had become.

"That's not fair." No matter how calm his voice was, her pulse was still rising.

"Neither is knowing your son could die." She pushed off the chair and stalked to the edge of the deck, stopping to grip the rail. She'd known that it would only be a matter of time before they would have this conversation, and yet she hadn't expected it to come this fast or hurt this much. "And it wouldn't change my love for Mason. I want him to have a normal life no matter what."

Dawson didn't respond, and she half feared the storm that was brewing.

Instead of yelling as she'd half expected, he was suddenly behind her and his arms encircled her waist.

"It's me, Melanie. You don't have to be angry with me." His deep timbre ran along the base of her neck, down her spine.

"I'm not," she lied. It was partly true.

"No. You're scared." His voice wrapped around her.

Despite wanting to fight it, to fight him, to fight the world, her body relaxed against his muscled chest. Because it was Dawson. And she felt safe in his arms.

"And I'm scared, too." His voice came out as a whisper against her neck. "But we can get through this together."

Then he kissed her. His lips so soft against the skin of her neck.

Heat swirled through her body.

She unclasped his hands, kissed each of them and then

let them go. Instead of falling at his sides, they landed on the guardrail, and on either side of her, pinning her.

She shouldn't allow this to go any further, and she knew that somewhere in the back of her mind. She was reaching the point of no return, and if he didn't stop she wouldn't be able to.

Melanie turned around. Her hip firmly planted against the rail. He leaned forward, resting his forehead against hers. And she could tell the instant her body changed from anger to awareness…awareness of Dawson's strength… awareness of his masculinity…awareness of the strong man standing in front of her.

So she didn't fight, couldn't fight when his lips crushed down on her, hungry. He groaned against her mouth. There wasn't much more that she could do except surrender to the heat, to the scorching flames engulfing her. Every part of her body came alive, sensitized, as she parted her lips for him and drove her tongue inside his mouth.

The cool breeze danced across her hot skin.

A thought struck. There were FBI agents watching the lake house.

It must've occurred to Dawson about the same time because he pulled back and then glanced around.

"You want to take this inside?" he asked, his gaze piercing through all her carefully constructed walls, shattering all her intellectual reasons why this shouldn't happen. This all came down to being a man and a woman, basic desire, and there was no man she wanted more than Dawson.

"Yes."

"Just so there's no misunderstanding. You realize what I'm asking," he said, and his voice was deep and gravelly.

"I already gave you my answer," she said. "Unless you think we shouldn't."

He twined their fingers and walked inside, closing and locking the sliding door behind them.

Flipping off lights as they moved through each room, she figured he was stalling, giving her time to change her mind. Did he want her to be the sensible one?

When they made it to the bottom of the steps, she tugged his hand. He turned around and she let go of his hand, wrapping her arms around his neck instead. She had to push up to her tiptoes to kiss him, but she did, pressing her body flush with his.

There was no mistaking that he wanted this as badly as she did when his erection pressed to her belly. That fired molten lava through her veins, melting any protests she might have had before they could take seed.

Yes, on an intellectual level having sex with Dawson would be a bad idea. It would complicate their situation even more if that was possible.

Physically, though, and from a place buried deep in her heart, those arguments didn't hold water. Being with Dawson made perfect sense and felt so incredibly right.

With his arms around her waist, he claimed her mouth again, deepening the kiss when she moaned against his lips. And Melanie melted against him.

He pulled back a little.

"Upstairs," he said, his mouth moving against hers.

"Yes. Now." She stepped around him and headed up first.

After quickly checking on Mason, who was sleeping peacefully in his crib, Melanie followed Dawson to his bedroom.

Her heart pounded, her skin tingled and there was something that felt a lot like ache penetrating her body.

She had never felt so intense, so much chemistry, so much heat—with anyone other than Dawson.

Mostly, because there was so much more between them than physical attraction, even though they had that in spades.

Did he feel the same?

Could she go through with this if he didn't?

"Dawson," she said.

When he turned to look at her, there was so much hunger in his eyes.

"We need to talk," she said.

Chapter Fifteen

"We need to talk?" Dawson echoed. Those four words were normally sex-drive killers. In Melanie's case, he'd make an exception and that was mostly because he had no control over his body's reaction to her. If she wanted to put the brakes on, he'd need one damn cold shower at this point. "Now?"

"I want…*this*." She sat on the edge of the bed. "But I need to know that it won't change things between us."

"In what way?" he asked. "Because I was hoping it would."

"We have a lot going on and I don't want to be walking on eggshells with each other," she said.

"Like we haven't been already?" he asked with a smirk. He had yet to be comfortable around Melanie since seeing her again and finding out they had a child together.

She burst into a smile. And it was about the sexiest thing Dawson had ever seen.

"Yeah, I guess you're right. It has been intense, hasn't it?" she asked.

"I'll understand if you've changed your mind about this." He glanced toward the bed.

Melanie stood and then pulled her shirt over her head. It didn't make a sound when it hit the floor. She stood there in front of him, wearing a lacy black bra. Her chest moved up and down quickly as he remembered the feel of her firm breasts in his hands.

Dawson closed the distance between them in two steps.

"You're beautiful, Melanie." That her cheeks flushed with the compliment stirred his heart. "And damn sexy."

Her gaze locked on to his when she shimmied out of her shorts.

Dawson groaned when he caught a glimpse of her panties. Black. Silky. Lined with lace. Just like her bra.

He ran his finger along the inside edge of her bra in a V. He remembered how sweet she tasted, and the urge to run his tongue along the same spot assaulted him.

"Dawson, I want you. *Now*." The urgency in her words turned him on. She made a move toward the bed, but he stopped her.

"I've thought about this moment for too long to rush." She wasn't making it easy. He tugged her toward him and kissed her, hoping to slow things down a notch.

It didn't help.

If anything, that kiss was like pouring gasoline on a fire. The explosion of need rushed through him just as out-of-control as the blaze.

Desire warred with his self-control, and his self-control was losing the battle.

He pulled back, eyes closed, and tried to think of something else…anything else…something mundane…like changing the oil on his SUV.

"You're not getting away with that, Dawson Hill." Melanie always could tell what he was thinking. "Look at me."

He opened his eyes at the same time her bra hit the floor, along with Dawson's reserves.

He spread his hand across her full breast, and her nipple beaded against his palm. Damn. Sexy.

Her tongue slicked across her bottom lip, leaving a

silky trail, and Dawson was mesmerized—mesmerized by the sweetness of her skin, the hold she had over him and the sense of belonging he felt when he slid inside her. Which, at this rate, wasn't going to be too long.

It only took another two seconds to strip his clothes off. Her panties joined the floor at the same time.

And there she was, his Melanie. Sweetness, intelligence and sex appeal rolled into one helluva blond-haired, brown-eyed package.

Dawson put his arms around her waist and lowered her onto the bed as gently as he could given how much restraint it took not to pick her up and drive himself deep inside her right then and there. Every muscle corded with tension, needing release.

And he'd only just begun.

He pushed himself up on bent knees and slicked his tongue down her chest until her beaded nipple was inside his mouth. Licking and sucking, enjoying every moan he got out of Melanie, Dawson slid his tongue down her belly, pausing long enough to kiss the stretch marks that had been created when she gave him a son.

And then he moved his mouth down, positioning himself in between her thighs.

Melanie tasted sweet, and the fact that she was already wet nearly sent him over the edge. He pushed the thought aside and delved his tongue inside her sweet heat.

"Oh, Dawson." He liked the sound of his name on her tongue.

Deeper. His tongue surged inside her as he used his thumb to draw circles on her mound.

Faster. He felt her body arch and tense and he knew she was nearing release.

"I want you inside me. Now." Melanie scooted toward the foot of the bed and then clasped her legs around Dawson's midsection.

He dipped his tip inside her and nearly lost all control. Her fingers dug into his back and he knew that she was teetering on the edge.

He drove inside her and she matched his stride.

As he thrust deeper, his own need was like a bomb about to detonate despite his best efforts to contain it.

When he could feel her muscles clench around his shaft, he allowed himself to release, falling off the edge with her.

Careful not to crush her with his weight, he eased her toward the pillow, not ready to pull out before it was absolutely necessary. And that was when he realized that they hadn't used protection.

"Melanie." Dawson eased to her side and pulled her against his chest. Their arms were still in a tangle and he could feel her racing heartbeat. "We didn't—"

"I'm on the pill. I won't get pregnant again this time," she reassured.

"Would it be so bad to give Mason a sibling?"

"Funny joke. I think our hands are full as it is, don't you?"

She thought he was kidding? Maybe she couldn't read him anymore. Because he knew in his heart that he meant it.

"I still love you. What more is there?"

Damn. Did he say that out loud?

And there was no reaction from Melanie.

Didn't he know how to quiet a room?

A quick jab to his arm came a second later. Melanie's laugh filled the awkward silence.

"Quit trying to be funny, Dawson."

He went along with the misunderstanding, ignoring the pain in his chest that she didn't believe him.

On second thought, maybe it wasn't the worst thing in the world right now. They were already heavily invested in feelings, they'd just had the best sex he could remember and love complicated their situation even more.

There were a lot of details to work out between them now that they shared a son. And maybe it was better that she didn't know he loved her, because Dawson had a feeling they didn't see eye to eye on a few important matters with regard to Mason. Until they sorted things out, it was best to take things one step at a time.

Besides, Dawson might have to play hardball to bring her to the light. And he would if that was the only choice she gave him.

Melanie softened his thoughts when she curled herself around him and fell into a deep sleep on his chest.

"I love you, Melanie," he whispered as he closed his eyes and then drifted off.

DAWSON MIGHT HAVE been joking last night, but Melanie's heart had stopped when he said he still loved her. Normally, she could read the man's mind, but her own confused feelings got in the way when it came to love, and her heart wished he'd said it for real.

Exactly the reason she needed to slow down and keep a level head.

Melanie untangled herself from Dawson's arms, thinking that was the best she'd slept in…she couldn't remember how long. She slipped out of bed and into the shower before Mason opened his eyes.

Once that whirlwind woke, Melanie had precious little time for herself.

She enjoyed the feel of the warm water. Since Dawson had come into their lives, she'd had several quiet showers.

By the time Mason woke and called for her, she'd dressed and had a few sips of coffee while standing at the sliding door, enjoying the view of the sun rising across the lake. This place was perfectly positioned to take advantage of sunsets, and she could easily see why the family had bought it. And she could also see why they wouldn't come back after they'd lost Bethany. This place had to have been special to her.

Melanie took the stairs, stopping at the top. She thought she'd heard Mason calling for her, but he was saying, "Dada."

And Dawson was a few steps away from his crib.

Her heart melted in her chest at the sight of them. Mason's wide smile. Dawson's outstretched arms.

She didn't want to intrude on the moment, so she tiptoed downstairs and poured a cup of coffee for Dawson.

This was nice. Was it even possible that this could be real? That it could last…no…it was almost too perfect. How long before the tiny cracks would seep through and break the facade?

And how devastating would that be?

With a normal man, Melanie could handle it. Not with Dawson. There was something too special about the bond they'd shared to allow that to happen.

All those negative thoughts shattered when Dawson appeared, shirtless, carrying a smiling Mason against his chest.

"Mama!" Mason exclaimed, happy to see her but not exactly trying to get down so he could run to her.

"Good morning, big boy," she said with a smile.

Dawson kissed her on the cheek and then Mason followed suit.

How adorable was that?

Melanie held out Dawson's cup of coffee when she heard a rustling noise at the door. Her first thought was one of the FBI agents noticed movement in the house and wanted to use the bathroom. But then, they wouldn't have a key, would they?

The back door swung open and, shock of all shocks, Alice Hill walked in behind Andy who wore an apology on his face. Dawson's father, Jack, trailed closely behind.

"The alarm company notified us of activity here at the house, so we decided to come see for ourselves what was going on. This agent interrogated us before allowing us onto our own property," Alice said coolly. Her ice-cold gaze stopped on Melanie, and disapproval was stamped all over her tense features.

"Again, my apologies, ma'am" Andy said to Alice. He looked at Dawson. "You have this under control?"

Dawson nodded before Andy excused himself.

"I didn't realize you'd brought a *friend* out here, Dawson."

Melanie stood there like a concrete statue, frozen in time, and she was sure her jaw had hit the floor. In no way and under no circumstances was she ready to face Dawson's mother.

Unable to breathe with that woman in the room, Melanie grabbed her son and bolted out the slider.

She vaguely heard Dawson calling her name, but she didn't stop until she reached Andy's sedan.

He turned toward her. "Everything okay, Ms. Dixon?"

"Yes. Sure. Will you take me and my son out to get something to eat?" she asked, pleading with her eyes.

Andy opened the back door with a knowing smile.

"You have a car seat already?" she asked.

"Have to be ready to go at a moment's notice," he said.

Right. Of course.

She buckled Mason in, praying that Dawson wouldn't burst out the nearest door.

He didn't, and she figured he was backed against the wall by his parents and trying to explain why the heck she was at their lake house with federal officers and their grandchild.

Melanie didn't need to see Alice's face again to know how much she disapproved of the pregnancy, of Mason. After all, that shocked image had been burned into Melanie's memory nearly two and a half years ago. Her words wound through Melanie's thoughts like weeds choking a flower. She tried to block them out, focusing instead on the gravel road leading away from the lake house.

"Thank you," she said to Andy.

"No problem," he replied before transmitting their change in location. "You looked like you'd seen a ghost."

"I hope I didn't freak you out or anything. It's just, well, that woman really knows how to get under my skin." How crazy was Melanie to think a life with Dawson and their child would work out? Alice was probably back there undermining Melanie before she even got out of earshot.

Then again, once she admitted to knowing about their son and pushing Melanie away, Dawson would have to see his mother for the...bully...she was.

Thinking about family was giving Melanie a headache. It was too early in the morning for this drama. Darn it. Family. Melanie hadn't remembered to bring her phone. She hadn't checked it yet this morning and she didn't know if Abby had called.

She would ask to borrow Andy's cell phone if she'd been smart enough to memorize the number. She hadn't. Everyone was a name in her contact list now. She couldn't remember the last time she'd memorized an actual phone number other than hers.

As soon as she returned to the lake house, she needed to find her phone and check to see if Abby had called.

"Has Sprigs been found yet?" she asked, knowing this operation would most likely be over if he had.

"No. We have people covering your place, though. If he so much as sets foot within a mile, we'll get him," Andy said.

"Is there still a possibility that he might be hurt or hiding?"

"There is." There was no commitment in his words.

And what that really told her was that Sprigs could be anywhere. She tightened her grip on her seat belt and glanced at Mason.

Andy's cell buzzed causing Melanie to jump at the sudden noise.

"Sorry," she said. "Guess I'm on edge."

"It's okay," he said with a smile. "I have a mother-in-law, too."

Melanie stopped herself before she said that she wasn't related to that crazy woman back there in any way, shape or form. She needed to watch herself in front of Mason. Like it or not, Alice was most likely going to be in her son's life, and Mason was a sponge. She didn't want him picking up on her dislike for his grandmother.

Besides, it would be Dawson's responsibility to make sure his parents saw their child. Mason could visit on Dawson's time, and Melanie wouldn't have to be anywhere around the woman who'd made it clear she didn't want to have anything to do with her.

Andy had pulled off to the side of the country road in order to take the call. He gave an apologetic look before holding the phone out to her. "It's for you."

"Why would that be for me?" She stared at the cell as if it were a bomb about to detonate, scooting back toward the door behind her. If she could crawl out the window to get away from that thing, she would.

"It's Mr. Hill. He asked to speak to you." Andy paused when she balked. "You want me to take a message?"

"Would you?" Her eyes pleaded again.

Andy nodded.

"Tell him I'm busy with Mason, but we'll be back soon," she said, realizing Dawson was most likely checking up on her to make sure she didn't disappear on him again. That hurt.

Andy said a few *uh-huh*s and *yes, sir*s into the phone before he ended the call and navigated the sedan onto the winding road.

"Sorry. We had a fight." It wasn't exactly a lie. She was pretty sure they were about to have it out when she got home. Or maybe Dawson would be too upset with his mother to be mad at her.

Alice would most likely spin the whole story to her advantage. And then what would happen after? The pressure to have Mason tested would be enormous. Melanie had planned to discuss the issue with her pediatrician. She'd been waiting…no… Dawson was right last night. She'd been too scared to bring it up.

She'd been ignoring the fact that a remote possibility existed that her son would be anything but perfectly healthy.

The pressure on her chest while thinking about it now was like a bull sitting on her ribs. Her thoughts were heavy and it was like a thick, dark cloud had settled over her brain.

Mason was in the backseat making raspberry sounds.

Seeing him, knowing he was okay calmed her below panic levels.

He was such a happy boy.

And she prayed that he would stay healthy, too.

Chapter Sixteen

Dawson was fuming by the time Melanie returned to the lake house. She could tell based on how red the base of his neck had become. She had to give him credit. He held it all inside as he greeted them.

She'd intentionally stayed away until his parents had gone, lying to herself by saying that she was giving them time to talk. Actually, she was being a coward because she wasn't ready to face Alice just yet. And especially not after what had happened between her and Dawson last night.

Tensions thickened between them while they played with Mason, fed him and then put him down for his afternoon nap.

"Where'd you go this morning?" Dawson demanded. He had every right to be mad. She'd done the same to him when he up and disappeared at her apartment last week.

"To breakfast with Andy."

Dawson's eyes sparked with anger. "Oh, it's Andy now?"

"What?" Was he jealous?

"Never mind. Why did you take off like that with Mason?" Dawson said, moving into the kitchen, and she realized that was the farthest point from Mason's room upstairs.

"Because it was awkward, okay?"

"You can't just run away every time things get tough, Melanie." A muscle in Dawson's neck bulged. Not a good sign. And he'd scored a direct hit with her.

"Hold on a second. I thought you would want time alone with your folks to explain what was going on."

"One look at Mason and they figured it out, Melanie."

She blew out a frustrated breath. Really? Seriously? Had Alice played it as though she didn't know about Mason?

"I'll bet they did," came out on a huff.

"What's your problem?" Dawson said, the muscle throbbing.

She could appreciate that she'd left him in an uncomfortable position to defend himself in front of his parents. And she could further acknowledge that it would be difficult to face Alice alone. The woman had scared Melanie half to death with her threats. But for Dawson to ask Melanie what *her* problem was, well, that was just ridiculous.

"That's not a serious question." She shook her head. "What did your mother say?"

"That she can't wait to get to know her grandchild."

Melanie balked. "I bet."

"What does that mean?" he asked, looking hurt in addition to being angry.

"I don't know what kind of game she's playing, but your mother does not want to spend time with Mason."

"What's your problem with her? What has she ever done to you to make you so bitter?" Dawson asked, incredulous. His mother really knew how to play him, which was odd considering that she hadn't been all that concerned about her son after Bethany died.

Melanie didn't respond. Couldn't respond. Anger filled her as she thought about the things Alice had said to her.

"Every time I bring her up, you have a reaction," he pressed.

"Leave it alone, Dawson."

"What? The fact that you hate my mother? Why should I? She's Mason's grandmother and she's going to be part of his life," Dawson said. "I know she isn't perfect, but she's excited to be a grandmother."

"Oh, that really does it." Melanie fumed. "Excited to be a grandmother?"

"That's the exact word she used."

"I didn't realize there'd be a snowstorm blowing through this morning to blind you, but you need to open your eyes, Dawson."

"To what? The fact that you can't stand my family? How can we have any kind of future together if that's the case?"

"I like your family just fine, Dawson. Or I did. Right up until the time your mother ran a pregnancy test on me when all I thought I had was the flu." She regretted those words as soon as they left her mouth. She hadn't intended to tell Dawson this way. His relationship with his parents had been so broken when Bethany died. They'd managed to repair enough of the damage to have a bond and she shouldn't take that away no matter how frustrated she got or how horrible his mother had behaved.

Dawson whirled around on her so fast she had to take a second to catch her breath. He would never hurt her, she would never have to worry about that, but she'd knifed him in the chest with her betrayal, and the hurt in his eyes nearly brought her to her knees.

"You went behind my back with my family?" he managed through gritted teeth. "What else have you been hiding?"

She deserved that. "Nothing. And I didn't want to tell you like this."

"Then how, Melanie? How did you intend to lie to me and break my heart again? Did you wait until I fell for you again on purpose? So you could rip my heart out and stomp on it? Again?" Dawson's fist pounded the tile countertop.

Tears stung the backs of her eyes as his image blurred in her vision. All she could do was be honest, put her cards on the table and hope that he understood.

"She threatened me. She told me that she'd take my child away if I told you about the pregnancy."

"I don't believe you," he said through clenched teeth.

Melanie kept going. "Said that I would be trapping you into a life of misery, especially if the baby inherited the disease."

"She would never say something like that," he seethed.

"That's the real reason I left Mason Ridge. I didn't want you to hate me and I knew you'd never be able to let it go if Mason inherited the disease, and it would destroy you."

"Even if she said that, and I don't for one minute believe any of it's true, why wouldn't you let me decide for myself?" he asked with hurt all over his tone.

She didn't have a good answer for that except that she remembered what Bethany's sickness and death had done to Dawson and couldn't force him to go through it again with his own child.

"After everything we've been through together, that's how little you thought of me when you knew me better than anyone else in the entire world?" he asked.

"I do know you, Dawson. And your mother said every

last word of what I just told you," she said, defensive. Melanie should've been honest with Dawson, that part was true, but she'd be damned if she'd allow him to go on thinking his mother would never do something like that and this was all her fault.

Dawson looked at her. The hurt in his eyes robbed her breath.

Had she done all this for Dawson? Or had a big part of her been afraid that she'd end up just like her parents...in an empty marriage?

"You're a liar." He walked toward the door without looking back, pausing as he filled the frame. "And if it weren't for Mason, I'd never want to see you again."

He left.

If Melanie could move, she'd drop to her knees. She couldn't. Instead, she stood there rooted to the kitchen floor for what felt like an eternity, stupidly wishing she could take it all back and start the day over. Hell, she wished she could go back and change all her bad decisions.

She couldn't.

If life had taught her one thing, it was that there were no do-overs. People made mistakes. Period. Wallowing in them wouldn't do any good.

Hurting Dawson hadn't been part of her plan. None of this had. She hadn't expected to be scared by his mother and pushed away. She hadn't expected to be stalked by a psychopath. And she sure as hell hadn't expected to reunite with the one man she loved. Loved?

That part was true enough. There was no use denying it. Being in his arms last night was the first time she'd felt truly alive since she disappeared from town.

Melanie could admit now that she'd committed serious errors in judgment. She'd give almost anything to correct them. Dawson would never forgive her. Between his mother and her own messed-up parents, Melanie was beginning to believe she would never be able to open herself up to another person again. How on earth had everything gotten so twisted?

When two hours had passed and he still hadn't returned, she packed up both her and Mason's things.

Andy had to call it in, but he was able to get permission from Randall to take her to another safe house.

Because Melanie couldn't stay in that house any longer. Not with the way her heart felt as if it would explode right out of her chest.

She scribbled a note for Dawson to let him know that she and Mason were moving to a safe house and that she'd be in touch to make visitation arrangements as soon as this ordeal was behind them.

And then she walked out the door.

This time, she looked back and her heart wanted Dawson to be standing there more than she wanted to breathe.

He wasn't.

And she had no idea when he would return.

DAWSON CIRCLED THE lake again, trying to walk off his anger. He'd learned at a young age that anger made everything worse and yet he couldn't stop himself. It was Melanie and he would've thought, would've liked to believe, that she knew him better than that.

He'd come down hard on her. It had only taken forty-six laps for him to calm down enough to realize it.

If what she'd said about his mother was true, and Dawson didn't want to believe it could be, then he owed her an apology.

They had a lot of work to do if they were going to make this…whatever *this* was…work. He thought they'd made strides toward being able to talk about difficult subjects and being able to depend on each other, so he'd overreacted.

If what Melanie said was true, then his mother should be the one to receive his fury. And he had every intention of sitting the woman down and talking to her about why she would pull such a stunt.

So much made sense about Melanie's actions after she'd learned that she was pregnant. And he'd been a first-class idiot with the way he treated her. He could only hope that she'd give him another chance.

As he was walking back toward the lake house, the first thing Dawson noticed was that Andy's sedan wasn't parked out back. Didn't that put a searing-hot branding iron through Dawson's gut?

He reminded himself to calm down even as his instincts had his feet moving faster toward that door.

Dawson broke into a run.

He didn't stop until he was inside the lake house. He called out for Melanie, but the place was quiet—too quiet because Mason should be wide-awake right now and running around. That boy was a flurry of activity, excitement and nonstop energy.

His absence pierced Dawson somewhere deep in his heart with painful stabs of loneliness.

The place felt so empty without Mason, without Melanie.

Dawson searched the upstairs, confirming what he already knew.

There was a note taped to Mason's crib.

I'm truly sorry for all the pain I've caused you, Dawson.

I never intended to hurt you. You're my best

friend and I've missed you beyond belief. You should know up front that I have no intention of keeping your son away from you. He needs you as much as you need him. Seeing the two of you together, the bond you've already formed, makes it that much harder to walk away right now. But until this is over, it's not safe. Mason is not safe.

As soon as Sprigs is caught, we'll be back. I wish I could tell you where we're going. I don't even know. But I'll do anything to keep our son safe until this is over and we can set up a normal routine—whatever "normal" means anymore.

Love,
Melanie

Dawson hadn't cried since Bethany died. Until a tear broke loose and streaked his cheek just now. He choked his emotion back and told himself to take a minute to toughen up.

He fished his cell phone out of his jeans pocket and called Melanie.

She didn't pick up and, on some level, he'd expected that.

His next call was to Randall.

"Where is she?" Dawson didn't bother to hide his anger.

"I can't tell you that, but I can tell you that she and Mason are safe," Randall said, an apology laced his tone.

"Send someone to pick me up," Dawson said. "Take me to them."

"I would if I could," Randall said. "That's not possible right now. I know you would never want me to jeopardize the safety of Ms. Dixon or your son."

Randall had that much right.

But Dawson had every intention of taking matters into his own hands.

Chapter Seventeen

Dawson paced while he waited for his parents to circle back and pick him up. The hour that had passed felt like an eternity, and he wasn't any closer to figuring out where Sprigs might be.

If he had to visit Alcorn in jail to pressure him for information, Dawson would.

There were other pressing questions with people closer to home that were about to give Dawson a headache. He needed to know the truth about what had happened between Melanie and his mother. He couldn't fathom his mother going behind his back, and at the same time he couldn't picture Melanie lying about something this important.

The second he heard gravel crunching underneath tires, he locked the door and met his folks as they pulled onto the parking pad.

"Can you take me to my SUV?" he asked immediately.

"Yes, of course," his mother said as Dawson climbed into the back of her Escalade.

His father was driving and that gave Dawson the perfect opportunity to speak to his mother without either of them being distracted.

"Was Melanie a patient of yours, Mother?" he asked outright as his father reversed out of the driveway.

Mother's jaw went slack, but she quickly recovered.

"I believe she did come see me once or twice." She looked to be digging deeply to recall the information.

There was another explanation that Dawson didn't want to consider. She was stalling.

"Which is it, Mother? Once or twice?" he pressed.

"I'm not sure. It was a while ago and I see a lot of people in town," his mother said.

"How many who come in with the flu do you end up running pregnancy tests on, Mother?"

Her face puckered like a prune as she stared out the front windshield.

Dawson waited for a response.

None came.

"Then let's narrow the field down to women I've dated," he said.

"Son, what exactly are you accusing your mother of?" Dawson's dad, who had been quiet up to now, asked as he spun the wheel, navigating the winding country road.

"Are you saying that you don't know already?" Dawson asked in return.

"I have no idea what you're talking about." Dawson's father paused. "Alice?"

Still nothing from her.

"Then let me tell you," Dawson began.

"Oh, all right," his mother said, cutting him off. "Melanie did come to my office saying she thought she had the flu. I knew right away what the real problem was, so I had the nurse ask for a urine sample."

Problem? Did she just refer to Dawson's son as a problem?

"The test came back positive, so I did what I had to in order to protect you," she continued, her voice so matter-of-fact it sent a chill down Dawson's back.

"You did this for me?" he asked, incredulous. "You threatened the woman carrying my child and kept my son from me for his first year and a half of life, and you have the audacity to say you did it *for me*?"

"Alice," Dawson's father said, sadness and disappointment in his tone.

"What choice did I have?" she defended, folding her arms.

"The best thing you can do for yourself right now is keep your mouth closed, Alice," Dawson's father said. "And pray that your son finds it in his heart to forgive you someday."

"I doubt that will ever happen," Dawson quipped.

"Tell me you don't mean that, son," Dawson's father said. "Your mother has done a terrible thing—"

His mother made a move to interrupt his father.

"Alice. Let me say my piece," he said quickly.

She harrumphed, picking invisible lint off her suit jacket.

"It's unforgivable to think she would do something like this. And I won't lie and say she had your best interest at heart, because I don't believe it, either. What I will say is that she believed she had your best interest at heart because she loves you. And losing Bethany changed all of us. Not all of it was for the better."

No one immediately spoke, and that was most likely because there was a lot of truth to those words.

Alice's chest deflated. "He's right. When he puts it like that, I realize how terribly I've overreacted. I didn't know how to fix it once I'd set things in motion. Then she disappeared and I tried my best to forget what I'd done. For all I knew she wouldn't follow through with the pregnancy, so I left it alone. You might never be able to forgive me, but I didn't lie about one thing, I'm beyond thrilled to have a grandchild. I hope I haven't messed up any chance I had to have a relationship with your son."

Dawson would forgive his mother at some point. And he wouldn't keep Mason from her in order to punish her. Too much time had been lost with the people he loved to allow that to happen. Still, he was going to need some time to absorb this news.

He leaned back against the seat and closed his eyes, wondering if the damage with Melanie was even close to repairable.

"I just want you—"

"Let him be, Alice," Dawson's father said. "Give the man time to think."

He was grateful for the interception. If his mother was genuine, and he believed she was, then he could find a way to forgive her. There were a dozen more pressing thoughts running through his mind right now.

His phone buzzed, indicating he had a text.

Dawson pulled it from his pocket and checked the screen. His heart raced when he saw the name, Melanie.

I can't reach Abby and they won't let me look for her. Said they'd handle it themselves. Please help.

It wasn't the message Dawson was hoping for, but it was a start. He wouldn't refuse her plea.

Can you tell me where you are?

He waited for a response.

No. I'm sorry.

He expected that and he didn't want to push it. He'd had to ask.

We're okay. Mason is asking for you.

Reading that message shattered the darkness inside him and filled Dawson's heart with light.

How about you?

He wanted to know where he stood with her.

She didn't respond, which wasn't necessarily a bad thing. She'd reached out to him in the first place and that was a positive step. That gave him something to work with.

Will check in with Abby and get back to you. Tell Mason that I'll see him soon, okay?

I will.

Came the response. Then she sent Abby's phone number.

Dawson needed to think. Where could Abby be? It was possible that she was somewhere there was no cell coverage.

There were plenty of places to camp in and around Austin that were off the grid. School was about to start and Abby could be having one last hurrah.

Of course, Texas temperatures at this time of year could be brutal, and even she didn't go camping in August, it was generally ten degrees hotter in Austin than in North Texas. Okay, camping might be out of the question.

Melanie hadn't said it, but he knew that she was worried about the same conclusion Dawson had come to... the possibility that Sprigs had her.

But then wouldn't he make contact? Try to use her as a bargaining chip to get to Melanie? He would only take Abby to draw Melanie out. Right? That was the only thing that made sense.

What about Abby's friends? Didn't Melanie say something about a boyfriend? Maybe Dawson could start his search there. Surely someone knew where she was.

Dawson could grab his laptop and log on to her social media account to locate her pals as soon as he got to his parents' place. Then he could do some digging to see where she might be.

The rest of the car ride was quiet.

By the time Dawson returned to Mason Ridge, he'd had a chance to think through a couple of options at locating Abby. He had his folks take him to their house, since that was the last place he'd been before all this started.

What had begun as him wallowing in his own anguish, watching Melanie's parents' house across the street, had turned into a crazy eleven days.

He'd become a father and his entire life had been turned on its head.

And he'd do it all again if it meant meeting his child and seeing Melanie.

"The Dixons had a break-in recently, so I want both of you to exercise caution, okay?" Dawson said to his parents as they parked in the attached garage. He touched his mother's shoulder. "For you, that means staying in the garage with the engine running until the door closes behind you."

She nodded and offered a hopeful smile.

"It's going to take some time, but I'll do my best to move forward after what you've done," he said to her.

"None of this was supposed to happen this way," she

said, and she sounded sad. "I'm not making excuses, but I panicked when I realized what was going on and made a huge mistake."

There was more to it than that, because she'd had a thousand opportunities to tell him since then. "Is it Melanie you don't like?"

"It's not her exactly," his mother said. "She seems like a nice girl, and the two of you were so close growing up. In some ways I guess I felt like she'd taken you away from us after Bethany…"

Dawson started to defend Melanie, but his mom stopped him.

"We had so much grief that we shut down. That wasn't your fault or hers and I realize that now," she said. "When I found out she was pregnant I also realized that I couldn't go through that again."

"Melanie's pregnancy shouldn't have been about you, Mother."

"You're right," she said. "Too much of our life has been about me since Bethany."

When he really thought about it, Bethany's sickness had been about his mother. She'd been the grieving doctor who couldn't heal her own child. The depression she'd succumbed to afterward when she couldn't get out of bed had been about her, too. She hadn't thought of her husband or her son. And it had almost ruined their family.

They had been able to move forward and repair their relationships.

Dawson was an idiot. He shouldn't have doubted Melanie earlier. And as for her knowing him better than anyone else, she did. But she was wrong about one thing. If Mason had inherited the gene, Dawson could handle whatever came with it. He was a father. And being a loving parent meant putting his child's needs first.

Dawson shook his dad's hand. It had been his father who'd finally pulled the family up by their bootstraps. He loved his wife and he must have seen it as his job to protect her.

On some level, Dawson understood. His mother was strong on the outside but fragile when it came to inner strength.

Melanie could take care of herself. But that wouldn't stop Dawson from loving her and wanting to take care of her. The image of her standing in front of him with a shotgun leveled at his chest on the back porch the other day brought a smile to his face.

A woman like that wouldn't cave under any circumstance and especially one that involved her child.

Dawson excused himself, went inside and booted up his laptop. He checked Abby's social media page. So much for narrowing down her friends. She had 1480. No one had that many friends. He scrolled through her photos, hoping that he'd be able to figure out who her closest contacts were. Figuring out who she actually spent time with was his best hope of locating her.

He scanned her page for any posts that might signify where she was. There was nothing identifying her location. Normally, he'd be happy about the fact that she seemed to practice internet safety. Under the current circumstances, he was less than thrilled.

As expected, there were only a handful of people that she hung out with regularly according to her posts. Much to his good fortune, she'd identified them by placing tags on them with their names highlighted.

One of whom he was able to deduce must be Abby's roommate. Her name was Tabitha and he knew that they shared a house in Austin near campus.

Abby last posted three days ago. There was a pic of

her and a guy who wasn't tagged with a name. He was good-looking, athletic.

The pair looked cozy. This must be the new boyfriend.

Maybe Tabitha would know. Dawson fired off a private message asking her to call him with any information she had about Abby's whereabouts. He identified himself as a friend of Abby's sister and hoped Tabitha would get back in touch with him soon.

Being away from Melanie and Mason made Dawson feel empty inside. He missed the little whirlwind that was his son.

Dawson was too far away to ensure their safety and he had a bad feeling about Sprigs being so quiet. If the guy had been hurt in the crash—and what were the odds that he wasn't?—then he'd had enough time to heal and get some strength back.

The feds had planted a woman at Melanie's place, but they didn't seem to be getting any bites there.

Sprigs might have been a loner, but he was intelligent.

Dawson knew so little about the guy, and yet they'd grown up in the same town together. What if he made a few calls? Tried to get to know the guy a little better? Didn't he used to live off Maddox Street? That wasn't so far from where Dawson was now.

Time was ticking and Dawson wouldn't get to see Melanie or Mason again until this whole mess was sorted out.

His first call was to his buddy Ryan. Ryan's brother was in the same grade as Sprigs. Maybe he would know something about the guy's background.

Ryan picked up on the first ring. "Dawson, where are you?"

"How's Lisa?" Dawson tried to redirect.

"She's doing a lot better, thanks. She's been worried about Melanie, though," Ryan said.

"Melanie's with me."

Ryan relayed the information to Lisa.

She must've had a big reaction because the line went dead silent.

"Tell her that I know about Mason and it's okay," Dawson said. "We're working things out."

"Who's Mason?" Ryan asked.

"Long story. I'll tell you later," Dawson said. "In the meantime, I need to talk to Justin."

"What about?" Ryan had good reasons for being protective of his brother after they'd learned that the sheriff had been targeting him for years.

"It's about Melanie. Actually, it's about Jordan Sprigs."

"Whoa. Hold on there. Jordan Sprigs?" Ryan asked. "Beckett Alcorn's partner?"

"The very same one."

"What does Justin have to do with him?" Ryan asked, hesitant.

"Nothing personally. The two were in the same grade and I'm hoping that Justin can tell me something about the guy."

"Hold on. I'll conference him in right now," Ryan said.

Dawson's social media page made a ping noise. He had a message. He opened his laptop. Sure enough, there was a message from Tabitha.

Haven't seen Abby in two days. She didn't leave a note. It was weird. I'm at work but I'll call you later.

A heavy feeling pressed down on Dawson. He typed a thank-you along with his number as Justin came on the line.

Ryan let his brother know that Dawson was listening, and then asked Justin if he knew Jordan Sprigs.

"Not really," Justin said after exchanging greetings with Dawson. "He was strange, though."

"What kind of strange?" Dawson asked.

"At first we thought his mom was some kind of witch because she always wore plain dark clothes when she came to school to pick him up. She was a scary-looking woman, wild eyes and stringy hair. And she was strict." Justin paused, thinking. "I heard rumors about some of her punishments."

"Was it anything like what we went through with Dad?" Ryan asked.

"Nothing at all. What we went through was normal compared to what this crazy witch did. She was all religious but not in the 'have a glass of wine on Friday and then go to church on Sunday' way. I heard she used to routinely perform exorcisms when he disagreed with her or got a bad grade on a test. At first, I didn't take it seriously because I just thought kids were being cruel, but then I noticed how bad he looked some days and could tell he was being tender with his bruises."

"That sounds like a breeding ground for a psycho," Ryan interjected.

"Most of it could just be rumor and exaggeration. You know how that stuff takes on a life of its own. Couple it with the fact that the guy didn't act like a normal person and the rumor mill goes wild," Justin said. "There's someone who would know for certain what went on at the Sprigs house, and that's Peter Sheffield."

"The reporter?" Dawson asked.

"Yeah. He's right there in town." Justin paused, and Dawson could hear shouting in the background. "Girls, Daddy's on the phone."

Giggles followed by an apology came through next.

"Sorry. They have a knack for finding me anytime I'm

on my cell. It's like they have me on radar or something," Justin said, but he didn't sound the least bit upset. Maybe it was part of the parenting territory and he'd grown used to it.

Dawson thanked Justin for the lead. "I'm in Mason Ridge, so it'll be easy to track down Sheffield."

The guy wasn't popular among Dawson's friends because of the way he'd hounded Rebecca for a story about her brother.

They ended the conversation with Ryan saying they needed to get together again soon.

A quick call to the station and within five minutes Dawson had Sheffield on the line.

"I've been told by Justin Hughes that you knew Jordan Sprigs in high school," Dawson started after identifying himself.

"I don't know how well I knew him. We were in the same grade, as was Justin. Why? What's this about?" Sheffield asked.

"Do you know anything about his background?"

"Not much other than the fact that his father died when Jordan was still young and then his mother snapped," Sheffield said.

"How so?"

"She was weirdly religious to begin with, but when his father died she really jumped off the crazy ledge." Sheffield was being guarded with his responses and Dawson knew the guy was holding back. "Everyone in law enforcement is looking for him now that Alcorn rolled. What do you want with the guy?"

"My reasons for finding him are more of a personal nature." Dawson didn't have a good bargaining chip, so he figured honesty was his only hope.

Sheffield seemed to perk up. "What did he do to you?"

"He's fixated on someone who is important to me. And if I don't find him, he might kill her."

"And who is this person Sprigs is interested in?" Sheffield asked.

Again, honesty was the only course of action that made sense. If Dawson had another route, he'd gladly take it. "Melanie Dixon."

Sheffield made a strangled cough noise into the phone. "I thought she moved away a couple of years ago."

"She did. Mostly, to get away from him." That part wasn't one hundred percent truth, but Dawson figured he could fudge a little under the circumstances. And what was up with Sheffield's reaction?

"Where is she now?" he asked.

"She's being watched carefully," Dawson said.

"You don't know or you won't tell?" Sheffield asked, picking up on the nuisance of Dawson's language.

"I honestly don't know." That was true enough. And he cursed the fact that he didn't. "Will you tell me what you know about Sprigs?"

"Are you close to the investigation?" Sheffield seemed to be hesitating, deciding.

"Close enough to let you know the minute Sprigs is in custody." Dawson figured he'd throw that in for good measure. It remained to be seen if he could deliver on the promise, but a phone call once Sprigs was locked up wouldn't hurt anything.

"That's a deal." Sheffield seemed to perk up even more. "Sprigs and I weren't friends, but I had to stop over at his house to take homework to him once. He'd been out sick and we had the same homeroom teacher. He lived two blocks over, so I got stuck with the job. Inside, the place was strange. There was a wooden altar that had been constructed in the corner of the living room. I'd heard rumors that he had to kneel at that thing until the devil left him. I thought people were making it up. Never in my wildest dreams did I imagine that could be true."

"Sounds crazy."

"He'd come to class looking zonked and some of the kids said he literally had to sleep kneeling the entire time some nights. He did something wrong and he had to pray." Sheffield paused. "No one said for sure, but there were whispers of abuse. Spare the rod and all that."

"What couldn't be removed by praying she'd beat out of him?" Dawson asked.

"Something like that. You heard that rumor, too?"

"It was all around school," Dawson said. "I didn't take it seriously."

"Me neither. Until I saw that house," Sheffield said. "Then I believed all the rumors. The one about her locking him into a closet for days on end to pray. The one about her starving him so the devil wouldn't have anything to feed off of. And especially the one about her beating him with a pickax handle."

"Sounds like the experience left an impression on you," Dawson said. He could only imagine what it would be like to grow up in a twisted house like that.

"The craziest times apparently happened when she used the candles on him," Sheffield said.

That was the reason he liked to burn things.

"What about his mother? Did you see her? Is she still around? She could walk right past me on the street and I wouldn't know it," Dawson said.

"Yeah, I did before. A few years ago she moved them to a trailer on the outskirts of town."

Now it was Dawson's turn to perk up. "You have an address?"

"Not exactly, but there aren't many places out there. It's

where Old Saw Mill Road meets FM 46. Sits on a couple acres. There isn't much else out there."

"And what about her? What does she look like?" Dawson asked.

Sheffield blew out a breath. "I haven't seen her in years, but I remember that she was fairly attractive before. Homely because of the way she dressed, but she had nice features, you know. Her hair was long, blond and she had big brown doe eyes."

Just like Melanie.

Chapter Eighteen

Dawson thanked Sheffield and ended the call. Randall had to have known about Sprigs's mother and chose to keep that information to himself. The logical reason was that Randall wouldn't be able to share information about an ongoing investigation, and Dawson realized that on some level.

Of course, given that his family hung in the balance, it still burned through him to realize information sharing was mostly a one-way street.

Maybe Dawson could interview Sprigs's mother. Get a clue as to where her son might be hiding. He loaded his shotgun and tucked it away safely on the floorboard in the backseat of his SUV.

It took forty-five minutes to drive to the area Sheffield had mentioned. A few wrong turns later and he managed to find a trailer that looked as if it belonged on an episode of a cop show.

His phone buzzed, so he pulled off to the side of the drive where he could keep an eye on the front door of the trailer while he answered. His phone didn't recognize the number.

"Hello, this is Tabitha." She had that perky college coed voice.

"Thank you for calling. I'm a friend of Melanie's. She's

worried about her sister and asked me to help find Abby." That was all the information Tabitha needed to make a decision as to whether or not she should trust him.

"When you find her, tell her the rent is due," Tabitha quipped. There wasn't a hint of worry in her voice. Maybe Abby had disappeared before? "She forgot to leave a check and I don't need this kind of stress to start off the semester."

"Will do." Dawson paused. "You have any idea where she could've gone?"

"None. And she's not answering any of my calls."

"There's a guy in the photos online and her sister thinks she has a new boyfriend," Dawson said.

"Oh, yeah. His name is Bradly. They've been spending a lot of time together lately. I should've called him first," Tabitha said.

"Does Bradly have a last name?"

"I'm not sure. You know who would, though? Carlton. Let me check with him and get back to you," she said.

"I'd like to hear from you as soon as you know."

"You don't think something's happened to her, do you?" she asked, and it was the first time she sounded truly alarmed.

"I hope not."

"She could be somewhere out of cell range, or there've been a few times she forgot her charger." Tabitha's voice rose the more she spoke. She was beginning to see the possibilities that both Melanie and Dawson feared.

He hadn't intended to scare Abby's roommate. But then, he needed some urgency on this, and that was one way to get it.

Dawson ended the call and then phoned Randall.

Staring at the trailer, Dawson figured he'd better go in armed with information.

"What do you know about Ruth Sprigs?" Dawson asked as soon as Randall answered.

"That she'd most likely do anything to cover for her son," Randall said. At least he didn't lie about it.

"So you interviewed her?"

"Yes. Her and everyone else I could find connected to her son." Randall's tone was matter-of-fact. "There's news out of Houston. Someone is watching the apartment and we think it might be him."

It was too early to hope, but if that was true then Sprigs couldn't be hiding out at his mother's trailer. Although that was probably too obvious anyway. "Is his mother involved in illegal activity?"

"No connection has been established," Randall said in a convincing tone.

"If I told you I was staring at her trailer, would you give me some advice?" Dawson figured it was now or never and he needed to know how concerned law enforcement was about her.

"Yes. Plenty. Are you alone right now?" Randall asked.

"Yes," Dawson said.

"Then get out of there."

"I've made it this far. I'm not turning back," Dawson said, and he meant it.

"Then wait. Let me send someone out there for backup," Randall said.

"You get anything out of her before?"

"No." Again, he was being honest.

"I might. I'm local and she might be more willing to talk to me."

"She's a few cards short of a deck," Randall said. "And I don't want you anywhere near that place."

"I might be able to help," Dawson said. "To end this once and for all."

"Let my people do their jobs."

Dawson understood Randall's position. It had been weeks since this whole ordeal began with Melanie and so much longer than that if they really went back to the beginning. What did anyone have to show for it?

Sure, Beckett Alcorn was in jail. At least for now. Wasn't it Randall who'd said it was only a matter of time before Alcorn's fancy lawyers got him out on some technicality? Stories like his littered the news.

Dawson couldn't risk it. His family was at stake.

"I gotta go," he said before ending the call to the background noise of Randall's protests.

The area was thickly wooded and the nearest major street was a good twenty minutes away. There was no way to sneak up because the road only led to one place, the trailer.

Even though the property consisted of several acres, there was a fence around the trailer, giving the impression of an enclosed front and backyard.

Dawson turned his SUV around and parked on the lane outside the fence. No one had opened the front door, which meant they were either content to watch him from the window or not home.

The trailer was old, the metal fence rusted. There was a beat-up tire tied to a tree in the side yard. It was the kind of place he expected to see a Rottweiler chained out front.

In fact, Dawson scanned the yard for animal feces as he breached the gate.

He took a deep breath and caught wind of something awful, a stench like rotting meat left out in 110 degree weather. The closer he stepped toward the trailer, the more pungent the odor. It was something worse than trash left to sour. There was something oddly sweet but overpowering about this scent. And it made him want to puke.

Dawson pulled his shirt over his nose and mouth to filter the air he breathed. It helped a little. He took the two makeshift wooden steps to the trailer in one stride and then knocked on the door.

There were no barking dogs and he sighed in relief. The last thing he needed was an encounter with a pit bull.

Then again, there was no noise at all.

He pressed his forehead to the glass, trying to get a look inside. The blinds were closed and with the bright sun to his back he caught a glare off the window.

The smell was about to double him over as he walked around to the back of the trailer. He hoped to see a metal trash barrel full of rotting garbage instead of what he most feared.

Melanie was fine, she was with Randall or one of his men. It was Abby he was worried about. And that was what prompted him to break the law and kick the back door open.

As soon as the door flew open, the stench cloaked him.

Dawson stumbled a step backward, tripping down the makeshift staircase and landing on his back. The wind knocked out of him.

Jumping to his feet, he curled his arm around his face, nose to the crook of his arm, to stave off the nauseating odor.

He gripped his cell in his other hand and called back the last number he'd phoned just as he glimpsed a female body slumped over in a plaid recliner. He couldn't get a good enough look at it to tell if it was Melanie's sister, and since he had no idea if the murderer was still around, he had no plans to run inside to check.

"There's been a murder," Dawson said.

"Get out of there," Randall said. "We're on our way."

Dawson jogged over to his SUV. It would be safe to

wait inside there and he needed a break from the over-whelming stench or he was about to toss his breakfast.

Even running the engine and turning the AC on high couldn't completely get rid of the smell that clung to his shirt like Louisiana humidity.

Staying alert, he waited for one of Randall's men to show.

Much to his surprise, the sedan that pulled in was driven by Randall. He parked next to Dawson and it looked as though he instructed Melanie to stay in the vehicle.

"We were the closest to you. I've alerted local law enforcement and they're on the way. We don't make a move until they get here," Randall said.

"She shouldn't be here," Dawson said to Randall as he exited the car and closed the door.

"We had a situation, so we had to transfer her to my vehicle," Randall said. "I couldn't leave you here alone or risk the crime scene being tampered with by the sheriff. Especially after learning about his relationship with the Alcorn family. This case has been mishandled dating back to the abductions fifteen years ago."

Dawson couldn't argue with that point. And he'd had his suspicions about Sheriff Brine's integrity along the way.

"We need to take a walk," Dawson said.

Randall followed to a spot where Dawson was sure Melanie couldn't overhear what he needed to tell the agent.

"Her sister is missing and I didn't get a good enough look at who was inside there to know if it was Abby," Dawson said.

"Based on the smell and the heat, this person has been

in there for a few days at least. I'm guessing there'll be significant decomposition given the circumstances."

"Meaning?" Dawson asked.

"Even if I walked inside right now, I might not be able to determine who it is."

"The body was too small to be a man's," Dawson said. "That much I could tell."

"Then we're dealing with a woman, his mother, or possibly a child," Randall replied.

Dawson's stomach churned as he thought about the possibilities. Given Sprigs's history, it could be either. Based on the size, Dawson's money was on a female.

"We'll bring in a team to analyze the crime scene," Randall said. "It'll take a little while to process. You leave messages with her sister?"

Dawson nodded.

"Then let's hope she calls back soon."

"She's been missing for three days." Dawson moved to the parked sedan. The door opened and Melanie climbed out, holding Mason against her chest.

"What is that smell?" she asked, wrinkling her nose.

"You might want to stay inside with Mason and keep the AC on," Dawson said, leaning in to kiss Mason's forehead and then Melanie's before urging them back inside. He didn't want to get too close while he had the dead body stench all over him.

"Dada." Mason's face lit up.

"I'm here, buddy." He looked at Melanie. "And I'm not going anywhere."

She squeezed his arm. "We need to talk."

"We will. Soon." He had no intention of letting her disappear again without knowing how he really felt about her and Mason.

"Did you find out anything about Abby?" she asked.

"Her roommate is trying to reach Bradly?"

"That's a good sign. She's done this before when she meets someone," Melanie said, looking a little relieved.

"She's planning to call me back here in a few minutes," he said. He hoped that was all there was to it. Abby had met a new guy and had fallen off the radar. If that was true then Tabitha could be calling back with good news soon.

Melanie smiled tentatively, nodding as she climbed inside the cab.

He closed the door and then instructed her to lock it, feeling a small sense of relief when he heard sirens in the distance.

By the time he turned around, Randall was on the phone. Good. Maybe there'd be an update about when other law enforcement officers would be there and Randall could take Melanie far away. Dawson had a bad feeling about her being anywhere near this place, and God forbid her sister be the one inside that trailer. The two were close and Dawson knew it would destroy Melanie if anything had happened to Abby.

The most likely scenario was that the body in there belonged to Sprigs's mother. And there was a less likely possibility that it was a child. In general, Sprigs and Alcorn took younger kids, three years old and younger. The only cases of older children being taken had to do with Kramer's greediness and nothing to do with the operation.

"There's a problem," Randall said to Dawson as soon as he ended the call.

Dawson didn't like the sound of that. He'd been catching the occasional whiff of something he couldn't immediately identify. He wrote it off as whatever was in that trailer.

"Emergency vehicles can't get through."

When he really thought about it, the sirens hadn't moved closer in the past few seconds. "What's going on? Someone blocking the road?"

"Not someone, some*thing*." Randall looked Dawson directly in the eye. "Fire."

The opening to the lane was far away and there were enough trees around to block their vision. Plus, the stench would mask the smoke, at least for a while.

And that meant one thing… Sprigs was there.

Dawson marched over to his SUV and pulled out his shotgun. "We'll have a better chance of getting out of here alive if we take my SUV."

"There's only one road in and out," Randall said.

"Then we'll have to make our own way out the back," Dawson countered. He ushered Melanie and Mason out of the sedan and grabbed the car seat with his free hand. He locked it dead center in his backseat.

Randall was on the phone again. "They're battling the blaze as they look for a way out for us through satellite pictures of the property."

"Being here isn't going to help us. I can get us through that clearing." Dawson pointed to a place opposite the entrance. "Find out where that'll take us, because we're not staying here. That's exactly what he wants and he could be anywhere."

The land was fairly flat in this part of North Texas, and that made traversing the terrain a bit easier as Dawson navigated as far away from the trailer as possible. The main problem was trees. They were getting closer together and Randall had already warned that there was a creek coming up that would block their path. Being inside the SUV offered some shelter and Dawson didn't like the idea of leaving its safety.

Sprigs would most likely know the woods, and Dawson

couldn't help noting that he was positioning them away from anyone who could help them.

Randall got another phone call, which he put on speaker.

"I've got more bad news. A couple more fires have been set. One is directly in the way of the new path." The voice belonged to Andy.

"Where are you?" Randall asked.

"We're doing our best to set a perimeter, but this is a lot of acreage to cover," Andy said.

Dawson didn't say what he was thinking out loud. This was the perfect setup for Sprigs. He was encasing them with fire. The question remaining was whether or not he'd stay inside the circle or bolt so he could find a place to watch them burn.

Dawson hit the brake at the edge of the creek and the SUV lurched forward. They couldn't go back. Trees to the left and right were too thick to drive through. As much as he hadn't wanted to consider the possibility, they had no choice but to get out on foot.

"How about following the water?" Dawson asked. Could they allow the creek to lead them out of there? As soon as he opened his window, the smell of smoke carried in on the breeze. The crackle of fire meant that it was close.

Well, Sprigs didn't get to orchestrate the perfect murder on Dawson's watch.

Randall took the call off speaker. He listened before ending the call, closing his eyes and leaning his head back on the headrest. "The blaze is all around us. We're not getting out."

"What about a chopper?" Dawson asked.

"By the time one gets here, it'll be too late. The dry

conditions have the fire moving too swiftly," Randall supplied.

"This is all happening too fast," Dawson said. "There's no way he's setting these fires by himself."

"The officers found a rig set up at the opening of the drive. He wired this place before and he's been watching," Randall said.

Which meant Sprigs might not even be there. He could be setting these fires using a remote. Dammit. Anger burst through Dawson's chest.

He had no plans to roll over for that son of a bitch and allow the fire to consume everyone he loved.

"If we follow the water source, there might be a way to get out," Dawson said.

"Everyone out. Grab the diaper bag," Randall instructed.

Melanie had been quiet up to now. She got out of the vehicle and held Mason to her chest. "Dawson, I'm really sorry about—"

"We'll have time to talk about it later," he said, his words meant to reassure her. No way was he allowing her to give up.

Randall pulled up the GPS on his phone. "Looks like the creek runs northwest. If we follow it long enough, we might be able to make it to FM 33."

"Good. That's the route we'll take. I have emergency supplies in my trunk." Dawson moved to the back of his SUV and retrieved his backpack.

He came back to the group and kissed Melanie's forehead.

"We're going to get out of here," he whispered.

Chapter Nineteen

Dawson led them along the creek for a good twenty minutes before he hit a thick wall of smoke.

Moving forward was no longer an option. Mason's lungs wouldn't be able to take much more.

A wall of fire blocked any chance of moving west, so Dawson had no choice but to circle back. They were beginning to walk into fire now. It was all around them.

Dawson didn't want to separate from the creek, but there would be no choice soon.

A fiery branch fell from above. Thick smoke was beginning to make Mason cough. And they were starting to walk in circles.

And then they heard it. A man's voice. A distorted laugh from the south. Sprigs.

"Go ahead, run," Randall said. "I'll slow him down."

Dawson hesitated at first, but Randall insisted. Even though Dawson wanted to stay back to help the agent, there was no way he would send Melanie ahead on her own.

Grabbing Melanie's hand, Dawson ran until a fallen tree blocked the trail, forcing him to move them east again.

"Let's stop here and rest." Dawson needed to check his phone to see if Randall had tried to reach them.

Besides, Melanie was out of breath and she needed a minute before he pushed them to keep moving again. There was a bottle of water in his emergency pack. He took it out and handed it to her.

She plopped down on the ground with Mason in her lap. He'd been such a good boy so far, taking in all the strange sights and sounds, no doubt thinking they were on a grand adventure.

On Dawson's phone was a text from Tabitha.

Abby just called. Said she'll check in with her sister to-night.

"Abby's safe. Her roommate just sent a message saying that she's been hanging out at her new boyfriend's place before the semester started and had lost her charger." At least he was able to give Melanie good news for a change.

"Once I'm finished with you, your sister will join you in hell," Sprigs said from behind them a good twenty-five feet away.

Dawson rounded on Sprigs, blocking his view of Melanie. The movement must've startled Mason, because he started crying.

"Randall?" Dawson shouted.

"He can't help you," Sprigs said, agitated.

"You're not taking her, Sprigs," Dawson said.

Sprigs fired a shot. Dawson grabbed his chest, and then he took a few steps back before falling to the ground. He felt wet and cold. He didn't move because for Sprigs to get to Melanie he'd have to run right past Dawson.

She let out a scream and, best Dawson could tell, tore off in the direction opposite Sprigs.

Sprigs cursed and Dawson could hear footsteps racing toward him. He had to time it just right…

When he caught sight of a tennis shoe six inches from his head, he twisted to his side, ignoring the shooting pain in his chest, and grabbed Sprigs by the ankle.

Caught off guard, Sprigs face-planted in the dirt next to Dawson. Another shot fired and Dawson prayed the stray bullet didn't hit Melanie or Mason.

"Run, Melanie," he shouted.

"Come back or I'll kill him," Sprigs threatened.

"Like hell you will. And if by some miracle you do, then I'm taking you with me." Dawson wrestled for control of the gun.

Sprigs was one of those wiry guys, surprisingly strong for his size. If Dawson was full strength, there'd be no doubt who would come out on top. As it was, he was losing a lot of blood.

Dawson wriggled his arm free, spun around until he was sitting on Sprigs's chest and punched him.

Sprigs's nose squirted blood as he fought back, jabbing Dawson where he'd been shot.

Blinding pain nearly caused Dawson to pass out, but he fought to stay conscious. He needed to give Melanie more time to get far away and he needed to make sure Sprigs would never bother her again.

Dawson highly doubted he'd get out of these woods alive given his condition and the lack of medical support. By the time he made it out of there, he would bleed out.

So he reared back and punched Sprigs one more time, knocking him unconscious.

Somewhere in the back of his mind, he heard Mason crying.

He pushed himself off Sprigs and rolled onto his back again, staring up at the canopy of trees. The crackle of the fire was getting even closer and it wouldn't be long before the smoke lulled him into a permanent sleep.

Melanie was fine. Mason was alive. That was all that mattered.

The crying grew louder and before Dawson could sit properly, he heard footsteps.

No. No. No.

Melanie was supposed to run far away. She was smart enough to realize that.

Reality dawned.

That meant one thing. She was trapped, too.

"Melanie," Dawson called out.

The footsteps came closer as Dawson pushed himself up to his feet, leaning against a tree for support.

"I'm here," she said, and her voice was like an angel's.

Dawson blinked and saw two blurry figures running toward him. One was holding Mason.

"Melanie, get out of here," he said.

"I'm not leaving you, Dawson," she said, putting his arm around her shoulder.

"Dada," Mason said, leaning toward Dawson. He wanted to hold his son more than he wanted to breathe.

"What are you doing? Now we'll all die," Dawson whispered to Melanie.

"I found a tunnel," she said. "It's how he got to us."

Randall was standing over a still-woozy Sprigs, his foot planted on Sprigs's back.

"Leave him," Dawson said as Melanie took Mason.

"Oh, no. This scumbag's going with us. Dying is too good for this jerk. He's got a lifetime date in a jail cell," Randall said as he cuffed the criminal.

"You won't keep me locked behind bars for long," Sprigs snarled.

"Yes. I will. And you know how I know you're going to have a long and painful life in prison?" Randall said, pulling Sprigs to his feet. "Because you're going to be very popular there. All those burly men in for life without parole are going to enjoy spending quality time with you. So you better plan to start talking and give up everyone you've been working with, every route you've set up."

Melanie led them through a tunnel that had been built as a water runoff in case the creek flooded.

There were medical personnel waiting on the scene as soon as they broke through to the other side onto the farm road.

Dawson dropped to his knees, exhausted.

"I love you, Melanie. I want to be a real family with you and Mason. Marry me and make me the happiest man alive," he said as EMTs flanked him and his eyes closed.

"THE SURGERY WENT WELL," Dr. Granger said, still wearing his surgical scrubs.

"That's good news," Melanie said. She'd been waiting, pacing for a solid eight hours.

Andy had been kind enough to offer to stay with her and Mason. He'd said he could use the practice entertaining a toddler. And he'd been great. Watching Mason with Andy made her miss Dawson all that much more.

"You can go in and see him now," the doctor said. "He's in room 210."

Melanie thanked him and walked as fast as she could without running.

She looked at Dawson, lying in bed with machines beeping and tubes coming out of him, and her heart stuttered.

All she could do was pull up a chair by his side and wait for him to open his eyes.

It took another three hours.

He blinked his eyes open and said something she couldn't understand.

"Hey, there, stranger," she replied. "It's okay." She squeezed his hand. "You don't have to talk right now."

He let go of hers and pointed toward the plastic cup of water.

"You're thirsty?" she asked.

He nodded.

She helped him position himself up so he could take a few sips. He blinked a couple of times and really looked at her.

"You didn't answer my question," he said clearly this time.

She looked around. "What? I already gave you some water. Do you want more?"

He shook his head like he was shaking out of a fog and then kissed her hand.

"I asked you to marry me," he said.

Melanie's heart filled with joy.

"Yes, Dawson, I will marry you."

"I love you, Melanie. I always have." He kissed her hand again.

"Confession?" she asked.

He nodded.

"It's you. It's always been you. I have wanted to marry you since we were ten years old and sat on the old stoop together." She didn't stop the tears from streaming down her face. "I have always loved you, Dawson."

Dawson pulled her toward him for a hug, kissing her on her forehead, her eyes, her nose, before pressing his lips to hers in a slow, sweet kiss.

He thumbed away her tears. "I understand what you were saying about Mason before and not needing to know. We don't have to get him tested."

"You were right, Dawson. I was scared before. I'm not

when you're with me. I think we need answers and I'm ready to face whatever life brings our way."

"No matter what happens, I'll be right beside you, loving you with everything that I am. We'll make it through this life together, making our own mistakes, and you'll never be alone again."

"I love you," was all she could manage to say through her tears.

Epilogue

"Don't you think it's a little too cold outside to fire up the grill?" Melanie asked Dawson.

When it came to weather this time of year in Texas, anything was possible.

"It'll be fine," Dawson reassured her. "Besides, this seems like a steak-on-the-grill kind of announcement."

She laughed as their friends began arriving couple by couple.

Everyone already knew to come around back, where she was playing with Mason on his new swing set.

Maribel barreled around the side of the house and Mason squealed the second he saw her.

Melanie helped him out of his swing. He ran across the yard until he and Maribel locked in embrace. They crashed into each other, fell down and rolled around laughing. Dylan and Samantha followed. And then Rebecca and Brody arrived, followed by Lisa and Ryan.

It was reassuring to see how much Mason loved other children.

The town had been through so much last summer and yet everyone seemed to bounce back.

There was a renewed feeling of life and a sense of relief after both Alcorn and Sprigs had been convicted and the sheriff had been removed from office, facing corruption charges. The rest of the ring had been busted and children played safely in their yards again.

Times were changing and Mason Ridge was beginning to feel the way it used to when they were all innocent kids. Or maybe there was a new wave of innocence breathing life into the place as a heavy cloud had lifted.

Alice and Jack walked around the corner and Melanie waved to them.

"What's going on?" Dawson asked, clearly surprised to see them.

"I invited them," Melanie said. She pushed herself up on her tiptoes and kissed her husband. "They deserve to know, too."

Bonds were still tentative, but Melanie wanted to make an effort.

Her own parents had pulled up in their RV an hour ago. Abby's semester was in full swing, so she couldn't make it to the party. Melanie had promised to fill her sister in on everything that went on later.

"I'll go wake your folks," Dawson said, patting Melanie's backside.

He returned with them five minutes later.

The sun cast a bright orange glow in the sky. Everyone gathered around the long wooden table.

Melanie couldn't think of a better night to share the news.

Dawson made sure everyone had a drink before taking his spot next to Melanie.

"We're glad everyone could make it tonight," he began. "We have a special announcement to make and we wanted our friends and family to be the first to know."

Friends raised their glasses in salute.

"Come here, buddy," Dawson said to Mason. "You want to tell everyone the good news?"

Mason grinned and nodded. He pointed to Melanie's stomach and said, "Baby."

Cheers rang out and hugs abounded.

Mason was right. There was a baby coming early next summer. Doctors had reassured them that both of their children were fine.

And Mason would live a long and healthy life with his little sister.

* * * * *

"You can go into my bedroom if you'd like."

Instantly he realized he'd made the offer sound suggestive. A Freudian slip if he'd ever had one.

Kelli did a half-snort laugh and retreated into the room. It could have been his imagination but it looked as if her cheeks had reddened. Then again, he could have been mistaken.

Mark stretched out his legs and realized just how tired he felt. Resting his head back on the cushions, he crossed his arms over his chest and closed his eyes. When Kelli was finished he'd offer her some coffee and make a very strong one for himself.

His thoughts went from coffee to the woman who had suddenly become a part of his life. Would she still be after they'd somehow found the justice they both wanted and so desperately needed?

And, more important, how would he feel about it?

FULL FORCE
FATHERHOOD

BY
TYLER ANNE SNELL

First Published in Great Britain 2016
By Mills & Boon, an imprint of HarperCollins*Publishers*
1 London Bridge Street, London, SE1 9GF

© 2016 Tyler Anne Snell

ISBN: 978-0-263-91902-8

46-0416

Our policy is to use papers that are natural, renewable and recyclable products and made from wood grown in sustainable forests. The logging and manufacturing processes conform to the legal environmental regulations of the country of origin.

Printed and bound in Spain
by CPI, Barcelona

Tyler Anne Snell genuinely loves all genres of the written word. However, she's realized that she loves books filled with sexual tension and mysteries a little more than the rest. Her stories have a good dose of both. Tyler lives in Florida with her same-named husband and their mini "lions." When she isn't reading or writing, she's playing video games and working on her blog, *Almost There*. To follow her shenanigans, visit www.tylerannesnell.com.

This book is for Lillian Grace and Katie.

Lily, thank you for being the coolest kiddo I know. One day you'll be able to appreciate there's a book dedicated to you. Until then I'm sure your mom will hide this sucker until you're older!

Katie, thank you for being a sister, a true friend, and giving me motherhood goals to aspire toward. Not to mention showing me such a strong bond between mother and daughter that it was almost easy to translate it to paper. I'll always love every bit of you and your family!

Chapter One

"Something's not right."

Kelli Crane looked at her husband and sighed. "Making fun of me isn't going to win you any points, Victor," she warned. "Don't poke the bear."

"Because she might poke back?"

He walked into the cabin's bedroom, where she had been lounging with a book, and took a seat at the edge of the bed. In his late thirties, Victor Crane had managed to hold on to his boyish grin with ease. Tall, almost lanky, he had short strawberry blond hair that looked like extensions of the sunlight that fell through the windows, and eyes that mimicked the blue of the sky. She could claim the same kind of brightness about herself, but slightly different—dirty-blond hair, green-gray eyes, a tan that could only be described as sunkissed—but sometimes when she looked at Victor, her own beauty felt diminished. Staring at her husband of a year and a half, she wondered what their children might look like.

"If you keep mocking me about wanting to keep you safe," she said, "poking back is the first thing I'll do."

Victor held his hands up in defense. "Whatever you say, my love."

She put down her book and smiled. She knew he had only indulged her paranoia by hiring the bodyguard two rooms away. For the past two weeks, he had tried to put her worries to rest. In his line of work as an investigative journalist, sometimes the crazies came out. That didn't mean they should run for help after receiving a few deep-breathing phone calls at the house. However, Kelli couldn't stop her anxiety from mounting as more than just a few calls had come in.

"How's the story coming along?" she asked, setting the book against her stomach. Her hand hovered there a second before she let it drop. "Please tell me you're almost done."

"The *news article* is nearly finished, yes. I should be done by tomorrow." He stood and stretched. "Then we can resume our normal lives."

"You wouldn't want to stay a few more days?" Kelli looked out the window. Victor's family cabin was a few skips away from a crystal-blue lake that looked like a painting, with a pier that Victor had probably walked down since he was a child. Her family had never had moments like that. Then again, if her parents had been alive, she was sure they would have tried. They had been good, loving parents before the car crash had happened when she was younger.

"If this was a vacation, then I'd say yes, but…"

"But you're here to work," she interrupted.

He nodded. "And when that work is done, I have to move on to the next assignment."

"One that I hope won't make me feel we need to hire another bodyguard."

Victor laughed. "Let's be honest. The only reason you hired him was for a little eye candy," he whispered.

He raised his eyebrows suggestively, joking with her. Kelli swatted at him.

"Dark hair and muscles galore?" she said. "Who would want that?"

Victor came to her side and bent low. He brushed his lips across hers for a soft kiss.

"Not you," he replied, laughter behind each word.

Kelli smiled. It had been a while since they had been able to spend more than an hour or two a day together. Since they had been married, Victor's assignments had taken him away from their home in Dallas.

But that was going to change soon.

It had to.

"Well, back to the grind. Do you need anything?"

Kelli pictured the ice cream in the freezer but decided against it.

"I think I might take a nap. I still don't feel all that great."

Victor gave her forehead another quick kiss. "Nap away, my love."

And then he was gone.

MARK TRANTON HAD watched the sun set as he finished his routine perimeter check. He might have had a history of traveling internationally and domestically, but this was the first client to bring him to a lakefront property. If he ever took his vacation time, he might consider coming back to a place like this.

In the dwindling light, the isolation felt serene.

He was almost glad that his boss, Nikki Waters, had more or less forced him to take on the weeklong contract with Victor. Even if both Nikki and Victor had said his presence was more for Mrs. Crane's peace of mind.

Since the Orion Security Group was in the middle of an expansion—thanks to a large contract completed two months before by Mark's good friend Oliver—the small company's caseload had tripled. Even though the closest contract start date was two months away. Including one for which Mark would be traveling to Washington for a three-week commitment.

Which was why Nikki had said accompanying the Cranes to a family vacation home in North Carolina was "the closest to a vacation" that Mark would take.

He couldn't complain.

They were on day three of the contract, and Victor and his wife had been nothing but pleasant.

"Are we in the clear?" Victor asked him.

Mr. Crane was standing in the kitchen, beer in hand, when Mark came back inside and locked the door. There was a lightness to his tone but no disrespect. He might not have shared his wife's fear for safety, but he didn't discount Mark's job. Mark respected him more for that.

"I think we'd hear or see someone coming a mile away," Mark answered honestly.

"This place is kind of off the beaten path, but that's why I thought it might do Kelli some good." Victor pulled out another beer from the fridge and started to offer it to Mark but caught himself. He switched out the bottle for water, which Mark thanked him for. Although he could have gotten away with one drink, he wouldn't. A bodyguard needed to stay alert at all times. No exceptions. "Kelli's normally not this anxious. But lately some things have happened that have…well, made her more emotional. I just want to keep her from getting all worked up."

"That's nice of you," Mark said.

"Well, I feel it's the least I can do. I've been working a little more than I should be."

"I can relate to that," Mark said with a quick smile, even though he loved his job. When he wasn't given a new client, he asked for one. He'd been working in the private security business since he was twenty-one. It was as much a part of him as the scars on his back and the muscles he had honed as a job requirement. Pretending that overwork bothered him would be just that.

Pretend.

"You know what I like about you, Mark?"

"Aside from my stoic nature?"

Victor laughed. He seemed always to be laughing.

"Aside from that, I'd have to say I'm surprised you haven't asked me what I'm working on. If I were you, I would have pestered me the last few days."

Mark shrugged. "Once Nikki vets a client, that's pretty much all I need to know. You're a freelance journalist working on a piece for a national news syndicate. I don't need to know the topic to make sure no one shoots you." Victor nodded in assent. "Plus, you said yourself that it wasn't anything that would ruffle anyone's feathers."

"True," he confirmed. "It's a piece spotlighting a private charity foundation based in Texas." It was Victor's turn to shrug. "Nothing too menacing sounding, am I right?"

"Yeah, I'd have to say that—"

The back of the cabin exploded in a fiery ball of glass and wood. The blast sent both men to the ground hard. Heat instantly filled the air, smoke hot on its tail.

Mark was the first to pick himself up, stumbling to his feet, trying to get his bearings. Looking to his right and down the hallway, he couldn't tell what the explosion's origin was. But he knew the outer wall that ran across the office, hallway and master bedroom and bathroom was definitely affected. Flames sprung up everywhere.

Mark went around the counter and hoisted up his client. Through the ringing in his ears, he could hear Victor yell out his wife's name.

The instinct to get the journalist to safety flared within him, but he didn't try to hustle him through the two doors or six windows they had access to. It wouldn't do any good. Victor loved his wife and wouldn't leave her. Mark wouldn't, either.

"Behind me," Mark yelled as he righted the man. Victor's eyes were wide, terrified. He nodded, and they began to move down the hallway as quickly as Mark was comfortable with.

Whatever had blown up had damaged the office opposite the bedroom the most. Through the open door, he could tell the wall was gone. The window in the hallway had blown out, and flames were in the process of devouring the frame. Mark sucked in a breath as he went into the bedroom.

Lying on the floor next to the bed was an unconscious Kelli. Smoke was already hugging the ceiling, billowing out from the bathroom. While Victor bent at his wife's side, Mark ran to see where the new smoke was coming from. The bedroom's outer wall wasn't on fire like the hallway.

He didn't have to look far. Flames were pulsing up the outside of the house, even stretching around to the right side where the guest bedroom was.

That's when Mark saw him.

A figure dressed in black ran around the perimeter of the house, right where Mark had walked minutes earlier.

"Someone's outside," he yelled. Kelli was in Victor's arms, limp. Mark wanted to help her, but he also needed to deal with the person responsible for starting the fire. Victor was about to say something when a horrible crack split the air.

With less than a second to react, Victor threw Kelli forward just as the outer wall crumbled. All Mark could do was watch as Victor was thrown to the ground beneath the wall and part of the roof. With the new source of oxygen, the fire expanded in a violent burst.

Mark went down to his knees, using his body to cover Kelli until everything settled. However, nothing did.

"Save her," yelled Victor. He was trying to move but, in that one horrible moment, both men realized that the weight would be too much for either of them to move. That didn't stop Mark from trying.

He quickly went to the journalist's side and tried with everything he had to lift the largest piece of wall and wood from Victor's back. It didn't budge. Not one bit.

"Save her," Victor yelled again. Another wave of heat rolled through the air. Mark looked around. The escape route into the hallway wasn't going to last much longer.

Mark met the blue eyes of his client, knowing it would be the last time he ever saw them.

"I can save you both," Mark said, though he knew it was a lie. Flames were licking at his back. If they didn't get out now, they wouldn't.

Victor yelled one last plea, making Mark decide the fate of three people all at once.

"She's pregnant!"

Mark didn't hesitate after that. He picked up Kelli and gave Victor one last look.

"I'll come back," he yelled, but the man didn't answer.

Mark kept Kelli to his chest and ran into the hallway. The state of the rest of the cabin confirmed his earlier fear. Someone had not only blown up the side of the house but also set the area around the entire structure on fire. Reason told him that the kitchen and its back door would be their best bet. The figure in the dark wouldn't have had time to get the fire going too strongly there.

Kelli stirred in his arms, coughing violently. He held her tighter and almost yelled in relief when he saw the back door wasn't crawling in flames. He threw it open and ran straight into the water a few yards away. The lake was low for the season, and the dock was high off the water. He splashed under the wood, giving them the only cover available in the backyard.

No shots had rung through the air and no attack had been initiated as they left the house. But that didn't mean the perpetrator wouldn't still try.

"What the—" Kelli started to catch her breath, eyes open and looking wildly at him.

"Are you okay to stand?" he asked quickly, already tilting her feet into the water. Confused, she nodded. "I need you to stay right here, hidden, okay?"

Again she nodded, but Mark knew it was only a matter of time before she realized her husband wasn't with them. She seemed to still be processing being conscious at the moment. Kelli caught her balance as Mark released her. He pulled his pocketknife from his pants and handed it to her, turning as soon as she grabbed it.

An awful sound filled the air, another in a long line of things that would haunt him about that night.

A fireball erupted from the kitchen and engulfed the rest of the cabin. Glass exploded and the ground shook. The house gave one final wheeze and, together, Mark and Kelli watched as it burned to the ground.

Chapter Two

Kelli slipped off her heels and padded quietly across the floor. Footsteps echoed in the hallway behind her, but she didn't stop. Sidestepping a few boxes left scattered around the room, she hurried into the open closet.

It wasn't deep, but it stretched wide. Empty save a few coat hangers, it didn't allow her much cover. On the other hand she could try to hide behind a stack of boxes in the corner. Though she'd have to really bend to remain hidden. The footsteps came closer, and she had to choose.

The closet would have to do.

Kelli pushed herself to the corner and slid down the wall until she was sitting with her knees pressed up to her chest. The light from the opened bedroom window lit even the mostly dark corner. She would be seen easily by anyone who looked inside the doors.

Silence filled the room.

For a second, Kelli worried. Had she been seen coming into the room? The shuffle of two feet let her know she had. The footsteps came closer, and Kelli held her breath. Her hunter was quick to search around the boxes and move on to the closet. The shuffling stopped a step from the opening. There was a moment of silence that felt almost tangible.

Then a tiny face peeked inside, and Kelli couldn't help but laugh.

"Boo," the little girl yelled. Smiling ear to ear, she squealed in delight as Kelli jumped out of her hiding spot.

"You found me!"

Grace Victoria Crane let out another round of giggles before running off. Kelli laughed as she followed the toddler through the house, knowing the little girl's destination.

Like mother, like daughter, Grace loved the library.

It was her fair-haired beauty's turn to hide.

Behind the wall-length curtains—one of the few things that hadn't yet been packed in the room—stood a pair of little blue shoes. They were covered in sequins, and Kelli knew for a fact that finding them in stock had been a miracle in itself.

"Hmm..." Kelli put her finger to her chin and tapped it. Moving slowly around the boxes and plastic tubs pushed to the side of the room, she made a big show of being confused. "I could have sworn I saw a little girl with chocolate on her mouth run in here!" Grace started to giggle. The sound made Kelli's heart swell. "I wonder who that could be!" She went to the curtains, ready to tickle the culprit, when the little girl jumped out on her own.

"Got you," she yelled. When Grace was excited like this, Kelli couldn't deny the resemblance between them. Although Grace's hair was a shade or two darker, their ever-changing green eyes were almost identical. Her facial features, however, all belonged to her father.

"You're the best hide-and-seeker I think I've ever played with," Kelli said, scooping up the toddler. She was about to unleash another round of tickles when the doorbell chimed. It echoed through the mostly packed up house.

"Me, me," Grace yelled, already trying to wiggle out of her arms and race to answer the door.

"Not without me," Kelli answered. She moved Grace to her hip and took a moment to marvel at how big she was getting. A year and seven months, almost to the day.

The past two years had flown by and yet, in some ways, Kelli seemed painfully stuck. As she moved down the hallway to the front of the house, she tried to commit to memory how the wood floor felt beneath her bare feet. She wondered what the next year would bring after all of the changes Grace and she were about to make.

A familiar face was bobbing in front of the windows in the front door, inciting a new excitement in Grace. Kelli put her down with a laugh and opened the door for the godmother of her child.

"You're late," Kelli teased Lynn Bradley. The short woman with black hair wore a pair of worn overalls with a long-sleeved yellow flannel shirt that contrasted with her dark skin. Kelli raised her eyebrow at the choice of wardrobe but didn't say anything. Lynn had been a bit eclectic ever since they were children.

"Listen, it's not my fault that you already packed up your TV, forcing me to choose between the end of *You've Got Mail* and the care of your child." The twenty-nine-year-old gave her best friend a smirk before bending down and enveloping Grace in a hug. "My, how you've grown! Look at you! Gosh, how old are you now? Three? Five?"

Grace put her hands on her hips and gave Lynn a critical eye. She held up one finger. "One!"

"That's my girl," Lynn approved. She mussed Grace's hair, and the three of them went inside.

"You were here yesterday, you know," Kelli said as they went into the living room. Lynn laughed.

"That doesn't discount the fact that that kid of yours is growing like crazy! She's going to be taller than me before you know it! She's not two yet and look at her!"

Grace, suddenly uninterested in their conversation, went to her makeshift play area in the corner. It looked like a graveyard for plastic dinosaurs, stuffed animals and Legos.

"I know," Kelli agreed with a smile. It didn't last long. Lynn had come over to help pack up the one room Kelli couldn't get through on her own.

Attached to the living room by a set of French double doors was Victor's home office. It was a small room but had managed to collect a lot of things in the six years he had lived in the house. Just looking into the room had sent Kelli into tears for the first six months after the fire. Then, slowly, she had been able to bear the sight of the room Victor had spent the most time in. Kelli supposed Grace had helped her with that. She had to stay strong for their child, who would never know her father.

Lynn's expression softened, but she didn't comment. Aside from Grace, Lynn had been the most constant part of her world during the past two years.

"Okay, well, let's get started." Kelli motioned to the bookcase. "You empty that and I'll start with the desk."

"Got yah, Boss." Lynn pulled the plastic tub over to the small bookshelf. Although there was a library in the house, the office shelves were filled with research materials collected over Victor's nine-year career as a journalist. Her husband had covered an array of subjects, freelancing from home, and working for newspapers and magazines around the nation. His next goal had been to work internationally, but then they had found out about the pregnancy. Victor had decided his family was more important than work.

Kelli sat down in the office chair, sadness in her heart.

Her thoughts slid back to the night at the cabin.

Sometimes she could still feel the heat of the fire. Smell the smoke in the air. Feel the cold of the water as they waited for help to arrive. The boy behind the fire had been caught, sure, but that didn't make the memories of what had happened any more bearable.

She took a breath. She didn't need to remember that night now.

Ten minutes into packing away the office's contents, Kelli found something she hadn't known existed.

"Hey, look at this."

The middle side drawer of the desk had stuck when she tried to open it. She pulled too hard, and the entire drawer slid out. Along with it came a small notebook that had been taped to the bottom of the drawer above it.

"What is it?" Lynn asked, walking over.

"I don't know. It was hidden."

The notebook wasn't labeled, but it was filled with Victor's pristine handwriting.

"It looks like work notes," Kelli observed. She flipped through it, scanning as she went. "I recognize some of these names...but I thought all of his notes were—" She cut herself off and rephrased. "He took them to the cabin with us. I didn't know he had kept notes here."

Lynn gave her privacy as she thumbed to the last few pages. Possibly the last notes Victor had ever taken. Kelli shook her head. She didn't need to travel down that road today.

"Wait." Her eyes stopped on a passage in neat, tiny writing. "This doesn't make sense."

Or maybe it did.

"WE NEED TO TALK."

Kelli's back was ramrod straight against the office chair. It wasn't made to be comfortable—those who sat across from Dennis Crawford, retired editor of the national online publication known as the *Scale*, didn't usually intend to keep his company long. Especially during house calls like this. She suspected that he had let her in only because of Victor. Dennis and he hadn't been friends, but they'd worked together on more than one occasion.

Including the last story of Victor's life.

"I suspected, considering I haven't seen you since—" He cleared his throat, trying to avoid the fact that their last meeting had been when her husband had been lowered into the ground. Kelli shifted in her seat. "How have you been?" he asked instead.

"Good. Grace is keeping me busy, but I'm sure that won't change for another seventeen years or so."

Dennis, an unmarried man with no children of his own, smiled politely. Victor hadn't told her the man's age, but she placed him in his early forties. Kelli couldn't tell if he was genuinely kind, but she could see he carried a lot of self-pride. Although gray was peppered into his black hair, his goatee was meticulous, along with the collared shirt and slacks he wore. Journalism award plaques, athletic trophies, and pictures of Dennis and other men dressed in suits decorated almost every available inch of the home office.

"So, what can I do for you?" His eyes slid down to the folder in her lap. There wasn't any use tiptoeing around what she had come to say.

"I was packing up Victor's office last night when I found some of his old notes." She slid the folder across the desk. "Including these."

Dennis raised an eyebrow—also meticulously kept—but didn't immediately pick up the folder. In that moment she was thankful she'd never had to work under the man. He fixed her with a gaze that clearly said, "So what?"

"They're his notes on the Bowman Foundation story—the last story he covered." That at least made Dennis open the folder, though his eyes stayed on her.

"Okay?" Dennis said.

Kelli shifted in her seat again. "I guess I'm wondering why the story you printed doesn't match up?"

His eyebrow didn't waver, but his gaze finally dropped to the photocopies she'd made of Victor's notes. The actual notebook was tucked safely into her purse. She didn't want to part with it, not even for a moment. Finding it after the past two years was like finding a small piece of Victor.

"What do you mean, 'doesn't match up?'" Dennis asked, voice defensive. "I used the notes he sent me."

"Not according to *those* notes, which are undoubtedly his." She leaned forward and pointed to the first section she had highlighted. "The names are different. I've already looked them up but can't find anything." Dennis pulled out a drawer and grabbed a pair of glasses from it without saying a word. He slipped them on and leaned his head closer to the paper. From where Kelli sat, she could see his concentration deepen.

But she could also see something else.

Dennis's eyes registered no surprise at what he was seeing.

"Normally I wouldn't second-guess this, but…well, it was his last story," she added.

"The names we published were pulled straight from the email I got from Victor," he said after a minute more of going through the pages. He set his glasses down and threaded his fingers together over the papers. The gesture also looked oddly defensive. "These were probably notes he wrote quickly, then later changed to be accurate. Perhaps it was even his way of brainstorming how he wanted the story to go with placeholder names."

Kelli didn't need to think about that possibility long. She shook her head.

"I think these were his backup notes. He always said he didn't like keeping everything electronically. I just thought his written notes were also with us at the cabin."

Dennis seemed to consider what she said but, by the same token, it felt as though he was putting on a show. What had been an off-balanced feeling of doubt started to turn dark in the pit of her stomach.

"I don't know what to tell you. I personally verified the information—just to be safe—before the piece was published." He shut the folder but didn't slide it back. "The Bowman Foundation publically thanked the *Scale*—and Victor—for the story. Because of the spotlight, they've received a substantial amount of funding since the article debuted. If any of the facts were incorrect, I would have been made aware of it—retired or not."

Kelli considered his words. Was she just overreacting? Was she looking for a reason to revisit the memory of Victor? Had finding his handwritten journal been too much of a shock to her system?

"Listen, Kelli." Dennis's expression softened. He took off his glasses and fixed her with a small smile. "I'm due to meet an old friend for lunch, but how about after that, I'll recheck these." He put his finger on the folder. "I'll call if anything weird pops up."

Despite herself, she smiled, too.

"Thanks. I'd really appreciate it."

Dennis stood, ending the conversation. He moved around the desk and saw her to the front door.

As she turned to thank him again, he said, "I'm sorry about Victor. But, word of advice? Maybe you should start looking to the future and not the past."

Kelli didn't have a lot of memories of her mother, but she knew being polite had been high on her priority list. That thought alone pushed a smile to her lips, while the knot in her stomach tightened. Dennis shut the door, leaving her standing on his porch with a great sense of unease.

You're reading way too into this, Kel, she thought as she turned on her heel. *Calm down and just forget about it all.*

"Hey, Kelli?" Dennis called when she was halfway down his sidewalk. She hadn't heard him open the door. "Do you have the journal those copies were from?"

Her purse suddenly felt heavier at her side. Before she could think about it, she was shaking her head.

"No, I just found the copies."

"Oh, okay, thanks."

She waved bye and continued on her way.

"Because if you did have it, I'd really like to see it," he called after her.

The feeling of unease expanded within her. Once again she turned to face him.

"Sorry. The copies I gave you were all I had."

Dennis shrugged and retreated behind the door. It wasn't until she was safely inside her car that she chanced another look at the house.

It might have been her imagination, but she could almost have sworn the blinds over the living room windows moved.

Chapter Three

Mark cracked his knuckles and swigged a gulp of his beer. Sitting behind the bar of a local dive, he kept his eyes glued to the television screen above him. An old football game was running, but he wasn't paying much attention.

He'd had one heck of a day, if he said so himself.

The construction manager had come in early with a mood that matched the unexpected storm that would mean no work for the next two days to a week. Then the concrete pourer—who had never driven in rain, it seemed—had backed up into Mark's Jeep, breaking a taillight and denting his bumper. The cherry on top was that when he decided to de-stress from an unproductive, unprofitable workday with a drink or two, he'd picked the bar from his past.

"Sorry, I had to take that call." Nikki Waters, founder of the Orion Security Group and his former boss, sat back on her bar stool and reclaimed her drink.

Mark smiled but felt no mirth. He didn't dislike Nikki. In fact, he had once considered her a great friend. However, the past two years had put a weight on the friendship. One that hadn't affected just their relationship but his entire life.

"It's fine," he said, trying to keep his tone light. He remembered meeting Nikki for the first time when she'd been a secretary at Redstone Solutions and he'd been a low-ranking security agent. She'd been quiet, unobtrusive, yet clever and kind. The latter two traits she had held on to, but the first two? Well, he knew from experience that if she was quiet, it was only because she was finding the right words to tell you exactly what was on her mind. And unobtrusive? If she thought people she cared about were making a mistake, she'd tell them.

She'd had *that* talk with Mark several times already in the past year.

"So, how are you, Nik? It's been a while."

The 33-year-old looked surprised he'd made the first conversational move, but she recovered quickly. She straightened her short, dark red ponytail before answering.

"Good. Busy, but good." She motioned to the bar around them. "I would actually still be at the office, but the storm knocked out our power. Jonathan told me it was a sign we needed to 'capitalize on Friday night.'" Mark mentally winced at the mention of Jonathan. Along with Nikki and Oliver Quinn, Jonathan Carmichael rounded out friends with whom he had all but severed ties since he left Orion. "I'd heard him talk about this place on more than one occasion, so I thought I'd give it a try."

"The service isn't great, but I can't complain about the price."

Nikki laughed. "I'll drink to that." And she did.

"What about you? How've you been?"

"Good," he lied. "Not as busy, but okay. Working

with a decent construction crew on a neighborhood south of the hospital. Keeps my muscles working," he joked. Nikki laughed again, but it was laced with concern.

"Listen, Mark," she started, but he cut her off.

"I don't want to come back, Nikki. I told you then that I was done with being a bodyguard, and I still mean it now."

"But, Mark, you have also told me before how much you love it," she pointed out. "You can't let one incident deter you."

"Incident?" he repeated. "A man died, Nik."

"It wasn't your fault. I don't know how many times everyone has to tell you that."

"My one job was to keep him safe, and instead I let some punk kid burn him alive." His voice rose as he said it, and the bartender shot him a look that clearly asked him to settle down. Nikki didn't flinch. This fight was an old one by now. He couldn't help it, though. Every time he thought about Darwin McGregor—the firebug—and his floundering admission to the cops that he had set fire to the cabin for fun, Mark's mood instantly turned heated. The nineteen-year-old had said that blowing up the large propane tank had been nothing more than an accident. He'd thought the tank was empty. He'd thought no one would be hurt, just scared. It didn't change the fact that Victor had died.

Or that Mark didn't believe him.

Images of the dark figure running away from the house flashed through his mind. He had been too tall and too wide to be Darwin. Though the cops, Nikki and everyone else had blamed this accusation on Mark's overwhelming guilt.

It was another reason he had quit Orion six months later.

"Yes, it's our job to protect people," she said, lowering her voice in an attempt to get him to do the same. "But that doesn't mean we can be everywhere at once." She stretched her hand out as if to touch his but stopped. "It was a horrible accident, yet even Mrs. Crane agreed that her husband's death wasn't your fault. You saved a woman and her unborn child. That has to count for something."

Mark took another swig of his beer.

"Don't you think we've talked about this enough already, Nik?" he asked, adjusting his voice back to a tone he thought was pleasant.

Again she started to say something but caught herself before nodding. She reached into her pocket and pulled out an Orion business card. There was a number already written across its back in pen. She slid it over to him.

"You're right. I'm sorry. This will be the last time I bring any of this up," she promised.

"What's this?" He nodded to the card. He didn't recognize the number.

"Let me preface this. I didn't want to tell you, considering everything you've been through, but she insisted she needed to talk to you."

Mark was perplexed. "Who needs to talk to me?"

"Kelli Crane."

Mark's mouth dropped open slightly. "Why?" he asked. "And when did she call?"

"I'm not sure why—I didn't ask and she didn't offer

the information up—but she called a few hours ago."
Nikki waved the bartender over. "All she said was that
she found something you might be able to help her
with."

"I—I have no idea what she's talking about," Mark
said more to himself than his former boss.

"Then you might want to call her back." She smiled
and handed her credit card over to clear out her tab. It
sobered Mark.

"I find it hard to believe that you happened to take
a message for me on the same day you just happened
to run into me at a bar. Did you come here to give this
to me?"

Her smile grew wide. "Let's just say, I'm hitting two
birds with one stone." She gave the man a pat on the
shoulder. "It was good to see you, Mark. I hope everything works out."

"Thanks, Nik. You, too."

Mark stared down at the number after she'd gone.
It was amazing how ten digits could affect him so pro-
foundly. He quickly looked around the bar, as if the patrons could hear his internal struggle. No one paid him
any mind. He slipped the card into his jacket.

Less than an hour later, Mark was sitting in his apartment, staring at his phone. There was nothing to be
afraid of about calling Kelli. She had, after all, wanted
to talk to him. But Mark couldn't get past the why of it
all. Why call? Why now?

"Only one way to find out," he announced to the
empty room.

Mark dialed the number before realizing how late
it was. He didn't know her child's name but knew she
lived with Kelli. The last thing he needed was another

reason for Kelli to be upset with him. Waking up her toddler was something he wanted to avoid if possible. He hung up on the third ring, deciding to call her the next day.

Again, he wondered why she wanted to talk to him.

Mark waited around for a few more minutes before deciding to take a shower. It was quick and refreshing, a great contrast to a not-so-great day. His new mood stuck as he got to his phone and saw he had a voice mail.

The number matched the one Nikki had given him. He put the message on speaker and listened as Kelli Crane's voice echoed off the walls.

"Mark Tranton? Hi, this is Kelli Crane. There's something I really need to talk to you about. Can we meet? Let me know." She paused. Mark almost ended the recording before she said one last thing.

"I don't think Victor's death was an accident."

THE NEXT WORKDAY was a washout, just as Mark had thought it would be. Thanks to a heavy rain in the middle of the night before, his construction site and crew were put on hold. That could have been a time to relax for Mark—they'd been working long hours before the storm came in—but he still wouldn't entertain the idea of a vacation. He was the kind of man who not only appreciated hard work but also craved it. When that work stopped, for whatever reason, he was left with a world of thought he'd rather not visit. So instead of lounging around—or, heaven forbid, sleeping in—Mark changed into his sweats and hit the gym.

The workout room was sectioned off in the corner of the bottom floor of his apartment complex, which gave the place a solitude that Mark liked. Or maybe it was the feeling of improvement that working out brought him. Either way, it was a ritual he could do anywhere, whenever he wanted. He didn't need permission. He didn't need advice.

Whether or not he was a bodyguard didn't matter.

"I don't think Victor's death was an accident."

Mark brought his fist back from the speed bag. Kelli Crane's admission had all but stopped him from breathing. Not because it was out of left field. No, because it was strange to hear his theory come out of the widow's mouth.

A theory that had been thrown aside by everyone he'd cared about and thought cared about him. Even Nikki had tried to talk him out of it until she'd been blue in the face. She was trying to protect him from himself, she'd said. But all she'd done was shown him that at the end of the day maybe she didn't believe in him as much as he'd once thought.

His fist connected with the bag again. He could feel the teeth of the past sinking back into him, and he had two options. Try to pry them off or ignore them until he couldn't feel their sting.

The second option had treated him well the past year. He snorted, knowing that was a lie.

Mark went through his boxing routine, trying to drown out his thoughts, but each time his skin connected with the bag, he seemed to fall deeper down the hole. The image of the mystery culprit—not the nineteen-year-old firebug—flashed across his mind.

"Whoa, what did the bag ever do to you?" Mark spun around to find his neighbor Craig go for the weights. He was grinning, but his smile fell when he saw Mark's face. "Everything okay?"

Mark realized his breathing had become rapid, his heart beating fast. His shirt clung to his chest, sweat keeping it flat against his torso. A dull ache in his hands began to register.

"Just blowing off some steam," he said, changing his harsh tone to one that could pass as conversational. It worked well enough.

"You already have steam? The sun just came up!" Craig laughed. "Must be about a woman."

Mark shrugged. "You could say that."

They talked about the weather and their jobs for a while before doing their own things. Mark's hands finally begged him to give it a rest, so he said bye to Craig and huffed back to his third-floor apartment.

It wasn't a big space—a studio with a box of a balcony—but Mark didn't need much. The only mementos he truly treasured were the pictures that hung on the walls. His parents and younger sister, Beth; friends from his hometown in Florida; and even one that had been taken the day Orion had officially opened. That one, though, he didn't really look at anymore. The rest of his valuables consisted of his home media center and laptop—both of which he had seldom used since starting his construction job. A homey place it was not, but it sufficed.

Mark walked to the glass door that led to the balcony and looked out. It was a cloudy seventy degrees and was expected to get chilly. A cold front was supposedly blowing in that night, but he wasn't about to put stock in anything the forecast projected. In his ten years of Dallas living, he had learned that if you didn't like the weather in Texas, you should just wait an hour. It often changed.

The quiet of his apartment crept around him the longer he stood there. He hadn't called Kelli back, and he didn't know if he would. After Victor had died—and in the year that followed—he had almost gone crazy following his gut, trying to find the figure in the dark who had started the fire. Even after Darwin McGregor admitted that it had been him.

Determination had turned into obsession. Walls went up around him as each of his friends tried to tell him it was his guilt that fueled the pursuit. Nothing more and nothing less. Then, on the one-year anniversary of the fire, he had decided it was time to let it go.

This was the first time, however, that Kelli had ever mentioned it.

He eyed his phone on the coffee table. Didn't he owe it to her to at least hear her out?

Chapter Four

The weatherman might not have been completely wrong. As Mark stepped out of his taxi, he wondered if he should have brought his jacket. His long sleeves might not cut it if the temperature dropped even further.

It was just after dinner, and he was back at the bar he'd been at the night before. He had a feeling the place would be seeing a lot of him in the next few weeks, especially if this meeting went south. He'd finally called Kelli back and was surprised when she'd asked to meet him somewhere later that night. Nothing more was said beyond that, and now here he was, showing up a half hour early. Nerves or anticipation? He couldn't tell which, but he made his way to one of the booths tucked into the corner. It gave him a clear sightline to the front doors.

From habit, he took in his surroundings. Men and women of varying careers were all dressed down to some degree—one of the women at the table next to him had on flats, though a pair of heels could be seen sticking out of the bag at her feet, while the other had let her hair loose across her shoulders; an older man at the bar had his tie undone around his neck, beer in hand and eyes on the TV; a group of yuppies had their blazers draped over chair backs while they threw darts next to the front door; a man walked in and immediately went to the bar, hand up, ordering a beer.

A few more patrons came in and before he knew it, the half hour had passed. Mark hadn't spent enough time with Kelli Crane to know if she was punctual or not.

No, he didn't really know her at all.

The Orion Security Group had done its homework on the now twenty-nine-year-old woman before the contract had started. It was imperative to do the research to make the protection side of the job most effective. He'd learned that Kelli Crane—formally McKinnely— had a degree in art therapy and worked with the elderly at the community center. She came from a small family that all but disappeared after a car crash killed her parents when she was young. Socially she had kept out of the spotlight, staying close with a childhood friend named Lynn.

In that regard, she was quite the opposite of her late husband. Victor Crane had been a networker, thanks to his job. He had more connections than even Orion's analyst had been able to uncover. Mark had tracked down as many as he could, trying to find a tie between the man's death and the fire, but it was hard to find a link when you didn't know what you were looking for in the first place.

Mark couldn't help but focus on the blonde as she paused to survey the room before meeting his gaze. There was no hesitation in her bright eyes. She made a beeline for him.

Although he'd recognized her easily, he had to admit she looked different from the woman he'd known through the contract. Kelli walked with unmistakable purpose. Her once-long hair was shortened to her chin with bangs that cut straight over her eyebrows. The dirty blond had lightened as her skin had darkened—she'd been getting sun. He'd bet her kid had something to do with that. Instead of the almost prim outfits she had worn at the cabin, she was dressed more casually—a blue button-up with jeans and black flats. There was no flashy jewelry—he noticed no wedding ring, either—and even her purse seemed more practical than pretty.

Seeing her made him wonder what he looked like in turn. Had he changed in the past two years?

"Hi," Kelli greeted him, sliding into the seat across from him without pause. Whatever was on her mind, it had her determined.

"Hi," he responded. Mark didn't know what to feel, seeing her so informally, as if they were old friends re-connecting. The only thing they shared was a tragedy. Did she feel the same self-loathing he did?

"Thanks for meeting me, by the way. I know it must be strange."

"It's the least I can do." He cleared his throat. "So, how have you been?"

"Good. Busy, but good."

Mark smiled. It was the same thing he'd said to Nikki the day before. He wondered if Kelli actually meant it.

In record time, the waitress popped over and took her drink order before they could dive in to their conversation. Kelli asked for beer and cracked a big smile. Mark couldn't help but raise his eyebrow at her expression.

"Sorry. I haven't gotten out much since Grace." She tamped her grin down a fraction. "And I certainly haven't been to a bar and ordered beer. I almost feel like this is a minivacation." Her smile instantly vanished, like a candle blown out. Silence followed as she dropped her gaze.

"Kelli, why did you want to meet?"

The blonde quirked her lips to one side as she concentrated. She was choosing her words carefully. Finally she found them.

"After the fire, the cops came. You told them you'd seen a man running from the house," she started. This time she didn't shy away from his gaze. "When they picked up Darwin McGregor—" she paused, eyes momentarily glazing over with emotion "—you said it wasn't the same person. At the time I didn't even think to question it—he admitted to setting the fire—but now…"

"But now?" he pressed.

"Well, I think I should have listened to you."

Mark was an impassive man. He didn't know if that was what had made him such a good bodyguard—before the fire—or if it had been the other way around. Sure, like anyone, he had emotions. He felt things like the next man. It was his ability to mask those feelings, those shifts in conversation that surprised him, that he had mastered through the years. However, as the words left Kelli Crane's mouth, once again he had to struggle to keep from gaping.

Not so much at their meaning. It was the implication behind them.

"I don't understand," he said honestly.

Kelli's drink arrived, but she didn't touch it. Her minivacation was apparently over.

"The story Victor was working on at the cabin—did you ever read it?"

"No." Mark didn't want to lie, but he also didn't want to admit why he hadn't. He'd tried before but even the headline had made his guilt expand. Reading the article was salt on the wound of not being able to save the man. If Kelli was offended, she didn't show it.

"The Bowman Foundation, a charity, had been operating anonymously in Texas for a few years but decided to go public. Victor did an in-depth spotlight on them—what they had already accomplished, what they hoped to accomplish, that sort of thing." She moved her hand to hover over her purse but paused before placing it back on the tabletop. "It was published a week after the funeral." Her smile was weak at the word. "While I was packing—we're moving to a new house— I found Victor's journal with a copy of his notes about the story. Now I've read the published article over and over again. I've memorized every detail."

"Okay…I'm not following."

"The two don't match up." He could tell she was getting frustrated, but at what or whom, he wasn't sure.

"The published story and the notes?" he asked.

Kelli nodded. "Names, not important in the grand scheme of the foundation."

Mark took a drink of his beer. "So they got the facts wrong. What does this have to do with anything?"

Kelli's fists balled slightly, a move that someone else might have missed entirely. Mark was suddenly aware of *how* aware he was of Kelli's movements.

"I talked to the editor of the *Scale*. He says it was Victor who was wrong, but I don't believe that. Victor was using that spotlight to show he was capable of writing more feature articles. He figured it would help him get local work so he wouldn't have to travel as much when Grace came. He wouldn't have made *that* many errors."

"I'm sorry, but I'm still not following."

When she continued, her voice was noticeably lower.

"I think Victor might have stumbled across something that he shouldn't have…and was killed for it."

MARK'S EYEBROWS STAYED STILL, and his lips remained in their detached frown, but Kelli saw a twinge of movement in his jaw. He was trying to pretend he didn't have a reaction to her accusation, but she'd seen it clear as day. She thanked two years of people trying to hide their pity for the widowed mother. She'd seen *that* look so many times that she had learned to read when most people were trying to hide what they really felt.

Mark had a reaction, but she didn't know what emotion was behind it.

"Do you have any evidence to back that up?" he asked, voice even. "Aside from the difference between notes."

Kelli remembered Dennis Crawford's sharp stare as his hand stayed firmly on the photocopies she'd brought to him.

"Have you ever had a gut feeling, Mark? One that starts out as a tiny doubt and then grows and grows until you can't ignore it anymore?"

"Yes," he admitted. "But having a gut feeling can only take you so far. What you're trying to say is someone targeted and killed Victor. You need more than a gut feeling to back that up."

"But aren't you convinced that Darwin didn't start that fire? What about the man you saw running from the cabin that night?"

Mark took a long second before he said, "Darwin admitted to it. Why would he do that if he didn't actually start it?"

"Maybe he was put up to it. Maybe he was threatened. Maybe—"

"Kelli." Mark's jaw definitely hardened, along with his tone. She must have reacted, because just as quickly he softened. "It was an accident."

"But you—"

Mark's set his beer down hard. "I was wrong, Kelli." The women next to them glanced over. He cleared his throat. "I'm sorry, but I can't help you with this."

It was an unmistakable end to the conversation.

Just as the pity of strangers had taught Kelli to read subtle reactions, her daughter had taught her the face of stubborn resolve.

"Then I'm sorry to have wasted your time." She pulled out some cash to cover her untouched beer. "Thanks again for meeting me. Good night."

Mark looked like he wanted to say something, but he didn't. Kelli left the table without a look back, not even pausing as she brushed shoulders with a man leaving the bar.

Her face was hot and the outside air did little to cool it down. The heat came from either embarrassment at not being believed, or anger for the same reason. Maybe a mixture of both. Or, maybe her emotion wasn't even meant for the ex-bodyguard.

Kelli took a deep breath.

Seeking out the only person who ever suspected foul play, and to have even him turn you down...

She let the breath out.

You really are overreacting.

Kelli followed the sidewalk, passing back by one of the bar's open windows. The farther away she walked, the more convinced she became that the whole conspiracy was in her head. Moving out of the only home she'd ever had with Victor while juggling work and Grace was a lot of stress to carry. She thought she'd been handling it well enough, especially with Lynn's help, but maybe she hadn't.

Time to put it behind you, Kel.

"Don't make a noise." The harsh command came beside her ear just as a sharp point dug into her shirt. A large hand grabbed her upper arm. Kelli's stomach dropped as her heart began to gallop. Before she had time to decide if she was or wasn't going to comply, the man yanked her into a nearby alley. It was empty. No one yelled after them. "Turn around and I cut you," the voice growled. "Make one move or sound and I cut you. Got it?"

Kelli felt her head bob up and down. She was facing the brick wall of a business she couldn't remember at the moment. Her mind filled with images of Grace. The thought of her child put a bit of spirit back into her, but not enough for her to be careless.

"Drop your purse," the low voice ground out.

Kelli slowly raised the arm that he wasn't holding and maneuvered the strap off her chest and shoulder. She tried to gauge the size of the knife, but her nerves were too frazzled. The purse was on the ground for less than a second before the man snatched it back up. She saw his black-gloved hand. It made the terror in her rise even more.

Instead of leaving, he applied more pressure with the knife. She winced but didn't make a noise.

"There. That wasn't so hard, was it?" His breath brushed against her ear. It sent a chill up her spine.

"You have what you wanted," she said, voice shaking.

The knife bit deeper. This time she let out a small yelp.

"Didn't I say *no talki—*"

"I have a gun," interrupted a cool voice from even farther behind her, definitely not her original attacker. "Hurt her and I'll—"

Kelli was pushed into the wall as the man let go of her arm and struggled with the newcomer. Pain burst in her cheek as it scraped the brick. She didn't pause to check it. She braced herself against the wall as she turned around.

Her attacker was a white man—she couldn't guess an age well enough—dressed in all denim and black with a red baseball cap. He wasn't tall but he was wide. In one hand he held her purse. The other was busy trying to fend off her savior.

Who just happened to be Mark Tranton.

"Give me the purse," Mark commanded. His arm was cut, but he was holding a knife. Apparently having a gun had been a bluff.

The mugger eyed what used to be his weapon before darting to the left and out of the alley, taking the purse with him. For a large man, he was lithe.

"Are you okay?" Mark asked, eyes roaming her over.

"Yeah," she breathed.

And then he was running.

Chapter Five

The man was fast. Like a jackrabbit, he cut across the road and disappeared into an alley opposite them with impressive speed. Mark was more of a hand-to-hand combat guy, but he held his own, only slowing down when a Mazda didn't brake, apparently not worried about hitting pedestrians.

He chased the mugger through the network of alleys that connected two blocks. Dumpsters lined the sides and debris littered the ground, but the man used neither to try to block or slow Mark down. Instead, he ran full tilt. Which meant Mark wasn't going to catch him unless he got creative.

His memory began to pull an aerial layout of the alleyways. The one they were running down had three turnoffs before forking into two paths. One went left into another busy downtown block, next to a chic restaurant that stayed open until midnight. The other torqued right between a Chinese take-out joint and a boutique. The way the man was running, he seemed set on a destination. He hadn't hesitated when passing the first two turnoffs.

Mark didn't, either.

He didn't break speed as he skidded around into the

first turnoff and ran the length of the short alley. It deposited him back onto a less busy sidewalk where businesses were darkened for the night. A few bystanders too drunk to drive and too broke to call a taxi dotted the sidewalks. Mark spun around a couple that stood and gawked at him. His breathing hitched at the extra movement, but he knew his body could handle the chase. He might not have been a bodyguard anymore, but he'd never stopped training.

The stretch of block ended, and he cut left around a closed café on the corner. Pumping his legs harder, he made it to the mouth of the alley.

It was empty.

"Dammit!"

Mark spun around, his eyes darting to all escape routes. There was no hurried motion on the sidewalks. None of the people milling around seemed alarmed. The mugger hadn't come out of the alley. Mark had misjudged.

Or had he?

With the knife heavy in his hand, Mark reentered the alley. He kept his body loose, ready to move if the other man jumped out. But no one did. He paused, listening for another set of footsteps, before bending to pick up what had caught his eye.

It was Kelli's purse.

BACKTRACKING THROUGH THE alley to the bar, Mark kept an eye out for security cameras or any obvious eyewitnesses who might have caught the face of the mugger. There were neither. He put the knife in his pocket as he neared the street; the bag was secured underneath his arm.

"Mark!" Kelli was standing outside the bar again with a manager he knew. The older man had a phone to his ear and nodded to Mark before retreating back into the business. Kelli waved him over. The obvious relief that painted her face at the sight of him made him uneasy.

"I think this belongs to you," he said by way of greeting. Kelli took her purse, but her eyes stayed on his.

"Thank you." The expression of relief turned to gratitude. Again, it made him uneasy. He nodded.

"Are you okay?" he motioned to her cheek. It was red, scraped, with a few spots of blood.

"Yeah. I'd rather have this than a cut from the knife." She quieted.

"Did the manager call the cops?"

"Yes. When you took off, I ran back to call. I would have used my cell phone, but it's in my purse." That's when she noticed the cut on his arm. He could feel its sting but knew it was harmless. "You're hurt!"

"Don't worry. It looks worse than it feels."

"Hey, you get a good look at the guy?" The manager had come back out without the phone. Mark didn't miss the bulge of a gun beneath his shirt.

"Not his face," he admitted. "But I do know he was sitting at your bar."

"He was in the bar?" Kelli asked, voice pitching high. The manager didn't seem too thrilled, either. Even in the dim light from the street lamp, Mark could see his face redden in anger.

"He was sitting at the end closest to the corner. I remember seeing the back of his jacket. He got up as soon as you passed him, leaving. He seemed a little too interested, so I thought I'd check it out." He looked at the manager. "He had a beer in his hand, so—"

"So we have him on camera. And maybe his card is on file, too," the man finished. "A cop is on the way. He'll want your statement, so you two stick around. A beer on the house for your troubles."

"Thanks," Kelli said, though she didn't follow the man back inside. Her attention was on her purse.

"Hundreds of muggings a year and you have the luck of the draw to get one of them," Mark said.

That pulled a snort from her. "Bad luck seems to follow me."

Whether she meant it to be a pointed comment or an off-the-cuff response, it sobered him. Standing a few inches shorter than him, Kelli looked suddenly fragile. He had to remind himself she was the same woman who'd stood her ground and kept calm when a lowlife punk had a knife pulled on her.

"What did he take?" he asked, not wanting to think about what might have happened had he not followed them.

Her eyebrow arched. "Nothing," she answered.

"What?"

She produced her wallet and phone.

"Okay, now *that's* lucky right there!"

"Is it?" Kelli's expression turned skeptical fast. "Why not take *anything*?" she asked. Opening her wallet, she showed him it was full of cash.

"I must have scared him off."

"Or—"

Her thought was cut off as a police cruiser pulled up behind them. The officer got out, and Mark went to meet him. This definitely wasn't how he'd anticipated the night going.

Twenty minutes later, Kelli was ready to go home. The officer took their statements and then went to look at the security footage with the manager. Mark wanted to go, too, but he couldn't see the reason behind it. Kelli was safe and had her belongings back.

"Are you sure you're okay?" Mark asked as they got to her car. Sudden guilt riddled him. The first time he'd seen her since the fire and she'd been attacked.

"I'm fine," she said with a kind, polite smile. "Thanks for everything, Mark."

They didn't say much more. Just the awkward goodbye two relative strangers exchanged without committing to seeing each other again. Mark watched as she drove away.

He was surprised at how the thought of never seeing her again struck a sour note.

Then, just as the feeling occurred, guilt followed it.

"I'm fine."

It was the second time Kelli had said it within the space of an hour, but this time it was to a very anxious Lynn. Her best friend was sprawled across the couch with a magazine open on her lap, and her eyes were saucers.

"Oh, my God, I can't believe you got mugged!"

"Hey, quiet. My kid's trying to sleep," Kelli warned with a smile. Seeing Lynn so obviously upset was starting to make her calm crack. She was surprised she had even been able to recount the entire story before Lynn interrupted.

"I know she's asleep," Lynn said, dropping the volume of her voice. "I'm the one who put her there and read that annoying counting-sheep book to her. Can we just get rid of that thing, by the way? Maybe 'misplace' it? Say the Easter Bunny needed it to keep on hopping, or maybe Santa needed it to fight crime or something? I think I've read that to her at least a hundred times already."

Kelli appreciated Lynn's attempt to calm her with a change of subject. The knotted stress within her lessened. She kicked off her shoes and leaned back into the pillows.

"And risk a never-ending tantrum? No way. I'd rather read it every night than endure *one* night without it."

Lynn seemed to reconsider her stance before returning to the topic at hand.

"I still can't believe you got jumped." Her face softened, lips turning down. "He could have really hurt you, Kel."

"I know, but he didn't."

Lynn's eyes slid to the scrape on her cheek. As Kelli had sat in the driveway outside the house, the light from the car mirror had shown her the small wound looked worse than it felt. Which is what Mark had said of his cut. Her thoughts switched to the man.

"I'm just glad Mark saw the guy follow me out," she admitted out loud. "Do you know he didn't even have a gun on him? The only weapon he had, he *took* from the guy."

Lynn whistled. "He's got my praise. So how *was* talking to the bodyguard after all this time? What did he want to talk to you about?" Out of all of the people who had ever stepped into Kelli's life, Lynn was the one person she'd always confided in without hesitation. From the crush she'd had on Billy Ryan in third grade to that one thing Victor had done in bed, there had never been a wall between them.

Until Kelli had found Victor's journal and started to investigate.

The urge to tell Lynn of her suspicions had been great, but something had stopped her. Whether that was fear of judgment or embarrassment at making something out of nothing, Kelli wasn't sure. Regardless, the excuse she'd made to meet Mark had been a lie.

"It was good. Nothing too special, just catching up." Another lie. Another shot of guilt. "But he's no longer a bodyguard," she added, needing a dose of truth to ease her conscience.

"What do you mean?"

"He quit last year." Nikki had told her that when she had called looking for him.

"Why?"

Kelli shrugged, but she could bet why he'd quit security. She couldn't ignore the way Nikki had sounded almost sad as she recounted the information.

Lynn switched subjects again. They talked about the latest episode of *The Bachelor*—which sidetracked them to the topic of Lynn's new neighbor, who had a "smoking body" but "not so much personality." Eventually both women's eyes started to shut, so they said good-night.

"Don't forget to let that kid of yours know who got sent home from my show," Lynn said at the door.

"You let her watch it?" Kelli asked, ready to admonish her. Lynn kept walking away with a wave.

"Just tell her it was the guy with the silly shirt. She'll know what I'm talking about."

Kelli laughed and shut the door after Lynn was safe in her car. She bumped her hip against the door to make sure it was shut all the way, threw the deadbolt and turned off the porch light. The cold of the hardwood floor made her pause. Moving across town to be closer to Lynn—and in a more affordable place—was definitely a move she needed to make, but...

She placed her hand on the door. It was polished and perfect. It reminded her of Victor picking her up and walking her over the threshold when they first got back from their honeymoon. He had insisted, even though they'd been living together for months.

Memories like that made her heart heavy as she walked through the house.

Heavy with love.

Heavy with loss.

She dropped her hand from the door and let out a long breath. Just because she was leaving didn't mean she was leaving the memories, too. With a weird ache tearing through her emotions, Kelli decided to go to the one place that often helped soothe the rising grief.

Since Grace's bedroom was mostly boxed up, the toddler had been sharing the king-size bed with her mom. Though the bed never seemed big enough if Grace got into a good dream. Kelli stood in the doorway and watched as the fair-haired child slept peacefully, unaware of her mother's tumultuous thoughts. The ache within her began to dissipate.

Without undressing, she climbed into bed next to the girl, wrapping her arms around her. Grace—a snuggler—burrowed closer to her.

You're okay, Kel. You've got all you need right here.

But even as she drifted to sleep, letting go of the hectic night's worries, Kelli couldn't help but pinpoint the one fact that felt off about her night's bad luck.

Why hadn't the mugger taken anything?

In the haze between wakefulness and sleep, her thoughts went to Victor's journal, hidden in a box in the kitchen.

Maybe he'd been looking for something more specific.

Chapter Six

Guilt hung heavy within Mark's chest. Lying in bed, he couldn't get the image of Kelli's scraped cheek out of his head. What was it about the Cranes that nulled his ability to keep them safe? It was a question that had pushed itself to the front of his mind during his cab ride home the night before…and it had still been there when he awoke.

"Get it together, Tranton," he scolded himself. "The past is the past." But even as he said it, he knew it wasn't true. The past had called him back to his favorite bar, asking him to avenge a man who died because of him.

The weather forecast was clear for today, but a storm was in the distance. He could smell the rain as he walked to his small balcony. Drought for months and then nothing but rain. Dallas was consistent with its weather inconsistency.

He moved through his apartment, trying to focus on anything other than last night. It wasn't working.

"Have you ever had a gut feeling, Mr. Tranton?"

Yes.

That Darwin McGregor wasn't behind the fire.

But he wasn't in the business of trusting his gut.

Not anymore. Not when it hadn't even twinged at the cabin that night.

Mark skipped his morning gym session and went straight for the shower. He managed to wipe his mind of any thoughts of the past. So much so that when he got out and looked at himself in the mirror, he took a moment to shave. Jonathan Carmichael would have been proud. Every time they had worked together during their time at Redstone Solutions or the Orion Security Group, he had always commented on Mark's five-o'clock shadow and lack of neatness. Facial hair hadn't been a point of fixation for the ex-bodyguard, and that had driven Jonathan a little crazy.

"You look like you're the one we're protecting our client from."

The memory made him snort.

And now I don't protect anyone.

His hand paused midmotion.

Once he had shaved, he decided Jonathan would've approved—he did have to admit it made him look better. He was heading to the bedroom when a knock sounded at the apartment door.

Eyeing the buzzer on the kitchen wall, he quickly went through a list of people already in the building who would want to pay him a visit. He wasn't pals with any of the tenants, but on occasion he would get asked to watch the game or go out drinking with Craig from the gym. As he walked to the door, towel around his waist, chest still bare, he marveled at the fact that he couldn't even recall Craig's last name.

Which was fine, since it was Kelli waiting at the door for him.

"Oh," he said, opening the door wide from its original cracked position.

"Oh," she repeated. Her eyes darted up and down his body. He pictured the pair of shorts and shirt on his bed that he probably should have put on before answering the door. "Sorry. Is this a bad time?" she asked, recovering. A slow pink had risen in her cheeks.

"No. I just got out of the shower." He motioned to the towel that hung low on his hips, just in case the droplets of water across his bare skin and his wet hair weren't enough proof to make his claim believable.

"Right. Um, could I maybe talk to you for a minute? I promise it won't take long."

Mark stepped back and waved her inside, cautious of how loose the towel felt as he moved. After everything they'd been through, he didn't think flashing Kelli Crane was the best way to start a conversation.

"Make yourself comfortable. Let me go get dressed."

Kelli nodded and took a seat on the couch, but only on the edge of it. She was uncomfortable, but why? Mark dressed in record time and sat in a chair across from the intriguing young woman, ready to find out.

"Sorry if coming by was too intrusive," she started. "I may have Googled your number the other night, trying to find your address." The blush from earlier came back, but not as strong. "I was in the neighborhood, meeting my realtor for some papers, when I realized how close your apartment is. So I decided dropping by might be better than leaving another voice mail." She gave a little laugh. "Now I see that maybe it was just creepier."

Mark still wasn't sure he could sum up how he felt at seeing Kelli again—especially in his apartment, wearing a pair of tight jeans and a form-fitting blouse—but he didn't feel creeped out in the least. He hadn't even thought to ask her yet how she'd gotten into the building.

"It's not creepy," he admitted. "But I am curious how you got in without buzzing up."

"A man asked me who I was here to see and waved me in." Her smile was small. "Said he was worried you hadn't shown up for the gym that morning."

He laughed. He really needed to learn Craig's last name.

"So what's up?" Mark asked when it was clear she needed a bit of prodding. "Did they catch the mugger?"

Kelli shook her head. "They told me they'd call if they did, but so far, no call. That's partly why I wanted to talk." She readjusted in her seat and seemed to take a breath before looking him in the eye. "I wanted to sincerely apologize for everything. I shouldn't have asked you to meet me after all this time just to spin a paranoid theory about a charity, of all places. I just— I guess I thought I'd accepted—to some degree—what happened to Victor. Finding his journal showed me that maybe I haven't fully."

She shrugged, sudden vulnerability showing in each movement. "After I had Grace, I needed to be strong for her—for us—to make it. I suppose I might have buried some feelings rather than faced them. Though creating a conspiracy in my head was probably the wrong route to take."

Her gray-green eyes took on a new shade as the conversation left the past behind. The vulnerable side of Kelli disappeared with it. The corner of her lips pulled up into a smile. "To apologize for trying to rope you into my crazy, I'd like to invite you to dinner tonight at my house. And before you say yes or no, I should warn you—my best friend, Lynn, will be there, and, of course, Grace. Most of the house is boxed up. So if you're expecting fancy, you won't find it there."

Mark tightened his jaw so his mouth didn't fall open in surprise. Once again, he hadn't expected their conversation to go the way it had. Being invited into Kelli's home to eat with her loved ones? No, he hadn't seen that invitation coming.

And he didn't know how to feel about it, either.

"Listen, I appreciate the offer—I really do—but you don't owe me anything, Kelli. You don't have to apologize to me." *Ever*, he wanted to add.

The blonde's smile grew. "Now, you listen to me. You saved me last night, and…well, it wasn't the first time." She pulled a small piece of paper out of her purse and handed it to him before standing. "I'd really appreciate it if you came, Mark. I'd feel a whole lot better knowing that—after I'd gone a bit crazy—you at least got a good meal out of it." She started to walk to the door before pausing. "Unless you already had plans? I—I realize I didn't even ask." Kelli's eyes quickly flicked toward the bedroom.

He smiled. "No plans here," he said.

"Okay, great. Then you really have no excuse not to come." That made him laugh. Kelli Crane was tenacious.

"Fine," he replied, copying her playful tone. "I'll be there with bells and whistles on."

Kelli's expression contorted to disgust. "I know that that's an expression but please, dear goodness, don't bring bells or whistles into my house. I have a toddler. She will want them and use them until we've all gone crazy."

Mark laughed again and followed her to the door. "Deal."

Kelli smiled and was gone, leaving him standing in his doorway with the paper in his hand. On it was an address and the starting time of seven. His eyes went back to the house number, and his memory sparked. Guilt undid the fun humor he'd lapsed into with Kelli when he realized she still lived in the same house she'd shared with Victor.

He was about to go to the house of the man he'd let die, to eat with his widow and daughter.

Mark rubbed the back of his neck.

He'd spent the past year trying to keep away from the past, and here he was, going to dinner with it.

LYNN HAD HER face so close to the window that her breathing was starting to fog up the glass. Grace, who had been copying her godmother's nosiness minutes before, was now sitting next to her feet, playing with Lynn's phone. Kelli rolled her eyes and wiped sauce off her hand onto a dish towel. She was a decent cook but lousy at keeping the ingredients off her. She wouldn't be packing the dish towels until they were out the door and on to the new house.

"You know, typically, when you invite guests to dinner, you're not supposed to watch for them so intensely," Kelli said. "That's what the doorbell is for. It lets you know when your invitee arrives."

Lynn turned her head and rolled her eyes. "First, don't act like you invite people over all of the time," she said, serious. "Second, I'm sorry if I'm insanely curious about the person you *did* finally invite over."

Kelli kept her smile firmly on her lips. They both knew the reason she hadn't been the most entertaining woman in the past year. Being a single working parent had limited her time. As far as her first guest being a man, well, that had surprised her, too.

Inviting Mark over hadn't been an impulsive decision. Instead, it had been one that grew from a thought seeded in her mind during the moments right before sleep. It wasn't until she was driving to meet the Realtor that she'd decided to act on the idea. Despite short notice, Lynn had been more than willing to help keep Grace entertained while they all ate. Even though Kelli had explained she truly needed to apologize and show thanks to Mark for saving her the night before, Lynn liked to tease her. She'd done it when Kelli wouldn't admit she'd liked Martin Ballard their sophomore year of high school, and again with his brother Tony a year later.

Not that Kelli liked Mark the way she'd liked the Ballard brothers.

Before she could stop herself, she pictured the ex-bodyguard with nothing but a towel around his hips. Her face heated instantly and Lynn's eyebrow rose as if she could read Kelli's thoughts.

"Want to come help me?" Kelli asked, attention turning downward to Grace, cutting off any questions that Lynn might start throwing out.

Kelli put the dish towel over her shoulder and went to her daughter. She picked her up, and Grace giggled.

"I guess I'll go powder my nose or something," Lynn said, resigned.

"Good," Kelli said. "Less smudging on the windows before our guest gets here."

Grace started to do her routine of toddler babbling and let her mom know really quickly that she preferred to stay right where she was on her hip. So Kelli tried her best to set the table while juggling the little diva. It didn't go as well as she would have liked. Grace had become fascinated with Kelli's dangling earrings.

"Pretty," she cooed.

"Nothing compared to you." The little girl had her hair braided in pigtails and wore a long green floral shirt and pink-and-purple-striped tights she'd picked out herself. The outfit, plus her innocent smile, brightened the entire room. Kelli was so distracted by the pure love she felt for the little human that she jumped when the doorbell sounded behind them. "Our dinner guest is here."

Grace started to squirm until Kelli put her down. She ran to the door and paused to glance back at her mom. Kelli peered through the peephole to confirm it was the ex-bodyguard before giving the girl a nod. Grace squealed, and together they opened the door.

Kelli felt a single butterfly dislodge in her stomach. It began to flutter at the sight of Mark. Even though he was fully dressed, there was a new attractiveness about him now. Wearing a white button-up and a pair of nice slacks, he looked as though he'd taken pains to style his short dark hair. Though she realized his face had been shaven when she'd visited him earlier, without the presence of his half-naked body she was able to appreciate how the clean look softened his otherwise hard expression. His dark green eyes scanned her face before falling to the child at her side.

A wide smile split his face.

"You must be Grace," he said, bending to meet her gaze. She was unapologetic in her stare right back, but Kelli knew she was reverting to the rare shyness she had only when first meeting someone. Her little arms wound their way around Kelli's leg. But surprisingly, Grace smiled. "Beautiful kid," Mark added, straightening.

"And she knows it, too," Kelli responded with a wink. She moved farther back into the entryway, inviting him in.

Kelli took a quiet, quick breath when their eyes met again. She wasn't sure what that butterfly was up to, but it was causing her to feel some things she probably shouldn't.

For a brief moment, she wondered about the love life of the man she'd just invited into her late husband's home.

Chapter Seven

Lynn managed to not lose her composure when she came into the entryway, moments after Mark shut the front door. What she didn't manage to do was keep her eyes from roving up and down the man. She cut a quick look to Kelli, who was at his side, before extending her hand.

"You must be Mark," she greeted him.

Mark took her hand. "And you must be Lynn."

The short-haired woman beamed.

"That's me—childhood best friend, keeper of all embarrassing stories, holder of everything secret. You know, the norm."

Mark chuckled, and Kelli swatted at her. Knowing her, she'd launch into one of those embarrassing stories if not adequately distracted.

"Why don't we go ahead and sit down?" she suggested, ushering the group into the next room. The table wasn't made up as fancy as she would have liked, but judging by what she had seen of his apartment, Mark didn't mind the lack of flamboyance. Like Kelli, he seemed to find pleasure in simpler tastes.

"You weren't kidding about boxes," Mark commented, taking the first seat he made it to. His back was facing the door but with a perfect sightline to a pyramid of boxes against the wall behind the table.

Kelli laughed. "I warned you."

"Yes, you did."

Lynn sat across from Mark while Grace climbed up on her lap. Normally Kelli would have said something, but the toddler had been in such a good mood that she didn't want to jeopardize it. Not that she thought Mark would have been angry if she had thrown a tantrum. He seemed to be a good man.

"I hope you like spaghetti," Kelli said, bringing in a pot full of it. "I'm not a five-star chef, but these two have never complained."

Lynn leaned in a bit but spoke loudly. "I just haven't told her that I'll never turn down free food."

Mark laughed, and the three of them launched into the small talk that happens when everyone isn't fully acquainted. Lynn brought up her disdain for her boss and, immediately after, her dream of owning her own marketing agency.

"I'd force this one here to leave her gig and get a job with me," she said, thumbing in Kelli's direction. "She can use those artsy skills to make a mean profit, helping me design pretty campaigns."

"You're still working in art therapy?" Mark asked after downing a mouthful of noodles. Kelli was surprised he remembered.

"Actually, no," she admitted. "I currently train others to use art therapy to help senior citizens with special needs. I used to be the one *doing* it, but now I teach those who will." She shrugged. "I have to say, it's way more flexible schedule-wise, which helps me take care of that little thing there." Grace's attention was on her food, even though half of it was on her face. "Though the pay leaves room to be desired." She glanced at the boxes stacked in the living room.

"It's great what you're doing, though," Mark replied once he, too, had glanced at another stack of boxes. Kelli wondered if he'd put together the fact that her new job and its lower pay was a big contributor to them moving. "Helping people can be a hard business."

"Speaking of helping people," Lynn chimed in, "Kelli tells me you're no longer working as a bodyguard?" Kelli's eyes shot daggers at her best friend. Always one to talk before thinking, Lynn's eyes widened. She'd finally realized the most likely reason behind his change of work. However, it was too late to take her words back.

If Mark was offended, he didn't show it.

"Yeah, I needed some time away from it," he said. He didn't meet their gaze but focused on his drink. "Don't get me wrong. Orion is the best place I've ever worked, but I'd been doing it for so long, I needed a break."

Kelli hoped what he was saying was true, that he'd changed careers for reasons that didn't involve her or her family, but she certainly wasn't going to pry into his motive.

"Orion. I just love that name," Lynn said, showing Kelli she wouldn't pry, either. That earned a smile from the man.

"The founder, Nikki, named it after Orion's belt. It was her way of remembering why she started the group."

"Why did she? What's the connection?" Kelli couldn't help but ask. Even though they'd hired Orion, she'd never heard their origin story.

"I'll warn you, it wasn't the best beginning," he said. "Nikki and I, along with two other agents, were working at an elite security agency called Redstone Solutions before Orion was even a thought. We did almost the same thing as Orion does now, but for a high price." Sadness crept across his face. Kelli realized that perhaps she'd jumped from one sore topic to another. "One day a woman named Morgan Avery came in, asking for protection while she traveled to the UK. She was competing for placement in an astronomy program that was really hard to get into. She said she'd been receiving threats and was terrified. We were told to turn her down—she didn't have enough money—but still she came day after day to ask again."

He paused. Instead of trying to find the right words, Mark looked like he was trying to forget them. "Her body was found in a ditch near the airport." Kelli and Lynn gasped. "That's when Nikki used the contacts she'd made as secretary to leave and start her own security group. She named it after Morgan's favorite constellation. She wanted to help those who couldn't afford it. Orion occasionally takes on wealthy clients to keep the place running, but the bottom line is we protect those who don't have the money for it." His frown tilted into a half smile. "And I went with her."

"Whoa," Lynn whispered.

Kelli couldn't help but agree. Warmth at the realization of why he helped people who couldn't afford it started to spread throughout her chest. Without a doubt Mark was a good man.

The conversation from there became lighter. A storm rolled in, and they found a more comfortable ground of discussing—of all things—the weather. It led to other

topics mundane enough that no one was forced to remember a tragic past but interesting enough that the
conversation stretched into an hour. Mark was more
than the quiet man she'd met before and met once again.
He livened up enough that she could see he wasn't just
a bodyguard—former or otherwise—but a normal guy
with a sweet smile.

He complimented her cooking and thanked her for
the meal. He talked directly to Grace as much as any
person could and even gave her a few compliments of
her own. Lynn must have decided she liked him, as well.
Without asking Kelli or Mark, she cleared the table and
replaced their dishes with wineglasses.

"It's storming outside, so it's not like you can leave
right now," she explained to Mark. "While we wait,
let's have a glass of this wine I was polite enough to
bring over."

Kelli found that she quite liked that idea.

"You said you'll never turn down free food?" Mark
asked Lynn, eyeing the bottle. "I won't turn down free
wine."

THE STORM DIDN'T DISSIPATE.

The longer they waited, the worse it got. If Grace
hadn't skipped her nap, she would have been terrified.
As it was, she was bundled up in Kelli's bed, fast asleep.
But with the growing volume of each boom of thunder,
she wouldn't be for long.

It was well past ten and Lynn, Mark and Kelli had
thoroughly exhausted all small talk. A majority of *that*
had been done by the vivacious best friend who hadn't
been shy with the wine she'd brought over. Whether she
was making sure to fill the conversational void con-

stantly or was just really excited for new company, Kelli couldn't tell. What she did know was that Mark had been nothing but polite. He hadn't been quiet, but she realized he hadn't said much about himself, either. The only time he'd momentarily opened up was about Orion before the wine. Past that? It was like talking to a ghost.

It made her wonder how he lived his life.

And how much of it he didn't.

"If you think I'm letting you two leave in this—" Kelli motioned to the living room's front windows "—then you're sadly mistaken."

Mark's head was tilted down over his phone, but he chuckled. "It isn't that bad," he said.

Lynn, who had taken up the other side of the couch, moved her head to see what he was looking at. "That's a very red radar," she commented.

Mark sighed. "Yes, it is."

Kelli stood from the chair opposite them and put her hands together. "Then it looks like we're all bunking here tonight."

Mark's eyebrow shot up so fast that Kelli instantly questioned her decision.

"Listen, you took a taxi here right?" she asked. He nodded.

"I realized my truck was running on empty," he admitted. "I thought it would be easier to just grab a cab here instead."

"Well, they aren't going to send someone out in this, and even if they did, would you trust them to get you home all right?" On cue, the sound of rain pelting the house intensified. She could tell the man was now reaching the same conclusion. "If you don't mind taking the couch, Lynn, you can bunk with me and the munchkin since her room is all packed up. Okay?"

Lynn reached over and patted Mark on the shoulder before standing with her empty wineglass.

"Don't fight it, man," she said. "That look she's sporting? That's her Mama Bear face. Right now she doesn't see us as people. We're her cubs." Mark laughed.

"Call it a side effect of motherhood," Kelli responded, hands going to her hips. She fixed Mark with a less intense stare. "I can't make you stay, but I assure you it's no inconvenience to us."

Mark glanced at the window and the dark abyss outside. He was hesitant in answering. "If it's really no trouble, then it might be a good idea to stay, at least till it passes."

Kelli smiled and Lynn clapped. The sound was drowned out by another *boom* of thunder. It didn't diminish her cheer.

"Haven't had a sleepover in years," she squealed.

Kelli promptly rolled her eyes.

THE DAY HAD been full of surprises, but now the night was trumping them. Mark settled back onto the couch, trying to get comfortable under the multicolored blanket. Kelli had said Victor had never been a fan of its brightness. Bringing Victor up, however relevant he was, had put a feeling of guilt and confusion within him once again.

Now the house was as quiet as the storm outside would let it be. The light kept on in the kitchen buzzed through the madness. Neither of these things kept Mark awake. It was the room across from him that grabbed his focus and kept it.

Victor Crane's office.

Kelli had mentioned it was the last room they had packed and as soon as she'd said it, her expression had darkened. That's where she'd found the notebook.

Mark let out a long breath and tried to readjust to a more comfortable position. Nothing was working. His mind was refusing to shut down for the night. After a few more minutes of no success, he pulled out his phone and checked the radar again.

"Desperate to leave?"

Mark sat up quickly, turning toward the hallway that separated the living room and kitchen. In the dim light, Kelli smiled.

"Sorry, I didn't mean to startle you," she apologized. "Unlike the two ladies passed out in my bed, I can't sleep through all of this."

"And here I thought I was the only one," he responded. His voice had dropped in volume to match hers, but every part of him had to focus to keep it from getting too deep. As she stood there in a tank top and plaid boxers, with no makeup, her short hair in a ponytail, Mark found himself admiring how beautiful she was.

"Well, since we can't seem to fall asleep, would you be interested in a late-night snack?" She grinned. "I know where Grace's mom hides the chocolate-chip cookies."

For the umpteenth time that night, Kelli made him laugh. It was not only a foreign feeling to him but also a sound he wasn't used to hearing.

"As long as you don't tell, I won't," he responded with a wink. Kelli's smile grew, and Mark followed her into the kitchen. Wanting to avoid another shirtless session with her, he'd been mindful to keep his undershirt on when he had first lain down.

The light above the sink was enough to illuminate the room. It showed Kelli climbing up onto the countertop next to the refrigerator. She looked back at his questioning look before opening up the small cabinet above.

"You really made sure Grace couldn't reach those, huh?" he whispered.

She laughed softly. "And Lynn." Kelli found the bag of cookies and passed it back to him. "Keeping any sweets in the house has proven to be a very difficult thing to—"

Another *boom* of thunder hit, but the sound that immediately followed wasn't storm-related at all. It was glass shattering. Both of them turned their heads toward the living room, even though the wall was in their way. Frozen, they listened.

Another crash was partially masked by the storm.

Every part of Mark went on high alert. He crept along the kitchen wall until he was at the doorway. Crouching so he wasn't at full height, he looked across the hallway to the room he had just been trying to sleep in. Past the couch and through the double French doors, movement caught his eye.

Someone was climbing through the office window. Judging by the flashlight in his hand and the mask on his face, it wasn't a person filled with good intentions.

Mark moved quickly back to Kelli. His face must have shown it all. She didn't question when he grabbed her by the waist. She put her hands on his shoulders, and he lifted her up off the countertop and set her back down on the floor. He took her hand and pulled her through the other kitchen doorway that opened farther down the hallway. The intruder couldn't see them as Mark rushed them to the master bedroom. But that also meant they couldn't see the intruder.

Once they were in the bedroom, Mark turned and quietly shut the door behind them. He threw the lock before turning to his hostess. The nightstand lamp illuminated her face. Acute worry shone clearly across it—so intense it almost gave him pause.

Almost.

"A man in a mask just broke into the office. I can't tell if he was armed," he whispered, taking his cell phone out of his pocket. He handed it to her and went to the bed where Grace and Lynn were fast asleep. He shook the woman. It took her a second, but her eyes finally fluttered open. He put a finger to his lips when she opened her mouth. "Take Grace into the bathroom and lock the door." Surprisingly, Lynn didn't argue. Without comment, she scurried out of bed.

Mark went back to Kelli, who was whispering into the phone. She watched with wide eyes as her best friend carried her still-sleeping daughter into the en suite. It was those wide eyes that he was looking into when the lamp and the bathroom light cut off. He could hear the dying whirl of the ceiling fan as it powered down.

He cursed beneath his breath before a hand reached out and took his.

"Either the storm or the intruder just cut the power," Kelli whispered to the 911 operator. Whatever the operator said back to her, he didn't hear. She squeezed his hand, pulling him closer. Suddenly her breath was next to his ear. "There's a flashlight under the bathroom sink."

It was Kelli's turn to pull him along. He didn't stop her. She knew the house better.

"Lynn, take the phone," Kelli whispered when they were inside the bathroom. There was noise, and then Lynn was the one whispering to the operator. The glow of the phone illuminated her sitting in the soaker tub, Grace asleep still in her arms.

Kelli didn't drop Mark's hand as she retrieved a giant flashlight from beneath the counter. She clicked it on. He was surprised to see that the worry she had exuded earlier had changed into something else. He couldn't place it and didn't have time to. She turned to her best friend.

"Stay here and don't open this door. And keep Grace safe no matter what," she ground out, turning the lock inside the door before shutting it and taking Mark with her into the bedroom. No hesitation lined her movements.

"There's a gun in the nightstand," she whispered, hurrying over to retrieve it. "But it doesn't have a clip." Her face fell. "I separated them just in case Grace found it…and I've already packed it up." Mark scanned the boxes that lined the wall.

"They don't know that," he said, taking the black 9 mm. It was undoubtedly empty, weighing significantly less than when it was loaded. He held the grip with one hand. With the other, he cupped the bottom, where the clip would normally be. If he kept it there, no one would be the wiser.

Until he needed to shoot it.

"What are you going to do?" Kelli kept the flashlight's beam on the floor. The beam bounced off the hardwood to give them just enough lighting to see the shadows on each other's faces.

"I'm going to go greet our new guest."

"But can't we just wait for the police?"

The storm kept its loud pace outside.

"I'm not confident in their response time," he said, already moving Kelli back to the bathroom door. "Stay and turn the light off."

"Be careful," she whispered.

The flashlight cut off. He waited a moment for his eyes to readjust to the darkness before creeping back into the hallway. The storm wasn't helping him hear exactly where the intruder was, but by the same token, the intruder probably didn't hear him, either. It helped he was barefoot.

Slowly he followed the cool hardwood back toward the living room. Without the kitchen light on, the house was bathed in darkness. The occasional lightning flash lit up his surroundings.

He mentally pulled up the layout of the house, thanks to a quick tour Kelli had given him after supper. The only way to get to the women was to go through him or the bedroom window. He doubted the intruder would go back outside just to break back in. If he did, he knew Kelli would let him know.

Mark slowed at the arch that opened into the living room. He heard rustling but couldn't tell where exactly it was coming from. Pulling the gun up as if it were actually loaded, he swung around into the room. Judging by the size and form, the intruder was a man. Broad shoulders couldn't be hidden by the black jacket he wore. He was no longer in the office but by a stack of boxes behind the couch in the living room. Mark had hoped to be quiet enough to surprise him completely, but the man turned at his presence.

Mark immediately noted the gloves and ski mask he wore.

And the knife in his hand. Even from a distance in the low light, he could see it was at least six inches in length.

"Drop the knife and put your hands up," Mark barked, making sure to keep his hand firm over the empty space where the clip should have been. He tried quickly to discern any details that might give him an edge over the mystery man if things went south. The intruder wasn't as big as Mark, but that didn't mean he didn't know how to fight. The flashlight he'd had when Mark had first seen him was set on the back of the couch. It partially lit up the room but not enough to piece together the intruder's expression or intention beneath his mask. "I said, *drop it*," Mark repeated, moving closer. He wanted to show the man he wasn't joking.

"And here I thought the ladies were alone." The way the man said it put Mark further on edge. There was no worry or remorse in his words. Almost as if he was stating a lazy fact.

"Drop the knife or I'll drop you." Mark lowered his voice to a level he hoped was pure threat. The man wasn't showing any signs of fear. He moved the knife to his other hand.

"'Drop me,' eh? Been watching a lot of cop shows, haven't you?"

"Can't say I'm the only one," Mark bit out. "Looks like you've been taking pointers from some lowlifes. I'd rather be the cop than the thief."

The man chuckled.

"I may be stealing something, but I'm no thief," he responded, starting to move slowly around the couch. Mark was surprised he was coming closer rather than trying to flee. He had no way of knowing there was no clip inside the gun. "But I don't have to explain myself to you."

Later Mark would be able to look back and realize that the small smile that brought up the corner of the man's lips right after he spoke was the exact moment he knew that the man was dangerous. That, without a doubt, the intruder was an immediate threat not only to Mark but also to the women in the house.

But in the moment, he felt his body act of its own accord.

He threw the gun at the man with all the strength he had. Clearly surprised, the intruder didn't duck out of the way. The gun hit his shoulder hard. The knife in his hand clattered to the ground.

Mark didn't hesitate.

Chapter Eight

The two men hit the far wall with enough force that Mark heard the man's breath push out. Mark wanted to get the man away from his weapon and subdue him. Tackling him into a wall seemed to be the best of both worlds.

However, it was Mark's turn to be surprised.

The man might have lost his breath, but he hadn't lost his fighting skills. He brought up his fist and gave Mark a good right hook. Pain burst behind his eye just as the man brought his foot right on top of Mark's instep. The combination made him waver enough that the intruder was able to push Mark backward into the couch.

"Is that it, bodyguard?"

How had he known Mark was a bodyguard? Ex or otherwise?

Mark balled his fists and brought his feet apart just in time for the intruder to lunge forward.

He swung high. Mark ducked low.

They went through another flurry of fists before the man threw a punch that landed so close to Mark's face that he lost his balance trying to dodge it. The intruder used the gap in defense to his advantage. He threw his shoulder into Mark's chest, and together they toppled over the couch.

Mark's head hit the coffee table, dazing him. The intruder pushed off him and made a run for his knife, lying a few feet from them.

"I don't think so," Mark hissed, scrambling to grab the man. He wasn't fast enough. The man picked up his weapon. He turned so fast that Mark froze.

"I'm no thief, but I don't mind fighting," the man said, brandishing the too-large knife.

Mark was so close that if the man jumped forward, he'd slice him with ease. Images of the three ladies in the bedroom flashed behind his eyes. He needed to get that knife away from the man, no matter what.

Just as he was gearing up to grab the man's wrist, something small flew over his shoulder. It hit the intruder's nose. He yelled in pain. Mark used the opening to grab the man's wrist and bend it backward. The knife once again dropped to the ground. Mark didn't waste time in retrieving it.

"Don't move," Mark ground out, knife in hand. The man's eyes—dark, Mark couldn't tell what color—darted from the weapon to a space over Mark's shoulder. Without another comment, he turned and ran back into the office. Mark tried to catch him but the man was fast.

He jumped through the window he'd broken and disappeared into the stormy night.

Mark wanted to follow him—to catch him—but a sound behind him drew his attention away.

Kelli stood in the living room doorway, eyes wide.

"I found the clip," she said, voice a few octaves too high. Mark didn't understand until he followed her gaze to the floor near the couch. Despite the situation, he let out a loud laugh.

"That's what hit him," he realized. "You *threw* the clip at him."

Kelli shrugged.

"I panicked," she admitted. "I thought he was going to stab you. I can't believe it actually hit him. I can barely see."

"We're quite the couple, then." Mark walked over to the discarded gun, partially under the couch thanks to the scuffle, and retrieved its clip. Working at Orion had trained him to shy away from using guns—there were other ways to disable an attacker—but he wasn't about to just leave it on the floor, either. He put the safety on and secured the gun in the back of his pants. "I threw the gun at him when I realized he wasn't going to give up."

Kelli let out her own little laugh, but it didn't last long.

Mark sobered. "The cops are on their way?"

"Yeah, the dispatcher said it might take a little bit because of the storm." Kelli took a few steps forward and extended her hand to him. Unsure of what to do, he took it. The light from the flashlight made shadows dance across her concerned face. The nerves boiling beneath his skin began to die down.

They were safe.

Kelli was safe.

"Are you okay?" she asked, not fazed by their contact. Mark wondered how well she could read him. Surprise at her thoughtfulness toward him was all he could feel for a moment. His slow response time only seemed to heighten that concern. "*Did* he cut you?"

"No, I'm fine. All he got in were a few punches." Pain in his head started to rise in his awareness. He glanced over to the coffee table. "But I think I might have cracked your coffee table."

Kelli didn't even turn to look. She squeezed his hand. "Thank you," she whispered.

He squeezed back. "Thank *you*. I have no doubt that he would have used this." Mark dropped her hand and held the knife up.

"Do you think his fingerprints are still on it?"

Mark shook his head, recalling the gloves the intruder had worn. "He came prepared."

Kelli grabbed the flashlight and pointed it to the office. Mark watched as she moved the beam across the now-open boxes from a safe distance.

"That's my laptop," she said, pausing in her movement. "I almost never use it. It's basically brand-new." She moved the light back into the living room to the open box that obviously held the stereo. "It's not a brand-new model, but it's worth money." The light moved again until it rested between them, showing him the clear expression of someone who has just discovered something they wish they hadn't. "Mark, I don't know why, but I think he was looking for Victor's journal."

Mark thought back to the purse snatching. The mugger had left the purse…and nothing had been taken. Now, in the dead of night, in the middle of a storm, a man decked out in black had broken in. What's more, he'd admitted he was no thief but was after *something*.

That was too many coincidences.

Sirens sounded in the distance. Mark met Kelli's gaze with certainty.

"I think I'm officially on the paranoid train."

THE POLICE BROUGHT in rain and mud and a lot of questions. Kelli, ready to deal with all three, was immensely thankful that Mark was more than willing to walk the cops through everything that had happened. Not leaving any details out. So when he got to the part about her throwing the clip at the intruder's head—an act of sheer panic on her part—the two men paused and looked her way.

Grace, now fully awake on Kelli's hip, waved at them. Mark was the only one who did a little wave back before taking the officers through the rest of the story. He stepped with them over to the broken office window, and together all three stood with heads tilted.

"This sleepover was almost as bad as Marcie Diggle's fifteenth birthday party," Lynn said from the dining table's chair behind her.

"Just because you found out Marcie kissed Tim Duncan," she replied.

Lynn snapped her fingers.

"Yeah, a week after he kissed *me*." She crossed her arms over her chest. The pajama set she'd borrowed had already been switched back to her earlier clothes. Kelli knew the way old friends do that Lynn was using humor to stay calm. She turned away from the men and patted Lynn's shoulder.

"You did good, Lynn," she said, tone void of any playful tease. "We're lucky to have you in our lives."

The dark-haired woman's expression softened. A small smile brought up the corners of her lips. She touched Kelli's hand.

"We're also lucky the storm kept Mark here." She glanced over to the ex-bodyguard. "He kept calm, really calm."

Kelli nodded at that. "It used to be his job."

"I guess it was good timing you invited him for dinner. Though maybe next time you invite him somewhere, you should go ahead and invite the cops, too."

Kelli wanted to tell Lynn right then that she believed the mugging and the break-in were a result of Victor's work, but at the same time she knew she wouldn't tell her. Lynn had been her confidant since before puberty. Apart from Grace, there was no one she loved more in the world. Telling Lynn that she might have stumbled across a conspiracy that had gotten her husband killed was getting the woman too close to danger. Lynn hurt— or worse—was an unimaginable danger she wanted to avoid at all costs.

Right then and there, Kelli made up her mind to keep Lynn in the dark.

"Kelli?" Mark called after the officers went back to their car to retrieve their camera. The ex-bodyguard, still shoeless and in his undershirt, met her in the middle of the living room with a face filled with concentration. Grace put her cheek back on her mother's shoulder but turned her head to watch the man speak. She was always curious. "They said they're going to take some pictures for evidence and finish taking both of our statements. They put out an APB for the man and have a patrol car looking, but if that guy is half as smart as I think he is, he'll have used the weather to hide." Mark paused, giving a quick smile to the little girl before sobering again. "That being said, I think it might be best if you don't stay here tonight."

"Oh, don't worry, we won't," she agreed. "Lynn already offered us her guest bedroom. Though…" Kelli placed her hand on Grace's back and began to rub it, the motion soothing her probably more than the girl. "I wasn't at home last night when I was mugged, Mark. What if we're right and someone is after the journal? What if they keep coming after me—after us—until they find it? Being across the city won't make a difference. We'll still be in danger."

It was a dark thought but also a real possibility. Keeping her family safe was all that mattered, and now she wasn't sure how to keep doing it.

Mark didn't immediately respond. His dark eyes were trying to have a conversation with her that she couldn't exactly understand. One that drew his brow together and thinned his lips before he finally spoke.

"Then we'll have to figure out who is after it and why," he decided. The decisive *we* he inserted filled her with an odd excitement. As well as relief. Sharing the burden of fear—no matter the degree of selfishness—made the situation less terrifying.

"But what about until we do?" She paused her rubbing motion on Grace's back. "How do we stay safe?"

"I know someone who might help with that."

Mark moved this way and that—trying to get comfortable. The front seat didn't give. He let out a long exhalation. Instead of trying a new position, he let his body become still again. The street outside Lynn's town house was quiet after the storm. He sat in Kelli's car. Lynn's neighbors paid Mark no mind if they saw him, which he doubted.

He'd been sitting there since he'd driven the tired women over. After the police had left and they'd put up a makeshift tarp over Kelli's broken window, Kelli had pulled him aside to let him know just how much she didn't want to involve Lynn. Not until they had concrete proof.

"I want to keep her safe, and isn't ignorance bliss?" she had said with fake humor. It had disappeared quickly. *"Plus, she's taken on a lot with Grace and me since Victor's death. I—I have to be certain before I drag her in."*

Mark saw the reason in her desire to keep her best friend in the dark. If he could, he'd keep Kelli out of the loop, too. But whoever was after the journal certainly hadn't thought twice about making contact with her. The fact that the man had known the house was filled with the young family and Lynn, and had come in armed anyway was something that made his blood boil.

The Cranes had already been through enough.

Mark rolled his shoulders back and stifled a yawn. His eyes fell to the journal on his lap. Kelli had offered the evidence to him so she wouldn't be alone in knowing what Victor had once known, too. It was strange to read the man's notes in a way. Seeing the words he had written and knowing that the journalist knew nothing of his tragic fate made the guilt in Mark rise to the surface. If only he could have stopped the man in black…

Just as another yawn was making its way through Mark, the front door of Lynn's town house opened. Kelli, dressed in a blue T-shirt from the Dallas Zoo and jeans, walked out with two cups in her hands. Her short hair hung darker, wet from an apparent shower, but she clearly had makeup on. A messenger bag was slung across her chest. The closer she came, the more he realized he was drinking in all of her details. Shifting in his seat, as if that could ease the sudden guilt, he unlocked the passenger door and pasted on a smile.

"I'm going to assume you're tired," Kelli greeted him, not pausing as she got in the car. "I'm also going to assume you're a fan of coffee with a lot of sugar." She handed the cup over, and he laughed.

"I'm not one to turn down free sugary coffee."

Kelli smiled, pleased.

"Nothing out of the ordinary here?" she swiveled her head around to see both directions of the street. He already knew what it looked like. The scenery would change when people began to leave for work.

"Thankfully it's been pretty quiet."

"How do you not lose your mind sitting here for hours with nothing happening? Let alone stay awake?" Kelli's eyebrows pinched in question. It was something he'd been asked countless times while on the job with Orion.

"Years of experience, I guess." He held up the journal as an example of some of what he'd done and passed it to her. She silently placed it in her purse, but Mark could see she wanted more, so he brought up another man from his past. "A friend I worked with at Orion, Oliver, used to tell me the key to keeping focused and sharp—no matter where or what case you were working—was to keep rescanning your environment over and over again as if it was the first time you'd seen it. Because, and I quote, 'It's the little things that change and bite you in the ass.'" He smiled. "Pardon my French, but that's pretty much how I've worked for years. Making sure none of the details go unnoticed can keep a person busy, even if nothing changes." Mark couldn't help but think about the night at the cabin. He'd done the same thing both inside and outside the cabin, and yet…

"Details. I'm not so good at those," Kelli said, taking a big sip of coffee. "I think having a toddler has fried my brain."

"She's pretty cool. Grace, that is." Mark motioned to the house. "She seems like a sharp kid for her age."

"Thanks. I think so, too."

A different kind of smile wound up the corners of the woman's lips. Pride mixed with unmistakable love. Guilt for not being able to protect the father of the family was replaced by an ache of loneliness within him. It caught him off guard. He didn't like it.

"So, what's on the docket for the day?" Mark changed the subject but was annoyed that the feeling stayed.

"Lynn is watching Grace—because she's a wonderful person—while I go to talk to Dennis Crawford. I told her we were tying up some break-in loose ends."

Mark's eyebrow rose. "That name sounds familiar," he said.

Kelli's expression hardened behind her coffee cup.

"He was Victor's editor for the Bowman Foundation spotlight," she explained. "He's also the only person other than you whom I've brought up my concerns to. And since I'm pretty certain you weren't the person who mugged me and then broke into my house..."

"You think he knows something," Mark finished.

"Or is our culprit."

"So you're going to go and—what—confront the man you think is behind it all?" Even as he asked, he realized that was exactly what Kelli intended to do. "Kelli, if this guy *is* behind this whole thing, then going to see him is dangerous."

Kelli fixed him with a pointed stare. "Good thing I have a bodyguard, then."

Her comment was playful, but it created a storm of

emotions inside him. As with his comment about her daughter being smart, he felt an ounce of pride, a measure of pleasure and the ever-present blanket of guilt beneath both. Without knowing what he was about to say, he was glad he didn't have to respond right away. A car pulled up in front of them. It drew Kelli's attention away from him.

"Speaking of bodyguards."

Chapter Nine

Jonathan Carmichael didn't look like a bodyguard at first glance. Although he was muscled and had an unmistakable set to his jaw that spoke of discipline and determination, he was leaner and taller than his original teammates, Mark and Oliver. From personal experience, Mark knew that even though the black-haired man looked slight next to him, his physical appearance didn't diminish the man's abilities. He was the rock of their once-close group. Always sensible, always strong.

Jonathan Carmichael was the guy who surprised everyone.

Seeing him cut his engine and get out of the car, waiting for Mark to make his way over, was definitely something Mark hadn't realized he missed. In a way it felt as though they were getting ready for a job—though he supposed that was kind of what they *were* doing.

"Long time, no see," Jonathan greeted him. He extended his hand and they shook. "I see your scruff has gotten better." He motioned to Mark's chin and his five-o'clock shadow. It made Mark laugh.

"I actually shaved yesterday. I was trying to do you proud," he joked back. Mark had wondered what their first meeting since the last time he'd seen him—at least six months ago—would be like. He was glad Jonathan seemed to be there with humor rather than anger. The past was more than creeping up on Mark. He couldn't take another problem to think about. "Thanks for coming on such short notice and with little to no explanation."

Jonathan shrugged, glancing at Kelli, who was still sitting in the car.

"We may not be hanging out like we used to, but I can still tell when you're spooked."

"I can't deny that this whole thing is...unsettling." It was his turn to look back at Kelli. "And that one is a firecracker. She won't back down, and I—well, I need to keep her and her family safe, and I can't do that by myself right now."

Jonathan, the middle ground between Oliver's compassion and Mark's normally stoic reasoning, nodded, while a twitch of his lips pulled up at the corner, moving his impeccable goatee.

"Well, I'm happy to help. But—" Jonathan lowered his voice, not to show he was trying to be secretive but instead to convey seriousness "—I'm able to be here because Nikki moved a contract around. She didn't question me getting out of work, but she expects an answer why. And we both know she deserves one."

Mark knew as soon as he'd called Jonathan the night before that eventually he'd have to talk with Nikki again. Still he sighed.

"I know," he admitted.

"Good. Now, tell *me* what's going on."

KELLI WAS TRYING not to pout. She was almost thirty, for goodness' sake, yet there she was, riding shotgun to the

Orion Security Group, trying her best not to show she was ribbed about not getting to go confront the potential culprit. Mark was quiet—ignoring the fact that she was upset she hadn't gotten her way.

"I remember him—Jonathan—from when I first came into Orion," she said when she could no longer stand the quiet. "His résumé was impressive, and if I remember correctly, he was one of the original Orion agents? Like you?"

Mark gave a half smile. There was no doubt in Kelli's mind that he'd been hiding his emotions since they'd reconnected—maybe a trade secret of the security business—but she could see his feelings for his friend were genuine.

"Yes, Jonathan and I were a part of the first team at Orion. Along with Oliver Quinn."

"The man who helped the private investigator catch a killer in Maine," she supplied. "That's how we heard of Orion in the first place. It was all over the news."

Mark chuckled. "Fun fact—that private investigator is now his wife."

"Really?"

"They were childhood sweethearts who reconnected after a long time. He now runs the freelance division of Orion, dealing with specialists and strategists who might be needed."

"What about his wife? Is she still a private investigator?"

Mark nodded. "Oh, yeah, you couldn't get her to stop if you begged. But Oliver never did. And between you and me, I think they help each other on their respective cases."

"Sounds like you're in with a well-connected crowd."

Mark's smile wavered.

"I was. Orion wasn't the only thing I distanced myself from when I quit." His jaw hardened as he said it. His eyes stayed on the road ahead. Kelli wanted to pry—to understand the motive behind him leaving—but she felt she already knew the reason. Mark had done so much for her in the past two days that she decided not to make him open old wounds.

Victor's death had changed more than just her life.

ORION SECURITY GROUP's main office looked more or less the same as it had all those years ago when it had first opened. A modest one-story standalone wrapped in brick and beige siding, Orion's name was painted in large white letters above the door that, as Nikki had said, made it feel as if Orion was watching over you as you entered the business. As they walked inside, Mark eyed these letters with nostalgia.

The lobby, like the building, was modest in size and decoration. A young Hispanic woman named Jillian sat behind a desk that broke up the space between the front door and the rest of the office. She acted as its part-time guard and had been there for almost three years. When she saw them, her already fifteen-hundred-watt smile brightened.

"Mark!" Within the space of a heartbeat, Jillian was around her desk and hugging him. Kelli raised her eyebrow but was soon enveloped in a hug of her own. "Hello, Mrs. Crane!" Mark shared a look over the girl's head that he hoped said, "I'll explain later."

Jillian backed off.

"Nikki told me you were coming in," she said, still all smiles. "It's been a long time since I've seen either of you." Her eyes flitted over Kelli. "I sent some flowers but I never got to tell you—in person—sorry for your loss of Victor."

Kelli didn't skip a beat. "Thank you."

Jillian turned back to Mark, somberness gone. "I'm glad you're back. It hasn't been the same around here without you."

"Thanks, but don't get used to this. I'm just here to talk with the boss."

She gave a small nod and threw her thumb over her shoulder. "She's all yours, but I'll warn you, she hasn't had her coffee yet."

Mark let out a breath. Just what he needed. A Nikki without her heavenly coffee.

"Who was that?" Kelli whispered. They were walking past Oliver Quinn's old office and Jonathan's current empty one. Mark's, or what used to be his, was opposite. Though Orion had expanded and no longer operated solely within teams, team leads still had their own offices. Even if they weren't around long enough to use them.

"Right before Orion first started its expansion, Jillian showed up asking if we had an internship program," he explained. "We didn't, but she made a compelling case. Now she's the part-time secretary while she takes college cybersecurity classes. She's a nice girl—tough as nails."

Kelli looked over her shoulder. A smile turned up her lips. "I can see why Nikki likes her, then."

They made it past the open area between the break room and the workout room—what Jonathan had once likened to the grazing field where agents would spend their downtime hanging out on the couches or watching sports on the wall-mounted TV—right up to the last office in the building. It was large, with three of its walls made of glass. Nikki's dark red hair could be seen bobbing behind the computer screen on the desk in the middle of the room.

"Should I wait out here? Or—" Kelli motioned to the couches behind them. Instead of looking as if she was afraid of the often intimidating Nikki Waters, Kelli merely seemed to be respectful of their privacy. But if he was ever going to sell his former boss on the theory that Victor's piece on a charity had gotten him killed, he needed the widow to back him up.

"If you don't mind, I think we should both tell her what's going on."

Kelli lowered her voice, even though Jillian and Nikki were the only other people they'd seen in the entire building.

"Do you think it's a good idea to tell someone else? We've already told Jonathan."

Mark had thought it over during the car ride.

"Keeping Nikki in the dark would be much harder to do since we're using Jonathan for help. She'd give us more trouble than we need right now. Plus, she can be one hell of an ally."

"All right," Kelli concluded. "I trust you."

Guilt exploded within his chest. Those three little words stabbed at his heart. Probing the spot that reminded him Victor Crane had also trusted him. He adjusted his smile—sure that it had sagged—and knocked on the door.

"Come in," his former boss called.

Mark took a deep breath, and together they went inside.

NIKKI'S HAIR WAS longer than when Kelli had first met her years ago, but she still had kind eyes, only hardening when needed. She came around the desk with her hand outstretched.

"Nice to see you again, Kelli," she said. Her grip was gentle yet firm. Nikki waved them to the seats opposite her.

"I'm glad you've come by," she started, bypassing any small talk. "To say I'm curious why you two are hanging out is an understatement."

Mark shifted in his seat. Kelli wondered if he was worried about whether Nikki would believe their story or just about her reaction to it. The woman who had gone from secretary to founder and boss of a successful—and moral—security group had to be tough.

How tough, Kelli was about to find out.

Mark straightened his back and dove right in. He rehashed his belief that Darwin hadn't set the fire and explained why they thought the mugging, the break-in and Dennis Crawford were all somehow connected.

"That's why I wanted to ask to have a check done on him," Mark said. "He knows something that could help us figure out what's going on."

Nikki threaded her fingers together over the desktop. "You have no evidence whatsoever that ties Dennis to the fire. You have a theory, one that's loose, and built *and* propelled by grief." She shared a look between them before stopping on Kelli. "I am truly sorry for your loss, and can't imagine what you have had to go through. I'm also sorry that the past few days have been less than great."

She turned back to Mark. "You spent a solid year

looking for your man in black. During that year you
quit your job, quit your friends and came up with what?
Nothing but a box filled with files that lead you to nowhere but self-isolation. I'm sorry, but I won't help you
go back to that world, if only for the basic reason that
you no longer work at Orion and will not receive its benefits." In one fluid movement, Nikki stood and moved
to the office door. She held it open. "There is such a
thing as coincidences and bad luck and timing, and I
think that's all it is."

Kelli didn't need look at Mark to know that the conversation was through. They would not be getting Nikki's
help. They would not be granted a reprieve. She followed
the man out with only a nod to Nikki as they passed.

Jillian didn't stop them as they left through the lobby,
and Mark didn't even say goodbye. Kelli couldn't tell if
he was mad, disappointed or embarrassed. Whatever he
was feeling, he was definitely silent as they drove away.

It was a silence that Kelli couldn't take for long.

"So, Nikki mentioned you had a box of files on the
fire that killed Victor?"

Mark took in a long breath before letting it go out
in a whoosh.

"Yes. Everything I collected in the year after." He
lowered his voice as if he was being scolded for a mistake. "I was looking for something—*anything*—that
could help me—" he paused "—understand." Kelli
knew the look of guilt he was trying to hide. It was
one she was starting to feel when looking at Mark. Not
because he couldn't save Victor, but because of what she
realized she was starting to feel for the ex-bodyguard.
Instead of trying to sort her thoughts out on the future,
she tried to focus on the present.

"I'd like to see that box, if you don't mind."

"Really?"

"Yes. Let's figure out why Darwin McGregor lied."

MARK DISAPPEARED INTO his bedroom for a few minutes. He wouldn't tell her where the box of files was, but she had a sneaking suspicion it was well hidden.

Kelli took the time to check in on Lynn and Grace. Both were watching cartoons in their pajamas. One reason why Lynn made such a great babysitter was that she was a grown-up child herself. Sometimes Grace had to let her know when *she* was done playing.

Lynn thankfully didn't ask too many questions. Kelli let the woman keep thinking she was dealing with the break-in and house issues for the day. Which wasn't too far from the truth. Finding out who wanted the journal was intrinsically tied to the break-in.

"Sorry," Mark said, breaking the silence. "I was a little too nondescript when labeling this. Not to mention I think I might have tried to hide it from myself." He put a box on the coffee table and took the seat next to her on the couch.

"I see what you meant about being nondescript," she commented. The box was devoid of any telling signs of what might be inside. It was an utterly ordinary brown with the top taped down. He pulled a pocketknife from his jeans but set it on the table.

"Are you sure you want to see all of this?" he asked, keeping his gaze on the box. "To say this isn't filled with bad memories would be a lie."

For one long moment, Kelli considered his words. She had been excited at the idea that Mark had files that could lead them to who was behind Victor's death and attempting to steal his journal. Yet it wasn't until that moment that she realized the past was neatly packed up a few inches from her. Was she ready to face tangible proof of the past instead of the memories that still haunted her at any mention or sight of smoke?

"No, I need to do this," she decided. "If not to find justice for Victor, then to ensure Grace's safety."

"Then, here we go."

Chapter Ten

"So give me *your* summary on all of this." Kelli waved her hand over the papers and pictures on the coffee table. They had spent the past half hour in silence, each combing through what Mark had collected. Most notable were the copies of the police report on Darwin McGregor, the rough sketch Mark had drawn of the man he claimed was responsible, and Orion's origin file on Victor and Kelli. She'd only glanced at that last one, pushing it to the side to look at later.

Mark ran his hand across the stubble on his chin and put down the pictures in his hand. They were of Victor's family cabin the day after the fire. She'd already glanced at those, too, but decided to keep her distance. On her darkest days, she could sometimes close her eyes and see the flames devouring the structure during the dead of night.

"On the surface it's simple," he started. "A dumb kid who likes starting fires sets fire to a cabin. In the process he blows up the propane tank. Which sets off a chain reaction that eventually destroys the entire place…and a man is killed because of it." He didn't pause, and Kelli was grateful for it. "He confesses in court that he intended to set the fire and—bonus—it's not his first one, so he's tried as an adult and sent to prison. Then everyone forgets about it. Well, you know what I mean."

He put his hand on the paper closest to him—the sketch of the man. "But I saw a man in black, bigger than the boy, spreading the fire. A man no one else thought existed." His eyes rounded a fraction. "A man I now realize bears a striking resemblance to the man who broke into your house last night." Kelli tried to interrupt, but Mark continued. "He set the fire, *intending* to have no survivors, and then disappeared. Darwin wasn't caught until the next morning, miles away from the cabin. Do you remember how he acted in court?"

Kelli didn't have to think hard. "Crude."

Mark nodded. "He certainly wasn't trying to sell that he was sorry for what he'd done. Even with his grandmother looking on the entire time."

Kelli remembered the young man's lack of empathy as he recounted setting the fires, later answering without pause that it wasn't the first time. He hadn't shown an ounce of regret despite claiming that he knew exactly what his actions had cost Kelli and her unborn child.

She cleared her throat. "I remember hearing her cry," she said. The sound of the older woman crying had created a background noise that had competed with Kelli's own sobs. Before Grace had been born, she hadn't always been rock solid. Then again, no one had expected her to be.

"She raised Darwin," Mark said. "I think he was the only family he had. I looked her up out of curiosity a few months after the trial. She's holed up in some lakeside retirement home."

That caught Kelli's attention.

"Lakeside retirement home?" she asked, pulling out her phone. "Do you know the name of it, by chance?"

"Uh, something about an apple? I can't remember, but I know it's just outside Wilmington, North Carolina. Darwin was a local there." Kelli pulled up the search browser on her phone. "Why?"

She put up a finger to tell him to wait. Her heartbeat started to speed up. Close to a clue? Reaching? She didn't know which was more accurate. But when she found what she was looking for she made a noise that was caught between an *aha* and a gasp.

"Appleton Retreat," she said, handing her phone over. The website for the retirement home was pulled up. Its gallery of photos were on a slideshow on the homepage.

"Okay…what am I looking at, exactly?"

"Darwin didn't hire a lawyer. One was appointed to him, right? Do you remember why?" She knew the answer but wanted to verify what she *thought* she knew.

"They couldn't afford one. Something about her medical bills before the fire."

Kelli motioned to the phone.

"And now, less than two years later, she's living in a retirement home for the wealthy?"

Mark quieted as he looked through the pictures.

"Darwin and she lived in an apartment together before the fire. I remember him being asked about his residence while on stand." She held back a shudder. She didn't like recalling so many details about the trial. Yet here she was trying to remember all of the pieces. "If she was in debt with medical bills and Darwin was truly her only living relative…"

"Then how did she get the money for Appleton Retreat?" Mark finished.

She snapped her fingers. "Maybe that's why you saw a different man spreading the fire, and why Darwin didn't argue with what was going on."

Mark raised his brow before he voiced it.

"Because Darwin McGregor was paid to take the fall," he said.

Kelli nodded so adamantly that her hair swished back and forth along her cheeks.

"How much do you want to bet that her medical bills disappeared, too? How can we even find that out?" Kelli's thoughts were going faster than her reason. She certainly didn't want to give the woman a call and ask. First, that would sound alarm bells for whoever was behind this newly formed yet becoming-more-real theory. Second, Mark and Kelli definitely were the last people who should be the ones to talk to her. Even if her grandson hadn't actually committed the crime, he was definitely paying for it. Just thinking about talking to the woman started a soft loop of her sobs from the courtroom playing in the background of her memory.

Mark rubbed at his facial stubble again, falling into deep thought. He was picking his words carefully when he finally spoke.

"I may have a friend who can help us answer those questions. Though…I don't know how legal it will be."

Caught off guard, Kelli chuckled.

"Let me guess, another bodyguard friend?" she asked, already picturing the imaginary man sitting behind one of the desks she had seen in Orion earlier.

"Close, but no cigar." He handed her back her phone and pulled his out.

"So, no Orion agent?"

"No. His wife."

"Acuity Investigations. Darling Quinn here."

Mark cleared his throat as a voice he hadn't heard in half a year floated through the earpiece.

"Hey, Darling, it's Mark. Mark Tranton."

There was a noticeable pause on the other end.

"I'm not going to pretend I'm *not* surprised right now," she replied. Her tone was light and, if he wasn't mistaken, he could hear a smile in her voice. Mark relaxed his shoulders a fraction. Oliver Quinn's wife had always been a vocal woman—even before they'd married the year before—never shying away from her opinion. If she had wanted to scold him for his lack of communication with Oliver, Darling wouldn't have held off to be polite. Instead, the light tone turned concerned quickly. "Is everything all right? Is something wrong with Nikki?"

"No, no! Everything—and everyone—is fine," he assured her. "I just have a favor to ask. I know I probably don't deserve one, but if you could at least hear me out, that would mean a lot."

There was less hesitation in her reply this time. Instead of concern or cheer, Mark could hear the woman slip into work mode. Darling Quinn was a private investigator and a damn good one.

"Shoot."

"We're looking into an old case," he started. Kelli's eyes were wide with anticipation. "We think someone might have been paid off to take the fall for a fire. But… well, we don't have proof. Just the theory."

"So where is the fall guy now?"

"Prison."

Mark could almost hear Darling's gears turning. He remembered the first time he had met the private investigator. He had flown to her town in Maine to celebrate Orion's impending expansion as well as Oliver's promotion to head of the new freelancer branch. Darling had been kind, hilarious and unstoppable. It was apparent that Oliver had found his other half—the perfect partner in crime. A thread of longing started to unravel in Mark as he remembered the thought. His eyes traveled to Kelli's. Swirling pools of green and gray stared evenly at him.

Could Kelli be a perfect partner for him?

Where had that thought come from?

"Mark?" Darling asked, bringing his attention back. He looked away from Kelli.

"Yeah, sorry. What did you say?"

"I said, why do you think he was paid off, then?"

"His grandmother—his only family and the woman who raised him—went from close to poverty to living in one of those retirement homes that price gouge. You know, the ones that have the resort amenities. All after the guy's trial happened and he was found guilty."

"Curious," Darling whispered. "So you need to see the grandmother's and grandson's financials to know if he got paid and then gave it to her, or if she maybe got directly paid."

"And, if you can, the person fronting the bill."

"I guess I shouldn't remind you that tracking financials on a case I'm not currently on and without permission isn't the most *ethical* thing to do."

Mark nodded, though she couldn't see. "I wouldn't ask if it wasn't extremely important."

Darling let out a long exhalation that he didn't miss. There was movement, and soon he heard the sound of fingers clicking against a computer keyboard. "You're lucky that Oliver is working something with Deputy Derrick right now. He'd tell me to ask more questions before I agree."

"Do you want to ask more questions?"

Darling snorted. "Too many questions sometimes degrade the degree of anonymity I like working under. Just give me the names of the grandson and grandmother, and the date of the trial."

Mark did as he was told. He gave Kelli a thumbs-up in the process.

"Thank you for this, Darling," he said after she repeated the information for accuracy. "It means a lot."

"Don't thank me—though you can later when I get back with the information. Thank Oliver. Although you've left him hanging, he hasn't stopped telling stories of the glory days."

Mark wanted to say something—something that would take away the guilt her words brought—but he couldn't find an explanation for the fact that he'd pushed his closest friends away. Instead, he thanked her again.

"I can't guarantee I'll have the info tonight, but I should be able to score it by tomorrow," she said, already typing again. "Like you, I have to call a favor in."

"No problem."

"And Mark, you know I can't keep this from Oliver," she added, voice serious. "But…there's no need to call him while we're both working. I'll just wait until he comes by after work."

"Thank you, Darling."

It was her turn to say, "No problem."

"So?" Kelli asked after they ended the call. "She'll look into the financials?"

"That's what she said."

"Wow. Just like that?" Mark scanned Kelli's face when he thought he heard a touch of jealousy in her voice. She merely tilted her head in question.

"I think Darling just likes a good mystery." Mark shrugged, hoping his expression didn't betray what he was feeling.

"Like the case against that millionaire in Maine?"

Mark laughed. "Exactly."

"I can't just wait for her to call back," she said with notable irritation. "I can't just sit still. I need to do *something*!"

Mark's thoughts led directly to the bedroom. It was so sudden and out of nowhere that he felt his expression change without the consent of his brain. How was it that the woman in front of him—wearing a zoo T-shirt and ready to pass out hell to anyone who threatened her family—could evoke such strong feelings apropos of nothing? How could he even entertain the idea of feelings for her, of any kind, when it was *his* fault that she was a widow?

Whether or not Kelli noticed the change in his demeanor, she didn't say. Instead, she slapped her hands together after a moment. A grin broke out over her lips.

"I have an idea!"

Chapter Eleven

"Can I go on record and say I really, really don't like this idea?"

Mark passed his binoculars back to Kelli, who was seated in the driver's side of her car. She was practically bouncing in anticipation.

"Believe me, you've already told me," she said with a quick smile. "Just remember—you could have said no to coming along."

Mark snorted. "Something tells me you would have still come."

He was right. She probably still would have come. But would she have gone inside? Without any backup? Probably not. If something happened to Kelli, then Grace would grow up without a mother or a father. That idea alone kept Kelli on edge as she took in the three-story building in front of them.

The Bowman Foundation's office was housed in a modern-style building on the edge of the Design District. One of the many relatively new buildings that had sprung up in the past ten years or so, the slick white office stood like a beacon of hope that welcomed those who passed by on their way to visit a market or bar, yet still added to the urban feel the District had cultivated perfectly. It was one of the many reasons the Bowman Foundation had blossomed as much as it had since Victor's spotlight had been published.

The Bowman Foundation wasn't just a charity aimed at eliminating poverty in Dallas. It was a welcoming destination to all who wanted to create a difference in the world.

"It makes you feel good when you look at it," Kelli commented, her eyes roaming the steel sans serif letters that composed the charity's name. "Doesn't it?"

Mark didn't bother lying. "It makes me want to help people," he admitted.

Kelli nodded, frowning. Could such an inspiring organization really be connected to Victor's death?

Mark placed his hand on hers. The contact caused her to jump, but not so badly that he addressed it.

"But I don't need to look at a building to want to help you," Mark said, squeezing her hand. The pressure started a fire that traveled up her arm and right into her face. With her cheeks fully heated, she gave him a small smile.

"We're going to find out what's going on," he said, "and we're going to keep you and Grace safe. This— this building—is just drywall and paint. You are much more inspiring."

Mark's voice was so firm, so sure, that it infused her with a feeling of confidence.

And something else.

He withdrew his hand and the moment, whatever it had been, was gone.

"Now let's go, as you said earlier, 'snoop.'" He shook his head. "I can't believe I said that."

The interior of Bowman was all clean lines, shiny

surfaces and pops of color. It was more trendy than its exterior. Kelli almost forgot for a second that they were inside the office building of a charity.

A woman with a low scoop-neck black blouse and cheetah-print pencil skirt smiled at them from behind a desk that stood next to the open stairwell and single elevator. She broke her conversation with a man in a suit to greet them as they walked up.

"Welcome to the Bowman Foundation. My name is Karen." She surprised Kelli by offering her hand to the two of them. They each shook. "How may I help you today?"

The man in the suit was polite enough to pull out his phone and seem busy. Kelli cleared her throat, jumping into the plan they had agreed upon on the ride over.

"Hi, my name is Kelli Crane and this—"

Karen's eyes widened in recognition. That also surprised Kelli.

"As in, wife of Victor Crane?" she asked. The suit looked up from his phone.

A twinge of sadness hit her as she answered, "Yes, once upon a time."

Karen sobered. "I'm so sorry for your loss."

Kelli shared a look with Mark.

"Thanks," she responded. "Forgive me, but I'm a little surprised you recognized me." Unless Karen was in on whatever was happening, Kelli thought a second too late.

Karen dropped her head a fraction. "To be honest, it was the name. I pass by that picture every day."

Kelli was confused. "The picture?" she asked.

Karen was clearly taken aback. "You haven't seen the press hallway?"

Kelli shook her head. "This is the first time I've been here," she answered honestly. She'd been invited to take a tour after their building opened to the public, but memorizing Victor's last article had been a lot different than visiting Bowman. Reading the words was easier than seeing the physical place they related to. But now that was the plan. "That's actually why we're here." Kelli motioned back to Mark. "This is my friend Mark Tranton. We both realized we had never taken a tour and were wondering if we could now?"

"Of course! Give me a quick second, if you don't mind!"

Karen hurried to the man in the suit, handing him a file before using her phone to call someone Kelli assumed was in the building. Not wanting to appear as though she was snooping—the whole reason she'd come—she fell back a step to Mark's side. The ex-bodyguard had gone tense. Kelli didn't know if that was because he was nervous or preparing himself. For what, she also didn't know, but she was grateful he was on her side.

"The press hallway?" he said through the side of his mouth.

"Yeah, I'm definitely curious now."

They waited as Karen spoke softly into the phone and the man in the suit retreated into the elevator. His interest in Kelli's name seemed to have only been a momentary thing. He didn't look up from his file as the door slid closed in front of him.

"Okay, if you're ready," Karen almost sang as she stood back up. "I'd like to start the tour by showing you the press hallway."

"All right." Kelli followed beside Karen while Mark

was a few steps behind her. She recognized his reflex to keep her safe. She wondered if that was a reaction specifically for her or if he would do it with anyone who might be in danger.

"The main floor of the Bowman Foundation is perhaps the most popular with the general public," Karen began, apparently *not* waiting until they got to the press hallway to start. "Bowman's CEO—Radford Bowman—believes that not only being out in the public but also interacting with them on a daily basis can make all the difference in keeping a community aware of its problems without bombarding them with guilt or scare tactics or propaganda to do the right thing."

The hallway they had been walking down opened into a large room. With floor-to-ceiling, wide, frameless windows on the opposite exterior walls, the space made what was clearly designated as a lounge area feel bright and airy. As though all your troubles wouldn't stand up against such cheery surroundings. Even the occasional art piece with a quote about compassion, helping people or volunteering didn't distract from what the place was trying to accomplish.

Subtle awareness. Ample comfort.

"Wow," Kelli said as they stopped to take it in.

"The Bowman Foundation allows for this space to be open to the public for a place to relax, hang out or chat with foundation employees about what they can do to help. As you can see, we have a game area that's being utilized right now." In a sectioned-off corner of the room were a Ping-Pong table, two chess tables and a foosball table. Two young guys sat at one of the chess tables, heads bent in concentration. "We host free events with the options of donating or volunteering here, as well. The community never ceases to surprise us. We've gotten more in terms of donations from our free events than those you have to pay to get into. I know it's a little strange to give free rein to nonemployees, but by the same token, it's helped build a mutual trust and respect with those who come and take advantage of what we're offering."

"What *is* it you're offering?" Mark asked, not a curious inflection in the sentence, just a flat question. He didn't seem to approve of the grandeur, or maybe of Karen. Kelli thought she spoke of Bowman and their method of getting their community aware as a cult leader might. Sure, their end goal seemed admirable, but she couldn't shake the feeling that something felt off about it all.

Karen didn't bat a perfect eyelash at the underlying current of criticism in Mark's voice. Instead, her smile grew.

"The information to change the world without leaving your comfort zone." She turned back to the room and sighed, starting to walk again. "Isn't it wonderful?"

Mark was suddenly next to Kelli's ear.

"It sure is something," he whispered. His breath brushed against her neck and ear with such electricity that she had trouble making her feet follow Karen.

Whoa, Kelli thought, body heating. A simple whisper had stirred something she hadn't realized could stir. At least not yet. Shaking her head to try and rid herself of the unexpected feeling, she moved forward and tried to focus.

They walked the rest of the way through the lounge and then into another hallway that turned right. Kelli thought back to Victor's article as Karen slowed. The

Bowman Foundation walked a fine line between the give-everything-we-own-to-help-people and let's-make-money-to-give-money mentalities. He had written that this struggle was a rare one for an organization headed by a wealthy man like Radford Bowman to have. A man like that—working his hands to the bone to rise from poverty and mediocrity, proving to everyone around him that he wasn't defined that easily—was a champion to those less fortunate. An everyday man who had become much more and could go live on an island drinking mai tais for the rest of his life but had chosen to try to make his city—his home—a better place for everyone to live. That was what made Radford Bowman a good man, and that's what made the Bowman Foundation a good organization.

Just recalling Victor's words gave her goose bumps. He had been a talented writer. He had also been a good man.

Now he was dead, and somehow the two were connected.

"The press hallway was originally supposed to be a room open to the public," Karen said as they took another turn. It brought them to a hallway that must have run parallel with the front lobby. More wide, wall-length paneless windows lined the wall to their left, while the wall to their right was covered in plaques, framed articles and pictures. "But Mr. Bowman thought it would be a better this way. He said that seeing what the foundation could accomplish shouldn't be a destination. It should be part of the journey—seeing what we can do, whom we can help—while on the way to meeting the team who could do it." She motioned to the door at the very end of the hallway. "Mr. Bowman's office."

"He doesn't use one of the other two floors?" Mark asked, clearly surprised.

Karen shook her head. Pride was evident in her reaction. "He wants everyone to be able to reach him. Sure, he could have a much bigger, better office suite upstairs, but that's just not his style." She practically beamed as she continued down the hallway to that door, pointing out a few of the articles on the wall. But Kelli had eyes only for one picture.

"Mr. Bowman thought it appropriate to dedicate a different space for this," Karen said, voice tender. They had stopped in front of a stretch of wall that squeezed Kelli's heart before she even could take it all in.

In Memory of Victor Crane was written above Victor's entire article, printed directly on the wall. Beneath that were inscribed the years he had been born and died, like his tombstone. Below that was a note that he had been survived by his wife and daughter, names excluded.

However, it was the picture that hung above it all in a beautiful golden frame that caught and held her attention so raptly. Without thinking, without being given permission, Kelli moved closer and touched the glass.

Victor Crane, frozen in time, smiled back.

And suddenly Kelli was crying.

"I'm really, really sorry again," Karen said. "I thought it would—I don't know—make her happy to see that we honored him, you know?"

But it hadn't. Kelli had broken down, only barely excusing herself to a nearby bathroom with tears streaming down her face. It was outside that bathroom that

Mark and Karen now stood. Karen, despite her cult-like love for Bowman, seemed genuinely upset in turn that she'd upset Kelli.

"Can you give us a second?" he asked, nodding to the closed door.

"Oh, yeah, sure. I need to check the front anyway." She pointed to a door in the middle of the hallway. "That leads back out to the lobby when you're ready."

"Thanks."

Karen cast one more worried look at the door before walking away. She pulled out her cell phone, already placing a call as she went through the door she had pointed out. Mark waited a few seconds before knocking on the bathroom door.

"Kelli, it's just me," he said, voice low. Mark marveled at how, after only a few days, he thought using "just me" would work. Seeing Victor's picture…seeing Kelli's reaction…reminded him that if he had saved Victor, too, he could have spared her the heartache. Ready to stand back and give Kelli her space, Mark was surprised when the door opened a crack.

"Come in," she said, voice low like his.

He did as he was told.

The single-occupancy bathroom was small but clean. Kelli backed up to the wall next to the sink and ran a hand over her eyes.

"I'm sorry," she said, voice still a little uneven. Mark shut the bathroom door behind him and moved uncertainly in front of her. He hadn't noticed until then that she'd been wearing mascara. Some of it had run beneath her eyes. "I just—I couldn't take it. Seeing that picture…" She put her hands over her eyes and bowed her head.

Mark, compelled by an emotion he couldn't quite define, closed the space between them. He put his arms around her. Never a man to put too much stock in his intimate actions, he hoped the contact—the embrace—would bring her a dose of comfort.

"It's okay," he whispered atop her head. He felt her body tense a moment. Maybe he *had* overstepped the boundaries of their new relationship.

Kelli wrapped her arms around the small of his back and buried her face in his chest. Soft cries filled the air, but Mark didn't interfere beyond holding her. If there was one thing he knew for a fact, it was that he couldn't protect her from the ache of missing her husband.

A pain that he was finding hurt him more than usual.

A few minutes went by before Kelli collected herself. Slowly she detached from him. Her mascara was really running now, but Mark found her impossibly beautiful.

"Are you okay?"

"Seeing Victor's picture…it opened an old wound, I admit. But I'm not sad. I'm angry," she explained, ice in her words. "I don't know a lot of things, but I do know one thing—my gut is right this time. This place—these people—they had something to do with Victor's death. And now? Now they have the gall to celebrate him with some kind of press gimmick?" Her expression turned fierce. Mark could clearly read her anger. "We have to figure out what's going on. And we have to do it now."

It wasn't until that moment that Mark realized the gravity of what they were trying to do. Or the lengths to which he would go to ensure that the Crane family got the justice they deserved.

And that Kelli and Grace would never be hurt again.

"You have my word, Kelli, that I will do everything in my power to help you. No matter what."

He meant every word.

Chapter Twelve

There was a man standing in the lobby when Kelli and Mark walked back in. She'd avoided looking at Victor's picture again. Her fear that her emotions would get the better of her again was too great. Especially considering the main emotion was unbridled anger. Mark led her out to Karen standing with the mystery man. He kept his back straight and fists slightly balled. Apparently the ex-bodyguard was now feeling that anger, too.

Kelli quickly touched one of Mark's hands before they stopped. It was her way of telling him to keep cool even though she'd just spent the past five minutes crying in the bathroom.

"I'm so sorry, Kelli," Karen said in a rush. "I didn't for one moment stop to think that seeing—well, that it might be hard."

Kelli held up her hand.

"It's not your fault," she said. "I'm sorry. I didn't realize it would be hard, either."

Karen seemed to take solace in that and gave her a little smile before turning to the man next to her.

Wearing a pressed gray button-up with a skinny black tie, a pair of pristine slacks and expensive-looking dress shoes, the man exuded importance. Older than Kelli, perhaps in his early forties, he had close-cropped black hair, brown eyes behind a pair of black-rimmed glasses and a dark complexion. His smile showed a mouth full of bright white teeth.

Maybe it was a requirement for working at Bowman.

"Kelli, Mark, this is Hector Mendez," Karen said. "He's the Bowman Foundation's publicist and PR genius."

Hector's smile widened as he shook their hands.

"I think you're taking privileges with that last title," he said, voice as cool as his attitude. "It's nice to meet you both and—" he exchanged a look with Kelli "—I'm sorry for our part in causing you any discomfort."

It was an oddly phrased apology, but she accepted it graciously. "Thank you."

"Now, Karen tells me you haven't been able to take the full tour?"

"No, I didn't make it past the hallway," Kelli joked, trying to lighten the anger she felt building inside her again. Whether it was lingering emotions or something altogether new, she couldn't tell. But she knew she wanted to leave.

"Maybe we can reschedule, if you wouldn't mind," Mark intercepted. His hand bumped hers, and she was surprised her hand was fisted.

Play it cool, Kel.

Hector didn't seem to notice the small movement.

"How about this?" The publicist walked over to Karen's desk and pulled an envelope from a drawer. He handed it to Kelli. "I know it's short notice, but the Bowman Foundation has a dinner each year to thank and celebrate those who have contributed to us. It's formal but lots of fun. It's tomorrow—again, sorry, short notice—but why don't you two come? We can certainly do another tour if you're feeling up to it then?" Before they could answer, he added, "Our fearless CEO will, of course, be there, as well as Dennis Crawford."

That caught Kelli off guard. She scrambled to close her mouth. Had Dennis asked the Bowman Foundation about the article even though he'd told her there was no story there?

"Dennis Crawford?"

Hector looked temporarily confused. "Oh, I'm sorry. I was under the impression you two were friends? He speaks highly of you."

Kelli was quick to hide her surprise this time. She smiled. "He was closer to Victor than me, but I'll look forward to seeing him tomorrow."

Mark cut his eyes to her before adding, "Thank you for the invitation. We can't wait."

"Great," Hector exclaimed, clapping his hands together. "It should be fun!"

They said their goodbyes, and Mark and Kelli went back to the car. They didn't speak until the Bowman Foundation's building was in the rearview.

"Well, that was a roller coaster of emotions," Kelli said, breaking the silence. Her mind was being pulled in several directions, trying to figure out which thought to focus on first. She chose the mention of Dennis. "When I talked to Mr. Crawford the other day, he assured me that nothing was wrong but then wanted to see Victor's journal. I get mugged and then the house gets broken into a day later by people who probably are after the same journal. And now the publicist for the Bowman Foundation pointedly mentions Dennis will be at the dinner?"

She ran a hand through her hair. A flowery scent wafted off, reminding her of the impulse decision to use Lynn's "sexy-scented" shampoo that morning. Her motivation behind *that* action made her face grow momentarily hot.

"As a former bodyguard, I've got to tell you going to the dinner tomorrow might be a bad idea," Mark said. "Especially if the one person we suspect has a part in all of this will definitely be there."

"But that's why we need to go!" Kelli stopped herself and amended her statement. "Thank you for standing by me in there, but you don't have to keep trying to protect me."

Kelli felt a shift in the mood as the ex-bodyguard's hands tightened around the wheel. As an afterthought, she realized with a tiny shock that he was driving her car without being asked. He'd seen she was upset and did it without mention. Just another detail that made her already scattered thoughts harder to pin down.

"You know, even when I was a bodyguard, I never *had* to protect anyone," Mark started. "I've never been forced to keep someone safe, and I'm not being forced now, either. So, yes, I know I don't *have* to try to keep you safe, but I really want to."

If his eyes hadn't been on the road, Kelli wasn't sure what she would have done with herself. Victor's picture floated behind her vision. It made her finally put the two men side by side.

Sure, looks-wise they were opposites. Victor was a lanky, almost red-haired man with a smile that approached goofy. Mark was wider—broad shoulders, solid muscles—with a no-nonsense cut to his brown hair and a little bit of a farmer's tan peeking out of his shirt. As for his smiles, they were all laced with something Kelli couldn't quite put her finger on but was finding she liked.

Personality-wise, were they also opposites?

Kelli did know one thing for sure. Victor and Mark shared one very important trait.

They had good hearts.

"I would say thank-you, but I seem to say that a lot," she answered after an awkward moment of silence had grown too loud. "So I'll skip right to the part where I ask, what's our plan?"

"Plan?"

"You know, the plan to catch the bad guy and restore justice to the world." She spread her hands out wide, making a pretend rainbow over the car's dash.

Mark laughed.

"You make it sound so easy," he commented.

She shrugged.

"If Grace can figure out how to play Candy Crush on my phone, then we can totally do this."

MARK DROVE THEM back to his apartment, where Kelli said they'd hatch their game plan. The trip to the Bowman Foundation had been much more eventful than he'd originally thought. Like Kelli, his gut had yelled at him.

There wasn't just one thing off—there were several.

"Do you mind if I go call Lynn and Grace?" Kelli asked when he'd settled into the couch, ready to brainstorm. "I'm not too good with separation from the little one." Kelli smiled a smile that clearly showed a mother's love.

"Yeah, no problem. You can go into my bedroom if you'd like."

Instantly he realized he'd made the offer sound suggestive. A Freudian slip if he'd ever had one. Kelli did a half-snort laugh and retreated into the room. It could have been his imagination, but it looked as though her cheeks had reddened. Then again, he could have been mistaken. Mark stretched out his legs and realized just how tired he felt.

Resting his head back on the cushions, he crossed his arms over his chest and closed his eyes. When Kelli was finished, he'd offer her some coffee and make a very strong mug for himself. His thoughts went from coffee to the woman who had suddenly become a part of his life.

Would she still be there after they'd somehow found the justice they both wanted and so desperately needed?

"Boo."

Mark turned his head toward the noise and slowly blinked.

Some small person was staring at him, only inches from his face.

"Boo," she said again, trying to whisper but failing.

Completely off his game and confused, he repeated the word. It made the little girl giggle.

"Grace!" The toddler whipped her head around to look toward the kitchen. She smiled even though Kelli's tone was scolding. "I told you *not* to mess with him!"

Mark, finally starting to connect the dots, sat up and rubbed his face.

"I fell asleep?" he asked, turning to face Kelli, also. His eyes widened at two things he hadn't expected to see—aside from the sudden appearance of the half pint who had gone back to staring at him. Kelli was standing over the oven cooking something—and it smelled delicious—while Nikki Waters sat across from her on a bar stool, beer in hand. "How long was I out?" he asked, alarmed.

Kelli laughed. "Um, a few hours at least," she answered with an apologetic smile. "I was going to leave to give you some privacy, but then Nikki showed up and we got to talking and lost track of the time." She motioned to Grace. "And then I started to miss that little one. Did I mention I have separation issues with her?"

As if on cue, Grace giggled. "Boo," she squealed.

"You were sleeping so solidly that I figured you'd be hungry when you finally woke up," Kelli added. "So I raided your pantry."

"And I stole a beer," Nikki said with a wink. Unlike the earlier, angrier version, this Nikki was all smiles. Her shoulders were even relaxed.

"Again, now that I say it all out loud, it sounds really creepy…" Kelli suddenly looked panicked, just as she had when she'd first stopped by his apartment. It made him smile.

"You can be creepy all you want if it means I can eat whatever that is you're cooking," he joked. His stomach growled loudly in testament.

Kelli relaxed. "Good," she said. "I wouldn't want to be kicked out before Nikki finishes this story."

"Story?" he asked when the two women shared a look.

Nikki laughed in response. "Don't worry about it."

So he didn't. Mark sidestepped Grace and the toy that had grabbed her attention and walked to the bathroom to try to lift the postnap haze of sleep. He splashed his face with cold water and took a deep breath. A fit of laughter met his ears from the other room. Aside from the past two days, Mark hadn't had anyone come to his apartment. Especially not to eat.

Was he upset that Kelli had decided to cook dinner for his former boss, her daughter and him?

He dried his face and gave himself a good look in the mirror.

No.

He wasn't upset at all.

"Do I even want to know?" he asked after he was finished. Nikki turned toward him with another smile. Her eyes took in his freshly shaved face, but she didn't comment on it.

"Let's just say that Kelli now knows why I've learned my lesson on sending you, Oliver and Jonathan on assignments together."

Immediately Mark pictured one long drunken night in Vegas. He cringed.

"Let it be known that we had already finished a contract when we decided to try our hand at gambling," he said to Kelli, walking to the refrigerator. He grabbed a beer and went back to the couch. Grace's attention had switched to a multitude of colorful building blocks she pulled from a bag.

Taking a sip from his beer, he watched the little girl try to piece two of the blocks together. Their parts didn't connect, and her frustration was evident. He set his beer down and slid to the floor next to her. With wide eyes she watched as he took the two blocks and found a long piece that connected them. He handed the new construction back to her and she smiled.

Slowly, as if asking for permission, he took a few more blocks from the bag and started to put them together. At first she seemed unsure of the intrusion. Then she started to hand him her blocks. She scooted closer to him, and together they faced the construction of what Mark hoped would be a little house.

"A builder, a bodyguard and a gambler? That's quite the résumé, Mr. Tranton." Kelli appeared beside them with a bowl of pasta. She held it out, uncertain. "Sorry, I know that last thing I cooked for you was pasta, but there wasn't anything else in the pantry. Also, I don't know the rules in this apartment about where we can and can't eat," she apologized.

Mark took the bowl and glanced at Grace, Kelli and Nikki. Each looked at him expectantly for much different reasons.

He smiled.

It was a definite change of pace for the bachelor.

Minutes later, all three adults were eating in a circle around a tiny block house. Grace had a bag of cereal and razor-sharp focus on a cartoon on the TV. Mark hadn't even realized he received the channel.

"Grace and I have gotten into the bad habit of watching TV after we eat," Kelli explained, sheepish. Even with the sound turned down, Grace didn't break eye contact at the mention of her name. "It quiets the toddler beast within her."

Nikki laughed. "My niece and nephew were the same way, so don't worry. Sometimes you just have to take your breaks when you can get them," she said.

"The joys of single parenthood," Kelli responded with an ounce of humor. It didn't last long, and the three seemed to remember why they were all there. Mark cleared his throat.

"Not that I'm against a visit from you, but what was

it that you came to say?" he asked his old boss. As soon as the question left his mouth, he saw the woman transform into Boss Nikki. Straight back, relaxation evaporating. She set down her bowl.

"First of all, I stand by my decision to not let you look into Dennis Crawford. Especially since you're no longer an Orion agent," she said firmly. "However, after hearing your theory about the fire and realizing that someone might really have tried to target Victor and by proxy my agent, I got maternal." She held up a hand to stop his comment. "Believe me, it was a weird feeling. But it was a good thing, considering it pushed me to look into Dennis personally."

Mark's and Kelli's attention zeroed in on the woman.

"As you both know, when Orion takes on a client, we do extensive background checks on the people connected to our client. We try to find threats before they happen—something we've learned to do better since the debacle in Maine with Oliver's contract a few years ago. Since Dennis was the editor on the story and had email contact with Victor, we made sure to include him on the list of people to check out. But…no matter how hard we look or how many hypothetical scenarios we run to prepare our agents, humans have this funny way of not always adhering to the norm. They become unpredictable."

Mark put down his bowl. Kelli leaned in a bit closer. Nikki's expression sharpened.

"Dennis, I've realized now, is one of those people."

Chapter Thirteen

Silence.

It enveloped the space around the three adults. Not even the *oink* of a cartoon pig in the background could penetrate their collective concentration.

Eventually Mark spoke.

"Dennis Crawford became unpredictable? How?" He tried to recall anything out of the ordinary about the retired editor back during the contract. The only contact he'd had with Victor was through an email the day before the fire happened. It had been solely work-related and hadn't raised any red flags.

"*How* isn't as important as *when*," Nikki answered. She looked at Kelli when she continued. "After the fire, I kept our contract open and tabs on you until it was ruled Darwin McGregor was behind it. I also kept an eye on those who were closest to the case. Nothing suspicious happened with any of the people I was watching."

"The people?" Kelli asked.

Nikki paused and for a moment looked apologetic.

"Your friend Lynn, Victor's friends at the various publications he had worked with, even the last of his family—the two cousins in Denmark, Dennis and the Bowman Foundation themselves."

That surprised Mark.

"You looked into the Bowman Foundation?"

"Yes, but a cursory look that suggested they were what they said they were. Nothing more, nothing less. Dennis also appeared to act normal, considering everything." She didn't have to pause for dramatic effect. Mark was already reeled in. "Until right after the trial, when he made a few uncharacteristic choices." She held up three fingers. "First, he hired a realtor in Florida."

"He was going to move?" Kelli's eyes widened.

"As far as I can tell, he never went out there," Nikki cut in. She held up two fingers. "Instead, two, he retired from the *Scale*—in my opinion—a few years too early. And then, three, right before he went quiet, he gave a sizable contribution to a national charity organization, namely *not* the Bowman Foundation."

Mark rubbed a hand across his clean-shaven jaw. He couldn't believe what he was hearing.

"Sounds like we've got another Darwin McGregor thing going on," he observed. Nikki gave him a questioning look.

"Darwin McGregor thing?"

"We think he was paid to accept the fall for someone so his grandmother would be taken care of," Kelli said.

"And it sounds like someone else might have been paid off," he observed. "Right after the trial, almost moving, retiring early and giving money to charity?"

"Or maybe it's a sign of something else?" Nikki offered.

"Surely that can't be a coincidence?" he said, mind already set on his theory. "Having two people making choices that dramatically change their lives, all surrounding the fire? They both seem guilty of being connected."

Nikki raised her index finger. "Connected, yes, but who's to say Dennis *was* behind it all?"

Mark tilted his head toward Kelli to see what she was thinking. A storm of thought was brewing just behind her eyes. He could have looked into them for hours and never lost interest. So beautiful.

He blinked and tore his gaze away. Now wasn't the time to realize he was much more attracted to the woman he was trying to help than he would have liked to admit. He needed to focus. He needed to keep her safe.

"Listen, I'm not suggesting Dennis Crawford isn't guilty," Nikki added before Kelli could voice any thoughts. "But I am trying to put myself into his shoes. Dennis is the kind of man who loves to work—loves his job so much it's become every facet of his life. He isn't married, has no kids and probably is low on friends. Why? He's always had his nose to the grindstone. He didn't earn his position at the *Scale*. He fought to get there. Then, all of a sudden, he's not only quitting but also trying to move away? That—to me—sounds like a man running from something."

"So, what are you getting at?" Mark asked, knowing her calculations had a bottom line.

"That maybe Dennis Crawford is a victim, not a perpetrator."

Another silence took over their group.

"While you mull that over, I need to check in on a contract." Nikki took her bowl to the sink and stepped out into the hallway, phone already to her ear. She shut the door behind her, leaving the two of them together with their thoughts.

"She's right," Kelli admitted after a moment. "Dennis could be just another victim of whatever is going on. But what the hell *is* going on?" Kelli's eyes cut to Grace, hoping the girl hadn't heard her word choice. Grace didn't even realize they were still in the room. "Whether or not Dennis is a victim doesn't change the fact that he knows something."

"Then we need to figure out what that something is." Mark stood and held out his hand to her. He lifted her to her feet. Suddenly they were close. A breath or two away from each other, hand in hand. Every part of Mark seemed to awaken at the contact. It made the job of his past bringing him back to reality—pointing out that he didn't deserve to be with Kelli, of all people—harder than it ever had been before. Mark dropped their hands and took a small step back. "So why don't we just ask Dennis tomorrow?"

Kelli's eyes widened, but she nodded. "Sounds like a plan to me!"

Talk about Dennis, the fire and anything else relating to the two died down. Kelli and Mark did the dishes, and Nikki came back inside and supervised while finishing her beer. Grace became bored with whatever cartoon was on and started to fuss. She rubbed her eyes with two tiny fists.

"That's my cue to leave," Kelli said after calming the girl down. "Someone didn't get a nap, thanks to Aunt Lynn's love of torturing me."

"She's not the only one tired," Nikki said with a

yawn. "Not everyone was able to take a generous nap today." She cut a look to Mark, and the three of them laughed.

"Hey, does it count if it was an accident?" he asked.

Nikki shook her head. "You sleeping doesn't make me any less tired." She turned to Kelli, who was packing up Grace's bag. "Speaking of sleep, Thomas is refreshed and ready to go. If you're still okay with it, he can switch out with Jonathan for the night."

Kelli nodded and smiled at Mark's confusion.

"When you were out, we talked about how it might be a good idea to give Jonathan and you a bit of a break. Orion Agent Thomas comes highly recommended and has said he's more than happy to help. So, before you offer to come watch the house, let me stop you and suggest you get more than a nap tonight. Tomorrow's a big day. We need to be well rested. Or as close to it as we can be."

Mark wanted to argue—*he* should be watching over her, not everyone else—but realized that want was partly selfish. He knew Thomas was a capable agent and trusted the man just as Nikki did.

"And to entice you further to get some rest, I'll follow you home, just in case," Nikki told Kelli. "It's on my way."

Kelli smiled. "Works for me!"

And just like that, the three of them went back to their own little worlds, leaving Mark alone in his apartment.

"You sure had a full house," Craig, the neighbor, said as Mark watched the three ladies get into the elevator at the end of the hall. He had a bag of trash hung over his shoulder, on the way to the disposal. It was probably the first time since Craig had moved in that he'd seen that many people leave.

"Just helping some friends," Mark hedged, though he didn't know why he was skipping around the truth. Nikki was definitely considered a friend—an estranged one of late, but once a great friend. Kelli? They had picked back up on an acquaintanceship and found a mutual trust as they worked toward a goal. Did that count as friendship or just two lost people looking for light at the end of the same tunnel?

As Mark went back into his apartment and looked around at its emptiness, he knew one thing for certain.

He was no longer happy with his isolation.

KELLI HELD THE two coffees in her hands as if they were anchors keeping her grounded. Not physically, of course. Her legs were moving at a good pace as she walked down a hallway that was becoming rapidly familiar. But emotionally, she imagined the coffees came with strings that attached to the feelings that she might or might not have been having for the ex-bodyguard, and the invisible anchors made to keep them out of sight and mind.

Because having feelings—any kind of feelings—for the man helping you bring justice to your murdered husband was just plain complicated.

So when she knocked on Mark's apartment door the next morning, she was trying to focus on the warmth of each cup of joe against her skin instead of the fluttering feeling of excitement that she got knowing she was about to see the man.

"Good morning," she almost sang when the door opened after the second knock. It was a little too enthusiastic a greeting. She felt her face heat slightly. Mark, bless him, didn't even look surprised. Unlike the first time she'd come over unannounced, he was fully clothed. Another fun realization for Kelli: she was a little disappointed at that fact.

"I was wondering when you'd come around," Mark said in return, humor clear in his voice. He smiled and made a grand sweeping gesture into the apartment. "Though how you got in again, I'm not so sure."

"Your building is very friendly," she admitted. "How'd you know I'd come around again?"

He laughed and tapped his temple.

"I've picked up on your routine," he said. "The last few days, you've ended up here, so it was only a matter of time. Though I have to say I hadn't foreseen the coffee." His eyes seem to brighten as he took in the cups. "It would be a massive understatement to say that you were lucky to find anything in my pantry last night. I haven't been shopping in a week or two. That means no coffee, and I could really use it right now."

Kelli handed him a cup and was pleased at the smile that continued to spread across his face because of it. "You mean you didn't get enough sleep last night? Even with your unexpected yet well-deserved nap?"

"I couldn't sleep that well after everyone left." He shrugged. "I guess it was too quiet."

Instead of walking straight to the couch, Kelli took up residence at one of the kitchen bar stools. She tried not to feel the pull on her heartstrings at Mark's subtle admission that he might have missed them after they'd gone the night before. It made her believe her theory that maybe he was lonely after all.

She wanted to catch the culprit behind Victor's death

not just for her family's justice but also, in some way, for Mark. The more time she spent with him, the clearer it became that he, too, had suffered.

"So, I'm guessing Jonathan is back with Grace and Lynn?"

Kelli nodded. "He came to relieve Thomas, who agreed to followed me over here on his way home," she answered. She had waved goodbye to the Orion agent through the lobby window before he'd even started to drive away. "You Orion guys sure are polite."

"I definitely can vouch for Jonathan and Thomas. Nikki trusts them, and so do I."

"And I trust you," Kelli admitted. It earned her an appreciative look.

Which darkened immediately.

It evoked another feeling she was trying to ignore— deep concern for the man in front of her. She took a sip of coffee and readjusted her focus.

"Okay, so, tonight's goal is to corner Dennis Craw-ford and get some answers," she started.

"When you say it like that, it sounds so simple."

"It may be a simpler goal to meet than the other one."

"The other one?" His eyebrow rose in perfect unison with his question. The small gesture pointed out, once again, how handsome the man was. She cleared her throat.

"To get fancy, of course."

His face blanked, and it actually made her laugh.

"You'd prefer cornering a man to dressing up, wouldn't you?" She already knew the answer. "And that's why I'm here. Do you have anything fancy you'd be comfortable wearing tonight? I looked up pictures from last year's dinner." She pulled up a photo on her phone and handed it over. "Just like their building, they sure don't hesitate in being upscale."

Mark's face pinched at the group picture of men wearing tuxes and women in dresses that probably each cost more than Kelli's car.

"I have a tux," he ground out, clearly unhappy. "But I haven't worn it in a while. I don't know if it fits."

Kelli clapped her hands. "Then let's see!"

Mark eyed her skeptically. "You came over here hoping for a movie-makeover montage, didn't you?"

"I came over here because Lynn said she could have Pretty Princess Day with Grace at her house while I saw to some errands. And you don't question when the babysitter volunteers. Though, yes, I did come over with this in mind," she admitted with a grin. "I guess Pretty Princess Day includes you, now, too."

Mark rolled his eyes skyward before shuffling back to his room, defeated. She'd already pegged him as a man who didn't take pleasure in any high-society conventions. Not that she did, either. Her thoughts slid to Victor and then his late mother. Claire had loved being a socialite. She'd attended many formal parties and events with Victor's father and then Victor with a smile on her face and happiness in her heart. Victor had told Kelli it was the confidence that she felt only when being dressed up with a purpose that had made Claire love it all.

It was a feeling Claire had tried to pass to her daughter-in-law. Before Kelli and Victor were even engaged, she'd bought Kelli a gorgeous gown so she could feel as beautiful as Claire did. She'd gotten sick and passed away before she'd ever seen Kelli wear it. Now the dress was boxed up and waiting for Kelli at the house, begging to be worn.

She only hoped she could do it the justice she should have done it years ago.

Waiting with her cup of coffee, Kelli let her thoughts do their own thing. Minutes went by before the bedroom door opened again. Kelli nearly dropped her cup. Turning without mentally preparing for what she saw next wasn't the best plan.

The mental anchors that held the strings attached to her off-limits growing feelings for the ex-bodyguard dissolved.

The tux did indeed fit.

And boy, did it fit well.

Chapter Fourteen

"That bad, huh?" Mark asked when Kelli couldn't seem to make her words work. She slipped off her stool with no amount of grace and resisted the urge to clear her throat.

Calm down, Kel! He's just a good-looking man in a good-looking suit!

"Bad? No," she exclaimed with a lot more enthusiasm than she was trying to convey. Her face burned, and she just hoped the dreary day outside helped hide the color that was surely painting her cheeks. "It's no Pretty Princess Day dress, but it definitely works."

The tux was a classic black one, tailored to his body type. It perfectly highlighted his broad shoulders while presenting his muscles in a way that wasn't showy or vulgar. It made the man beneath the clothes go from handsome to downright sexy.

Kelli hadn't thought she'd ever find a man who made her feel this way again.

Yet here he was, fumbling with his tie, unaware of just how wonderful he looked.

"Here, let me," she said, walking over and taking hold of the open tie.

"Try and tell me you aren't surprised at the fact that

I don't have a clip-on," he joked as she took both sides of the tie in her hands.

"I plead the Fifth."

Being so close to him wasn't helping her current frame of mind. She could smell his aftershave—something sharp yet pleasing—without even trying. Her hands bumped against the solidness of his chest.

"So, do you have an outfit picked out for this shindig already?" he asked, eyes straight forward.

"Yes, but it's at the house. I also haven't tried it on since before Grace, so there's no telling how it will actually look."

"I'm sure you'll look great."

Kelli smiled at the compliment.

"We'll see. I still need to swing by there to check the job the window guy did on the office. I'm sure the new owners wouldn't like it if I left the house in bad condition." She paused, and a surge of excitement flooded through her. "Hey! Would you like to see my house?"

Mark raised his brow.

"I have?" he said uncertainly.

She laughed. "No, I mean, *my* house. The new one! Granted, it definitely isn't as big or nice, but I like to think it's cute and cozy." An odd look crossed the man's face as she finished. One that wasn't wholly bad but gave her pause. Had she overstepped a boundary? She pinned her gaze on finishing his tie. "You don't have to," she added quickly. "It has nothing to do with Dennis or the fire or anything like that. I just—" She managed a quick look up into his eyes. Their even stare pulled the truth right out from between her lips. "I wanted to share my happiness." She gave him an apologetic smile. "Sounds cheesy now that I say it."

The corner of Mark's lips lifted up. He took her hands, paused in midair and gave them a small squeeze.

"I think we both could do with more happiness in our lives." His voice dipped low as he said it, almost into a whisper. Kelli's mind jumped around as she wondered about the meaning behind his words coupled with the warmth of his skin against hers. Maybe it was her imagination wanting something she probably shouldn't have, but Mark seemed to be moving closer. Changing an already established connection to mean more.

Kelli tilted her head, angling her lips to what she wanted to be so much more than a simple kiss.

But reality decided it wasn't meant to be.

Mark dropped her hands and stepped back. Just like he'd done the night before.

She hoped she hid her hurt.

"Let me get back into some real clothes, and we can head out," he said, voice back to normal. The smile, however, was gone.

Maybe Kelli *was* just reading into his words.

HER NEW HOME was in Lake Dallas, a charming suburb that was a lot more affordable than some of the others she'd seen, and cute as cute could be. In relation to Lynn's town house, it was about a twenty-minute drive with no traffic—another reason Kelli had loved the location—but it was a good deal farther from Mark's apartment.

The latter point, she realized with a bit of chagrin, was a blemish on an otherwise perfect home, in her eyes.

Wrapped in gray siding, the two-bedroom home featured light hardwood floors and an open floor plan that would keep Grace in her sight from anywhere in the living room or kitchen. It was small, as she'd said to Mark, but for their little family, it fit just right.

"I like it," Mark said after she'd given him the tour. "It's charming."

"Ha. That's the polite way to say it *is* small."

"It's also the polite way to say it's charming," he countered. They were moving from what would be Grace's bedroom to the kitchen.

"Now, I know it needs a few upgrades and certainly some paint." Both their eyes cut to the olive green living room walls. "But right now we can live happily with this."

"When do you start to move in?"

Kelli sighed at that. "Technically, I could do it now, but I booked movers for next week. Apparently I picked a popular time to move."

"You know, I'm sure I could round up enough men to help get the job done," he said, trying to be sly. "My ex-job happens to be with a bunch of bodyguards, and my current job is with a bunch of construction workers. Free labor, if you don't mind all the sweaty men."

Kelli was about to respond with a clever quip—at least, she'd try to make it clever—when Mark's attention dropped to his pocket. His cell phone was doing its vibrating dance. He held up his finger.

"Excuse me a second." He pulled out the phone and went into the backyard. Apparently he needed privacy, which was fine by Kelli. But it did make her curious as to whom he was on the phone with. Mark had admitted he was single, but that didn't mean he didn't have admirers. Aside from Nikki and Jonathan, she really didn't know if he had a social life.

She surely didn't.

While Mark was on the phone, Kelli did another sweep of the house, trying to picture where everything would go the next week. She wasn't halfway through mentally piecing together the master bedroom when a knock sounded on the front door.

Perplexed and slightly nervous at meeting who was probably a neighbor, she hurried back through the living room and opened the door.

Her stomach dropped.

"Dennis?" She asked, "What are you doing here?"

Dennis, dressed casually with a pair of sunglasses on, didn't smile. Every muscle in Kelli's body tensed. Apart from her Realtor, Lynn and now Mark, no one knew where her new house was. So why in the world was Dennis here now? Had he followed them there?

"I need to tell you something, and you need to listen," he ground out. Anger was evident in his last four words. It made Kelli step back, trying to soak up the comfort of her new home to offset her growing fear. "You need to stop digging into the past. Drop this story—it isn't one you need to tell."

"Why?" she asked, voice giving a little. "What's going on? What did Victor really find?" Determination pulsed through her at each question. She was gearing up to ask him everything right then and there.

"Victor's dead, Kelli," he interrupted with a harsh whisper. It pulled all of the air clear out of her lungs. "He found *nothing* and he still died. And now you want to know what got your husband killed? Why? So the same thing can happen to you *and* your daughter?"

"Don't you *dare* talk about *my* daughter," she said, fury filling the space left behind in her lungs. She stepped forward, aware that she was two seconds from attacking the man.

"Do you know how easy it was to find this place, Kelli? How long do you think your bodyguards will protect you and your loved ones?" That deflated her a fraction. "Can they even really protect you every minute of every day anyway? Look what happened to Victor. Who's to say it won't happen again?"

"Is that a threat?" she whispered, her confidence draining quickly.

"It's food for thought for the young mother." He bent his head down to meet her gaze. His voice was dangerously low when he spoke. "Don't go to the dinner tonight. Don't dig anymore. And give me that damn journal."

Kelli believed in a lot of things. She believed in determination and the power of self-confidence. She also believed that emotions had the absolute power to derail the other two. So Kelli, thinking of Grace and of Victor and Lynn, grabbed her purse from beside the door and pulled the journal from it.

"Don't you ever come here again," she said, pushing the journal at him.

Dennis took it but didn't smile.

"Hopefully I won't have to."

Kelli didn't wait for him to get back to his car by the curb before she was running through the house and through the back door. Mark turned at the noise and barely took her in before his entire demeanor changed.

"Let me call you back," he said into his phone, closing it immediately after. "What's wrong?"

"Dennis just came by," she blurted out, pointing wildly. "I—I gave him Victor's journal." Kelli put a hand over her mouth, instantly regretting that decision. Mark grabbed her shoulders, moving her focus back to him.

"Are you okay? Did he hurt you?"

She shook her head and then he was gone, running through the house.

Who's to say it won't happen again?

Kelli hurried inside and grabbed her phone. She dialed Lynn's number and waited for what felt like a lifetime for her to pick up.

"Is Grace with you? Can you see her?" Kelli practically yelled.

"Of course she is and yes," Lynn answered. Just like Mark, she could read the shift in the woman's mood. "Where else would she be? What's wrong?"

Kelli pulled the phone away and placed it against her chest. She took a deep breath before continuing.

"Lynn, I need to tell you something, but first I want you to promise me you'll stay inside until I get back. Please?"

Lynn, bless her, had known Kelli long enough to trust her vagueness. And to pick up on her fresh fear.

"Okay, I promise."

Mark came back as she ended her call.

"I should have fought him instead of giving him the journal," she said without any segue. Mark grabbed her hand, a look of ferocity on his face.

"No, I shouldn't have been in the backyard on the phone. I should have been protecting you." He looked around them as if he was ready to throw whatever he could get his hands on. Luckily, there wasn't a thing to grab.

"It's not your fault he's a horrible man," she assured

him. "It's not your fault I couldn't let this go. Oh, God, what have I done?" Now she was panicking. "What if Grace or Lynn or *you* get hurt because of the decision *I* made?"

Mark put his free hand behind her neck, tilting her head up. Before her panic could mount into tears, he pressed his lips against hers with such force she nearly lost her balance. The kiss wasn't entirely a kiss, she'd realize later. Like the coffee from before, it served two purposes.

One was to address the elephant in, apparently, both of their rooms. An attraction that had grown through the past few days. A bond that had been established by shared tragedy.

The second purpose was, in the simplest of terms, to focus her. To throw a cup of water in her face. To bring her back to reality.

To remind Kelli she wasn't alone and didn't have to protect everyone by herself.

A lesson she didn't think Mark had learned yet.

Mark ended the short kiss with fire in his eyes.

"It's not *you* who's in the wrong. I promise you we'll nail the guy who is."

"How?"

"I'm getting my job back."

Chapter Fifteen

"I want it to be noted *somewhere* that I think this is a bad idea." Lynn sat at the end of Mark's couch with her arms crossed over her chest, giving the eye to everyone around her. As she still wore her Pretty Princess Day pink dress and matching plastic beaded necklaces, her disapproval was almost humorous. "Heck, it isn't even really an idea, when you get down to it."

Mark had to agree with her there. His eyes traveled to his bedroom, where Kelli was putting Grace down for her nap.

"My friend at the station said that if we can prove Dennis is a threat, then we'll be getting somewhere," Nikki chimed in from her spot on a bar stool. Jonathan sat beside, her eating leftover pasta. He nodded.

"Dennis seems to be one of those guys who needs to talk," he said, careful not to speak with the food in his mouth. "It seems like all you will need to do is just walk up to him and talk. That recorder will do the rest." Everyone looked down at the little black circle on the coffee table, courtesy of one of Nikki's Orion contacts. Another benefit of Mark being employed as an agent again—Orion and its founder had quite the stash of resources. "When he incriminates himself, then just fall back to me and we'll go straight to the cops."

Lynn huffed. "So we're going to ignore the many unknowns here?" She turned her gaze to Mark. "What happens if—I don't know—he has a gun or a knife or something and decides to stop you two once and for all?" The lines in her face sharpened, her brows slamming together. It was clear she didn't even like to voice a hypothetical in which harm came to her best friend. He didn't like to picture it, either.

"I won't let that happen," Mark assured her.

"And I can't imagine Dennis would do that," Jonathan said.

"Why?" Lynn wanted to know.

"He hasn't done it yet, and he's had the opportunity. Why would he do it now *and* in front of an audience?"

Lynn slumped back into the couch cushions. "I still can't wrap my head around all of this. We still don't know *what* it was that Victor even found. What if it's all been one giant misunderstanding? A series of coincidences, and we're too paranoid to realize it?"

"I thought the same thing," Nikki said, casting an apologetic smile toward Mark. "At first I thought it was grief clouding judgment, misplaced guilt. You know, seeing signs that weren't there." She turned to Lynn. "But then we found out that Darwin McGregor received enough money to get his grandmother out of debt and into a wealthy retirement home while still giving him money in his savings a day after the trial." She held up her finger. "*That* plus Dennis's strange behavior at the same time? Whatever is going on, that man is pulling some major strings to keep it quiet. Who's to say he'll stop just because Kelli says she will?"

The room quieted at that.

Mark recalled the fear on Kelli's face as she'd told him about Dennis's visit. He had ended his call with Darling only to call back after he officially accepted his job. He'd talked to her husband.

"I'm going to skip over the fact that you called my wife and asked for help and didn't bother to at least clue me in to what's going on," Oliver had said, not giving Mark room to make excuses or apologize. "Instead, I'm going to give you a warning. I know Darling confirmed your suspicions about Darwin. He got paid. But what she didn't get was a chance to tell you she has no idea who did that. There wasn't a trace of the purse holder at all—she looked all night and morning. We even looped in Derrick with his law-enforcement connections and still couldn't come up with a name or place. Whoever is behind this—whether or not it's Dennis—they're good. They're dangerous. Watch yourself and be careful."

Now he was sitting in his apartment with the best bodyguard he knew, his boss, a very concerned best friend, a toddler and a woman he'd kissed in a heated moment. All of them creating a plan to end whatever was going on.

If he thought about it too much, Mark started to see the cracks that their plan could fall between. Lynn was right, but that didn't mean they could all just sit there and pretend everything could go back to normal. Not after Dennis had shown up at Kelli's house. Not after he had talked about Grace.

"I think this is what they make beer for," Lynn finally said. Despite their moods, it earned a laugh from the room. The weight of the unknown dangers started to lift.

"You know, I'm just curious to see what Mark's going to wear," Jonathan said. "I think the last and *only* time I saw you spiffed up was Oliver's wedding. And even then I think you changed between the ceremony and the reception."

Nikki laughed. "He did! One minute he was wearing his tux and the next he was wearing flannel," she added.

"Flannel?" Lynn asked with a grimace. "I'm a fan of flannel, but I don't think it's meant as wedding attire."

Mark held up his hands. "Hey! I didn't wear flannel to the wedding. Just the reception and, to be fair, the reception was small and at their house."

"Everyone was wearing their fanciest clothes and here comes Mark looking like a lumberjack," Jonathan jumped in, smiling at the memory.

"Please tell me you got a picture of this," Lynn said. She grinned. "I really can't picture the glory of Lumberjack Mark."

"Oh, we made him take a picture with Darling just so we'd never forget," said Nikki. She turned to Mark and her expression darkened. "Do you still have it or…"

Or did you get rid of that when you decided you didn't need friends? Mark finished her unsaid thought in his head. The past few days had shown him how easily he could fall back into step with those once closest to him. When they hadn't believed him after Victor's death it had hurt, but now he really understood their viewpoint. They had been trying to protect him from himself—from his guilt and grief—by trying to get him to move on. To stop chasing a ghost and get back to living his life. Instead of seeing it from their eyes he'd decided to believe they didn't trust him—didn't believe in him. Now, looking around at their faces, eager to help,

Mark wished he could change the way he'd just shut down around them. When this was all over, he needed to do right by them.

"Of course I still have that. I still have pictures from the wedding of all of us. Including one of Jonathan trying to break-dance," he answered with a grin. Jonathan groaned in response. "Let me grab them really quick." He wanted to prove to Nikki and to Jonathan that he hadn't completely written them out of his life during the past year or so. Plus, he wanted to check on Kelli. Not being able to see her for this long didn't sit right with him. Dennis Crawford's earlier appearance had set him on edge more than he liked to admit.

The bedroom door was cracked open. Slowly he pushed inside, not wanting to knock and wake Grace if she had finally fallen asleep. The room was dark but the light from the window—even though it was cloudy—lit it enough that he was able to make eye contact with Kelli when he walked in. She and Grace were both lying down. Grace's arms were wrapped around Kelli, and her eyes were closed.

Mark pointed to his closet and tried to get there as quietly as possible. Within the walk-in he found the shoebox he'd labeled as Doliver—his name mash-up for the Quinns—and started to slip back out of the room.

"How's it going in there?" Kelli whispered. Her voice cut through the silence like a knife. He turned, surprised she had said anything at all. "Don't worry. Once she's like this, we could sit here and recite every episode of *Dora the Explorer* and she wouldn't wake up. This one sleeps hard." She smiled. "Want to keep me company until the octopus decides to detangle from me?"

Mark stifled a laugh and nodded.

"If that's a pickup line, I can honestly say I've never heard it before." He kicked off his shoes and put the box down on the floor before carefully lying down on the opposite side of Grace. Both adults watched her with wide eyes. She stirred but didn't wake up and didn't detach from her mother.

"Bullet dodged," Kelli said once Grace had stilled again. "She may seem like a pretty chill child, but if you wake her up before she's had enough rest, she'll show you just what war looks like. And we have enough on our plates right now. Speaking of war, how are our troops out there?"

Mark settled his head back on the pillow and looked at the ceiling.

"We've gone over the plan enough—not that it's complicated—and everyone's ready. Lynn thinks we shouldn't go, and I don't think so, either," he admitted.

"You think it won't work?"

"No, it probably will. Jonathan thinks Dennis will say something to us when he sees we came despite his warning. I agree."

"So, why shouldn't we go, then?"

Mark turned his head to face her. Her green-gray eyes still managed to be clear in the low light of the room.

"Because Lynn's right, too. What if he pulls something and *does* try to hurt you?" Mark felt the backup of words behind his tongue. Words that needed saying, emotions that needed out. But was it the time? Was it the place? Would it ever be?

"Then you'll stop him. You'll protect me," Kelli answered simply. The uninhibited trust she placed in him was so pure that Mark couldn't stop what he said next.

"I couldn't protect Victor." Kelli blinked. She hadn't expected him to say that. He could see the surprise clearly on her face. He took advantage of the lag and continued. "If I had, you wouldn't need protecting now. Not by me. I'm so sorry, Kelli."

The anguish—the guilt since the fire—had finally burned its way through his skin. Lying there with Victor's wife and daughter was too much for the bodyguard. He needed Kelli to know that *he* knew he had let her down in an unimaginable way. He could no longer deny that he had feelings for the beautiful blonde. Like his admission now, the kiss earlier had sprung from an inner desire he could no longer suppress.

Expecting her to finally see reason—her trust might really be misplaced—Mark started to get up. It shifted the bed enough to jostle Grace. Before he could clear her reach, the toddler flipped from her mom and grabbed his arm. He froze, and like the little octopus she was, she looped her arms around his and buried her face against his shirt.

Mark remained steady until it was clear she had gone back to sleep. He wanted to do at least one good thing by Kelli, even something as small as not waking up the toddler. However, he wasn't used to affection from a child. Even if that child was fast asleep. He looked at Kelli uncertainly.

She smiled, and the room around her seemed to brighten.

"Mark, I'm only going to tell you this once, so please take it to heart." She put her hand in his, resting them both against the sheets. "I *never* blamed you for Victor's death and I *never* will. In my eyes, you did your job perfectly." She squeezed his hand before moving hers over Grace's hands on his arm. "Do you want to know why I think—no, why I *know*—that?"

Mark nodded, transfixed by her words.

"Because, no matter what else you did that night, at the end of it you saved me. Which means you saved Grace." Without heeding her own advice not to move her child, Kelli leaned across the girl and brushed her lips against Mark's. The kiss was so soft he almost thought he'd imagined it as she pulled away. "And for that, I am eternally grateful. So, as Victor's widow, I have to ask you to stop blaming yourself for every wrong thing that has happened and might happen. If Victor could talk to you now, he'd tell you the same thing. I *promise*. It's time for you—and me—to stop living in that tragic past." She paused and looked down at her daughter. "It's time we start focusing on a more beautiful future." She reached up and took his chin in her hand. "No more of this tortured-soul stuff. Okay?"

A chuckle rose in his throat as if her touch alone had absolved him of a burden he'd carried for two years. Ever since the first night he'd held her in his arms and carried her to safety.

"Okay," he agreed. A smile that felt better than any he'd had in a while pulled the corner of his lips up.

Kelli mimicked it.

"Good." She backed away from him slowly, rolling over and carefully getting out of bed. "Now you stay with the octopus while I take a look at you as a lumberjack." She went straight for the box he'd put down.

"Were we that loud?"

She mocked surprise. "Oh, I didn't tell you? Along with mom separation anxiety I also have mom hearing. It's a bundle thing." She opened the box and pulled out the photo album. "We know you can pull off a tux, but now let's see if Mark Tranton can pull off flannel."

Chapter Sixteen

Afternoon quickly turned into night, and the humor the small group had been enjoying quickly disappeared. It was getting time to put their plan in motion, even if not all of them thought it was a good plan to start.

"This concern comes from a place of love," Lynn said from the edge of the bed. She had made a clothes run and had now changed out of her Pretty Princess attire and into a pair of jeans and a white-and-yellow blouse that contrasted beautifully with her dark complexion. Her half of the best-friend necklace Kelli had bought them when they were in high school hung around her neck in plain view. Occasionally they would don them when they were nervous about something involving one another. The last time Kelli had worn hers was when Lynn had a job interview. The last time Lynn had worn hers was when Kelli had gone into the hospital to be induced for labor. In a way it was like a good-luck charm.

"If you weren't concerned, *I'd* be concerned," Kelli said. "But we need to stop Dennis. I don't trust him, Lynn."

The other woman sighed and nodded. "Yeah, yeah, I just…" She pursed her lips, seemingly choosing her words carefully. "Remember when you asked me to be Grace's godmother?"

Kelli laughed. "Of course. You baked a cake for us to celebrate."

"Exactly! I was so excited—so honored—to get the title that I didn't really think about what it meant until today. After you told me what was going on." Kelli tilted her head in question. "If something happens to you, God forbid, I'll raise that kiddo so well, you would be proud. That's a promise I made, but it's not one I *want* to fulfill." Her eyes started to mist as she continued. "You and Grace are my little family, and if something happens to you—"

Kelli closed the space between them, enveloping her friend in a warm embrace. Lynn wasn't a woman to cry easily. She didn't look down on the emotional, but she wasn't typically gushing about her own feelings. To see her almost cry—to hear her sniffling back tears— almost brought Kelli to her own.

"He might come after Grace, Lynn," Kelli said. "I won't sit around and wait to see. I have to do this, but I need you in my corner. I need your good vibes."

"Then let me come with you two," she said, pulling back to look Kelli in the eye. "I have that obnoxious orange dress back at home that I could wear!" But then Lynn stopped herself. "Grace," was all she said.

"I trust Jonathan and Nikki, but Grace trusts you. I need you here and so does she."

Lynn hung her head a fraction and sighed again. "I guess I should start up with those good vibes, then."

Kelli clapped, and just like that they were on the same page.

"That's the spirit," Kelli exclaimed. "Now, let's start with this dress, or was it a mistake to put this thing on?"

Kelli went to stand in front of the closet door. The full-length mirror showed her a reflection she wasn't used to seeing.

Her hair hung in loose curls, framing a face with impeccable dark eyeliner and red, red lips—thanks to Lynn, despite her concern—and coupled with long, skinny silver earrings. Though how could anyone focus on her face when she was wearing the dress?

Constantly getting dolled up and stretching her socialite muscles might not have been Kelli's forte, but she couldn't deny her appreciation for the dress wrapped around her. Navy blue silk slid across her body, starting out strong with a breathtaking deep-V back and ending with a small but elegant train. It also dipped into a much more modest V at her chest, showing limited yet undeniable cleavage. The sleeves were short and cupped the top of her shoulders while the rest of the dress hugged her body, forcing her to rethink her undergarments when she'd first put it on. Her shoes— which couldn't be seen beneath the rich fabric—in no way compared. They were fifteen-dollar black pumps that had more than one spot where a marker had come into play.

"Is it too much? Or am I underdressed?" Kelli asked, recalling the picture of the women from the past year's dinner.

"It's just beautiful," Lynn answered. "You're going to make it really hard for Mark to concentrate."

Kelli turned at the humor in her voice. Lynn smirked. "Don't think I've missed this—" she waved her hand in the air at Kelli "—getting all weird when he's mentioned or in the room."

"Weird?"

"It's a good weird. I just haven't mentioned it yet because I wanted *you* to bring it up, but—since you didn't and you're about to go talk to a psycho while wearing a ball gown—I'll go ahead and tell you that I think it's time you grabbed some happiness of the intimate kind." Lynn's smirk transformed into a caring smile. "I approve of this Mark character. He's a good guy, you know. But that doesn't mean we aren't going to talk more about this when it's all over."

If it had been anyone else, Kelli might have blushed. However, it was Lynn, so she just laughed. Of course the other woman had picked up on the change between her and the bodyguard.

"Deal."

"Good! Now let's go showcase this elegant-as-all-get-out dress!"

Kelli gave herself one more look in the mirror. The dress truly made her feel beautiful, but beauty wasn't the goal for tonight. Getting a man to admit to his sins was their true endgame.

Instead of Lynn letting Kelli simply walk out into the living room where Mark and Grace were, she decided to announce it.

"Lady and gentleman, may I present to you Pretty Princess Kelli!"

Mark stood from the spot where he'd been playing blocks with Grace and not so subtly looked her up and down.

"You're beautiful," he said, face openly appreciative. Heat swarmed up and filled her cheeks.

"You're not too bad yourself." She motioned to his outfit. Like earlier that morning, he was the perfect picture of sexy in the classic tux.

"Sure beats your flannel," Lynn said.

"Har, har." Then, like flipping a switch, his mood did a complete one-eighty. "Jonathan went ahead to find a good spot to wait and watch," Mark said, brows drawn in focus. "Nikki is on her way up. All we need to do now is put this on and head that way ourselves." He scooped up the recorder and looked her up and down again. She could have sworn she saw him turn a bit red.

"I'm pretty sure that thing won't be able to fit in there or stay," Lynn commented.

"We still need it on you just in case Dennis decides he'll only talk to you when I'm not right beside you."

"She's right," Kelli agreed. "*I* barely got in this thing."

A knock at the door paused whatever Mark was about to say. He checked the peephole—twice—before opening the door to let Nikki in. She looked between the two of them and whistled.

"Well, don't you two look nice?"

"Thanks, but we've apparently hit a snag. There's not a good place to hide this." Kelli pointed to the recorder. "I guess I could always put it in my clutch but, depending where I set it during dinner, that might look suspicious."

Nikki held up her hand. "I think I have a fix for that." She walked over to the kitchen counter and set down the bag she'd been carrying. The three of them huddled around her.

"Orion is all about using nonlethal methods to ensure client safety, because we believe our agents can handle any type of fight," she said, sounding rehearsed. "Our agents are well trained and experienced so the clients don't ever have to make contact with their aggressors. However, sometimes exceptions can be made." She pulled out what looked like an older cell phone and looked at Kelli. "It's a stun gun," she said. "On the off chance you need—or feel like you might need—some help. It looks somewhat like a phone, so it will blend."

"Somewhat?" Kelli shared a matching look of surprise with Lynn. "If you hadn't told me, I would have tried to make a call on it!"

Nikki laughed. "Don't worry. I would have stopped you."

Mark cracked a smile. "I would have, too, if it's any consolation," he said.

"And I appreciate that, but what does a stun gun have to do with hiding the recorder?"

Nikki held up another item from the bag. Black cloth and elastic made up a two-inch circle with a small slit in the middle.

"Is that a garter?" she asked.

"Of sorts." Nikki took the stun gun back and slid it into the slit so it wouldn't fall out. She took the recorder and put it into a small pocket on the back Kelli hadn't seen before. "These are popular with women who want to carry their phones or cash without having to take their purses around. We're just tweaking that idea with stun guns and recording devices." She handed the garter to Kelli. "Now to try it on."

"I FEEL LIKE A SPY."

Kelli patted her silk dress above her right thigh. The

light from the city filtered through the Jeep's windows and showed a slight bump beneath her hand.

"Just make sure when we sit down to put a napkin over that, Ms. Bond," Mark said, eyes sliding back to the road. Kelli snorted.

"Is it bad I'm kind of hoping I can use the stun gun? I've never used one before."

"As long as you don't use it on me, we'll be fine."

Kelli stopped fidgeting with the garter filled with goodies and started to rub her hands together instead. She was nervous and trying to hide it. Mark wanted to tell her it would be okay, but he knew it wouldn't do any good. In her mind, they were going into enemy territory, and he couldn't exactly disagree.

The rest of the car ride was spent in silence. It wasn't unpleasant, just two people caught in their own thoughts. Mark wondered what the woman was thinking about. *He* should have been thinking of the situation at hand, but his mind seemed to be sticking to her.

When he had told her she was beautiful before, it had been partially a lie. What he should have said instead was that she was the *most* beautiful woman he'd ever seen. It wasn't because of the dress or the way her hair curled. It was the smile of modesty and the dose of vulnerability that had made every part of his attention attach to her. Kelli Crane was a strong-willed, fascinating woman. She continued to surprise him with her loyalty and concern for others. Also able to see his internal pain, she'd had the compassion to try to quell it.

And she had.

And then some.

Her speech and her kiss had dislodged an affection for the woman he was finding he would like to keep beyond whatever happened tonight. But did she feel the same? Was it just the heat of the moment moving them down this path? Could they be together once she didn't need protecting anymore? The bodyguard didn't ask any of these questions.

Now wasn't the time.

They had work to do.

The Bowman Foundation was lit up like a Christmas tree. Even at night, it felt like the epitome of hope, bright and promising to those who needed it. None of this surprised Mark as he parked the Jeep and took in the surroundings. Cars filled the parking lot. Two men in suits stood outside the doors, clipboards in their hands and smiles on their faces.

"Hopefully we're on the list," he said, trying to get her attention away from wherever her mind was focused. It worked. She laughed a little and turned. Unease lined her expression. It was a look he didn't like at all. "Kelli, we don't—"

"Mark, this is possibly the best way to get Dennis to condemn himself," she interrupted. "So, we do have to do this. I don't want Dennis ever to show up at my house again. I won't live in ongoing fear for Grace's safety."

She patted her thigh one more time and got out of the truck. Mark took a deep breath and followed.

Aside from the men at the door, he didn't spot anyone else outside the building. Jonathan was doing a good job at hiding.

"My lady," Mark said. He held his arm out.

"It's been a long time since I walked in these heels, so I truly thank you," Kelli said, laughing. She linked her arm through his.

Together they walked right up to the lion's den.

Chapter Seventeen

Kelli's head swam.

Pain and confusion. That's all she could wrap her mind around at first. What had happened? Where was she? Why did her head hurt so much?

Darkness invaded the space around her, clinging to her skin like a blanket. Blinking several times didn't help. She still couldn't see a thing. The darkness was thick. Unrelenting. Terrifying.

Where was Mark?

She desperately tried to remember what had happened. The life before this darkness. But she was too panicked to concentrate. The pain in her head didn't help matters, either.

Calm down, Kel, she thought sternly. That phrase was becoming her mantra, she realized. What she also realized absolutely killed any attempt at calming down.

She couldn't move.

She was tied to a chair.

"Oh, my God," she gasped. Her wrists were pulled behind her, tied together. She tried to move them but they were anchored to the back of her seat. As she twisted her hips, her stomach dropped. She was tied to the front two chair legs from her shins to her ankles.

Wherever she was, it wasn't good.

"Hello?" she asked timidly—afraid of who would answer, afraid that no one would.

"Kelli!"

If her stomach dropped before, it absolutely crashed through her and the floor at the voice beside her.

"Lynn? Oh, God, is that you, Lynn?"

"Yes! Yes, it's me."

Kelli almost cried in acute fear. She forgot to breathe for a moment.

"Grace?" she asked, every hope and prayer in her world resting on one name.

"She was still in the apartment with Nikki. She should be okay," Lynn said hurriedly. "I was the stupid one who left it."

Relief flooded the mother's heart. She wasn't completely calm, but she was in a better state of mind to work with whatever happened.

"Are you okay?" Kelli asked.

She could hear the other woman trying to move around. "He beat me up pretty good—I think my lip's busted—but I'll live." Lynn paused, then added, "I think."

"Who beat you up?"

"I don't know his name—all I was doing was taking out the trash—but he shoved me into the elevator and just attacked." Lynn's voice wavered. "I shouldn't have left the apartment, but I was trying to be nice since Mark let us stay in his place! I'm sorry, Kel. I should have stayed with Grace."

The maternal voice of reason within Kelli agreed, but the woman who loved her friend like only family could defended her.

"Nikki will realize something is wrong. She won't leave Grace to come get you. She'll call the cops," Kelli reasoned. She hoped it was true. She prayed it was true. "Do you know where we are?"

"No, the guy slammed my head into the elevator wall, then nothing but stars. Are you okay? What happened?"

Kelli tried her restraints once more. They didn't move an inch.

"My head hurts a lot," she admitted, giving up. "Everything's fuzzy. I remember walking into the Bowman Foundation with Mark. We talked to a few people—everyone was mingling before the dinner actually started—" She closed her eyes tightly, trying to remember. "We were looking for Dennis but ran into the publicist guy who said he hadn't shown up yet. Ugh, my head." A wave of nausea passed over her. She opened her eyes, but the darkness kept her disoriented.

"What else?" Lynn prodded.

"I went to the bathroom and—and it was out of order," she continued, words coming faster as her memory was catching up. "I was told to use the one up the stairs." She remembered leaving the second-floor meeting room and walking into the hall. Her heels had been loud as she hurried to the steps. The publicist had said it wasn't too long a trip. She'd see the bathroom door as soon as she reached the top and turned. "I got to the top but there was a man there! He was waiting for me!"

"Who was he? What did he do?"

Kelli shook her head, instantly regretting the action.

"He was wearing a mask—a ski mask." Then it clicked. "He was wearing all black, too, just like the man who broke into the house...just like the man Mark said he'd seen at the fire." A sick feeling began to spread throughout her. "I tried to run," she continued after an involuntary gulp. "But I didn't get far. He threw a punch that I apparently didn't dodge." Now the pain in her head made sense.

"We both were knocked out, brought together and tied to chairs," Lynn summarized. "But why? And where do you think we are?"

Kelli didn't answer. Instead, she listened for a moment.

Silence.

"I can't hear anything," she whispered, "and our mouths aren't bound like the rest of us. And I really can't move—whoever did this took their time—so for them not to gag us, too?"

"Means we're probably not where help could hear us if we screamed," Lynn answered.

"Right." Kelli felt panic flare. Her heartbeat thumped much faster than normal.

"The guy who grabbed me wasn't Dennis Crawford," Lynn whispered. "I didn't recognize him at all."

Kelli let out a long breath that shook at the end. "That means our plan was never going to work," she admitted. "All of this was pointless. We don't know what Victor found, we don't know why it's bad and we don't know who put us here. We're not even back to square one." Kelli's fear bled into the tears brimming in her eyes. "I'm so sorry for getting you mixed up in all of this, Lynn."

"No. Don't you go all soft on me," Lynn shot back. Her voice was hard, pointed. "We aren't going to sit here and play the blame game, especially since none of this falls on either of us. Okay?"

Kelli nodded but remembered the woman next to her couldn't see her. "Okay."

Another bout of silence fell between them. Kelli tried her best to keep her thoughts away from her daughter and the fact that if anything happened to Kelli and Lynn, Grace would end up an orphan. Thoughts of the bodyguard weren't any better. Worry clutched her heart as she wondered where the man was and if he was okay.

You can't lose it now, she tried to yell in her head. *Mark will save you. He'll rescue both of you from the dark. You'll see Grace soon.*

But no amount of self-assurance could stop the sheer terror that seized her body at what happened next.

Another voice sounded in the darkness, so close she could feel the breath the words rode on.

"I guess it's time to break this silence and tell you why exactly you're here," he said. "And why you definitely won't be leaving."

Light filled the room. Kelli blinked past her fear and focused on the man across from her.

"Oh, my God."

THE WOMAN CHATTING his ear off was named Maria Something-or-Other. Mark tried to be polite as he scanned the ever-growing group in the large room, but the older woman was starting to grate against his already sensitive nerves. Kelli had taken the easy way out and escaped to the bathroom. He'd tried to follow but had found it trickier than it should have been to detach from the older woman. When Kelli came out she'd be surprised to see the two partygoers chatting right outside the door.

"It's nice to see the younger people start to give

back," Maria said after another large sip of her champagne. "I only wish my son were as charitable. Do you have any kids, Mr. Tranton?"

If she hadn't said his name, Mark probably would have just kept nodding along.

"No, I don't."

"Good on you," she said with vigor. "Enjoy as much as you can before your wife and you decide it's the right time. Me? I wish I'd waited a few years. Traveled and such." Maria kept on with that thought, not giving Mark the room to interject that he wasn't married. Not that he'd tell her that, though. She—along with a few other guests whom they had talked to after first coming in—had made the assumption Kelli was his wife. And that didn't really bother him, he was finding out.

Mark scanned the large room once more, taking in the new and old faces of the fifty or so guests who had arrived already. Round tables with white tablecloths and centerpieces made up of succulents and burlap—something Kelli had pointed out was simple yet beautiful—took up the entire room, leaving only enough space against the far wall for a grand piano and its pianist to perform while everyone mingled. They had wondered why the dinner wasn't served in the chic lounge downstairs. Publicist Hector had answered that question when asking if they liked the more "intimate" setting. The room was indeed smaller than the lounge. It forced people to talk to each other instead of doing what Mark was trying to do. He just wanted to stand in the corner and not talk to a soul who wasn't Kelli while waiting for Dennis finally to show.

Maria was somewhere in a conversation that involved the topic of margaritas on the beach when Mark flipped from nonchalance to outright concern.

"Maria," he interrupted, making her pause midword, "can you do me a favor and go check on Kelli? She's been in there for a few minutes."

Whatever offense she might have taken at being interrupted was lost when she realized she was needed. She smiled wide.

"Isn't that sweet," she almost cooed. "Of course I'll go check up on her."

The older woman swished her long dress away with her, disappearing into one of the two public bathrooms next to the meeting room opening. Mark kept his eyes glued to the partygoers. The dinner wouldn't start until the CEO made his grand entrance. Apparently he couldn't be bothered to mingle. Dennis was still nowhere to be seen.

If he didn't show, they'd have to come up with a different plan.

"Are you sure she went in there?" Maria asked a moment later. Mark looked down at her, confused.

"She said she was going to the restroom," he answered, replaying Kelli's words in his head. But he hadn't actually seen her walk in there, had he?

"Well, we would have seen her leave," Maria reasoned. "So my guess is, she never went inside."

Mark let out a breath that was filled with bad, bad words and left the wide-eyed woman behind. If Kelli wasn't in the bathroom, and he knew she wasn't in the meeting room, then he had no idea where she would be. Guilt and shame coursed through him as he pulled his cell phone from his jacket pocket. He shouldn't have let her out of his sight—bathroom be damned.

Moving out into the hall, he fully planned on calling Kelli and, if she didn't answer, bringing Jonathan in, but apparently the bodyguard *and* their boss had already called several times.

"Son of a—" he ground out, realizing he'd silenced his phone by accident. Such a small mistake might cost him big. Temporarily ignoring the missed calls from Jonathan, he called Kelli.

Her phone went straight to voice mail.

Mark fisted his hands, already starting to walk down the hallway. There were a few offices on this side, in the opposite direction of the main stairs. He called Jonathan while he quickly looked in each one.

"Jonathan, I need you to—" Mark started as soon as the phone picked up.

"Mark, Lynn was taken," Jonathan interrupted.

The bodyguard stopped in his tracks.

"What?"

"She apparently decided to take the trash out and didn't come back."

"Is Grace okay? Nikki?"

"Yeah, Nikki didn't want to chance leaving her alone, so she locked up and called me. I'm over here now."

Mark's relief made him start to move again.

"How do you know Lynn was taken?"

"There was a bag of trash from your apartment strewn next to the elevator…and in the elevator there was some blood."

"Did you call the manager to look at the security feed?" Mark knew each floor had cameras positioned at the ends of the halls. The apartment complex prided itself on safety.

"Yeah. Too bad the room where the feeds go was

broken into and vandalized," Jonathan said, clearly unhappy. "I called the cops, Mark. With or without proof of what Dennis has been doing, a woman was kidnapped."

"No, you did the right thing," he assured his friend. No sign of Kelli down this side of the hallway. He turned back and hurried for the stairs. "I can't find Kelli," he admitted, grit in his voice. "She went to the bathroom and never made it inside. I lost her, Jonathan. I had one job and I lost her."

It was Jonathan's turn to suck in a breath.

"I'm on my way."

"No, you stay with—" Mark stopped midsentence. Past the open stairs that connected all three floors, walking out from around the corner of a hallway was none other than Dennis Crawford.

Meeting Mark's stare, he stopped.

The bodyguard felt rage boil within him.

Dennis wore a tux, much like Mark, but with one blazing difference—he had a bloody nose. Like someone had busted it trying to fight back.

Before Mark could deal with what his next step would be, Dennis turned tail and ran.

The bodyguard was right behind him.

Chapter Eighteen

For the second time in as many days, Mark had to rely on speed rather than brawn. Dennis had run back down the hallway he'd come from—a hallway that was long, narrow and straight—giving Mark enough time to reach the retired editor at the end of it.

"Where is she?" Mark roared. He grabbed the man by the scruff of his jacket and pulled back. It was an attempt to throw Dennis to the ground—to stop him—but the man was quicker than he looked. He spun around and threw a punch that landed squarely along Mark's jaw. The pain made him let go of Dennis's jacket. He braced for another hit.

It didn't come.

Dennis pushed through the door next to them while Mark scrambled after him.

The door led to the service stairwell—concrete steps and metal railings—and Dennis seemed to know exactly where he wanted to go. Instead of taking the easier route to the first floor, he started to jump the steps two at a time to go to the third. Mark didn't have time to question the motivation behind the more difficult escape route.

He just wanted to find Kelli.

Dennis jumped three steps and was out the door to the third floor door so fast, Mark was afraid he would lose Dennis completely if Dennis knew the layout of the building. Mark ran up the stairs, feet pounding. The sound that echoed back was almost deafening.

But not so loud that he missed the gunshot that rang out ahead of him.

On reflex alone, Mark stopped and ducked down, waiting for the second shot off. Instead, what followed was an eerie quiet.

How had Dennis gotten a gun so fast? Had he been hiding it?

Something wasn't adding up.

Mark crept up to the open door and looked down the hallway, ready to duck back in at a second's notice.

What he saw *definitely* didn't add up.

Dennis was leaning against a closed door a few feet away, hand holding his side. He was facing the empty hallway ahead of them. Mark waited a moment to see what else would unfold. With his free hand, Dennis pawed at the door handle next to him. He was hurt— that was plain to see.

Confused yet cautious, Mark hurried up behind him, still ready to react if needed.

"I just realized what you said down there," Dennis said, voice low. "You asked where she was. You're the bodyguard." The man turned slightly, keeping his hand on the knob. Mark was about to restrain him when he saw the blood beneath his other hand. He'd been shot in the side. Mark's eyes whipped up and over the older man's shoulder toward the end of the hallway. Who had shot him? No one else seemed to be around. "Unless you have a gun, I suggest we hide," Dennis said, managing to get the door to open. Mark got ready for the ambush he was sure was going to come from the other side but instead was met with a dark office.

"What's going on?" Mark didn't understand anything. "Who shot you?"

"I did," a voice called.

Mark's training made him react faster than his brain could process the man in black stepping around the corner at the end of the hall. He grabbed Dennis and pulled him inside the office as another shot rang out. Mark slammed the door shut, locking it. He threw the light switch and turned on Dennis.

"What the hell is going on?" he asked again. They were standing in a small office with a wooden desk in the middle, two lounge chairs against the wall and a potted plant in the corner. There were two doors in the wall to their right. One open to show a sink and the other closed with a plaque that read Connie Cooper, IT.

Mark immediately went to the latter and cursed when it was locked. He looked back at Dennis, waiting for a response.

"I was trying to protect Kelli and Grace," he said, face contorted in pain. "And myself."

"From what?" Mark wanted to know. If Dennis wasn't the kingpin behind everything, then who was?

The man in black—who had become Mark's nemesis in every way—yelled in the hallway. "It's time we had a little talk, Mark. There are a few things I'd like to say!"

Mark felt his eyes widen. The night kept getting more confusing.

"What?" Dennis asked, apparently alarmed by his change in expression.

"I know that voice," Mark whispered. Recognition

turned to disbelief and then to anger. The man in black was Craig. "He's my neighbor."

KELLI BLINKED AGAINST the harsh light, but the man in front of her was as clear as day.

The Bowman Foundation's own publicist genius, Hector Mendez, was grinning ear to ear.

"My, don't you look lovely," he said, voice sickeningly sweet. "And yet how troublesome you are."

"I don't understand," was all Kelli said.

Hector straightened his tie and shrugged. "And yet, you continued to try and figure it all out," he said. "You can only dig so long before you're just left with a hole that needs to be filled."

The analogy sent a shiver up Kelli's spine, but she held his gaze firmly. Hector tilted his head to the side. It made him look unbalanced, which she was figuring was an accurate assumption to make about him.

"Even now you're trying to work it all out, aren't you?" he asked. "Though who can blame you at this point? Let me start by saying a quick hello to Miss Bradley." He looked at Lynn. "My apologies for my associate, who seems to have gotten a little too happy bringing you in."

Kelli turned to look at her friend. Her lip was indeed busted, there was a cut along her eyebrow and blood had dried on her forehead, along her hairline. Kelli felt her maternal instincts flare. She wanted to protect her best friend—wanted to ensure her family's safety—but couldn't do either if she stayed as scared as she was. Seeing Lynn's wounds was a shock she needed. She rounded on Hector.

"Let her go," she demanded. "She never did any of the digging. It was all me. She knows nothing."

Lynn started to say something, but Kelli shot her a look that froze the sentiment on the tip of her tongue. Kelli didn't know what the outcome of this bleak situation would be, but she needed at least to ensure Lynn's safety. Kelli needed her to be all right. And so did Grace.

"Sadly, I'm not going to do that," Hector said with little empathy. "From what I can tell, even if I were to let Lynn here go, she'd never let *this* go." He motioned to the room around them. It was used as storage. Boxes lined the wall. "Her best friend tortured and killed in front of her? Yeah, I doubt you'll let that go. What do you think, Miss Bradley?"

The anger Kelli had felt changed to dread.

"You bastard," Lynn growled.

"I've been called worse, trust me." Hector detached from his spot against the wall and threaded his fingers together. Moving them quickly, he popped them and sighed. Their current situation had him unfazed. Like *this* was a normal day at the office for him.

And maybe it was.

"I don't understand," Kelli tried again. "How are we a threat if we don't even know what's going on?"

"Threat?" He snorted. "You aren't a threat. An annoyance, but not a threat. Your husband wasn't even a threat, really. He was just a damn fine reporter." Kelli felt her body tense. Hector didn't miss it. "Does it please you to know that you were right about Victor's death? Does it make it hurt any less?"

"So you did set the fire?" Kelli ventured, anger starting to grow.

"I didn't, but yes, it was my call. An unfortunate but necessary precaution."

Kelli shook her head. "Why? What did he find? Was it because of the names in the article?"

Hector's smile shrank. He pinched the bridge of his nose, clearly annoyed, and closed his eyes.

"He found an error in judgment. One I made and refuse ever to pay for." He massaged from the bridge to the top of his nose before opening his eyes again. "I'm afraid I'm not answering your questions to the best of my ability, am I? Well, too bad. It's time for you to answer me some questions. For starters, who all have you talked to about your theories? How many people have you shown the journal to? I need to know exactly how many loose ends I need to tend to."

Kelli set her jaw. "If I tell you, will you let us go?" she asked.

Hector laughed. "Let you go? Oh, no, we're way past that," he sneered. "I don't like loose ends and you definitely need to be tied up."

Another series of shivers danced up Kelli's spine.

"Then why would I answer any of your questions?"

"Simple." He moved over to stand in front of her before bending down so his eyes were level with hers. "This—all of what's about to happen to you—will be a demonstration of what I will do to your daughter if you don't answer *every single question* to my satisfaction. Is that clear?"

She had no time to answer—no time to let the words or anger or absolute, all-consuming fear to sink in—before a distant *bang* made all three of them look toward the door.

"What the—" Hector was up and at the door in a

flash. He pulled his cell phone from his pocket, dialed a number and put it to his ear. Whoever picked up, it was fast. "What's going on out there?" There was a man on the other end, but Kelli couldn't make out what he was saying. She chanced a glance at Lynn. Her eyes were wide with fear. "Your incompetence is outstanding," Hector practically yelled. "Take care of it. I'll send you backup, but I'm leaving." He ended the call with force. "It looks like no torture tonight," Hector said, obviously upset.

Another *bang* echoed in the distance.

"Or at least, I won't be the one to do it."

Without another word, Hector opened the door and left, closing it behind him.

"Those were gunshots, Kel," Lynn said. Her voice was low, terrified.

"I know."

They waited for another shot to sound. It didn't. After a moment, Lynn spoke again.

"Again, remember Marcie Diggle's fifteenth birthday party?" Surprised at the question, Kelli looked at her friend. Her eyebrow rose, but she nodded. "This isn't as bad. Unless they—whoever 'they' are—suggest we play spin the bottle with Gordon Taylor again, we'll be okay." Lynn gave her a smile. It was small and weak, but it was a smile nonetheless. "Despite our current situation, all I can think about is that boy's excess saliva. Yeah, this has nothing on that nightmare."

Kelli couldn't help the laugh that escaped. It was also weak. The world had become horribly complicated in the past few days. "We've sure been through a lot."

Lynn nodded. "Whatever happens to us, Grace will be fine," Lynn assured her.

Kelli felt tears start to prick behind her eyes. She jerked her head to say she agreed. An image of the little girl smiling back at her filled her head.

"I love you, Lynn," Kelli choked out, her composure cracking.

"I love you, too, Kel." Lynn's voice wavered.

It hurt Kelli's heart.

"Now, let's agree on something," Kelli said, trying to tamp out the tears.

"Okay."

Kelli cleared her throat. "We fight like hell when they come for us."

MARK KICKED THE door clear off its hinges with the idea that practice makes perfect. Connie Cooper would not be happy on Monday.

"We don't have a gun," he said to Dennis, walking away from the downed door. His leg was slightly sore, but the pain wasn't anything alarming. He was happy to know he had done it without any issues—that he was strong enough to do it on his own. "And we don't have another way out."

He moved back to the door that led to the hallway. No thundering footsteps, but Craig was still coming their way.

"Do you know if the girls are up here?" Mark whispered.

Dennis stood in the bathroom doorway, a hand towel pressed against his bullet wound. He was growing more and more pale.

"Yes, but I don't know which room."

That was all Mark needed. He unclenched his fist,

still holding the phone from his call to Jonathan, and tossed it to Dennis.

"Call the cops. Then call the contact named Jonathan Carmichael. Tell him everything you know," he ordered. "Got it?"

Dennis caught the phone with his free hand and nodded. "What are you going to do?" he asked.

"I'm going to save Kelli."

There was no time to elaborate. The doorknob started to turn. Mark took up position.

"Why don't we get this over with M—" Craig started. Mark didn't let him finish. Praying the man wouldn't shoot, the bodyguard reared back. He kicked the door for all he was worth. Instead of coming off its hinges as easily as the last—his practice door—this one largely splintered. Mark pushed forward, using the top half of the door as a projectile aimed right at the gunman's head. It caught Craig off guard, giving Mark enough time to kick the bottom half of the door out of the way. He launched forward and kept the top half against Craig, forcing him down to the ground.

Mark rolled to the side once the dust settled, ready to fight the man for his life. But Craig wasn't moving. Mark scanned the wreckage for the gun. He spotted it on the other side of Craig, inches from his open palm. The bodyguard didn't waste time in grabbing it.

Training his new weapon on the man at his feet, Mark kicked off the piece of the door. Craig had thrown his mask away already, confirming exactly who he was and how much damage he'd just taken. With a busted nose matching Dennis's, he also had a busted eyebrow and cheek. Mark had hit him with a lot more force than he'd originally thought.

Craig moved his head to both sides before opening his eyes. They looked enraged.

"What? Going to shoot me, neighbor?" he seethed.

Mark put his shoe on the man's chest to keep him from jumping up. "Where are they?" Mark ground out.

The downed man chuckled. "Even if I told you, would it matter? It's not like I came alone."

Mark's eyebrow rose, silently questioning him, when footsteps sounded in the corridor Craig had come from. Mark wasn't going to catch a break.

Two men popped around the corner, and Craig yelled what clearly was an order at them.

"Kill Kelli Crane!"

Chapter Nineteen

When the men came for them, Kelli and Lynn were both on the floor, having tipped their chairs over toward each other in a fruitless attempt to escape.

Now, staring up into the faces of two strangers in suits, Kelli understood that fighting wasn't an option either woman had.

"Watch the door," said the man closest to Kelli. His partner nodded and went back outside. The first man pulled a gun from beneath his jacket and pointed it down at her. *Grace is safe*, Kelli thought, closing her eyes. Lynn started to yell at the man, tears in her throat.

Bang! Bang!

Kelli's eyelids flew open. The man outside the door dropped, his upper body falling in the middle of the doorway. The man above Kelli redirected his aim.

"Who's out there?" he called.

Like a savior descending from the sky, Mark Tranton answered.

He ducked around the door frame and shot.

The bullet hit the man's arm, forcing him to drop his gun.

"Move and I'll shoot again," Mark warned. But the man didn't listen. He let out a guttural growl and charged the bodyguard. Mark had lied. Instead of shooting him again, he stepped back when the man was close enough and clocked him a good one upside the head.

The man crumpled to the ground.

"Kelli? Lynn? Are you okay?" he asked, rushing inside. He knelt by Kelli and began to work on the rope around her wrists.

"We're a thousand times better now that you're here," Kelli almost cried, relief coursing through her veins.

"Man, do you know how to make an entrance," Lynn added, just as clearly overjoyed at his timing.

"It's Hector Mendez, Mark," Kelli said after he freed her hands. He set her right side up and then moved to Lynn while Kelli started to work on freeing her legs.

"The publicist?"

"Yes. He wouldn't tell us why he's doing this, but he definitely seems to be the mastermind."

Mark untied Lynn's hands just as Kelli freed her legs. Her head was still swimming, but she managed to help Mark right Lynn and untie her legs.

"A different man grabbed me, though," Kelli said.

Mark nodded, disgust showing in his face. "He's my neighbor. I've already had a run-in with him."

"Does that mean we're at the apartment complex?" Kelli realized she still didn't know.

With Lynn's restraints off, the three stood.

"No, we're still at Bowman. On the third floor."

"What about Grace? Is she okay?" Kelli found all of her hope riding on the outcome of his answer. She wasn't disappointed.

"I talked to Jonathan. He said she's safe with Nikki and the cops." Kelli was enveloped by a hug from Lynn.

"Thank God she's okay," Lynn cried.

Mark reached out over her friend's shoulder and took Kelli's chin in his hand.

"I agree."

Kelli felt her lips pull up into a small smile. Mark mimicked the sentiment before dropping his hand.

"Now let's get out of here."

They stepped over the two still men, following the bodyguard closely. Kelli knew that what she'd heard earlier were gunshots and she'd even seen Mark shoot the man in the room with them, but still she wouldn't look at their bodies to confirm if they were dead or not. Knowing, she guessed, would welcome in even more panic at their situation.

"Are we going to take the stairs?" Kelli whispered. She didn't think they'd be able to get out of the building undetected if they took the stairs that split the building in half. There was no telling how many people wanted their silence. They needed to get out of Bowman and fast.

"Yes, but the service stairs," Mark said, picking up on her concern. "We need to make a quick pit stop first."

The two women didn't question him.

They hurried down the length of a small hallway, past offices and a lounge, until it turned right. Mark came to a stop before they rounded the corner. He motioned for them to stay back and pulled the gun up, ready.

He peeked out.

Kelli tensed in worry.

"Son of a—"

Lynn grabbed at Kelli's hand while Kelli fisted the other. She hadn't been ready for the man in black earlier, but now there was no question about how far these people would go. If Mark hadn't come in when he did…

She squared her shoulders.

Now she was ready.

"HE'S GONE."

Kelli gave Mark a look split between confusion and fear. Lynn met his words with an equal amount of both. Seeing the two of them look up to him, count on his words and his protection, filled him with a determination so fierce that he doubted he'd need the gun to get them out of the building.

"Who?" Kelli whispered. There was blood dried near her scalp. She'd been hit there hard.

"Craig," he answered, looking back down the empty hallway. "Stay behind me," he reiterated. No one complained.

Slowly, yet not too slowly because he had no idea how many people were working with Hector, the three crept down the hallway to the debris pile. Mark spotted blood on the carpet, but there was no way to tell where Craig had gone from there.

"What happened to him?" Lynn asked, eyeing the splintered pieces of wood.

"I threw the door at him."

"You threw the *door* at him?"

Mark didn't have time to explain further. He held his hand out to get the women to stop. Peering around the empty door frame, he looked into the office for the man in black.

It was empty.

"Dennis?" he called, still trying to keep his voice low.

"Dennis?" Kelli asked, voice *not* low. It made Mark turn back to her.

"He's on our side."

Kelli's eyebrows went sky-high. If Lynn hadn't had one of her hands, he was sure she would have put them on her hips.

"And how the hell do we know that?"

Movement out of the corner of his eye pulled his attention back into the room. The closed bathroom door in the office opened. Dennis met his gaze and gave a weak smile.

"Because Craig shot him."

Mark moved the party into the small room and took his phone back from the wounded man. Even though the bodyguard hadn't been gone long, Dennis's condition had undoubtedly worsened. Pale and covered in sweat, he kept his hand and the towel beneath it pressed firmly to his side.

When he saw Kelli and Lynn, Mark saw relief wash over him.

"I don't understand any of this," Kelli said to the room. Her expression had softened at Dennis's obvious pain. But not by much.

"We need to leave, now," Dennis said, ignoring her and talking straight to Mark.

"What we *need* are answers," Kelli persisted. She detached from Lynn and walked around Mark. Her anger—her frustration—was running over. Shoulders straight, jaw set, eyes unblinking. Mark wanted answers. Kelli needed them.

Now.

Dennis let out a long, shuddering breath. It made him wince. He refocused on the woman in front of him.

"In short, Hector Mendez has been using the foundation as a cover for drug running. Even shorter—half of the organization is in on it, which means that half of this building probably wants to kill us." He turned to Mark. "Which, again, is why we need to leave. Right. Now."

There was a moment of stunned silence. One that Mark was guilty of partaking in. The Bowman Foundation was a cover for drug running? Who was privy to that knowledge? Who was working for Hector?

The situation, although already on the bad side of the scale, seemed much more dire.

Mark grabbed Kelli's hand.

"Did you do what I said?" he asked Dennis.

"Yes. I called the cops as well as that Jonathan guy. I told him the short truth but then had to hang up." He looked past them to the door debris. "I heard him moving." Dennis looked apologetic. "I didn't want to get shot again."

Lynn, who had fallen back to the door, let out a weird squeak.

"Guys, hear that?" she asked, eyes wide.

Mark listened.

The footsteps were heavy and loud. At least two men were running down the hallway they'd just come from. No doubt thanks to Craig.

"Someone's coming," he said. "We need to get out of this damn building!" Mark pictured waves and waves of men with guns spreading through the building like a virus, trying to find the four of them. At best he had three bullets left. Even if they decided to hide until the cops came, there wasn't any insurance that they would be safe. They were in Hector's territory, not his.

"The only way out is down the service stairs," Dennis pointed out.

Mark nodded. He didn't want to have a standoff now and waste bullets that he might need later. Plus, he didn't think he'd ever be able to recreate his Hulk smash through the door. "Let's go!"

Mark ran into the stairwell through the still open door. Quickly scanning the concrete steps and listening, he deemed them a much better option than where they currently were. He motioned to his flock to move inside the stairwell and start descending. Kelli and Lynn were fast. Surprisingly, Dennis wasn't too bad, either.

Mark shut the door and reestablished himself as the leader.

He needed to be on point if he wanted to protect them.

To protect Kelli.

They managed to clatter all the way past the second-floor door when the third opened with a *bang*.

"Stop," a deep voice bellowed above them. The space between the stairs was wide enough that Mark could see two faces—two *new* faces—peering over the railing. He could also see a gun pointed down.

"Go, go, go," Mark yelled.

Loud cursing from above filled the air as their small group was steps away from the door to the first floor. Mark reached out, ready to open it, when a bullet hit the concrete a step away from him. He recoiled and redirected his feet down the rest of the stairs to the last landing, out of view of their pursuers. The door was labeled Basement, Employees Only.

Mark flung the door open and ushered Kelli, Lynn and Dennis inside.

The basement—a floor he hadn't thought existed—was the complete opposite of the building that stood above. It was cold concrete with dim lighting. Mark bet that not many of the Bowman Foundation employees ventured to this uninviting place. Also unlike the rest of the building, this floor didn't seem to have long parallel hallways. Instead, everything was disjointed—more doors than seemed necessary chopped up every walkway.

Mark went to the left and started to navigate through the layout until he was comfortable there were enough doors between them and their hunters to talk.

"I don't think the elevators reach this level, so I'd have to hope there's a second set of service stairs," he said, slowing to look around another turn before making it. "We reach it, get to the lobby and get the hell out of here."

Mark glanced back at his motley crew. All three were out of breath, but Dennis was panting. Bent over slightly, he put his hand against the wall when they paused.

Kelli didn't miss Mark's summarizing look.

"He needs help, now," she whispered, grabbing Mark's hand and squeezing it. Whatever anger she'd harbored against Dennis seemed to be ebbing away.

"We have to keep moving," Mark answered loudly enough for the other two to hear. "They can't be too far behind us." He squeezed her hand back and pulled her along as he continued forward. Their shoes became a desperate rhythm as they hurried toward a stairwell that might or might not have been there.

The hallway forked and gave them the option to continue forward and turn right, doubling back, or turn left.

Mark definitely didn't want to double back. Hiding on the third floor was an entirely different ballgame from hiding in a dark, empty basement. Its lack of easy access was enough to put the bodyguard even more on edge. So Mark took the second option and peered around the corner to the left.

"Found the stairs," he called back. The door marked Stairs was like a light at the end of a tunnel. "Let's go!"

Finally, he thought, *some good news.*

"Mark," Lynn shrieked.

The bodyguard spun around in time to see Dennis stumble sideways, eyes barely open. Mark moved backward to catch him under one arm while Lynn caught the other. He wasn't fully unconscious, but his knees were buckling. The towel he'd been holding fell to the floor, a bloody mess. Kelli didn't hesitate to pick it back up.

"Keep pressure on it," she told Lynn. Lynn was about to do just that when the stairwell door banged open.

Craig's chest heaved. Blood trickled down his face. Mark's good news hadn't lasted long at all.

Craig smirked.

It made something in Mark break.

"I see you still have my gun," the man said with obvious disapproval. "Are you going to shoot me in cold blood in front of these fine young ladies? Or maybe you can use one of these doors instead?"

Mark's hand twitched. The gun felt heavy in it.

Shooting Craig, no matter how badly he wanted to put the crazed man out of commission, wasn't a good move. Not only did Mark want to save what ammo he had left for the unknown trek across the lobby, but also he didn't want Kelli and Lynn to see him shoot the man. Plus, they still needed answers.

Mark hadn't missed Kelli's attempt to not look at the men he'd already hit upstairs.

No, he thought with determination, *I can take him on my own.*

"Kelli, take this and go hide," he whispered to her. Surprised but perhaps on the same wavelength, she took the gun he held out. Mark dropped out from under Dennis's arm. Kelli replaced him, bolstering the weight of the nearly unconscious man between her and Lynn. "Use it if you have to," Mark urged her.

Kelli looked as though she was going to say something, but Mark didn't have time to listen. They were in a building potentially filled with men who *needed* their silence.

Mark, however, had no intention of staying quiet now.

Chapter Twenty

If Kelli had known how active her night would be, she definitely would have purchased a more flexible dress. As it was, she shuffled along a new corridor, trying to balance Dennis's weight with the pressure to find a hiding spot, and quickly. She hadn't forgotten about the men who had originally forced them into the basement.

"Let's get into a room," Kelli said to Lynn. The shorter woman was having a more difficult time supporting the tall man. It would be much easier to hide him and then hide themselves…but Kelli was realizing she didn't want to just leave him behind. She still didn't know the full extent of his involvement with what had really happened, but Mark had seemed to trust him. Plus, her maternal instincts were in full gear.

Dennis was hurt. Badly.

He needed to be protected.

"In here." Lynn nodded to a door near the end of the hallway. Kelli held most of Dennis's weight as her friend slowly opened it and peeked inside. "It's dark."

"Good."

They struggled inside before Lynn shut the door behind them.

"Should I try the light?" Lynn whispered. Fear

coated her words. Kelli couldn't deny that the darkness made her heartbeat race even faster. The last time she was in a dark room, Hector had been there.

Waiting.

"Yeah, just to see what we're dealing with."

Lynn fumbled against the wall for a moment before flipping the switch.

"Oh, my God," Kelli breathed.

It was a long room that—if she had to guess—was the heart of the basement. That wasn't the only thing it was the heart of—it was easy to see the room housed an insane amount of drugs. Bags of white were boxed across a long table that ran most of the length of the room. Scales sat on the cabinets that lined the wall opposite them, along with boxes that were closed, taped up and marked Bowman Foundation, Providing Hope, Providing Light.

"Why wouldn't they lock *this* door?" Lynn whispered, more panicked than before.

"We need to hide in a different room," Kelli responded instantly, already trying to open the door again. Dennis didn't move with her and instead went completely limp. Kelli wasn't prepared for the dead weight, and together they fell to the floor. Like the rest of the basement so far, it was just painted concrete. Pain exploded in Kelli's elbow as it connected with the floor that just wouldn't give. Dennis slumped on top of her. At least she'd been able to break his fall.

"Crap," Lynn squealed. She crouched down and tried to pull Dennis back up. "He's so heavy for such a lean guy!"

Kelli wasn't going to argue with that.

"Let's set him up against the wall," Kelli said after

taking in a few breaths. Together the two heaved and pulled the man into a sitting position, propping him up as best they could against the wall next to the door. Kelli moved the man's jacket out of the way to see the extent of his wound.

"Oh, man, oh, man," Lynn chanted beside her. "That doesn't look good."

"Don't pass out, please," Kelli scolded. She took the towel Dennis had been using and pressed it against the wound, setting the gun down next to him.

"I almost passed out once when I accidentally *saw you giving birth* and I've heard about it forever," Lynn said in mock offense. She was trying to lighten the mood. "We're in a room filled with cocaine in the Basement of Doom and I'm still hearing about it."

Kelli wanted to smile—she wanted to laugh—but Dennis wasn't looking good. And Mark…

The last she'd seen was him walking toward the man who had killed her husband. She hadn't wanted to leave him, but at the same time she'd known that staying would distract him. Plus she needed to get Lynn and Dennis safe.

"Put your hand on this," Kelli ordered, her mind wholly on Mark. He'd saved her life and now was fighting to keep it safe. Lynn, despite her aversion to blood, did as she was told.

"What do we do now?" Lynn asked.

Kelli stood and surveyed the room. She really didn't like that they had chosen it to hide in. Aside from the door they had just come through, another door at the far end led back out in the direction of the first set of stairs. Another door was opposite it, nearer her. Did it connect to the hallway Mark and Craig were in?

She had to find out.

Kelli nudged the gun on the floor with her foot. "Put that in your hand and shoot anyone who tries to shoot you," she said, another order in a voice she hoped was stern.

Lynn's eyes widened. "Where are you going?"

"To help Mark. I can't just leave him to fight for us." As the words left her mouth, she felt a surge of emotion swell and surround her heart. "I can't leave him," she said more softly.

Lynn could have pointed out that there wasn't much Kelli might be able to do. That he'd made them leave. That she was a distraction. All of the things that Kelli was currently thinking...but Lynn didn't.

"Shouldn't you take this, then?" she asked instead, holding the gun back out to her.

A weird clicking noise cut off Kelli's response. The two women turned toward it.

"No," Kelli whispered in anguish. Someone was turning the doorknob at the other end of the room. The one farthest from Mark. The other men who had chased them had found them. The knob twisted, and both women fell silent in fear. However, the door was locked.

"What do we do?" Lynn whispered. "We can't just leave him here, can we?" She looked down at the defenseless man. His breathing was shallow but he *was* still breathing.

"No, we can't. Come with me," Kelli snapped. "I have a plan and it's probably really stupid."

Lynn didn't question her. She put Dennis's hand against the towel on his side and quickly followed Kelli right to the door. The knob had stopped turning, but jingling could be heard from the other side. They were going to unlock the door.

Kelli hiked up her dress and put Lynn's hand on the fabric.

"Pull," she ordered. Momentarily confused at the weird demand, Kelli caught on quickly. The two pulled their handfuls of fabric in two different directions. They didn't stop until it ripped open up to Kelli's thigh.

Where Kelli could grab Nikki's stun gun with ease.

She pushed Lynn to the side so she wouldn't be seen when the door opened.

"Use the gun if you have to," Kelli whispered.

The jingling of keys stopped as Kelli slid off her shoes and aligned herself to the left of the door. She gave Lynn one quick nod and turned off the light.

The sound of metal scraping metal filled the large room.

Kelli tightened her hand around the stun gun and waited.

Keep calm, Kel. You can do this.

The door unlocked and opened. Even though Kelli would realize later that what happened next was quick, in the moment everything slowed down. Light from the hallway came into the room, but not enough to tip the men off that two women were waiting for them. The man in front took a step inside and reached toward Kelli to flip the light switch.

That's when she acted.

Squeezing the buttons on both sides, she pushed the stun gun into the man's chest. It crackled to life. The man never saw it coming. He dropped the gun in his hand and spasmed to his knees.

"What the hell?" his partner yelled from behind.

Kelli turned, ready to zap him, too, but he was faster. He caught her wrist and twisted hard. She screamed in pain and, like the other man's gun, the stun gun fell to the ground. Kelli brought her foot up in an attempt to kick the man away from her, but he anticipated the move. He slung her down to the ground next to his partner using only her wrist.

Pain once again exploded within her elbow as it connected with the ground.

But pain was nothing compared to the fear that washed over her.

For the second time that night, a man had her on the ground, gun in hand.

"It's amazing how one woman can be such a pain in the a—" he started.

"Ahh!"

Lynn let out a war cry as she rushed the man. Even though she was short in stature, the force of her body hitting his slammed him into the opened door. Kelli scrambled to her feet and lunged at the man's gun hand. She tightened her grip around *his* wrist and tried to shake the weapon free. He thrashed around, dislodging Lynn and nearly knocking Kelli back down. If he moved like that again, she'd lose her grip and he'd surely shoot them both.

So Kelli took a page from the Grace toddler handbook, craned her neck over and bit the top of his hand.

"Are you serious?" the man roared in pain. Kelli bit down harder just as he used his other hand to grab her hair. He yanked back, which did the trick. She yelped in pain, releasing her hold. "It's not so fun, is it?" he spit out. Kelli was sickened to hear a touch of humor in his voice.

"It sure isn't!"

Two *thuds* sounded.

Then Kelli's attacker crumpled to the floor.

Chest heaving, breathing painfully quick, Kelli stumbled over the man she'd shocked and felt for the light switch. When she finally found it, she winced at the pain in her wrist.

The men—the same ones dressed in suits who had chased them into the stairwell to begin with—were sprawled out next to each other. The first one who had been shocked was facedown, arms bent awkwardly away from his gun. The other was slouched against the open door with blood on his temple.

"Why didn't you use your gun?" Kelli asked Lynn. She scooped up the stun gun and the first man's weapon. The stun gun went back to her garter. It was warm to the touch.

"I did," Lynn exclaimed.

"You pistol-whipped him!"

Lynn bent to retrieve the other discarded gun.

"I panicked! Excuse me for not being all Miss Bad Butt Stun Gun Lady," she said with a huff. "But hey, we started with one gun. Now we have three, so that has to be helpful, right?"

"I sure hope so."

MARK SLAMMED INTO the wall so hard that for a moment all he saw was stars. It didn't help that Craig wasn't giving him any breathing room to defend himself—let alone hit him back. Since Kelli, Lynn and Dennis had gone to hide, the man in black hadn't let up.

Apparently he'd been partaking in a lot more gym sessions than Mark had realized.

The bodyguard ducked to the side as Craig aimed a punch his way. Instead of connecting with his face, it hit his shoulder. The pain that came from that added to a growing list of aches radiating throughout his body.

He brought up his bloody knuckle in an undercut to the man's stomach. Craig wheezed and staggered backward. He wasn't unstable for long.

Craig was fast—Mark would give him that—but he was also arrogant. Mark had been in a lot of fights throughout his life and he knew Craig's type. He fought with the confidence that no one else could win. That he was invincible. That, even though Craig's eye was bloody, his torso probably sore and his knuckles bleeding, Mark was still going to lose.

He was wrong.

Mark met him in the middle with a one-two punch to his jaw. Craig blocked before his fist could connect beneath his chin. The bodyguard countered at the same time Craig threw his punch. Mark's fist hit the other side of his jaw just as Craig dealt a jab into Mark's brow.

Mark felt the blood before he even felt the pain.

Both men broke apart, each in their own worlds of hurt. Warm liquid streamed down into Mark's left eye, stinging it. He wiped it away with the back of his hand and cringed at the pain. He could have sworn he'd heard a crack but hoped Craig had only busted his eyebrow.

"You know, I could have killed you more times than I care to count over the last two years. I should have." Craig backed up a few steps, rubbing the length of his jaw. "But no, Hector said you didn't know anything. That you were harmless." He laughed and spit to the side. Blood mingled with his teeth. "I bet he'll be singing a different tune when he finds his men upstairs."

"So—what?—Hector paid you to kill Victor and then become my neighbor? Sounds like you're whipped," Mark shot back. As much as he wanted to end the fight, he needed to catch his breath. If that meant keeping the man talking for a second and finding out some answers, then so be it.

Craig's nostrils flared.

"Call it an offer of convenience. I needed a place to stay and he needed someone watched for a while. Don't mistake that for blind obedience. I don't work for anyone," he seethed.

"But I thought Boss Hector *was* pulling all of the strings?" Mark prodded. "Or is breaking into a house to steal from a woman and child something you like to do as a hobby?"

"Like you, bodyguard, I have *clients*," he said, a smile starting to seep through his words. "Unlike you, I know how not to destroy their lives completely." His tone gave way to a wide grin. "They don't resent or pity me."

Mark recalled the soft touch of Kelli's lips earlier that day.

The all-consuming guilt he'd felt for the death of Victor was one he'd never forget. However, that didn't mean it would keep him from living. Trying to cut Mark down by reminding him he hadn't saved Victor wasn't going to work. Not anymore.

If anything, it made his resolve stronger.

"You're right," Mark said. It was his time to smirk.

"You should have gotten rid of me when you had the chance."

This time Mark was the faster of the two. He grabbed the man's shirt collar with both hands and head-butted him hard. Craig let out a howl of pain and fell to the ground.

Ready to finish the fight—to knock the man out of commission—Mark went for him again. Craig didn't try to back away or move to the side. Instead, he grabbed at his ankle and produced something that went beyond leveling the playing field to downright demolishing it.

Craig held the small revolver steady as he struggled to his feet. There was no smile left in him.

He was all pissed.

"You had another gun?" Mark asked, frustration and anger clashing inside of him.

"Welcome to Texas!"

Chapter Twenty-One

The good part about fighting in such a narrow space was that the only way Craig could easily escape was by backtracking several feet before fleeing through the stairwell door. On the flip side of that coin, Mark was in the same boat. To get out of view or range of the gun in Craig's hand, Mark would have to run backward and hope he could turn around either corner before the crazed man got a shot off. The other option was to rush him but, by the look in Craig's eyes, Mark knew he'd be shot in the process.

So Mark quickly weighed his limited options as Craig got to his feet. His gun never wavered. He raised his hand a fraction, getting a better bead on Mark's head. The bodyguard tensed.

He needed to move—to disarm the man—or else Mark wouldn't be able to protect the people in the basement counting on him.

To protect Kelli.

"I'm done with this," Craig ground out. Blood stained his teeth as he spoke. "You're not worth all of this trouble."

Mark bent, ready to charge, when a loud *bang* sounded. He froze. He hadn't been fast enough. He was too late.

Craig had shot him and now he was going to die.

Mark waited for the pain or the darkness that introduced death to overtake him.

But it never came.

Craig dropped his gun arm to his side and fell awkwardly to his knees. Even though he was wearing black, the bodyguard could see blood blossoming right above his stomach. Craig's wide eyes traveled over his shoulder.

"Drop the gun or I'll shoot higher next time," Kelli demanded, voice even. Mark whipped his head around.

Kelli Crane was absolutely fierce.

She stood barefoot, legs braced apart, both hands holding the gun with an almost perfect stance. Her hair was wild, and he couldn't help but notice that her dress had a new slit showing almost all of her bare leg. He wasn't as thrilled about the blood he could see dripping from her elbow, but there was no doubt that Kelli was holding her own. And then some.

Mark's attention went back to Craig as he dropped his gun. That got Mark moving. He closed the space between them and picked up the weapon. The sound of Kelli's bare feet slapping the concrete echoed around them as she surprised Mark once again. She pushed past him, put her foot on Craig's chest and kicked.

He fell backward with a groan.

"That's for threatening my daughter and hurting Lynn." She reared back and kicked him in the groin. He rolled over with a yell. The bodyguard cringed. "That's for hurting Mark." She lowered the gun at him. "That bullet is for me," she whispered, voice so cold it froze Mark to his spot. Was Kelli really going to kill Craig? Would he try to stop her? Could he?

She took a deep, shuddering breath. Luckily, he wasn't going to have to find out. Without turning, she handed the gun back to Mark. "And the fact that I'm not going to kill you right here and now is for Victor. He'd give you mercy, a courtesy you didn't extend to him or his family."

Kelli turned to Mark with one unmistakable expression written across her face.

Relief.

"Are you okay?" she asked. Her tone had warmed up considerably.

"Thanks to you."

A small, tired smile tugged up the corner of her lips.

"Do you think you can carry him into that room?" Kelli motioned to the door behind them. It was offset to the right so he had to move to the side to see it. That was probably the reason Craig hadn't noticed Kelli walk up at first.

"Yeah, but I think we should get going before anyone else catches up to us," he advised. The two men who had chased them into the basement must be somewhere close.

Kelli's smile grew a fraction.

"Believe me, I think we have enough firepower between us now that we'll be okay until the cops get here." She sobered. "Dennis is fading. I don't think we need to move him any more."

Mark nodded after some consideration. The possibility that they'd be met with more force in the lobby—or even the stairwell—was high. At least they had two guns now. If they holed up in a room, then waiting wouldn't be as stressful.

"Don't worry about being gentle with him," Kelli said when Mark reached for a still-writhing Craig.

"It didn't even cross my mind."

KELLI HADN'T EXAGGERATED when she said they had enough firepower. She watched Mark's surprised expression with a bit of pride as he took in Lynn standing near the two downed men with a gun in each hand. After calling Jonathan and updating him on their location, he got the entire lowdown of what had happened from Lynn.

"Maybe you should think about joining Orion," he said.

Kelli shrugged. "When you back Mama Bear into a corner..."

Mark laughed. She realized how happy the sound made her.

A few minutes passed before a sound she *wasn't* happy to hear met their ears. Footsteps were pounding across the concrete in the hallway they'd just left.

In a flash, Mark raised the handgun Kelli had used to shoot Craig, Kelli grabbed the revolver Craig had almost used to shoot Mark and Lynn pointed both her guns all at the doorway. They were done messing around.

"Whoa, whoa! I come in peace, guys!" Jonathan Carmichael held his hands up in surprise at the scene when he opened the door. "When you said you had this, I was assuming you were just trying to seem manly in front of the ladies, but damn!"

With Jonathan came a flood of police and two EMT groups. One dispatched upstairs to check on the downed men there. The second came for Dennis and the others.

"Take him first," Lynn said to one of the EMTs. She pointed to Dennis. "He's the good guy, not them."

And they did just that.

Finally, escorted by Jonathan and the head of police himself, Kelli, Mark, Lynn and Dennis made it out of the Bowman Foundation. Lynn gave her statement in the parking lot before asking to be dropped off at the hospital so Dennis wouldn't be alone, while Mark and Kelli went straight to the station. There they told the entire story.

When they'd finished, Kelli said, "And if you don't believe us—" she maneuvered her dress around under the table and pulled the recorder from her new favorite accessory "—pretty sure we recorded the entire thing."

Luckily the police already had believed them. The recording only solidified their next actions. An all points bulletin went out on the missing Hector Mendez. The CEO of the Bowman Foundation, along with almost all of the staff, were quickly brought in for questioning. Radford Bowman, despite his importance within the foundation, appeared to have no idea what his publicist was up to while on the clock. The lackeys who *had* been working with Hector confirmed Bowman's innocence while condemning those who were not innocent in the least, each trying to swing a deal for their knowledge against Hector.

Mark and Kelli didn't stay long enough to get a head count of how many were in on the scheme. They got the okay to leave with the promise they'd be back the next day.

The sun was coming up by the time Mark and Kelli made it back to his apartment. Nikki greeted them with tight hugs and congratulations for "kicking serious butt." Jonathan had given her the CliffsNotes over the phone and she, too, jokingly offered Kelli a job.

Mark stayed in the living room to fill the woman in on everything else that had happened while Kelli excused herself to the bedroom. Finally able to take off the dress she had ruined—but knew she'd always keep— Kelli snagged one of Mark's long shirts and unapologetically crawled into his bed.

Grace, feeling the movement, reached for her mother. Kelli reached right back.

"THIS PLACE IS a dump." To prove his point, Jonathan grabbed the railing and freely wiggled it. The movement nearly took it clear off. Mark rolled his eyes. "I'd never stay here," Jonathan continued.

Mark was with him there. The motel was as rundown as they came. A far cry from what a man like Hector Mendez was probably used to. Yet they had followed him here to the small Florida town's decrepit motel that not even tourists used. It was a perfect place to hide.

If he wasn't being pursued by Orion agents and a private investigator wife. Oliver and Darling Quinn had used every connection in their combined books to follow his trail right to the outside of the one-level motel.

It had been two days since Hector had fled, and Mark was itching to finally take him down. It was a three-way race between Hector fleeing the country, Mark and Orion getting Hector before that, and the FBI agents who had taken over the case catching Hector before anyone else. The Feds had booked it to a town three cities over following up on a reported sighting of the man, along with a credit card used in his name, but Darling had said the information was wrong. She knew more than a few people on the shadier side of the town and was able to track the man to the motel instead. She'd asked if she should let the Feds know of their location but Mark had told her that if and when they caught their man they could give them a ring then.

"Just don't do anything illegal or I'll arrest *you*," the local beat cop, Cara Whitfield, had warned on the ride over. She had talked to the police in Dallas and had been filled in on the possibility that Hector had fled to her small town. It was a possibility she hadn't liked at all. She'd agreed to accompany and help them despite the fact that they weren't truly law enforcement.

Now she stood with the two of them as they stopped to discuss a plan.

"How do you want to play this?" Jonathan asked. Their target was in the room farthest from the office.

"We could always pretend to be housekeeping," Mark offered. "Works for Darling on some of her cases."

"Unless you have a convincing female voice, I don't think he'll answer the door," Jonathan insisted.

"Hey, men can do housekeeping, too," Mark scolded. "Thinking otherwise is sexist."

Jonathan nodded. "True," he admitted. "Let me say it, then."

Cara made a noise that clearly indicated she was unsure whether or not to be amused.

"Or we can use this," she said, waving a key in the air. "The front-desk clerk said a man fitting Hector's description was the one to pay for the room."

That sobered the men.

"Lead the way," Mark said to the officer. She pulled her gun from her holster.

"Let's try not to get anyone shot."

The three of them sidled to the left of the door. Although Hector was dangerous, the best Cara would let them do was have their stun guns—not cell phone–shaped—as weapons. That was fine by Mark. He wanted to lay hands on the man. Not bullets.

Despite her annoyance at their antics, Officer Whitfield didn't use the key right off the bat. Instead, she rapped on the door.

"Housekeeping," she called.

No one responded.

"Housekeeping," she tried again.

This time there was a loud crash and scuffling on the other side of the door.

"He's running," Cara yelled, putting the key in the door.

Instead of sticking behind her, Mark turned and ran around the building. He'd already noticed that each room had a back window.

Sure enough, Hector was climbing through it.

"I don't think so," Mark yelled. Hector thumped to the dirt and scrambled to stand.

It didn't work.

Mark threw a punch that put him back on the ground.

Cara was yelling something through the window, but Mark didn't hear it.

"Your luck just ran out, buddy," Mark said.

Hector cradled his jaw, eyes wide in fear. "Let me go and I can make you a very rich man," he said quickly. "You could have everything you've ever dreamed of."

The bodyguard didn't skip a beat.

"Sorry, my dreams can't be bought."

"How about your happiness, then?" Hector whispered angrily as Cara and Jonathan ran up. "You can have *whatever* you want."

Mark pictured Kelli and Grace and smiled.

"What I truly want in life, money can't buy."

Chapter Twenty-Two

Kelli hadn't been in the hospital since she gave birth to Grace. She wasn't afraid of them. She just wasn't comfortable in them. However, she voluntarily walked through the sterile-smelling hallways with determination.

It was time she had a talk with someone.

She finally found the room she was looking for and knocked, oddly nervous. Talking followed by laughter floated out as the door was opened.

Lynn was a little dressier than normal, wearing an orange-and-white floral jumper with matching flats. Her hair was even teased out a bit, with her prettiest hair band secured around her head. It was her smile, though, that was the most beautiful part of her outfit. She was happy, no doubt about it.

Kelli raised her eyebrow at her friend, who promptly averted her gaze.

"Hey, Kel," she greeted her. "Is it time already?"

Kelli smiled. "Yeah, the movers get to the house in an hour," she said. "Everything is all ready to go except Grace's toys and some random knickknacks."

"Where's Mini-You?"

Kelli felt her lips stretch wider. She didn't bother hiding the bigger smile. "She's at the house. She was trying to get Mark to play Pretty Princess with her when I left."

Lynn laughed. "I'll go try to save him," she said, reaching for her purse against the wall. When she straightened, she glanced back in the direction of the hospital bed Kelli couldn't yet see from her spot in the doorway. "Do you want me to stay for this or…?"

"You can leave," Kelli assured her. "I'll be fine."

"Oh, I wasn't worried about you," Lynn shot back with a wink. "I've seen with my own eyes you can handle your own."

They said goodbye, and Lynn left after a few words to the patient over her shoulder. Kelli took a deep breath and went farther into the room.

Dennis Crawford was propped up in bed, hooked up to machines, but also looking a thousand times better than he had when he'd been brought in. One emergency surgery and lots of bed rest had done the man wonders. She even rethought her earlier assumption that he was forty.

"I was wondering when you'd come," he said.

"Apparently life didn't pause itself while we were unknowingly taking down a drug-running operation." She shrugged. It made him laugh, but not too long. He seemed to still be uncomfortable with his healing wounds.

Dennis motioned to the chair next to the bed. It was really close and smelled like Lynn's favorite perfume. Kelli made a mental note to ask her about this new relationship she seemed to be starting. But Lynn had been through a lot recently, so she wouldn't tease her too much just yet.

"How are you feeling?" Kelli asked, unsure of how

to talk to the man she'd thought was the ultimate evil just two weeks beforehand.

"Sore but alive. I'm told that you refused to leave me in that basement." He gave her a half smile. "Thank you for that."

"I heard I was returning the favor." She shifted in her seat and stopped dancing around what she wanted to ask. "Tell me everything. Lynn offered, but I wanted to hear it from you."

Like her visit, it seemed Dennis was anticipating Kelli's desire to have him explain as much as he knew. He leaned back against his pillow but held her gaze as he spoke.

"In the beginning, I was contacted directly by Bowman's CEO, Radford, to do a spotlight on the foundation," he started. "It seemed like an open-and-shut story, and I truly thought it was. Until the fire." He averted his eyes for a second, pained. It was an emotion he'd masked well in his office when she'd first confronted him. "Radford came to my office the next day to offer his condolences. I told him I still wanted to honor Victor by printing his last story. He thought that was a great idea. He left, and then a few hours later, Hector showed up. He told me Victor had gotten some names wrong in his story. I didn't believe him. Victor was one of my best writers. Very thorough, especially so close to turn-in. Hector also started acting very strange as he tried to convince me otherwise, but I insisted Victor wouldn't have made that mistake."

"What did Hector say to that?" Kelli found herself leaning in a bit.

"He got angry. Stood up and shut my office door. Then he laid it all out for me."

"He told you about running drugs? Just like that?"

Dennis smirked. It wasn't in humor.

"He was proud of what he'd done. I think he wanted someone who knew what it was like to be successful to be in awe of the success *he'd* achieved." Kelli realized she wasn't that surprised. She could picture Hector's arrogance with ease. "And, in all honesty, I was impressed in a strictly objective way. Turning half of a charity into a cover for running drugs in direct competition with the cartel? That takes serious guts and absolutely thorough planning."

"And a good dose of stupidity," she added. If the cartel had found out they had lost business because of Hector, he—and everyone connected to him—would have met a very bad end.

"That, too. When he realized that Victor had actually snagged the names of two ex-cartel runners who helped make his venture possible, he panicked. Especially when the calls to the house didn't so much as make Victor think twice. To say Hector escalated quickly is an understatement." He frowned.

"Did he admit he hired Craig to start the fire?"

Dennis nodded. "Those weren't his exact words, but he heavily implied it. He told me he was a well-connected man who wouldn't hesitate in burning me…like Victor had burned." Kelli's jaw tightened. She fisted her hands on her lap. Dennis paused, then continued, voice low. "However, now I know that he wasn't actually all that well-connected. There are very few people who would directly run against the cartel, in direct opposition. And, if he had been so well-connected, I have no doubt that all of us would have met our ends some time ago. Instead, Hector personally visited me and talked to me about covering up the article that could put him in the spotlight. I think his venture was a start-up of sorts and too new for him to really have any allies yet, aside from the lackeys beneath him. Either way, when he came here he must not have believed me when I said I'd keep my mouth shut and change the story—which was good, because I wouldn't have—so he gave me a new incentive."

"Grace," Kelli whispered. After the fire, the secret of her pregnancy had become public.

"And you." His expression softened. "In my line of work, I've had to become a lot of things—hardened, blunt, often seemingly without an ounce of empathy— but something in me seemed to soften, to almost break. What if I did report the real story and wasn't able to get the evidence to put Hector and the whole business away? What if the FBI swooped in and still couldn't manage to get anything to send Hector away for life? I didn't even have Victor's original notes and didn't even know they existed at the time. Every way I looked at it I realized that, for once, I couldn't take a chance on everything falling through. I couldn't gamble with your lives. I wouldn't. So I changed the names the way Hector wanted and hoped you'd never look into it." He gave her a wry smile. "But then you showed up with Victor's original notes and an unwavering amount of loyalty."

That relaxed her a bit. She gave him an apologetic look. "Sorry," she said, not at all meaning it. Dennis waved his hand to dismiss what he also knew was a lie. "How did they know I had the journal?"

Dennis didn't hold back his anger for the answer. "When I came to speak to you at your new house—to try and get you to stop—I had already been visited by

Hector. He said if I didn't get you to stop and get the notebook, then you'd pay. He also let me in on the fact that apparently my house was bugged so he could ensure I wasn't up to anything. Something I had suspected but hadn't been able to prove yet. He may have been arrogant but he was also clever."

"So at the Foundation dinner—" she started.

"I gave him the notebook and told him to leave you all the hell alone." He motioned to the fading bruise across his nose. "He wasn't happy."

"I'm sorry," Kelli said, meaning it that time.

"In the end, it turned out better than I could ever have hoped. I heard Mark was able to be the one who grabbed Hector from Florida, right?"

Kelli loved being able to nod at that.

"Mark and Jonathan tracked him down and now the FBI have him back in town. I've since been assured that no amount of money will keep him out of a life-long prison sentence. I also learned that, thanks to some publication that has been blasting the story all over the internet, the Feds publically confirmed that Hector's entire operation has been shut down while all of those that followed him have admitted to their part in everything. I also couldn't help but notice that my name and Grace's were never mentioned. I think the publication is called the *Scale*?" She smiled and cocked her head to the side. "You wouldn't happen to know anything about that, would you?"

It was Dennis's turn to lie. He shook his head. "I've been attached to this bed since they brought me in. I wouldn't even be able to do that."

Kelli laughed, and just like that, the weight of the unknown lifted. She finally had the entire story behind

Victor's death. Justice had been brought not only to the man at the top of the operation but also to those who had helped build his tower.

"Thank you, Dennis," she said, holding his gaze with a look of absolute sincerity. "If Victor were here he would thank you, too." She took his hand in hers and squeezed it.

He squeezed back. "He was a good man."

"Yes, he was."

KELLI PULLED UP to the house for the last time and got out with a much lighter heart. The Dallas weather had been kind enough to revert to its normal heat instead of the freak storms that had plagued the city the past two weeks. If Mark hadn't resigned from his construction job to become a full-time Orion agent again, he probably wouldn't have had work for a while. Kelli couldn't help but smile when she thought about the bodyguard.

After he and Kelli had gotten back from the police station, he'd told Nikki she could go home. He had—with permission—fallen asleep next to Grace and Kelli. Kelli had awoken hours later to the sound of Mark and Grace playing blocks in the living room. Since then, the three of them had fallen into a groove of being together.

One that just felt right.

One that, without saying it aloud, they'd both decided to continue to explore.

One that Kelli hadn't expected but absolutely loved.

"Hello?" she called into the boxed-up house.

"Back here, and please bring your camera," Lynn called.

Kelli, not one to question Lynn's excited voice, pulled

her phone out and hurried to Grace's bedroom. Once there, she almost doubled over in laughter.

Mark sat on the floor, a bright pink boa wrapped around his shoulders, a plastic crown on his head, cheeks tinted with blush. He had a plastic teacup in his hand while Grace—also wearing a crown and blush—sat in Lynn's lap across from him.

"I see someone just had his first taste of Pretty Princess," Kelli said around her fits of laughter. She quickly snapped a picture while she spoke. She looked at Lynn. "I thought you were supposed to help save him?"

Lynn put her hands up in defense. "I tried!"

Mark snorted. "By *tried* she means she tried to get me to wear some of your lipstick," he said. Kelli almost hooted at that.

"Hey, listen here, buddy, I was trying to offset the blush we had to put on to match your boa," Lynn shot back.

Grace just giggled between them.

"Is this my life now?" Kelli joked.

Mark's lips stretched into a grin. "One can hope," he said.

His words made Kelli's stomach flutter.

Lynn stood and picked up Grace. "Okay, gag me, guys," she said. "You're all over here making Pretty Princess somehow *romantic*. I think it's time we go outside and look for bugs or something, don't you, Grace?"

Grace nodded so hard that her crown nearly fell off. Kelli adjusted it and kissed her forehead before the two left the room.

"Do you want to keep that on or take that off before the movers get here?" Kelli asked the bodyguard.

He shrugged. "I don't know. I think it's a really good color on me," he joked.

"Well, how about I make you a deal?" She walked over to him and took the boa from his neck, her hand lingering beside his cheek. "Help me box the rest of this, and Grace's toys, and I'll let you play dress-up with us whenever you want."

Mark laughed. "Deal."

Together they finished boxing the last of the house's stray contents. Kelli spent the time telling him what Dennis had said. He also admitted his opinion of Dennis had gone up exponentially.

"Lynn's been spending a lot of time at the hospital with him, I've noticed," he added when they had finished.

Kelli put her hands to her ears.

"Yeah, yeah, don't get me started on how weird that is," she said. "But after today's talk, maybe I can come to terms with the possibility of them spending more time together. Then again, when have I ever been able to stop Lynn from dating a man she likes?" She paused, then elaborated, because Mark probably didn't know that answer. "Never."

They conducted a walk-through to make sure everything was ready for the movers. When Kelli was able to confirm that it was, they found themselves standing near the front door in a house devoid of sound. Mark took her hand in his and pulled her close.

Bending down a fraction, he met her lips with a kiss that took her breath away. It put fire in her body and passion back into her heart. He pulled away too soon, much to her disappointment.

"How about I make us all some dinner tonight?" he asked, voice transitioning from husky to an attempt at a normal tone. "I make a mean mac and cheese I'm pretty sure Grace will like better than yours."

Kelli tossed her head back and let the laughter come from her gut.

"I'll believe that when I taste it!"

"Then it's a date," he said, all smiles.

"It's a date."

Mark kissed her forehead and let go of her hand.

"I'll give you a moment," he said without even asking if she needed one.

He already knew she did.

Kelli watched him walk away until the front door closed behind him. She let a moment go by before slipping off her shoes. The hardwood kept her feet cool as she started one truly last walk-through.

The hallway Grace had learned to walk in. The one Victor had carried Kelli through after coming home from their wedding.

The master bedroom where Grace often slept with Kelli when she was afraid of being alone. The same room where Victor had held Kelli until they'd both fallen asleep countless times.

The bathroom with the tub that Grace had dubbed "the rubber duckies' home" with its awful green walls that Victor had promised he'd paint "one of these days."

The spare bedroom that had become Grace's haven. The room that had been waiting for Victor and Kelli's future child.

The kitchen that Grace always ran through, unaware of her mother's worry of falling. Where once upon a time Victor had tried to convince Kelli his burned lasagna was, in fact, edible.

The living room where all three Cranes had lived, laughed, and loved together and separately.

Kelli paused in the opening of the nook attached to the heart of the home.

The office that had been solely Victor's. She imagined the man at his desk, bent over his laptop with a look of pure concentration on his handsome face.

Kelli couldn't help but smile.

"I love you," she whispered to the quiet.

The urge to say goodbye to the house—to him—faded as she made her way to the living room window. Outside Lynn was doubled over laughing while Grace chased Mark around the yard. He slowed down just enough to let her catch him before turning around to tickle the toddler. She couldn't hear the girl's laughter, but she felt it in her heart.

She would never stop loving Victor—or their only home—and the life they'd had together, but now it was time to be somewhere else.

As if on cue, Mark turned toward the window. His expression softened, and his smile was genuine. Like her daughter's laughter, she felt it in her heart.

One last time, Kelli tried to memorize the cool hardwood against her feet before slipping her shoes back on. She patted the front door and opened it wide.

They would never forget the past, but it was time to start moving toward the future.

As Kelli shut the door behind her and walked toward the laughter of her diverse little family, she knew it was exactly what Victor would have wanted.

* * * * *

MILLS & BOON®

Why shop at millsandboon.co.uk?

Each year, thousands of romance readers find their perfect read at millsandboon.co.uk. That's because we're passionate about bringing you the very best romantic fiction. Here are some of the advantages of shopping at www.millsandboon.co.uk:

* **Get new books first**—you'll be able to buy your favourite books one month before they hit the shops

* **Get exclusive discounts**—you'll also be able to buy our specially created monthly collections, with up to 50% off the RRP

* **Find your favourite authors**—latest news, interviews and new releases for all your favourite authors and series on our website, plus ideas for what to try next

* **Join in**—once you've bought your favourite books, don't forget to register with us to rate, review and join in the discussions

Visit **www.millsandboon.co.uk**
for all this and more today!

MILLS & BOON®

Why not subscribe?

Never miss a title and save money too!

Here's what's available to you if you join the exclusive **Mills & Boon® Book Club** today:

- ✦ *Titles up to a month ahead of the shops*
- ✦ *Amazing discounts*
- ✦ *Free P&P*
- ✦ *Earn Bonus Book points that can be redeemed against other titles and gifts*
- ✦ *Choose from monthly or pre-paid plans*

Still want more?

Well, if you join today, we'll even give you
50% OFF your first parcel!

So visit **www.millsandboon.co.uk/subs**
to be a part of this exclusive Book Club!

MILLS & BOON®

Helen Bianchin v Regency Collection!